7

BREACH
OF
TRUST

Also by D. W. Buffa
in Large Print:

The Legacy
The Judgment

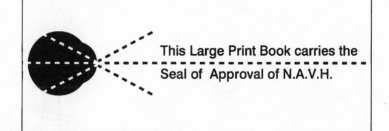

BREACH

OF

TRUST

D. W. BUFFA

Thorndike Press • Waterville, Maine

Copyright © 2004 by D. W. Buffa
A Joseph Antonelli Novel

Published in 2004 by arrangement with G. P. Putnam's Sons, a division of Penguin Group (USA) Inc.

Thorndike Press® Large Print Americana.

The tree indicium is a trademark of Thorndike Press.

The text of this Large Print edition is unabridged. Other aspects of the book may vary from the original edition.

Set in 16 pt. Plantin by Elena Picard.

Printed in the United States on permanent paper.

Library of Congress Cataloging-in-Publication Data

Buffa, Dudley W., 1940–
    Breach of trust / D.W. Buffa.
       p. cm.
    "A Joseph Antonelli novel" — T.p. verso.
    ISBN 0-7862-6702-X (lg. print : hc : alk. paper)
    1. Antonelli, Joseph (Fictitious character) — Fiction.
2. Attorney and client — Fiction. 3. New York (N.Y.) — Fiction. 4. Portland (Or.) — Fiction. 5. Large type books. I. Title.
PS3552.U3739B84 2004
    813'.54—dc22   2004053662

For Morley Winograd

As the Founder/CEO of NAVH, the only national health agency solely devoted to those who, although not totally blind, have an eye disease which could lead to serious visual impairment, I am pleased to recognize Thorndike Press* as one of the leading publishers in the large print field.

Founded in 1954 in San Francisco to prepare large print textbooks for partially seeing children, NAVH became the pioneer and standard setting agency in the preparation of large type.

Today, those publishers who meet our standards carry the prestigious "Seal of Approval" indicating high quality large print. We are delighted that Thorndike Press is one of the publishers whose titles meet these standards. We are also pleased to recognize the significant contribution Thorndike Press is making in this important and growing field.

Lorraine H. Marchi, L.H.D.
Founder/CEO
NAVH

* Thorndike Press encompasses the following imprints: Thorndike, Wheeler, Walker and Large Print Press.

1

They must have thought me mad, all those solemn-eyed art lovers, all those exhausted, lost-looking tourists, all those weary New York faces struggling to get past me while I stood in front of a painting that looked like someone I once knew. An elderly woman tugged at my sleeve and asked if I would mind if she got a closer look. I stepped back, my eyes still fixed on that strange canvas. Holding a shopping bag in her left hand, her head tilted slightly to the right, she examined each brush stroke as if that might yield a secret. After a few moments, she turned to me and, as if I had acquired some right of possession, or rather, as if she understood how quickly attachments are formed to things we have only just seen, thanked me before moving on to the next painting, something by Cézanne. It seemed incredible, but she seemed not to have noticed the striking resemblance — the uncanny resemblance — to one of the most photographed faces of our time.

I moved closer, put on my glasses and bent forward. I read the brief description: *The Boy in the Striped Sweater,* painted by Modigliani in 1918. Amedeo Modigliani, born in 1884, died in 1920, had marked in advance his own mortality with the admirable and arrogant epitaph: "A short, but intense, life." I heard it first when I was in college. Because nothing appeals to the mercurial temperament of young men quite so much as defiance of death, I remembered it with a kind of nostalgia for certain vague and romantic dreams of my own.

It was only a matter of chance that I had found myself suddenly in front of the Metropolitan Museum of Art; only a matter of chance that had made me turn into one exhibition hall and not another. Only a matter of chance, and yet there was a strange suggestion of inevitability, as if no matter what I had done, no matter what turn I had taken, I would have ended up here, in front of this painting, to be reminded of what he had been like when I first knew him, before that awful thing happened and we were no longer friends.

The colors were vibrant, alive, making me feel it again, the way things had always seemed so much more vivid and intense when he was around. I had never been able to bring it all back, see it with the clarity that I could now, my once-upon-a-time friend, seen through the gifted eyes of Amedeo Modigliani who had been painting someone else. The Boy in the Striped Sweater bore the same expression, the same look I had so often seen on his face. It was an attitude, an aspect of his character that for all the pictures I had seen of him had never been caught on film. It was too subtle, too much the impression of a kind of immobility that only struck you, or struck you most forcibly, when he was talking, when his eyes were alive with the thought he was trying to express, when his hands were in motion and his face all lit up. It was the part of him he always held back, the secret observer who watched without either sympathy or contempt, but with a kind of vast amusement, the small ambitions and the sad pretensions of the world around him. Modigliani had caught it with his brush.

The boy in the striped sweater sits at an angle on a chair with his legs apart and his hands clasped between them. He has greenish blue eyes with thin curving eyebrows arched high above them. He has a long nose decidedly off center, red lips and ears that stick out as if they cannot wait to hear what you want to say next. The face is all angular half circles, with a small protruding cupid-shaped mouth twisted a little to the side. There is a smirk on his lips, as if he is thinking of something he thinks you will probably find amusing. There is a gentle sadness about that mouth, as if he has already lived life in advance and knows that nothing will ever go wrong. It is the absence of any expectation of surprise. His hair is thick and bushy, parted high up on his head, reddish brown — chestnut, I suppose you would call it. And his head — yes, well, it was the way he held it that told you who he was; that told you he was different than what you were used to; that told you he was from a world you only imagined you knew something about, a world in which privilege was a thing ordinary and commonplace. The head, large in proportion not only to his narrow, sloping shoulders, but to his ample waist, reflecting, as it were, the relative application of interest and effort, inclined a little to the side, pulled back just a bit, watching you.

There was nothing he wanted from you — that was what that look conveyed — but he understood that others would al-

10

ways want something from him. He did not resent it, this knowledge that he was seen by other people as someone who could do something for them. You could see it in that look, that unquestioned sense of what he was and what he had it in his power to do, a power so great that he could refuse to give you what you wanted and by that same refusal give you something that you wanted even more: to have him listen in that attitude of perfect calm to whatever you wanted to tell him about yourself.

I left the Metropolitan and though I had only an hour to get ready walked along Fifth Avenue as if I had all day. Perhaps I would be a little late; perhaps I would follow my first instinct and not even go. Four or five hundred people were going to be there; only one of them would notice my absence and I could not imagine he would think about it twice. He had asked me to come, but only after one of his people had called first and I had said no. We had not talked since the day it happened, years ago, when he still looked like that painting by Modigliani and I still looked like — well, a lot younger than I do now. He seemed to find it amusing that I had not just refused to come, but had turned down the chance to introduce him

11

at the dinner when he spoke. He sighed and laughed and told me I had no ambition; which, he confided, was one of the reasons he had asked. Then he said in a solemn, serious voice, that he would let me beg off the introduction but it was important that I come, and that he would view it as a personal favor. He added, when I did not answer, that he looked forward to seeing me, and that so did his wife. In the silence that followed, I could almost see him sitting in that languid pose, his legs apart, his hand resting in his lap, his large head tilted slightly to the side. Then he said the words that told me he had not forgotten what had happened and that the memory of it still hurt.

"It's going to be at the Plaza. It would mean a lot to me if you were there."

I cut into the park, following the asphalt path under the high arching trees and through the sloping green grass lawn. For all the tightly packed buildings and the frenzied swift moving crowds, this was the place that made me feel, not the energy or the excitement, but the elegance and the beauty of New York. On one of the dark green wooden benches that lined the sides of the twisting path, a man with curling gray hair and shrewd blue eyes, wearing a tan windbreaker and clean canvas shoes, stroked the tousled head of a boy in a blue sweater and short pants. They were laughing as each tried to keep up with the ice cream melting in the waffle cones they held. He was old enough to be the boy's grandfather, but here, in Manhattan, where money could always banish age, the proud, comfortable look glistening in his eyes left no doubt that the boy was his son. There was an empty space next to him, apparently where the boy had been sitting, because next to that was a young woman who by an instinct that must have taken generations to breed kept her back arched and her head held high while she bent forward to tease the boy about the ice cream dribbling down his chin. She was beautiful, captivating and she had a voice that touched your ear the way silk feels across your hand. I caught her eye and smiled and for just an instant she glanced back. Someday, if she had not yet, she would have affairs, and if the men were only twice her age she would think them still young.

Just ahead, with their mouths drooling open, like five thirsty drunks stumbling out of a bar into the light, five small dogs with ugly flat faces and obscene piglike tails were coming right at me. Their paws scratched against the hard asphalt surface as they strained against the leashes held in the resentful hand of a lean and muscular Hispanic woman with dark, murderous eyes. I stepped out of the way and listened to a guttural language that even had I understood it could not have conveyed a more ominous sound.

I reached the circle where the heavy hoofed horses wait in front of open carriages for the next couple who want to be driven through Central Park. Across the street, in front of the Plaza Hotel, the police had already barricaded the front entrance. Around the corner, at the side entrance, facing the park, a long line of limousines had taken possession of half the street, forcing traffic to an angry, horn-smashing crawl. I still had half an hour, plenty of time to get there if I hurried; or plenty of time to change my mind and go out to dinner by myself, see a show, do what an occasional tourist might do who just wanted to see the city and have a good time.

I tried not to look at the Plaza as I walked along the sidewalk next to the park. I heard the cabdrivers cursing and pounding their horns, edging their way a few inches at a time. I glanced across at the side entrance, keeping my eyes level with the street. Men in tuxedos and women in long expensive dresses moved with the air of people who went to these sorts of things all the time. Someone would call out a name in a voice full of surprise. Someone would stop, a look of eager anticipation in their eyes, and then, shaking hands, slapping the other on the back, making a quick round of affable introductions, laughing at their own hesitation before they remembered the right names, they would step inside where the same ritual of recognition would repeat itself over and over again as all these strangers tried hard to pretend they had once been great good friends.

I had never been to a class reunion, not high school, not college, certainly not this. I had never been much for the formal ceremonies that mark the end of things. When I graduated from the University of Michigan I was anxious to get back to Oregon and I had them mail my diploma home. When I graduated from the Harvard Law School I was in such a hurry to get out of Cambridge, I did not care if I had that piece of paper or not. I had not liked law school, but that was not the reason I had wanted to get away as soon as it was over.

The crowd was growing by the minute

on the sidewalk near the door. Maybe they did all know one another; maybe they had all been great good friends; maybe . . . My eyes began to drift away, to go higher, to look up one story at a time until . . . I sat down on a bench, wondering at the madness of it all, to have a mood dictated by something as strange and impersonal as a place. It was the end of April and the warmth of the air felt later than that, but my hand went to my throat as if it were still December, and the air was crisp and cold and snow was falling. My eyes were back in motion, reaching higher and higher, the third floor, then the fourth. I forced myself to stop. I got to my feet and calling myself a fool walked away, staring down, afraid to look up, afraid that if I did I would see her, Annie Malreaux, still falling to her death.

I got back to the hotel and changed into my tuxedo, struggling with the cuff links and the endless studs, wondering whether what you used to see in the movies — that married women helped their husbands do this — had ever been true. It was only three blocks to the Plaza and though I would not have much minded if I had been late, I was on time. I got into the line that passed through security and then stood in another line to register. A young woman put her finger at the top of a typewritten list and immediately found my name.

"Joseph Antonelli." She looked up. "You were almost first."

"That's a nice way of telling me I lost."

She handed me a name tag. "From what I hear, that doesn't happen to you very often."

She was young, in her late twenties, rather pretty, with straight brown hair and even-set intelligent eyes. She worked for the alumni association. It was her job to know things about the people who had gone there, to the fabled Harvard Law School, to know what they had done and how much they could give. I looked at her for a moment, returning her smile.

"But it always hurts," I said in reply.

She nodded as if she knew the truth, not because she had ever tried a case in the criminal courts, or had ever practiced law, but because no matter how much we talk about winning, no matter how important it may be, we all have much more experience with being on the other side, the one that doesn't quite make it, the one no one remembers when the game finally comes to an end.

I did not know anyone, and everyone

17

seemed to know me. It was really quite funny, that look of almost stunned surprise. Every time I turned around in that vast, crowded ballroom I was face-to-face with another stranger. Balancing a drink in one hand, nodding a kind of hassled acknowledgment of someone they did not know, they read the name on the tag. It was usually when they said it out loud, announced it for the purpose of letting you know they were prepared to admit that you really did exist and had somehow gone to Harvard, too, that it hit them: Joseph Antonelli was famous, and in some quarters notorious. The person I could not remember invariably assured me that of course I must. We had been in this class together, or that class; we had studied together, had gone out for a beer together. The enigmatic smile on the face of a still quite striking woman changed into mocking disappointment when she asked: "Have you forgotten that night?" I was saved by the long arm of her husband who from another conversation turned around to shake my hand.

"The night all six of us studied straight through till morning for that civil procedure exam?" I replied, watching her over my drink.

Heads began to turn as my name, the name that had not meant anything when I was another anonymous face in a law school class, spread through the room like a widening circle in a pond. For most of them I was simply a curiosity, someone who had become famous, not someone they were all that eager to know. A glance, a few questioning remarks among themselves — not all of them flattering or kind. No one felt easy around criminal defense attorneys, especially other lawyers who never went to court because they constructed legal labyrinths by which to protect their Wall Street clients from anyone who might want to look into how the money was made. It was what they had wanted to do from the beginning, before they ever showed up at Harvard. They wanted money, and the law seemed the best way to get it. You knew who they were right away. They wanted to concentrate on the basics, on the rules, on the facts, on the things you needed to know to become adept at the craft. The first mention of justice, or fairness, or how the law could or should be changed and they were checking their watches. They were intelligent, focused, habitually well prepared; they knew everything about being lawyers and from the moment you first heard them reporting the facts of a case you began to doubt there was any effective difference between them and a machine.

There were others, of course, who had higher aspirations, who looked upon the law, or at least a law school education, as an opportunity for something more. They wanted to be lawyers, but only, or mainly, so they could become judges, or hold other, perhaps higher offices instead. In the sixties, Harvard Law School was filled with future governors and senators, men and women who thought they could, in that phrase that now seems so quaint, make a difference. Two members of the class in which I graduated had been elected to the United States Senate, though one of them had been defeated for a second term. There had also been two governors, both of them in the Rocky Mountain States, and three — or was it four? — Cabinet officers, including one attorney general. Two had gone much farther. One, Elias James Reynolds, was an associate justice on the Supreme Court. The other one . . . Well, the other one was the reason I was here.

The crowd kept growing until whichever way you looked you were in someone's

20

way. Holding my empty glass against my chest, I mumbled apologies as I turned toward the nearest bar.

"Hello, Joseph Antonelli."

I looked up into the tired, exhausted eyes of a man I did not know. A frail, well-intentioned smile lurched across his gaunt, troubled face.

"James Haviland," he said in a quiet, unassuming voice. The smile grew broader, more confident, as we shook hands. "Jimmy," he reminded me.

My first reaction was astonishment; my second, regret that I had not been able to hide my surprise.

"You didn't know I came back and finished, did you?"

I could never forget his name, but I did not remember his face. Cheerful and outgoing, everybody's friend, somewhere in the great amorphous middle of his class, but the first person anyone who knew him would think of when they needed someone they could trust, he did not look anything like this cautious, hesitant man who could not look directly at me for more than a fraction of a second at a time. Everyone looked different — everyone was twice as old as they had been — but age alone could not account for this. Something had

21

happened to Jimmy Haviland, and I knew what it was. What had happened that winter day in New York, that day Annie Malreaux died, still had him by the throat.

"It wasn't your fault," I said, realizing only too late that it was the last thing I should have said. Under the din of the enveloping crowd perhaps he had not heard me — or perhaps he had. From the distant expression in his furtive eyes, I could not tell.

"I went back that next fall. I only had a couple of classes to complete. I don't even know if I'm supposed to be here. I came in with this class, but that isn't how I ended."

"What are you doing now?" I asked, bending my head forward to hear.

"When I left I didn't think I'd ever come back. Then I decided I had to do something and that maybe I shouldn't just throw it all away."

"Are you here — in New York? Or did you go back home? Pennsylvania, wasn't it?"

He sipped on his drink, subjecting me to such a close scrutiny that I felt a little awkward. Did he want me to bring it up? — Or did he just want me to know that he knew that I remembered; that, like him, I'd never been able to forget.

"So I came back to good old Harvard. The next fall. I might not have, except I knew that then . . ." His voice trailed off as he looked around, like someone who is not quite certain where he is.

"Except you knew that then . . ." I tried to remind him when he turned back to me, a blank expression on his lost, unfamiliar face. He blinked, then narrowed his eyes, looking at me as if he had already forgotten who I was. His head began to nod up and down. With a glance he hoped I did not notice, he looked at my name tag.

"I always knew you'd be different than the rest of these . . ." Breathing contempt, he surveyed the room. "I knew you'd do something worthwhile." He smiled down into his glass. With his right hand he reached up and scratched his ear. "I've never come to one of these before. Have you? I wouldn't have come to this one, except that . . . I thought maybe I had to. It's the first time I've been back in the hotel." His eyes became remote.

The crowd began to make their way to the dining room where at assigned tables of ten we would celebrate who we were and who we had been. And amidst all the understated pride and all the modest bragging, Jimmy Haviland would sit there, thinking about something that had happened half a lifetime ago in a suite at the Plaza Hotel, eight floors above, on a white winter day in New York.

"I thought I had to. Come back here. If he was going to be here, I had to be here, too." Haviland gave me an odd look, as if he were sure I knew what he meant. "If he was going to be here, I had to. Don't you think? You're not surprised what happened to him, are you? I'm not. We knew that about him, didn't we? The only thing surprised me is that he isn't yet at the top. You watch, though. He will be."

What was left of the crowd began to move with a kind of reluctant urgency toward the other room.

"I'll see you again," said Haviland, touching my sleeve as we went our separate ways.

I found my place at a table in the second row from the front. I tried to find where Jimmy Haviland was sitting, but there were too many people and there was not time. All the places on the dais were filled, all except one. The dean of the Law School, almost giddy with excitement that he was presiding over a dinner with the members of his own graduating class, made the short, formal announcement. Standing at the microphone, a huge smile on his narrow crimped face, he looked down at the curtained entrance at the far end of the room.

"Ladies and gentlemen, please join me in welcoming another member of our class, Thomas Stern Browning, the vice president of the United States."

2

Thomas Stern Browning. The vice president of the United States. Everyone was on their feet, applauding, the ballroom of the Plaza engulfed in a crescendo of tumultuous, dignified noise, every eye straining to get a closer look at the man they had all come to see. There were probably not more than a few dozen who had actually known him, but as I watched the beaming self-assurance on their faces, that look of reflected glory by which they seemed to share the achievement, I imagined that most of them had made reference to the fact that they had not only been at Harvard together but had been in the same class. It did not matter that they might never have exchanged a word, they had been there together, and if some of them had become more famous than others, that only added to the memory they all shared of the place. They might not agree with his politics, they might not belong to the same party, but they applauded Thomas Stern Browning with the intensity, the heartfelt enthusiasm, reserved for the approval we give to one of our own.

With a kind of collective sigh, the force of its effort spent, the crowd settled back, taking chairs turned now at different angles, facing the front. A wistful, bashful smile trembled over Browning's small oval mouth. He looked all around, a slow, searching glance, as if he wanted to make sure that he did not miss someone he knew. The smile became a little more pronounced. He lowered his eyes as if he could not otherwise stop from laughing at something enormously funny that had just crossed his mind. Abruptly, without warning, his head dropped to the side. His left hand came up to his hip. The smile became broader, more difficult to control. Suddenly, his head snapped straight up. His eyes sparkled with defiance.

"And if every one of you had voted for me, I could have had it all!" he roared to the crowd's delight.

With his chin tucked in, he rolled his head to the side, directing a sly, sidelong glance at the dean who waited, helpless, with a nervous smile.

"And I want to thank Dean Conrad for the very nice letter he was kind enough to write congratulating me after the New

Hampshire primary. But I kept waiting for the check," he added with a grin framed with so much thoughtful kindness that the dean was allowed the easy escape of laughing harder than anyone else.

"Two years ago, when I announced my candidacy for the presidency, and during the long months that followed, in a campaign that took me from one part of the country to another, and sometimes into three or four states in the space of a single, endless day, there were few things that kept up my spirits more than the letters of encouragement I received from so many of you, men and women who, like myself, were among those fortunate few able to call Harvard home."

He paused, lowered his eyes, that same ingratiating smile bubbling on his mouth. It was as if he could barely contain this thing that was pushing up out of his soft round-shouldered chest. His head bobbed from side to side; his arms began to shake.

"And the delicate, lawyerlike precision with which so many of those letters disclaimed any interest — any 'immediate' interest — in having your name considered for the next opening on the Supreme Court was, I thought, modest in the extreme."

Browning narrowed his eyes into a pugnacious glance. "I'm afraid I can't do that much for anyone now. I lost the South Carolina primary, and after that everything went downhill. And while I was glad to have the chance to run on the ticket and become vice president, there isn't anything I can do to make sure that if there are appointments to make on the Supreme Court of the United States any of them go to men or women from Harvard. All I can do," he said, breaking into a huge smile, "is to make damn certain none of them go to anyone from Yale!"

It brought down the house. The dean was on his feet, clapping his bony-knuckled hands like some deranged fanatic, leading the applause. What is it that makes the destruction of a rival more gratifying than even a victory of our own? Is it because we have always secretly envied, and perhaps feared, his strength? The only thing worse than not winning the prize is having someone else win it instead?

The smile on Browning's face faded almost as soon as the applause began. I watched him closely, wondering how much he was still the same, always so much aware of the effect he had on others. He was reaching down onto the table next to him for a typed manuscript inside a black smoke transparent cover. His eyes never left the audience while he picked it up and spread it open just below the yellow lectern light. The crowd was wild with applause, reacting less to what he had said than to the way he had said it, the cheerful arrogant insistence that you were the best and that though you could never say that to outsiders you could say it among yourselves. Browning was waiting for them when they finished.

He began to read from the prepared text. Three sentences into it and you knew that whatever he did on other occasions, he had written, or at least had edited, this one himself. There was none of that reliance on those familiar phrases that invoke all the things in which everyone believes. Nothing about what a great country this was, or how Americans had always risen to the challenge and always would. There was nothing about freedom and democracy and the God-given right of everyone to make as much money as they could. He did something quite uncommon for a man who held high office and, it was reasonably certain, had not yet surrendered all hope for higher office still: Halfway through a speech about the state of the law in

America, Thomas Stern Browning told this audience of affluent and important members of the bar that the way they led their lives was all wrong.

"Let me tell you about the kind of lawyer we need more of today. We need men like Louis Brandeis — the inventor of what came to be called the 'Brandeis brief.' You remember, of course, what that was: a brief submitted to a court by someone not a party, because the decision reached in it would affect the community at large. It mattered, when a court had to decide an issue about whether a particular young woman had been compelled to work twelve or fourteen hours every day in an airless room, that the court knew how many women in this situation ended up exhausted, malnourished, beaten or dead. Brandeis supplied the kind of information that proved that what might otherwise have been thought an isolated situation causing no great harm was a cancer threatening the very existence of society as a whole."

Browning paused, furrowing his brow. His head swept from side to side, an ominous look in his eyes. Taking one step back from the podium, he placed his hands on his waist. His shoulders hunched forward, he rocked back and forth.

"There are in this audience tonight some of the best lawyers in the country." He lifted his head. A thin smile ran flat across his mouth. "And some of the most highly paid. I'm sure you've earned it. And now that you've earned it, now that it's yours, you might start thinking about devoting some of your time to doing something a little more important than simply trying to make more. You might try to remember that there were once lawyers — men like Louis Brandeis — who thought the words *pro bono* represented a lawyer's highest calling and not," cried Browning with withering contempt, "some poor haggard wretch with her hand stretched out. Do you know — do any of you know — what Brandeis really did?"

Browning grasped the sides of the lectern tight with his hands. The tension in his short neck tightened, the muscles bulging out. His mouth turned down at the corners. There was anger in his eyes.

"Brandeis did not just do it all for free; he did not just give away all that time he spent writing, researching, consulting, on those famous classic briefs. He paid for his own time. He paid the firm of which he was a member for the time, the money he did not make. Do you understand me?

Can I make it any more plain? Louis Brandeis was of the opinion that his time belonged as much to his partners as it did to him and that the twofold obligation — to the public interest and to them — could only be fairly met by reimbursing the firm for what he could otherwise have earned."

Waving his left hand in front of him, Browning vigorously shook his head. "It was not always my view that lawyers — or anyone else, for that matter — should do anything except what was to their own financial advantage." A shrewd smile stole across Browning's soft, pliable mouth. "My grandfather did not build cars to give them away. It was only when I came to Harvard to study law — because to tell the truth I had not yet decided what I wanted to do — that I first encountered anyone who did not seem to think the same way. 'I'm Antonelli' — that was the first thing he said, the roommate I did not know I had before he showed up at the dormitory door. 'I'm Browning,' I replied, wondering as I said it why I was following his example and whether we would live all year together and never learn each other's first name.

"It must have been sometime that first week — the first week of our first year —

when I asked him if he had yet given any thought to the kind of law he wanted to practice, what kind of lawyer he wanted to be. I assumed of course that he would say something about corporate, or tax, or perhaps, if he had more imagination than most, something about admiralty or international law. Instead, he said that he was going to be a criminal defense attorney. When I suggested diplomatically that I thought it really did not pay, he said he could not see what difference that could possibly make. As you can imagine, I knew then that I was in the presence of someone quite as strange as anyone I had ever met."

Around the table at which I was sitting, faces turned, looking at me with new interest, as they listened to Thomas Browning describe someone I did not remember. He was changing things, giving them a subtle reinterpretation, lending the present an illusion of coherence by making it seem the inevitable consequence of the past.

"I took him home with me at Thanksgiving to see what my grandfather, who had a gift for the appraisal of men, thought of my new friend." Browning paused, looked around the room, took a step to the side of the lectern, picked up a glass of water and drank. "Now, I don't know how many of you remember old Zachary Stern." Browning's eyes were fixed on his hand as he put down the glass. "But he had a way of looking at you that made you think that you must have done something wrong. He gave that look to Antonelli — and it did not do any good at all. Antonelli thought my grandfather's baleful silence was an invitation to say what was on his mind. Do you know what he said, this first-year law student from Michigan and even farther west? 'We had one of your cars when I was just a boy. It kept breaking down and they could never fix it and my father, who was a mild-mannered man, said if he ever met the famous Zachary Stern he'd tell him a thing or two.' I thought my grandfather was going to explode. He grew red in the face; his body tensed and shook; and then, suddenly, he laughed. Laughed, mind you! Zachary Stern, the man they said had never smiled. He laughed. And then he leaned closer and confided something I had never heard him confess before: 'We had a bad year. Problems on the line.'"

Browning drew himself straight up. A look of baffled amusement spread over his face.

" 'What year was that, sir?' Antonelli asked, the same way, I imagine, he takes a question of a witness on the stand. My grandfather looked at him, startled, and then laughed some more. 'Now that you mention it, might have been more than one.' "

Women were looking at me with the lost affection that, had they only known, they would have lavished on the young man whose innocent bravery had brought the great and formidable Zachary Stern to heel. It was a wonderful story, made better yet by the masterful way he told it, with those rich, rolling periods, accompanied by just the right gesture and always, at each point one was needed, the perfect pause. It was a wonderful story, and not one word in it was true. Browning had not reinterpreted my conversation with his grandfather at their baronial Grosse Pointe estate, revisited it in a way that put me in a better light: He had made it up, all of it. I had never had a conversation with Zachary Stern. I never met him. I had not been invited there that first Thanksgiving; I was there the Thanksgiving after that, in our third year, the one after the summer in which the old man died.

I sat in the darkness, no longer a face

in the crowd, but a silent, unwilling co-conspirator in this utter fabrication invented by Thomas Browning and given out as nothing more than the simple truth.

"I was always glad I brought Joseph Antonelli home with me that Thanksgiving; glad he had the chance to meet my grandfather a few months before he died. 'Watch him,' my grandfather told me. 'He's the kind who does well. It's the ones who start out looking for money who seldom get rich.' Then my grandfather added something that tells it all: 'The money means nothing. It's the work that counts. It's what you can do with your head and your hands, the things you can build, the things you can change.' "

Browning looked out over that vast audience and in that rich voice that swept you up in it like a great, flowing river reminded them of what was important and what was not.

"We remember Zachary Stern for what he did, for building an industry, for changing the way we live, not for how much he was finally worth. I remember him of course for other things as well, none of them with greater gratitude than that lesson he taught me that last Thanksgiving of his life: that if you want to know which among you is going to do well, look for those, if you can find them, who want something so badly that if they had to, they would do it for no money at all. And that, I daresay, is why my friend is the most famous lawyer in the country and makes more in a month than most of us — especially those of us who work for the government — make in a year."

The echo of his voice slipped into a silence so complete that the sound of a chair creaking under a slight shift of weight could be heard from far across the room.

"And every year he gives much of it back. He still takes cases no one else will, cases in which the accused has no money and no way ever to pay. And he does it — well, why does he do it? Because he can; because he knows how; because he was trained as a lawyer and remembers something most of us forget: that he never once heard from any of his teachers in law school that the justice of a cause had anything to do with how much it paid.

"I never did anything for the money, either," he insisted with an innocent stare that produced first laughter, then applause. "It's true, I started out with certain . . . modest advantages; but I tried to follow my grandfather's instruction; I tried to follow my friend Antonelli's example; I tried to think only about the work and not about the money — but while they both succeeded beyond anyone's dream, the best I could do was wind up second, which in America, you know, is the same thing as last." The grin grew broader, the effort at suppression part of the game. "But perhaps, on some future occasion," offered Browning with a teasing sparkle in his eyes, "I may be able to appear before you without that awful word *vice* in front of my name."

Browning had other things to say, solemn, consequential things, about the country and where it was headed, and what could be done about it, and why we should try, but I was too caught up in my own thoughts and emotions to listen to much of what he said. This was the first time I had seen him since I left Harvard, the first time I had been in the same room with him since that crystal cold day, years ago on Christmas Eve, here at the Plaza Hotel. Why had he been so insistent I come? And why, of all places, here? There are some people — most of us, I suppose — that you might see every day for years and not really notice when they're gone. There are others who, even if you only glimpsed them once — a face you passed late one night on a city sidewalk; someone stepping brightly off a daytime curb — you never forgot. The memory of it stays with you forever. Annie Malreaux was that and more. I knew her, and I liked her, and every time I saw her it was like seeing her for that unforgettable first time. She had a voice, a silver tinkling voice that even now, when I thought about her, I could hear all over again. If I had not been in love with her, it was because she was always with someone else, first Jimmy Haviland and then Thomas Browning at the end.

I glanced around the darkened ballroom, all the anonymous well-tended faces lifted toward the front, listening to Thomas Browning's memorable speech. I felt the hard leather soles of my shoes push against the hardwood floor, and I remembered the sensuous feel of it, when there were no tables and an orchestra was playing and I was dancing with a girl in my arms, a different girl, staring down at the light glistening on the fine polished floor from the glass chandelier high overhead. When the speech was over and the audience rose in a standing ovation, I slipped away through the crowd. It had been a mistake to come.

Jimmy Haviland was waiting for me as I got to the door that led to the thick-carpeted hallway outside. The lights had just come on. The applause that had risen to the ceiling was followed by the bois-terous noise of hundreds of voices talking all at once, of bumping shoulders and scraping chairs and bursting high-pitched laughter, of shouted partings and mum-bled greetings among those who thought they recognized one another but were not really sure. Amidst the swirl of eager, smiling faces, Jimmy Haviland looked quite alone, a passing stranger, watching from a distance a spectacle that had nothing to do with him.

"Reminds me a little of Churchill, the way he gives a speech," observed Haviland with a gaze wistful, scornful and detached.

My mind had been on too many other things to make comparisons between Browning and anyone else. At first, I did not see it, but a moment later, I realized he was right. When you got beyond the ob-vious differences: that Churchill was so much associated with the war, the war that my generation was born into and that, in ways we never quite understood, shaped our lives, the similarities were so striking you wondered why they had not been noticed before. The deep, rolling cadence, the balanced phrasing, the steely-eyed pause, the gesture done for dramatic effect, the playful teasing, the last-minute change in direction that gave a double edge to his words. It was all there, a kind of practiced imitation, not intended to be identical, but close enough that if you caught it there would be no mistake who his model had been.

"He's even started to look a little like him. He always had those sloping shoulders, and he was never much at staying in shape."

"There wasn't much he could do." I caught myself before I said anything about Browning's lame left foot. Haviland would not have heard me anyway: He was too intent on his own emotions.

"I survived it," he announced. "Annie died, but I survived it."

His eyes held a faint glimmer of hope, like the light in a sinner's eyes, that promise of redemption after the last thing lost. His gaze started to move from side to side, gradually picking up speed. He began to rub his hands together, harder, faster, as he balanced high up on his toes, like someone outside on a freezing winter day waiting desperately for a cab.

"Jimmy, how would you like to get out of here and go somewhere for a drink?"

He stopped at once and with a grateful smile asked if I meant it.

"Who else in this crowd would I want to have a drink with?" I replied with the cynical edge with which loners like us beat back the empty darkness of the night.

Haviland started for the hotel bar. I shook my head and kept moving toward the lobby.

"Everybody will be in there," I explained. "The same people we're trying to get away from. What hotel are you in? Let's get a drink there."

He mumbled something evasive about it being the other end of town. I kicked myself for not realizing that he was probably in some cheap, out-of-the-way place that took an hour to get to and was difficult to find.

"I'm just a few blocks up — the Warwick. They've got a good bar. You mind if we go there?"

We were through the doors and down the awning-covered steps, outside on the sidewalk, just turning away, when I looked back over my shoulder and saw the Secret Service moving Thomas Browning toward a waiting car.

"Did you think he was staying at the Plaza?" inquired Haviland from a few feet away. I turned and caught up with him. "They usually hold these things later in the spring, or sometime in the fall. They did it now because it worked with his schedule. And they did it here, at the Plaza, because that's where he wanted it to be."

We were walking at a brisk clip in the cool night air. I was glad for the exercise after sitting cramped inside for so long. Haviland stopped, wheeled toward me, and searched my eyes.

"Why?" he asked in an anguished voice. "Why of all places would he want to have it there?" With a shudder, he turned away and with his hands plunged deep into his pockets, kicked at something unseen in front of him. He began to walk with an angry stride.

At the corner, a block away from the Plaza, a hand out of nowhere took hold of my arm. "Mr. Antonelli?"

"Yes?"

A man in his late thirties with short-cropped hair and a face I can only describe as anonymous looked straight at me. It was not raining, but he wore a tan raincoat over his coat and tie. A thin wire ran from outside his shirt collar to a clear plastic plug in his ear.

"The vice president would like to see you," announced the Secret Service agent in a matter-of-fact monotone.

"When?"

"Now."

I smiled. "Can't. I'm having a drink with a friend."

The agent blinked. He was not amused.

"The vice president of the United States would like to see you, sir. The car is waiting."

Out of the corner of my eye I saw Haviland starting to move off. With a sharp look I told him to stay where he was, that this would take only a minute.

"I can't see him now. I have something else I have to do."

"Sir, I . . ."

"I'm not trying to make your life difficult, but I'm not going with you. It's as simple as that."

He decided I was serious. Nodding to himself, he moved half a step away, whipped out a thin handheld phone and in a worried voice reported in. After a few moments of muted conversation, he put his hand over the phone and gave me a quizzical glance.

"When could you come, sir?"

Haviland had inched his way back into the shadows. His only thought was to avoid trouble.

"I'm having a drink with a friend. About an hour, I suppose. — Or sometime tomorrow," I added with indifference.

"Where are you going for your drink?"

"That's really none of your business, is it?"

A grudging, but not unfriendly, smile crossed his firmly set mouth. "Where would you like me to pick you up?"

I told him the Warwick, smiled back at him, and shook his hand. It was all in the attitude.

"You shouldn't have done that," insisted Haviland after we had ensconced ourselves in the Warwick bar. He gulped a double whiskey and water with a sense of something close to panic. "You don't just ignore a summons like that." His mood was changing from timidity and fear to anger and confusion. He leaned both arms on the bar and, with his head sunk between his shoulders, stared bitterly into his glass. "I shouldn't have come. I knew it would be a mistake."

As quickly as it had come, the anger vanished. He laughed and turned to me, a baffled look on his honest, open face.

"I'm always doing that: doing things I know damn well I shouldn't do. It's because I'm a coward, and when you're a coward you do stupid things because the only reason you can think not to do them is you're afraid. I've always been like that," added Haviland as he tossed back his head and gulped down what was left. The hollow glass struck the bright polished bar with a lonely echo. "Another," he instructed the bartender whose lackadaisical eyes had been drawn automatically by the all-too-familiar sound.

"Was like that as a kid. Long as I can remember, I was like that. It's why everyone liked me." He pulled the leg closest to me around the leather stool, hooking it on a metal rung. His elbow rested on the front edge of the bar. His face was inches from mine and I had to make an effort not to turn away from his stale, deathlike breath. "That's the truth, you know. Everyone liked Jimmy Haviland because there wasn't anything Jimmy Haviland wouldn't do."

It is always a sign of trouble when men start to refer to themselves by their own names. Tired drunks and breast-beating politicians do it most often, but whoever does it, it is usually the beginning to an endless orgy of self-pity and worse.

47

"Listen, Jimmy," I said as I stood up, "I better get up to my room. I have to change into something different before they come to pick me up."

With surprising strength, Haviland gripped my wrist. "I'm trying to tell you something."

The bartender set a second drink in front of him. With a thoughtful gaze, Haviland lifted it to his lips, but he did not take a drink, or if he did it was barely a touch. He held the glass pressed against his lower lip, the smell of it mixing with the air, the familiar scent of late-night musings on things he should not have done. When he put it down, he did it with a kind of regret, as if he had run out of excuses by which to postpone what he thought he had to say.

"It was my fault what happened. It was what I told you before. I always do things I know at the time I shouldn't do. I shouldn't have come to the Plaza that day," he said with a bleak, rueful expression. "I knew what Annie would say when she saw me; what she'd say when I told her that I wanted a second chance. That's why I had to do it, why I had to come." Haviland shook his head, as if after all these years, he still could not understand why he was the way he was; why he always had to prove something to himself. "The only reason I could think of not to tell her that was the fear of what she would say. And that's why it happened — because I did that."

It did not explain anything, but he did not understand that, not at first. He looked at me, waiting, I think, for me to give him some kind of absolution, to say something that would finally give him some relief. We stared at each other, locked in an awkward pause.

"They were standing there, she and Browning, talking so intently they did not realize I had walked into the room. I told her I loved her more than Browning ever could, that I wanted her to give us another chance. She told me I shouldn't have come, that we could talk about it later, but not now, not there." With a distant smile, Haviland stopped.

"That we could talk about it later. That was all the hope I needed. I was not going to lose Annie twice. I told Browning what I thought of him: that he was a liar and worse, and that he didn't have the right to do the things he had; that he didn't love Annie, that he didn't love anyone except himself. That's why it happened, because I walked in there where I didn't belong, and because I had to say the things I said. She ran after me, tried to calm me down. She blamed herself for the way I had become. She was like that, wasn't she? She blamed herself, I think, for letting me fall in love with her, as if there was anything she could have done about that.

"She told me I had better go, that Browning was upset, that we could talk later, that everything was going to be all right. Then, after she went back to see Browning, there was something else she wanted to tell me. That was how it happened — or that's how they said it happened — she was leaning out the window, looking for me. They said — Browning said — that she lost her balance and before anyone could reach her, Annie fell eight floors to her death."

I put my hand on his sleeve and looked directly into his damp, reddish eyes. "Browning told you that she was trying to look for you at the window?"

Haviland blinked his eyes. "He told me it was my fault. He told me he never wanted to see me again."

"Browning told you that it was your fault? And you believed him?"

"It was my fault. It wouldn't have happened if I hadn't gone there and said the things I did."

There was something about the way he said it, something in the haunted expression that he could not quite control that told me there was a secret he was hiding, a secret he wanted me to know.

"But you don't think it happened the way he said, do you?"

"No, I don't. I never did. I think Browning was angry because of what I had done. I think they got into an argument over it. I think he pushed her. I think that's how she died."

I felt a tap on my shoulder. I looked up into the waiting eyes of that same Secret Service agent. I had an appointment with Thomas Browning, an appointment that suddenly seemed long overdue.

3

Outside the Warwick Hotel, the Secret Service agent stepped into the street and hailed a taxi. After three days of waiting for a call that never came, this is the way I had finally been summoned for my meeting with my famous former friend: in the filthy backseat of a New York cab. I had flown three thousand miles, not because I had wanted to, but because Thomas Browning had called me himself and put it in a way that made it impossible to say no. Come a few days early, he had suggested; that way we might have more time. And like a fool I believed him. I sat in the hotel, waiting for a call, each time I went out certain that it would come before I got back. A lot of messages were left, but never one from him.

The agent gave the driver an address, and then, pointing with his finger, told him where to turn. Out of habit, his eyes kept moving back and forth, searching the garish bright-lit sidewalks for anything out of the ordinary. The movement of his head slowed, hesitated, stopped. A half smile of interest started on his thin straight mouth. He looked at me through curious eyes.

"You mind my asking?"

I was as much interested in what the question might be as he could have been in the answer.

"You've known him a long time?" began the agent tentatively. "In law school together." I waited in the rumbling silence for him to go on. "I was there in the room tonight. I heard what he said about you."

The cab turned onto Fifty-eighth Street, between Central Park and the Plaza Hotel. A long line of limousines was still waiting outside the hotel. Some of them, I imagined, would be there for hours while members of my law school class, Browning's challenge to do more for public service all but forgotten, spent their way into the promised illusion of their own importance.

"I've been on this detail two years, since he got the nomination. He isn't what you'd call free with praise. I've never heard him say anything like what he said about you."

We rode in silence as the cab headed up Madison and then cut across to Fifth Avenue.

"Anyway, I just wondered — that's all,"

he remarked presently.

"Wondered what?"

The agent pressed his lips together and shook his head, baffled by something I did not understand. "Why you turned him down. No one's ever done that before. We were just pulling away from the front of the hotel. He must have spotted you heading down the street. He wanted you to ride with him."

I looked out the window at the stone wall that bordered the park and the dark mass of trees sheltering in mystery everything below. Sometimes I thought I did not understand anything, other people, other places, least of all myself. Anyone else would have been jubilant with pride, no other thought in their mind than not to let it show too much. I sat there listening to a glowing tribute and discovered in it only grounds for suspicion and a reminder of things I would have preferred to forget.

"Sometimes . . ." I stopped and looked across at the agent. "You have an old friend? Someone you've known since you were a kid? You know how sometimes something gets said — you take it one way when it wasn't meant that way at all?"

The suggestion that it had been a misunderstanding between friends and that the

54

fault had been mine alone seemed to satisfy him.

"When I told him what you said, that you had other plans — were going out for a drink with a friend — he laughed, and said: 'That's Antonelli, all right. No one ever could tell him what to do.'"

Antonelli. That is what Browning called me the first time we met. It was not what he had told the crowd. I had learned it from him, not the other way around. I had been raised in Oregon; I had spent four years in Ann Arbor at the University of Michigan, which still thought itself an outpost of civilization in the untrammeled wilderness of the West; and now, finally, I was on the East Coast, at Harvard, where, I assumed, everything had a reason and tradition went back to a time before anyone thought there ought to be a Great Republic in which people like me could come to a place like this. There is nothing the ardent democrat is more eager to learn than the custom of a royal house. From the first day we met, one bright, crisp mid-September New England afternoon, I was Antonelli and he was Browning and I felt I might finally have found a home.

He even referred to his grandfather by his last name. A few months after we became roommates he made one of the strangest remarks I had ever heard.

"Jesus gave you Christianity, but Stern gave you the car." Browning's eyes bubbled with mirth. "Jesus gave us Christianity and, according to some, enfeebled the human race; Stern gave us the car and ruined any chance we had left."

We were sitting in the commons late in the afternoon, after our last class, one of the few we had together. Browning was reading the paper. He put it down.

"You think that's not true?" he said with a challenging look, though I had not said a word and, so far as I knew, had not changed expression. The truth of it was, I had barely heard what he said. I was stirring a cup of coffee with one hand while I jotted down in a notebook something from class I was afraid I would otherwise forget.

"It's true, Antonelli. Every word of it." Browning leaned back, raising his chin. His eyes fastened on something out the window, something he saw in the swirling late-autumn snow. A wry grin, the look of someone remembering a shrewd remark he had once made — or perhaps had wanted to make, but had to hold back — a remark that if he had made it might have had some tremendous, but not entirely unexpected, consequence, started across his small, rather impish mouth. "Think of it! The automobile! It was supposed to be this great liberating phenomenon. Freedom. Everyone could go everywhere — whenever they wanted. Freedom. And it became the means by which we imprisoned ourselves."

Browning's eyes came back to mine, but did not stay. He stretched out his legs, wedged his hands between his thighs and bent his head to the side. A pensive smile played at the soft corners of his mouth. He looked out the windows. The snow was coming harder in the dying light, like white stars falling on a slate gray night. He looked back, not at me, but at the rows of law students, their jackets still on, sipping hot coffee, hunched over their books like quick-fingered scriveners bent to their task.

"I did not read it myself — though I should — the whole thing, I mean; but a teacher of mine once read to me . . ." His eyes darted to mine, an apology grinning in his eyes. "Read to the class a line from a letter of Jefferson's in which he complained that the Americans were becoming soft and effeminate by spending too much time on horseback. An Indian, Jefferson insisted, could cover fifty miles on foot faster than a white man could on horse." He paused, a languid expression on his face. "I get a little tired just thinking about walking through this damn blizzard back to the dorm."

He glanced out the window and winced. Straightening up, he put both elbows on the table and lapsed into a brooding silence. I began to scribble another fragmentary thought on the notebook page.

"It doesn't make much sense, does it?" I looked up and found him nodding at what I was doing. "Civil Procedure." A look of disgust swept over his face. Then, as if he had become aware of his own reaction, and that it was more, far more emphatic than he had meant, he laughed. "It doesn't make any sense. Before anyone knows anything about the law — what it is — they insist on trying to teach you the process by which it is applied. You have to know a thing — what it looks like — before you can take it apart. Stern knew that. Seems simple enough — you'd think everyone would."

Slowly, Browning sagged back against the chair, like a balloon that had been blown full up but had not been tied, the air gradually, almost imperceptibly, allowed to escape. His legs, rather spindly from the knees down but thick in the thigh, stretched straight out. He crossed his right ankle over his left, the way he always did. It was never the other way around, always right over left and always rolling his hip slightly in that same direction, balancing himself with an exquisite sensibility on the front edge of the chair. He folded his arms, or rather, let his left hand dangle palm up in his lap while he grasped the elbow of that arm with his other hand. With his head bent to the left, his eyes traced a path down to his oxblood loafers. It did not matter how cold it might be, or how hot, whether it was raining or snowing, whether the sun was baking the sidewalk chalk white, Browning wore that same pair of shoes.

"I like them," he said with a shrug of indifference the one time, in a feeble attempt at humor, I made some remark. I did not know that Browning's left foot was slightly misshapen and two sizes larger than the right. The loafers, however, were exactly the same length. All his shoes — and he must have had dozens of them, but he had only that pair and the ones he wore when he had to get dressed up at school — had been specially constructed to appear the same size on the outside. Browning walked slowly, a lazy, unhurried gait, and, as I only later discovered, was in constant pain. The same shoe that masked the size, twisted the ball of his foot back toward his heel and held it there in a viselike grip.

Browning's head sank down on his chest, rolling back and forth. His eyes, half closed, seemed bent on some calculation behind those narrow slits. The cupid-bow mouth, pushed farther out by the concentrated effort of the task, took on the rueful aspect of a parrot's crooked beak. He began to speak in that low, distant voice he had. It was uncanny, the way it held you, rapt and attentive, straining to hear. It was like stumbling across someone in the night, holding forth in some private dialogue of their own. No, that leaves something out, something important. It was like a soliloquy by one of Shakespeare's characters, talking out loud to himself, knowing that he was surrounded by an audience intent on listening to every word. The only spontaneous remarks Thomas Browning ever made were, I suspect, always well rehearsed.

"That was the dream," he was saying. "It's always been the dream in America, the dream of the freedom to go, to leave everything behind, to go on to the next dream, and the one after that; to find that place where you can have the life you've always wanted, the one that deep down you know is yours by right."

The snow outside was falling in clumps, lit by the lights that flickered and died and flickered again from deep inside the darkness on the far side of the Charles River, a quarter mile away.

"Stern — the old man — always thought he was an instrument of God. He did not believe in any organized religion." Under his breath, Browning emitted a helpless laugh, a commentary on the bewildering beliefs of men. "That would have meant admitting the possibility that God had not been waiting all this time for him. It was the way he explained his genius, the fact — the seemingly undeniable fact — that he had almost single-handedly changed the world. Him! An immigrant from Wales who had come here when he was twelve — an orphan whose father died in the mines, whose mother died giving birth to one of her innumerable sons — sent off to America by some distant relative with a ticket in steerage and one change of clothes. He never went to school a day in his life. He learned to read and write somehow on his own. So how do you explain going from that to becoming the principal architect of the modern world? Do you think he ever thought it was just by chance? — That it was an accident that it was he and not someone else? That's what it was, of course; but it's easier to believe that it's because you've been chosen, given something no one else has been given so you can do something no one else could do. So Stern believed in God — but, mark you, only because of his absolute conviction that God believed in him."

I looked at Browning, watching the way he always seemed to keep his eyes focused somewhere else, as if beneath that affable exterior he was a little afraid of letting anyone get too close.

"You talk about him — your grandfather — as if he were already dead."

Browning raised his head and looked at me. He was not irritated by what I had said or offended that I would say it. He seemed to be thinking about whether it was true, and what it meant if it were.

"You think he was ever alive?"

Browning pulled his legs up beneath the table and placed the flat of his hand on top of it, ready to get up. I thought he was going and I turned back to the notebook, trying to remember more of the things I should have written down.

"You take almost verbatim notes in class," remarked Browning as if he were puzzled anyone would think it worth the time. "Why do you then take more, sit there like this after every class and write and write as if your life depended on remembering everything that was said?" Something on the page caught his eye. He grabbed the notebook, turning it toward him so he could see it clearly. "Good God, Antonelli! You're writing down the questions some other student asked in class?"

He must have realized how it sounded, disparaging the effort of someone for whom law school at Harvard was the chance of a lifetime and not something that could be left or taken on a whim. He became suddenly expansive and generous.

"You're right to do it like this," he said with a smile full of warmth. "And you're lucky, too — to want something bad enough to work so hard." His head moved slowly to the side. His eyes swept cautiously around the commons. "Everyone here works hard, but not for the same reason. You want to be good at it. Most of them," he said, jutting out his chin at the crowd, "want what comes from doing well at it."

Browning pushed the notebook back. He began to get up, and then, with a grudging, self-deprecatory smile, sank back into the chair.

"Listen to me — passing judgment on what other people want to do with their lives. As if I had ever made any better decision about my own." He crossed his good foot, his normal foot, over the other, covering it from view. "As if I had ever made any decision about much of anything."

The cup of coffee he had brought to the table and from which he had taken one or two sips had long since grown cold, but he had forgotten, or I thought he had. Staring straight ahead, he lifted the cup slowly to his mouth and took a drink and then put it down, completely oblivious of either its temperature or taste.

"There was no choice." I looked up. Browning had not moved. He was still staring into the middle distance, as if he had just remembered something that explained what he had been trying to say. "Not once it started. Don't you see? Once it started, no one could stop it. That's what the old man never understood: that it wasn't Stern that did it, that he wasn't on some mission from God — that once it started what happened next was inevitable,

64

and that it really was just a matter of chance, and that if it had not been Stern it would have been someone else. He was right about this, though: He was an instrument, not of God, but of a power, a force, that had been brought into the world and set into motion a long time before the old man had ever thought about building cars, a long time before he was born."

Thomas Browning, the third-generation Stern, the first lineal male descendant, the one whom the old man had as it were picked from the cradle to be his heir apparent, rested his weight forward on his left arm.

"But if he had known that, known that he was as much a replaceable part as any of the things that were mass-produced for one of his machines, it would not have been him. That's the illusion, the great self-deception, the belief in your own importance — this astonishing egotism that makes you think you're the chosen instrument of providence — that excuses every ruthless cruelty you commit, wiping out your competitors, destroying anyone who gets in your way. And doing it all without a second thought. Who knows how many men old Stern drove to suicide? I doubt he ever noticed; and if he did, believe me, he did not care. It was the rule of life: Conquer or die."

Browning paused, hesitated, reconsidering what he had said. His face was right in front of mine, bent close. He looked over first one shoulder, then the other.

"No, I think I'm wrong," he said. "I think he did notice; and I think he did care. I think he cared a lot when he drove someone first to bankruptcy and then, because of it, to death. I think it gave him a thrill to feel that he had that much power, that if he put his mind to it he could leave someone with no other way out. It was the look on his face, the empty depravity in his eyes, the way a wolf waits, waiting for you to grow weaker and more afraid, before it moves in for the kill." Browning raised his eyes from the floor and then, in a brief show of defiance, raised his chin. "I saw that look a lot when I was growing up. That look was meant for me. He needed me because he had to have someone keep what he had made alive; he hated me because in his twisted mind, he was sure there should have been some way that instead of me, it could have been him. He hated me because he was an old man and I was not."

Browning leaned back against the chair,

made a vague gesture with his hand and shook his head.

"You said he was as much a replaceable part as any of the things he ever produced for one of his machines."

I was not sure Browning was listening, but as soon as I finished, his head snapped around.

"And you can recite from memory the question that moron asked in class, can't you?" he remarked with a good-natured laugh. "You have a kind of instant recall for things you hear, don't you?" he asked seriously. "Not a photographic memory — more like a . . . 'phonographic ear.' You're cursed, Antonelli. You'll spend the rest of your life with all these things people have said — things they can't remember ever saying — floating around in your brain. The noise will make you crazy." He squinted at me, as if he wanted to examine me more closely. A flash of light came into his eyes. "Or can you switch it off and on at will? Like a phonograph record — turn it on, play the part you want, then turn it off. Is it like that?"

I cut him off. "As much a replaceable part," I repeated as I bent forward, insisting on a response. Browning raised his eyebrows and drew the fingers of his left hand across his mouth, moving them slowly back and forth until he had clearly in mind what he wanted to say.

"Once you could move things — once things could move themselves — inanimate things — then there was no turning back. The first car — a few miles an hour, that was all; barely enough to keep ahead of someone moving at a normal walk. But that did not matter. It was too late. Ever read Adam Smith and the part about the pins — remember? When each man made a pin from start to finish: cutting the wire, rolling it round, sharpening one end into a point, flattening the other into a head, sticking each one he made into a paper that held a dozen or more, each man in a day could make, let us say, X. But now, change things around. Let one man do nothing but cut the wire, another do nothing but sharpen points, another flatten heads; in other words, divide everything into the simplest tasks and make each man do only one and production rises to a hundred, or five hundred times, what it was before. And that was something that involved nothing but human hands. Now add to that the power to move things to the people who worked on them, so they can stay in a single spot and not have to waste motion, that is to say, time, moving from one place to the next. We're not making pins anymore; we're making machines, making them on assembly lines. The machines are being moved as they are being built. The production itself is in motion. The motion produces the machines that produce the power of — motion. That's what I meant. That's what Stern never understood: Once inanimate things were given the power of motion, there was a new force in the world, a force that nothing could resist. The machines would keep getting better, while the human beings who made them, each of them performing a narrow task, too tired at the end of it to think of anything, would get worse. Stern did not think about any of that. For him they were all part of the vast machine that made the machines. Stern worried only about how he could keep the whole thing in motion after he was gone — as if he or anyone else could have done anything to stop it. That's why I've always been a failure in old Stern's eyes: because I could not see the point in any of the things he thought it was so important I do."

Browning pressed his lips together and tightened his eyes. "He couldn't stand it that I might have a mind of my own. When you get right down to it, he did not really think anyone did. They were all machines to him."

4

The cab stopped in front of one of those sedate gray buildings in which the forgotten descendants of fabulously wealthy and sometimes notorious people lived in the private splendor of rooms with high ceilings and the most valuable thing in New York: a view of Central Park. In the late afternoon, while being nearly struck dumb by the uncanny resemblance between what Amedeo Modigliani had seen in a young man of his acquaintance and what I remembered of someone I once knew, Thomas Browning had been here, or could have been here, just a few blocks down the street.

The doorman, dressed in a green jacket with gold braid, greeted the agent by name. "Good evening, Mr. Powell," he said as he held open the door. "You're expected."

I was not surprised that Thomas Browning was here, on the top two floors. Riding up in the elevator, it seemed odd that I had not put it together before.

71

Browning had never really lived anywhere else. Michigan, where Zachary Stern helped build the auto industry and make the country the dominant industrial power in the world, was what Hudson Bay had been to John Jacob Astor or what the oil fields of Pennsylvania and Ohio had been to John D. Rockefeller: the place where they came from, the place where they made their money; the place where some of them, like the Fords and the Sterns, built enormous mansions that dwarfed everything around. But they did not stay there, not the second generation and certainly not the third. They came to New York where they lived as part of the only aristocracy America allowed, in which neither nobility, something acquired by birth, nor talent, something useful only if it was something you could sell, but money and massive amounts of it gave you your place.

From the time he was old enough to escape the iron discipline of his grandfather, Thomas Browning had probably not spent more than six months in the state he never failed to call home. He had gone to Princeton for his undergraduate degree, and then straight to Harvard to study law. He spent his summers and most of his holidays in New York, and if I had not thought anything about it at the time, it was because I had been more interested in the life I was leading than in what he was doing in his. After Harvard he went to England where he studied at the London School of Economics, or at least attended classes, because he had not gotten a degree. He went a few other places as well.

The first time I heard of him being back in Michigan was when he took over the company, the one built by his brilliant and crazy grandfather, the one intended to perpetuate his name. When I read the accounts of Thomas Browning's first speech to the shareholders as the new president of Stern Motors, I wondered if he had been tempted to change it and let the memory of the old man die a well-deserved death. I did not think there was any particular significance in the accompanying report that the new president would maintain offices in both Detroit and New York.

When Browning ran for the Senate, many of the places he visited he must have seen for the first time. You would not have known it, though, from the eager willingness with which he listened to every small-town complaint. He was the heir of great wealth, but he had been born to something else besides. He had that instinct, that

73

touch, that sparkle of human kindness that can never really be taught. He made people feel that whatever they said he knew just what they meant, and that once they said it he would never forget. He made them think that whatever problems they faced, he was there to help. In his Washington offices all the pictures were of Michigan, and the Christmas cards he sent out each year were always of some snowbound Great Lakes scene. But the senator preferred New York.

The elevator doors opened onto a marble crescent-shaped entryway. On each side of two paneled double doors, a Secret Service agent stood with his hands folded in front of him, legs spread shoulder distance apart. Behind each of them was a sculpted dark gold chair with the look of furniture that is never used. The agent on the right, his grim eyes fixed on a point straight in front of him, stretched out his arm and opened our way through the massive glass and bronze-stamped door. We were inside a long, rectangular hallway with muted, recessed lighting from fixtures set at regular intervals just below the high curved ceiling on the rosewood walls. Another series of lights, each of them shielded inside a lime green shell-shaped case, had been built into the wall a foot above the floor, bathing in a soft, golden light a hardwood floor laid in a zigzag pattern in which there was no beginning and, so far as the eye could see, no end.

There were two doors on each side of the hallway, each flanked by white column pedestals with lush green plants on top. The doors were shut tight and we walked on ahead, all the way to the end where a set of doors swung open in front of us like the stone in front of Ali Baba's cave. We were in a room of colossal proportions, filled with furniture scattered in groupings, like the library in one of those old and exclusive downtown clubs where in the days before equality the men who were members might retire for a quiet hour of brandy and newspapers and an occasional cigar. On the far side of the room, a wall of continuous glass rose two stories tall, and each story at least twelve feet high. Across the treetops the skyline of Central Park West shimmered ghostlike in the darkness. I was in the middle of millions of people jammed into broad crowded streets that never stopped moving and tiny congested apartments that vibrated all night with noise; yet standing here, looking out over the best of it, I was overwhelmed with the immense solitude of the place.

I turned and started to say something, but the agent had vanished without a sound. I was on a landing, two steps above the floor. A few lamps had been left on, but all the chairs were empty and all the sofas bare. I had been left to wait and no one had told me how long. It was like being locked in a museum after hours. I went out on the terrace and found a stone bench. Rocking slowly back and forth, my hands wrapped around my knee, I filled my lungs with the rich scent of money and New York, smiling at the memory of what I thought I had discovered when I first came here, when I was still young, when there was still a romance about everything, and I had not yet learned that for everything we get there is always something we lose: that the only way to live in New York was to live here rich, because with money you could live how you wanted, here, on the park, above, and no longer part of, the crowd.

"Does it remind you very much of our room at school?"

Thomas Browning's hand pressed against my shoulder. I kept staring out across the park, out over Manhattan.

"But we had something to look forward

to then," I remarked as I took his offered hand. "What do you have to look forward to from this?"

His small eyes danced circles in the night. The warmth of his hand engulfed my own and then let go. With both hands he grabbed my shoulders. Beaming, he looked me up and down.

"You haven't put on a pound. You look just the same." He laughed, and quietly the laughter died away. "I meant what I said tonight: You're what every lawyer should be." He peered into my eyes, while he held me between his two outstretched hands, nodding his head to tell me that he was telling me the truth and that he had not done it simply for effect. I believed him, or thought I did; but then, before it would have been too late, I remembered, and, re-membering, drew back.

"I never met your grandfather; I never had a conversation — I certainly never had the one you said I had — with the great Zachary Stern."

I waited for an answer, a denial of any illicit intent, an apology for being carried away into what he was afraid must have been a mistake, or at least an honest attempt at evasion. He put his arm around my shoulders and led me inside.

"I remember it all quite distinctly," he began to explain. "It was at Thanksgiving, the year before the old man died. He liked you enormously. That was very unusual for him. He hardly liked anyone at all. He certainly never liked me. But he liked you and never stopped talking about it: what you had said to him, and how much he admired the courage — the sheer guts of it, is how he put it — of standing up to him, of speaking your own mind."

Browning stopped halfway across the enormous room. He looked at me with a kind of worried regret, an acknowledgment of the way the longer you live time can play tricks with your mind.

"And you really don't remember that?" he said as he turned and with his right hand draped over my near shoulder began to guide me forward again. "How strange; how sad — when it made such an impression on old Stern — that you should have forgotten that."

In his calm, artful presence, I began to think that perhaps he was right after all, and that it had happened just the way he said it had.

He took me into his study, a more modest, book-lined room with windows that also faced onto the park, but set farther back from the street, like an alcove built into the side of the building. There was a small awning-covered private terrace with a chair and table and a single chaise lounge, a place where he could relax and be alone. The study itself was like that, a place private and reserved, suitable for a single person at work. There was a partner's desk; one, I learned later, that had belonged to his grandfather when Stern Motors had its first permanent headquarters out on the southwestern edge of Detroit. Stern had never had a partner and perhaps the desk, which never had a chair on the other side of it, had been to remind him that he never would. A brown upholstered chair, comfortable and obviously well used, sat behind it. The only other chair in the room sat with its round wicker back and brown leather cushion, stiff and unwelcoming, off to the side. The shelves were filled with books, many of them clean, burnished leather, books that though hundreds of years old looked new, books of the sort that belong to serious collectors who do not have to bother about the expense. On the shelves closest to the desk, where he could reach something without rising from his chair, were books newer and more used. It was my impression that they were mainly about American history and politics with a heavy emphasis on biographies. There was a fair number of British titles as well.

The few photographs intensified the sense that this was a private room, seldom seen by an outsider, or even a very close friend. However different he might be from the common run, Browning was after all a politician, one of the most successful of his time. If his picture had been taken once, it had been taken thousands of times, not just with candidates for every imaginable office, but with most of the important public figures here and abroad. It seemed strange that there was not a single photograph in which he didn't stand next to someone also well known. There was a photograph of his grandfather, the gaunt cruelty of his mouth barely hidden behind a cadaverous grin, and there was one of his parents. There was a picture of his wedding, he and his bride dashing out the front of a stone church, laughing as they tried to shield themselves from a shower of rice. There were pictures of their children taken in the pleated skirts and buttoned blazers worn at exclusive private schools. The rest of the photographs, which I now realized followed a logical line of progression, traced his life and career. It stopped at what seemed a curious point: a photograph in which, angry and bitterly disappointed, Browning is caught turning away from a microphone, clutching in his hand a crumpled piece of paper.

"The day I withdrew," said Browning, stretched back in his chair. He was still dressed in his tuxedo, but he had taken off the jacket and put on a silk dressing gown. It was something a British politician before the war, a member of the governing class, would have done; men who did not give a thought to what they wore because their clothes were always laid out for them by servants who knew how they were supposed to dress. I wondered if somewhere, back in this maze of well-appointed rooms, someone had done the same for him.

"That's why it's there: to remind me that I lost, so that I won't yield to the easy vanity of thinking that there isn't any serious difference between second place and . . ."

Browning shoved his hands down between his thighs and drew his head back just a little, an inch or so, to the side.

"How are you, Joseph? I mean, really? It's been such a long time. I'm glad you came.

"Did you think of Annie tonight, when we were there at the hotel? I did. Talking about you brought it all back. I've been at the Plaza of course many times since, but you haven't, have you? I wondered what you were thinking. Whatever it was, I was sure it had to be about her."

He bent his head back a little farther, inviting a response. But I was older now and had lost the desire to make him think I was someone he might want to know. I sat as straight as I could at the front edge of the chair, reminding myself that whatever we had once been, we were now more strangers than friends.

"You did not ask me to come all the way to New York to talk about that." I tried to sound assertive, but it rang a little hollow and a little forced. Browning looked down at his hands, a bleak expression on his mouth.

"I was in love with her, you know."

He said this as if it were a confession, something he had never admitted before. He stared at me with the puzzled suspicion of someone suddenly afraid he may have gone too far.

"I was in love with Annie; I never loved anyone else in my life."

Is that why he had me fly all the way

across the country, sit three days in a hotel, go back to where it happened, bring me here to Xanadu? — Because he wanted to hear himself say it — say it out loud — to the only person who would remember her the way he did and not think him a fool? I slipped back in the chair, smiled sympathetically and waited to hear what he would say next.

"I wanted to marry her," he insisted as if there was something inherently incredible about it. "Everyone thought — she thought — that because of who I was — the name, the money, the business, all of that — that nothing could ever happen, that it could never be serious."

Browning stood up and walked over to the glass door that led out to the small terrace. He slid it open, took a half step out and breathed in the cool night air. He bent his head and with a glum expression scraped his shoe against some loose gravel that had fallen from a planter onto the terrace stone floor. In the muted yellow light cast by the lamp inside, Browning's hair, graying at the temples, still had the thatched unruly look that it had when it was all a golden reddish brown.

"If you wanted to marry her, why didn't you?" I asked. "What stopped you?"

With a helpless shrug, Browning laughed softly into the night. There seemed to echo back the faint, youthful laughter of a young girl's voice.

"Everyone was a little in love with Annie," I heard myself saying. Browning did not hear me.

"God, I was mad about her," he whispered quietly, his gaze become moody and intense. He looked down, twisting his head to the side as he brushed a pebble with the side of his shoe, caught by the carelessness of things. "I wonder sometimes what would have happened if things had been different: if it had just been the two of us, without any of the rest of it . . . if she'd lived."

He moved back to his desk and sank into the chair. Reaching his left hand across his chest, he gripped his right shoulder and for a long while sat thinking.

"I wanted to tell you that," he said finally. "That I was in love with her, that I wanted to marry her — that I would have married her." His eyes drifted away from me, out through the open door, back somewhere into the past. "And I wanted to tell you that you were right, what you said back then — that it's my fault she's dead."

"I never said I thought it was your fault."

He dismissed my objection with a wave of his hand. "She was supposed to meet someone. That's what she said. She was supposed to meet someone and she was late. I kept insisting she stay. I kept telling her to stay just a while longer, have one more drink . . . We'd all had too much by then as it was. You remember that, don't you?" he asked suddenly.

It was as if he had been transported back in time, watching it all unfold before his shiny, eager eyes. He moved forward, placing his elbows on the desk, resting his chin on his two folded hands.

"The Christmas party at the Plaza that had gone on all week. I don't remember if we had one suite or two or if in a moment of reckless abandon — trying in my arrogant stupidity to impress her with the very thing that never would — I had taken the whole damn floor. There were people there I didn't know, people I'd never seen, milling around, coming in and out. We must have been drinking for days. You were there; you remember. You remember how it was: the way we studied all the time, went to class, and whenever we got the chance to get away, came down to the city, found a few girls, or took a few with us, and went off on a binge."

I tried to remind him that he was not talking about me. "I worked here one summer, and then that Christmas . . ." But he blinked his eyes without comprehension and continued calling what he remembered back into being as if he were simply reporting what he could actually see.

"There were people everywhere, coming and going. It was like one of those kaleidoscopes I had when I was a boy, all those shifting, changing, wonderful colors forming one shape and then another. God, I was mad about her, about Annie, about the way she looked, the way — that lithe, long-legged, slim-waisted way — she moved. I was in love with her. I would have done whatever she wanted — anything, if only she had said yes. That's why it happened: because I was that much in love with her and I could not let her go. I just wanted five minutes alone, five minutes to tell her I'd do anything she wanted if she would just give us a chance. But she kept saying she had to go, that she had stayed too long already, that . . ."

"And then Jimmy Haviland walked in and suddenly he was telling Annie that you didn't love her and that he did," I interjected. "Then Haviland left and Annie went after him to make sure he was all right. What happened — when Annie came back?"

Browning looked at me with puzzled eyes. "Who told you that? — Haviland?"

"Yes, of course. He was there tonight."

"I see. What else did he say?" asked Browning with a look that suggested he knew it had to have been something bitter and cruel.

"That Annie told him they could talk later, that everything would be all right."

I was not sure I should tell him everything Haviland had said, but Browning kept looking at me, certain there was more.

"He said that Annie went back to see you, that there was something else she wanted to tell him, and that she leaned out the window, hoping to see which way he had gone, and that's how it happened, how she fell to her death. He said you told him that, and that you said it was his fault Annie died."

I bent forward, peering intently into his eyes. "Is that what you told him, that it was his fault Annie died?"

Browning stared down at his hands, folded in his lap. "I probably said a lot of things I should not have said. But what Haviland told you isn't quite the truth.

Annie did not go after him. Haviland didn't leave. I did."

"You?"

"Haviland was out of his mind. Everyone had had too much to drink, and so had he. Annie was trying to calm him down, but he wouldn't stop screaming at me. I left them alone so Annie could talk some sense to him."

"But you went back?"

Browning raised his head and nodded. "Haviland had left. Whatever he had said, Annie was very upset. That's why I said what I did to him, that it was his fault. She wanted to go after him, to tell him he was wrong — the things he had said. That's why she was looking out the window when she fell."

There must have been something in my eyes, a look of skepticism, a moment's doubt. Browning saw it and knew immediately what it meant.

"He doesn't believe that, does he? That she fell. He thinks . . . ?"

"That you were angry because of what he had done; that you were angry because of what she had said to him; angry because she wanted to come after him. He thinks you must have pushed her. He doesn't think it was an accident; he thinks you killed her."

I had thought Browning would be outraged, or at least upset, that at a bare minimum he would begin to protest; instead, he treated what I had just said like the answer, or the beginning of an answer, to something he had been struggling to understand. His pensive gaze moved around the private, book-lined room, as if he sought in some unopened volume the rest of what he needed before he could finally solve whatever riddle had been posed.

"It's late," he announced presently. He straightened up from the hunched-over position into which he had gradually sunk. "You're staying here tonight. All the arrangements have been made," he said before I could object. "In the morning we're flying back to Washington and you're coming along."

He started to rise from his chair, but saw that I had not moved. He seemed to recognize that I would not be put off, that I was not going anywhere until he explained.

"They've started an investigation," he said, narrowing his eyes.

"An investigation?"

Browning's eyes widened. His small, closed mouth moved to one side then the other. He bent his head to the side and for a moment seemed to study me.

"An investigation into the circumstances of Annie's death." He gave me a strange look. "Can you think of a better way to destroy someone's political career than to have him accused of having been involved in a murder?"

Annie's death had been ruled an accident. There was a police report to prove it.

"Haviland? You think after all these years he decided to say that it was not an accident, that it was murder? That Annie didn't fall, that she was pushed? I know what he said to me, but . . ."

"There is a witness. I don't know who it is, and there may be more than one. Remember, I was there when it happened, when Annie died. It was ruled an accident — it was an accident — but if they make it sound like murder . . ." There was a flash of impatience in his eyes. "They don't have to accuse me. Don't you see? If they charge anyone, then I had to have been involved. If someone murdered Annie, then I must have been part of a cover-up, a conspiracy to protect whoever did it. If that happens — if they charge someone with murder, if they get a conviction, I'll either have to resign or I'll be impeached."

"Who are you talking about? Who are

these people who are going to convict an innocent man of a murder that never happened because they want to ruin your political career? And what is it you think I can do?" I asked, searching his eyes. "Are you looking for some kind of legal advice?"

"I want you to take the case."

"What case? There isn't any case; there might not even be an investigation. This might be nothing more than rumor."

There was something in his eyes, an almost imperceptible enlargement, a silent acknowledgment that he had anticipated, perhaps word for word, the question, the objection, the statement of possibility. I had not finished talking before he was making his reply.

"They'll have enough of a case to take to a grand jury. There will be an indictment. I guarantee there will be a trial." His eyes became cold, immediate. "It's the only way they can bring me into it. I was there. How could I not be called as a witness for the defense?"

"If they're not going to charge you — whom are they going to charge? Who else was there? Who else can they accuse?"

Browning was only thinking of one thing. "Whomever they charge, I want you to defend him."

That was not up to me, and it certainly was not up to him.

"If someone is indicted, he'll choose a lawyer of his own."

Browning slapped both hands hard on the desk and sat bolt upright in the chair.

"Good God, Antonelli! You're the best there is. Why would anyone accused of murder — especially a murder he didn't commit — want 'a lawyer of his own'? In addition to everything else, you knew Annie, you were there, you know it was an accident. Of course he'll want you."

Browning was on his feet, moving rapidly around the desk. His arm was around my shoulder, guiding me with his earlier ebullience down some well-lit corridor to another endless series of rooms. He stopped in front of an enormous gray hammered-metal door.

"Come with me to Washington. We can talk more about this then."

"I can't go to D.C. tomorrow," I protested. "I have to get back home."

Browning nodded, but not because he agreed with what I had said or had even paid attention. There was something else, something he had just remembered that he wanted to add.

"Joanna is expecting you. And no one

ever says no to Joanna," he remarked with a warning smile.

"I thought she was going to be here — in New York."

"Something came up, and she couldn't come." It was the kind of vague, meaningless explanation that passed for politeness among people who were not in a position to question it.

"How is she, anyway?" I asked as he turned to go. He stopped, and for a moment appeared to think not only about the question but also about all the different answers he could give. A smile like a shared secret floated over his mouth.

"The same as when you saw her last."

5

―――――

"Have you ever been here?" asked Thomas Browning in a quiet, indulgent voice.

"To Washington?" I asked, turning toward him with a blank expression on my face.

"No, here — to the White House."

The limousine rolled to a stop in a small parking lot hidden between the West Wing of the White House and the Executive Office Building next door.

"It was always the 'Old Executive Office Building,' the 'OEOB,' " remarked Browning with a disparaging glance. Someone quickly opened the door on his side, and I followed him out. He gestured briefly toward the gray monstrosity looming overhead. "Then during the Clinton administration the name was changed to the 'EEOB.' "

A tightly controlled young man with black, resourceful eyes reminded him that he was running late. "It can wait," said Browning. The assistant began to protest.

Browning stopped him with a look. "It isn't that important. It seldom is," he added in a whispered aside as he sent him on his way.

"Remember John Nance Garner?" Browning asked. "He did a number of interesting things, but the only thing he's remembered for is his very apt description of the office he and I have both had the honor to hold: The vice presidency 'isn't worth a warm pitcher of spit.' I've thought about that," he said, laughing softly as we began to climb the long steep steps to the entrance of the EEOB. "I've taken a pen, and sat at my desk, staring at a blank piece of paper, trying to come up with a better way of saying it. I must have tried it a dozen times, but I couldn't do it. 'A warm pitcher of spit.' By the way, what Garner really said was that it wasn't worth a warm pitcher of piss. But no one would print that then. Now everyone would, wouldn't they?"

A few steps from the top, Browning halted. "You've never been here — to the White House? Good. I'll give you the tour."

He looked at me the way he used to, when he was about to propose something that might not be entirely within the rules, something you did on a dare.

"Come on," he said as he began to climb the steps with renewed vigor, "let's see what they've done to me while I've been away."

He reached the landing on top, stepped ahead and caught the door, holding it open while I went through. "This mausoleum was always the OEOB — the Old Executive Office Building — but then, after the Republicans got control of Congress and they changed the name of the airport from National to Reagan, they decided they would rename this as well. Hard to say which is most astonishing: the sheer effrontery of people like Gingrich and Armey and all the rest . . ." Browning stopped in midsentence, struck by how strange and incongruous the world could be. "They were a curious bunch — third-rate academics who had taught at second-rate schools. No uncertainty about anything because they are so damnably certain of themselves. They were going to change the world — save Western civilization — that's what they said." Browning lowered his head and gave me a shrewd glance. "You might have thought they would start with something smaller, like saving the United States; and even then, been a bit more careful about claiming so much more than they could do."

We moved through a long, depressing hallway to another flight of stairs. We could have taken an elevator but, as Browning later explained, he wanted me to get the full nineteenth-century flavor of the place. Each time we passed someone, they would stop to make way, smile, and make themselves a little crazy wondering why they did not know who it was he was talking to with such friendly affection and apparent respect.

"So they decided to show who was really running things. The Old Executive Office Building became the Eisenhower Executive Office Building. I suppose we should be grateful that in their relentless attempt to change history they didn't decide to name it after Harding or Coolidge."

We reached the door to the vice president's second-floor office.

"And Clinton did not do anything to stop it. He probably wanted everyone to think it was his idea."

Browning opened the door and, with a cheerful growl to the staff who rose to greet him, barreled through the outer office. He opened the next door, the one to what was formally known as the ceremonial office of the vice president. Before he went in, he turned around and, with a gleam in his eye, announced: "This is my old friend and classmate Joseph Antonelli. Mr. Antonelli will be visiting with us for a few days. Please treat him with the same disrespect and condescension with which you usually treat me."

Browning ducked inside, took two steps, then went back to the doorway and called out: "Tell them over there that I'm going to be coming by a little later, that I have someone I want to show around."

Shutting the door behind him, he stood next to me, certain he knew what was going through my mind as I stared at a long table, varnished to a hard reddish gold luster, that took up half the room. At one end it was flanked by a sofa facing a fireplace on the mantel of which models of triple-masted sailing ships, the kind that once fought the nation's wars, were arranged. At the opposite end, the vice president's desk waited, clean and immaculate, only a telephone and a single, thin stack of papers at the side.

"If it doesn't look like anyone works here," said Browning with a grunt, "it's because hardly anyone ever has. This is where they banish people once they've served their need. Here, let me show something."

He pulled open a drawer and had me look inside. There was nothing there, not a scrap of paper — nothing. He told me to look closer. Then I saw the deep, definable scratches, the different letters of names and initials carved into the wood. Browning could scarcely wait to explain.

"It's hard to think what to call something that no one knows anything about," he mused aloud, listening to his own voice like someone practicing a speech, a set of remarks, he wanted to sound just right. "It can't be a tradition if it's a kind of private secret. And you can't exactly call it a rite of initiation when instead of at the beginning it happens only at the end. It's more like a schoolboy prank: grown men, acting like teenage boys, carving their names and initials in a bathroom door. That's what it is, the secret of the least desirable club I know of: vice presidents of the United States who didn't have a damn thing else to do."

Browning gave a nod to respectability. "It's a bit more serious than that. Every vice president since Truman has done it: carved his name or initials in the same drawer of this same desk on the day he left office. If it had not been for the fact that

Truman left to become president the day Roosevelt died, I would have suspected that it began as a kind of protest against anonymity, a way to leave a record — or at least a mark," he added with a low chuckle, "to prove they had actually once held the office."

Browning straightened up. "Not every vice president. They wouldn't let Spiro Agnew do it." Raising his thatched eyebrows, he wrinkled his nose in disgust. "If Agnew had opened the drawer on his last day, it would have been to look for more cash."

I had finished looking, or thought I had. Browning insisted I look again.

"There — not next to Nixon, but close to Truman — 'H.S.T.' What do you see?"

"T.S.B.?" I said, glancing up from my bent position over the drawer. "I thought you said the last day . . . ?"

Browning's eyes became hard, relentless, the eyes of someone with a deep grievance that was never far from his mind. He began to pace behind the desk, three steps one way, three steps back. Abruptly, his head jerked back and he stopped.

"I did it the first damn day I was here. I did it to tell myself that as far as I was concerned my first day here was my last."

There was a slight, almost imperceptible movement; a quiet, inward turning; a silent shift of attention from what he could blame on others to what he blamed on himself. He looked at me, and for an instant I thought he had forgotten who I was; then he appeared to forget everything he had just said.

"There is something else not too many people know. When Nixon was vice president, he kept a tape recorder in the desk," said Browning, shaking his head in amazement. "All he had to do to start it was press his knee against a button. There have been some strange men elected to the presidency. . . ." With a meaningful glance, he let me know that he did not exclude the present occupant. "But Nixon had to have been one of the strangest of them all." Browning sank into his chair. "I've read a lot of the biographies. None of them has gotten close to the truth of what he was." Browning's eyes wandered listlessly around the strange, time-bound room. "It's the mistake we make about a lot of people: to think there is something there when there isn't."

The room grew quiet, still, the bleak prospect of futility hanging heavy in the air. Browning took out a black fountain pen and began tapping it, slowly and methodically, against the hard wooden surface of the desk.

"I think that must be right," he said presently. He held the pen upside down in five fingers, tapping it over and over again. "It's the office."

He was not talking to me anymore; he was talking to himself, trying to make sense out of things.

"You can't really think about someone who occupies it the same way you did before. You knew this guy when he was staying in cheap motels and lying to any three people he found on the street; you knew him when there wasn't anything he wouldn't do — any promise he wouldn't make — to get the money he needed to win. You knew he was a ruthless, sanctimonious bastard so convinced of his own rectitude he could put a knife in your back and believe it was self-defense. You knew all that, but now he's the president of the United States, and you think about Lincoln and Jefferson, Washington and Roosevelt, and all the others who were great, and you think something about the office has to rub off and make whoever holds it bigger and better than they were."

The words echoed in the varnished silence. Browning rolled his head to the side, a look of amusement glowing on his soft, round face.

"Funny how much we cling to our illusions even when we know that's what they are. The truth of it is that the office doesn't change a thing: It just magnifies whatever virtues, whatever vices, were there before." He bent forward, his shoulders above the desk, his hands plunged down between his thighs. "That's the key — to understand that. Listen to what the president says — read it in the papers — then imagine that someone else — the proverbial man on the street — had said it instead and see if it isn't just about the stupidest damn thing you ever heard in your life. But none of that matters, because it's the president, after all, and what the president says is important."

Browning raised his eyes to the ceiling and made an expansive gesture with his hand. A smile spread over his mouth, creased his cheeks and headed for his ears.

"It's like hearing all that terrifying God-like thunder coming from on high, then pulling aside the curtain as Dorothy did and finding that the wizard behind it was just a harmless old man blowing a lot of hot air in the formidable name of Oz."

Browning bolted to his feet, a mischievous glint in his eyes. "Which for some reason reminds me: I promised you a White House tour."

He left me alone for a few minutes while he went into another room to confer with someone on his staff. When he returned he was visibly annoyed, grumbling to himself in a way that made me think that it was part of his ongoing frustration with the role he had been forced to play. By the time we started across the parking lot to the West Wing he had begun to find some humor in it.

"There are spaces for forty or fifty cars in this lot. The vice president's office has been allotted two of them. Good thing I'm such a shrewd negotiator. The original offer was one."

Browning caught me straightening my tie. He seemed to think it an appropriate, and perhaps undervalued, reaction. Though born into circumstances so different some would have said we came from two different worlds, Browning and I were both of that generation when mothers told their sons they could grow up to be president, when that was considered the ultimate honor and not a disgrace. We were born in the days when Franklin Delano

Roosevelt was in the White House and even his enemies had to concede that he was larger than life. It was before Johnson and Nixon, Carter, Ford and the others — some of them men of decency, but none of them great — presided over our long, gradual decline. If democracy was our civic religion, the White House had been our sacred shrine.

Browning took me first into the Roosevelt Room because, he explained, there was a story he wanted to tell.

"When Truman was president the place was falling apart. Literally falling apart. Truman moved out, went over to Blair House for a year or so while they completely renovated the place. He wanted a room next to the Oval Office that could be used for meetings and some press briefings — things like that. It was Truman's idea to call it the Roosevelt Room. It's the only room in the White House named after one of its occupants. The Lincoln bedroom isn't really named that — it just happens to be where Lincoln — and later on a lot of rich contributors — slept. Well, that was fine for Truman, but what was Eisenhower to do? Today someone would insist on the right to rename the room. Eisenhower was too subtle for that," said

Browning, beaming at the general's cunning and craft. "He simply replaced the portrait of Franklin Roosevelt with one of Theodore Roosevelt. Genius lies in simplicity. My grandfather first taught me that. Eisenhower is president and the Roosevelt Room is still the Roosevelt Room, but without a word to anyone it no longer belongs to FDR.

"Eisenhower started a tradition, like the Army-Navy game, or some other big collegiate rivalry: The winner gets to have the picture of his choice. And it went on that way, the Democrats putting up one Roosevelt, the Republicans the other — until Clinton." Browning gave me a baleful glance. "There wasn't any tradition he wasn't willing to break. He didn't put FDR back up. He left Teddy hanging there." Browning shook his head thoughtfully. "Perhaps it was because he thought of himself as a progressive like TR; or perhaps he thought the best way to position himself for reelection was to make Republicans think he was really one of them. Whatever the reason, he could not bring himself to take it the whole way. He had to give himself an edge, an angle, a way to show that he wasn't really breaking a tradition — he was starting another one."

Browning lifted his right eyebrow and threw back his head; his mouth turned down at the corners as he weighed in the balance what had been done.

"And why not? For the Clintons and the rest of that generation born after the war, history and everything else begins and ends with themselves."

The lines on Browning's forehead, scarcely visible when he wore his normal expression, etched deeper into the skin. He lowered his pensive eyes and began to twist his mouth back and forth. His gaze moved haphazardly across the floor and around the room, inching its way up until, for one brief moment, it met my own and then, once again, wandered away.

"There was something duplicitous, even cowardly, about the way he went about it." Browning took a breath, not quite a sigh, but long enough to underscore the point he was determined to make. "The way it always is with half measures, when you're too afraid of offending anyone to act in an honest, straightforward fashion that, whether or not they agree with it, people will at least respect. Clinton could not just let Teddy Roosevelt's picture stay there. It was not enough to identify with the Republican, rather than the Democratic, one.

There was a third Roosevelt who was famous as well. Yes, exactly — Eleanor." Browning's eyes blazed open. He started to laugh. "He wouldn't put Franklin's portrait back over the mantel," Browning explained, nodding toward the portrait of Teddy Roosevelt, "but he could put a bust of Franklin's wife right under the picture he left."

Shoving his soft hands into the pockets of his blue striped suit coat, Browning rose up on the balls of his feet, an expression of thoughtful amusement lying idle on his mouth.

"Can't you almost hear the gears turning, the wheels twisting around in that eager, calculating brain? Someone had probably told him the story about Eisenhower and how he had changed the meaning without changing the name. There's something essentially small-minded about a thing like that," mused Browning as he started to lead me out of the room. "Thinking yourself clever for imitating what someone else has done."

As we reached the door, he glanced over his shoulder at the empty fireplace mantel. "There's an interesting end to the story, a strange irony in that rather crass attempt to associate himself with FDR's remarkable wife. The day Clinton made that memorable statement — perhaps the only memorable statement he ever made — that first, angry, denial, shaking his finger at the camera, insisting with such savagery that he had never had sex with 'that woman — Ms. Lewinsky'? He did it right there, in front of the fireplace, right in front of the bust of Eleanor Roosevelt. It's a wonder the bust didn't roll off and crash to the floor, shattered in a thousand pieces."

From the Roosevelt Room, Browning showed me an office next to that of the White House chief of staff.

"Yes, Mr. Vice President?" asked a middle-aged woman with suspicious eyes and an unsmiling mouth. She placed her hand over the telephone. Browning ignored her. She went back to her call, but her eyes stayed on him, watching him, as if he were trespassing in a place he had no right to be. Browning held the door open just long enough for me to get a look.

"That was where the last several vice presidents have had their working office." With his hand still on the door handle, he nodded toward a corridor ahead. "Next to the president's chief of staff, just around the corner from the Oval Office itself. There was not a promise they were not willing to make," he said, lowering his voice at the approach of someone leaving the office of the chief of staff. "And not one they've kept."

Browning's head came straight up. "Hello, Arthur," he said in a firm, businesslike voice. "How are you?" They shook hands and then Browning made the introduction. "Arthur, I want you to meet an old friend of mine, Joseph Antonelli. And this, of course," he said, turning to me, "is Arthur Connally, the president's chief of staff."

There was a blank expression on Connally's round and strangely featureless face. My name meant nothing to him, and I had the feeling that even if it had, he would not have let it show. He worked for the president, and everyone else was judged in relation to that. He looked back at Browning before he had finished shaking my hand.

"What brings you over, Tom? Anything I can do?" asked Connally in a distant, preoccupied voice. His eyes darted down the corridor. He started to walk, expecting that Browning would follow; Browning did not move. Connally stopped, looked back, impatient, anxious to go.

"I thought you might prefer to discuss it

in private," said Browning in a civil but, as it seemed, slightly ominous tone.

Clutching under his left arm a voluminous folder, Connally explained that he was already late for a meeting. Browning fixed him with an icy stare.

"Tell the president that I need to talk to him."

Connally shook his head as if they both knew that was not possible. "He won't be back for three days. And after that . . . Well, you know how difficult it is." He shook his head again and hurried off, slowing only for a moment when Browning called after him, "Then tell the president that I tried."

I wondered what it meant, but it was not my place to ask. It was obvious, however, that whatever it was had been building for a long time. Browning had made an attempt at civility, the smooth polished politeness that at least allows enemies to talk; Connally — and if the look of that secretary was any indication — and others in the White House would not do even that.

"Does he always do that?" I asked, playing a hunch.

"Connally? Yes. Whatever it is you're asking — yes, he always does that. He is nothing if not consistent. So, yes, whatever it was — it's always the same. What particular ill-bred thing did you especially notice in that most ill-bred of small-minded men?"

The irrepressible puckish grin was back on Browning's face, the charming gleeful commentary on his own irreverence, the smile that came like a flashing neon advertisement for his own best-considered work.

"Tell me, Antonelli — tell me," he urged as we made our way out of the West Wing and gulped the thick humid outside air. "I can't wait to hear what particularly struck you about that monumental . . ."

"Does he always look at everyone like they don't exist?"

Browning twisted his head to the side. The mischief vanished from his eyes. He thought about what I had said, turning it over in his mind.

"Yes," he said quietly, and, as it were, to himself. "Always; except of course when he looks at . . . But then," he went on as if this had just occurred to him, "a lot of them over there do that: They don't really see anything except what they think they already know. And one thing they know for sure," he added with a deadly grin, "is that they have to get rid of me."

A couple of people, members of his staff,

tried to get his attention. He waved them off like a swarm of meddlesome flies.

"Sit," he ordered perfunctorily as he plopped into the chair behind that all-too-ceremonial desk. His chin sank down on his chest; he stared at me from under his lowered brow. He had the look of an innocent schoolboy forever plotting mischief in his mind. The fact that he was hated, the fact that the president's people and, presumably, the president himself wished he would somehow disappear, had the effect, perhaps not altogether strange or unprecedented, of enlivening his senses and bringing all the color back into his face.

Browning's eyes caught a document that during his brief absence had been placed discreetly on the corner of the desk. From the faint expression that began to form around his mouth, I could tell it came as no great surprise. He pursed his lips, rolled his eyes heavenward, and then, with the tips of three fingers, pushed the document in my direction.

"Read that," he said, a strange, bitter smile tracing a line between his lips. "I was the head of the third-largest company in the world," he began, the words coming from deep in his chest. His eyes began to shine with a kind of vehement, vengeful delight. "I was a member of the United States Senate for damn near ten full years," he went on, the voice growing louder, fuller, more insistent. He sprang forward in the chair, his face full of defiance and humor. His small hands made into petulant fists, he pounded on the famous second-place desk. "I would have been president if that treacherous gang of cutthroats over there had not engaged in such unspeakable conduct — a campaign of poisonous half-truths and outright lies. I took this on, agreed to the vice presidency, because without me they could not carry Michigan, and without Michigan they could not win. And after all that," he roared, his voice echoing off the walls, "this moron over there has the temerity to tell me that yet another speech that needs to be given — cannot be!"

Browning began to march around the room, beside himself with angry jubilation at the stupidity of these people he despised. He stopped, whirled around, looked at me as if he knew that at last there was someone who would understand.

"I was going to make a few remarks, reminding people as gently as I could, that the notion some people seem to have that the country owes reparations for slavery reflects a certain ignorance of a small matter called the Civil War. The president is against it; everyone in the administration who has been asked about it is against it; but I'm not allowed to say that because someone might find it offensive.

"Isn't it wonderful! You have an entire generation growing up whose only knowledge, whose only understanding, of history come from movies and everyone is too lazy, or too stupid, to ask what these people demanding reparations think the Civil War was all about. What do they think would have happened if the North — if Lincoln — had not been willing to lose the lives of hundreds of thousands of men to save the Union? What kind of reparations would anyone be talking about now?"

With a doubting, troubled look in his firm-set eyes, Browning loomed over the varnished table that ran the length of the room. "Everything would have changed," he said in a low, reflective voice. "Slavery triumphant. The North — a fraction of what the United States has become. The wars of the twentieth century — what result? Germany undefeated. Black slavery; Jewish annihilation." Browning pulled his head back as if to scrutinize more closely what he knew. "Lincoln did not just save the Union: He saved the world. — And he knew it, too. No one seems to understand that: Lincoln knew! That's what he meant when he said we were the last best hope of freedom — the last chance, really, of 'government of, by and for the people.' " Browning's mouth curled back in disdain. "Reparations? Read Lincoln's Second Inaugural. Go see the graves, at Gettysburg, at Antietam." He sighed and shook his head. "When you can't talk about Lincoln and the Civil War, then you might as well give up hope that this country stands for anything more important than how to make money and how to get rich. But try telling that to the people over there," he said, nodding toward the White House next door. "The only thing they understand is what they think they need to do for the next election." He paused, and then, with a subtle half smile that seemed to hold the key to everything, added: "And of course the next one after that.

"Lincoln," Browning murmured to himself as he again took his chair. "Wilson understood." He glanced at me. "Did you know that Woodrow Wilson wrote a history of the United States? You are looking at the only man alive who can honestly claim to have read all five volumes of it.

It's a curious thing, this phrase Wilson uses over and over again, trying to describe what was going on after the war was over and the Union had been saved. That's when it began, when the forces of industrialization were suddenly let loose and the country began to build itself into what it became. Wilson — an academic — could only see it from the outside. He kept using this phrase — 'men on the make.' He was trying to understand what drove these people to risk everything to build all those factories and plants, those mills and refineries, that whole infrastructure that changed not only who we were but, more important, what we thought we should be. 'Men on the make.' It's not a bad phrase: It captures the frenzied, driven quality of what it must have been like."

When Browning was talking about something over which he had often pondered, he would narrow his eyes and with the fingers of his right hand pressed against the side of his chin, scratch or pick at the end of his lower lip. It was a gesture that bordered on anxiety: the finger working over and over, faster and faster, until, suddenly and quite unexpectedly, it would stop. The hand would fall away, settle usually into his lap, while his eyes resumed their normal, almost languid pose: large half circles that looked at you with the detached irony of someone who knows there are limits to what he could ever hope to explain.

"It's probably better I've been banished from the White House to this place. This, by the way, was the secretary of the Navy's office after the Civil War. For a time the building held the departments of the Navy, the Army, and State. At the time of its construction it was the largest office building in the United States: five stories high with another two floors underground." Browning's eyes grew larger. "It's what the Civil War did — what Lincoln did — make the national government so much more powerful and important than the states. Lincoln re-created America — something that probably needs to be done again," added Browning with the kind of shrug that suggested it was nothing more than a turn of phrase, a way of expressing dissatisfaction with the way things had become. Yet, beneath the surface of the words, I thought I heard something more, an ambition that, while distant, was never out of sight. It seemed to fit with the disdain he had been quick to exhibit when he described how only the next election had any meaning or importance to the people who ran things in the next building over.

"The curious thing," continued Browning without a pause, "is that something happened that right from the beginning expressed the tension between the efforts of human foresight and the scientific revolution that was just getting under way. Just look at these walls," he said, marveling at more than their size. "Six feet of solid concrete, built to withstand — what else? — a cannon assault. But then, in eighteen seventy-two, just a year or so after construction was completed, it became possible to build skyscrapers out of steel. Don't you see the great irony in that — that the biggest thing, not just that government, but that anyone had built, was obsolete the day it opened?" Browning emitted a low, wistful laugh. "Rather the way I was the day I was sworn in."

The telephone on his desk rang in a muted tone. Browning answered.

"Yes? I see. Very well. In that case, I'd like to have someone take Mr. Antonelli around. We can tie up again at that thing early this evening . . . the ambassador of . . . ? Yes, that's it. That shouldn't take long. Would you call Mrs. . . . ? What time? Oh, I see. Very well. Yes, right away."

Browning hung up. With his hand still

on the receiver, he stared straight ahead, as if he were intent on organizing his immediate impressions, remembering what he had to and forgetting what he could. He let go of the telephone and flashed a polite, helpless smile.

"I'm afraid I have a minor rebellion on my hands." He nodded toward the door to the outer office. "We'll meet up again late this afternoon. Some country you've probably never heard of has just spent half their gross national product on a new embassy, and I'm scheduled to make a few remarks." He looked at me with a playful grin. "Or maybe I'll just introduce you and you can make them instead."

He began to walk me toward the door, but after a few hurried steps, he slowed down. His mood became pensive and a little dark. When we reached the far corner of the long varnished table, he placed his right hand on top of a chair. He studied me with a sudden severity, as if he were questioning some assumption he had made. Then, apparently satisfied that he had not been wrong after all, he seemed almost to apologize with his eyes.

"What we talked about . . . last night in New York. I'm afraid it's true. There is going to be an indictment. It may be coming sooner than I thought. And when it does," he said, placing his hand on my shoulder and looking me straight in the eye, "I am going to need your help."

Browning nodded twice in quick succession, then he opened the door, and with a broad smile to those who stood waiting, sent me on my way.

6

I was taken around Washington, perhaps not quite a tourist, but still someone very much from the outside, by Elizabeth Hartley, who, as she made a point of letting me know, was also a graduate of the Harvard Law School.

"Like Browning," I said, smiling to myself. "Though I imagine you got much better grades." She was driving past the Smithsonian, and had just begun to say something about a recent exhibit. The remark about Browning's grades caught her attention.

"His grades weren't very good?" she asked with an amused expression.

"His grades were fine," I replied. "But it was never important to him to make *Law Review* or finish at the top of his class. You were on *Law Review*, though, weren't you?" I asked.

She nodded with a thin, polite smile, anxious to hear more about Browning. She was smart and pretty and amazingly quick, but she was too close to what she wanted to see it from the distance that would have shown it from all sides. Eventually, she would learn that, but for now, despite the long silences and the friendly looks, it was a little too obvious that she never rested, that she never had a thought except what her next move should be.

"Browning had too many other things he wanted to do. He went to Harvard because he wanted to learn something about the law; I went to Harvard because I always knew I wanted to be a lawyer. There's a difference. And, no," I said before she could ask, "I wasn't on *Law Review*, either."

She invited me to have lunch in Georgetown, but I took her instead for a hot dog at the bottom of the stairs that led up to the Lincoln Memorial. I had seen it before on other visits to Washington, and I wanted to see it again.

"How long have you worked for Browning?" I asked. With the back of my hand I wiped the mustard that had dripped onto my chin.

"A long time," she replied, frowning into the sun. "More than two years. I started in New Hampshire, in the campaign."

"Why Browning?"

She finished her hot dog; crumpled up

the napkin she had not used and tossed it into a wire trash can. "Do you always call him that?" she asked, as I took the last bite and wiped my mouth clean. I did not understand the question. "You always use his last name."

I was not sure I wanted to tell her. "What do you call him?"

"The vice president."

"What did you call him before that — in New Hampshire, before the first primary was held, at the beginning of the campaign?"

"The senator." She was completely serious.

"What did you call him behind his back? When you were making fun of him, mocking something he had done?"

She studied me with what I can only describe as professional curiosity. I felt like a member of some lost tribe under the slightly astonished gaze of an anthropologist, a Trobriand Islander encountering the patronizing neutrality of Margaret Mead.

"You never made fun of something he had done? Never laughed a little at the way he sometimes gets out in the middle of a very long sentence, so caught up in his own enthusiasm that he suddenly doesn't quite remember where it was he wanted to go?" I cocked an eyebrow and tried to find even a hint of comprehension in her impenetrable eyes. "You're going to tell me that Browning never did that — never got tangled up in what he was saying — never started laughing because he thought the way he had botched things up was just about the funniest damn thing he had ever heard?"

There was a faint glimmer of recognition, a first hairline fissure in the ice. "Self-deprecation. Yes, that was one of his greatest strengths. We worked on that a lot."

"Browning," I said, shaking my head as I began to climb the steps.

"Yes?"

"You asked me why I always called him that."

"Yes," she said, still interested.

"Because that's how we talked then."

"Yes?"

"Yes."

A puzzled expression entered her disciplined eyes. She did not understand. That was not what she was worried about. She did not understand why she did not understand.

"We wanted to talk the way people who knew things worth knowing talked, and that meant with a certain formality; so we made, I suppose, a kind of game of it. Instead of using first names, we used last names, because it reminded us that we wanted to be serious and do serious things. I called him Browning; he called me Antonelli."

We reached the top. The statue of Lincoln, his knees bent close together and his huge hands draped over the arms of the chair, towered above us. The words inscribed on the white marble wall reminded me of something I had not thought of in years.

"In the fourth grade I had to memorize that. If I had to, I could recite it, or most of it, even now. In those days, everyone had to do that, memorize the Gettysburg Address. But when we were in law school, Browning memorized Lincoln's Second Inaugural. He had this fascination with American history, with the way the country had changed. He had, I think, a greater sense of connection with it because of what his grandfather had done, with the kind of changes that had taken place after Lincoln and after the war. I'm only guessing, but I think he thought those changes had come with a certain cost, and that the only way to know what that cost had been was to go back, see what things had been like before, try to understand what the people who brought those changes about thought they were doing. So while the rest of us were plodding through Contracts and Property and Conflict of Laws, Browning was reading things all of us should have read, but never quite found the time to. But then, Browning could always do things other people could not."

She nodded that she understood, and I knew that she did not understand at all.

"No, I don't mean what I was saying before: that Browning had come to Harvard to learn some law, but not to become a lawyer. His mind never stopped working; his curiosity was insatiable. He took things in at a glance I never got at all. He memorized Lincoln's Second Inaugural. He recited it verbatim late one night. When I asked him why he had done it, he said that he loved it so much he wanted to make it his own. And then he told me something that I've often thought about because what he said keeps getting more and more true. He said that that speech, the last major speech Lincoln gave, was the high point; that there would never be another American speech like it, and that each succeeding generation would fall farther and farther behind."

I had been carried away by the memory of things from a past only dimly remembered; by Lincoln's brooding presence and the reminder of what we had once been and might become again; by the innocent and perhaps misguided desire to impart something of value to someone young and intelligent. I felt a little like a fool, and did not mind so very much that I did. If she did not understand what I was telling her, or thought it a boring irrelevancy in her busy and ambitious life — I had at least the satisfaction of having told the truth. Or as much of it as I knew, because of course the truth, the whole truth, about anything involving Thomas Browning was far beyond any capacity of mine.

"I have Lincoln's Second Inaugural," she said with a kind of eager certainty. "I have all of Lincoln's speeches — in my computer. I can call up any one of them I want. I can even type in a key word — say, *freedom* — and pull up every place Lincoln used it. Not just Lincoln, of course, but Roosevelt, Kennedy — pretty much every speech, every presidential speech, ever given." With what seemed genuine sympathy, a physician's lament for the miracle drug that, had it only been discovered earlier, might have saved a favorite patient's life, she added: "He wouldn't have had to spend all that time memorizing the Second Inaugural. He could have just typed in a word."

It brought me back to my senses. I glanced at my watch; Elizabeth Hartley glanced at hers. We moved down the steps, jostling our way through sweaty, wide-eyed tourists getting out of a bus as we headed toward her car.

"Tell me something, Elizabeth," I said as she turned on the ignition and checked the side-view mirror. "I was with the vice president this morning at the White House. Why do those people seem to hate him so much?"

She darted a glance in my direction, then looked back at the road. This was a question lodged squarely in the present. She gave me a second glance, reminding herself that it was safe, that I was the vice president's old and trusted friend. Still, she wanted to feel sure.

"I read the vice president's speech, the one he gave last night in New York. Did you know he was going to say what he said about you?" She asked this with a smile that suggested she had known about it for weeks.

"No. All I knew was that he wanted me there. That's the only reason I went," I admitted. "Because he asked."

"The office called?"

"No, Browning — I mean, the vice president — called. Why does Arthur Connally in particular dislike him so much?"

"You remember how Kennedy picked Johnson, and how all the people around Kennedy, the ones closest to him, were against it?"

She knew something after all.

"Bobby especially," I said, shaking my head as I pondered how easily enemies could become friends when it was the only way to win. It was not the principals, but the people who worked for them, the people who believed in them, who were usually the most difficult to convince that former enemies would not become enemies again.

"This is like that, only worse. Nobody really thought Johnson was smarter than Kennedy, or that he would be a better president; everybody knew Thomas Browning was enormously intelligent and that almost anyone would be a better president than the boy idiot from North Carolina."

"The 'boy idiot'?" I asked, laughing.

"Well, we had to mock someone, didn't we?"

Turning a corner, she parked on a long, narrow, tree-lined street below the Capitol. "I thought you might like to see a little of the Capitol. Or we can just walk around — or find a place to sit and talk."

We walked up the road, circling around the Capitol until we were across the street from the white marble front of the Supreme Court.

"Have you argued a case in front of the Court?"

"No, I never have."

"Do you wish you had?"

A little uncertain, I shook my head. "I don't think so. I'm a trial lawyer. I've never done much appellate work. I wouldn't know what I was doing."

"Did you know Reynolds? You were in the same class at Harvard."

I had told her perhaps more than I should have about Browning; I was not going to breathe a word about Reynolds and what I knew about him. Reynolds had been a liar and a cheat, a nervous wreck who studied with maniacal devotion and then, afraid of forgetting something under pressure, took crib sheets into final exams. He was never caught, but everyone knew what he had done. And now it was Justice Reynolds and, so far at least, none of us who had known him had told anyone what we knew.

"No, not really. I think we were in a class or two together. That was about all," I said with a shrug.

We walked across to Union Station, restored from its shabby decay to the look it had when the only way to get to Washington, D.C., was by rail. At a café inside the high vaulted dome, we got a cup of coffee.

I wanted to know more about what was going on; about why, if Browning was right, someone was willing to go to the extraordinary length of inventing a case of murder out of an accident, an accident that had happened so long ago that there were probably not more than half a dozen people left who still remembered Annie Malreaux. Browning seemed certain that it was a conspiracy to force him out of office, but why would anyone care that much about whether he was vice president? Elizabeth Hartley did not know anything about what had happened in a New York hotel room a few years before her birth, but she knew a great deal more than I did about the present circumstances of Thomas Browning's life. I thought she could tell me things that Browning seemed unwilling to tell me himself.

"What happened? Why did Browning lose? And why did he take the vice presidency? Thomas Browning is the last person I ever thought would settle for second place."

She had invested so much of herself, so much of her own shining ambition, in Browning's quest for the presidency that though age might bring a certain distance, and even a kind of ironic detachment, she would never be able to think of it without a sense of something lost, a once-in-a-lifetime chance that she had missed.

"We didn't want him to take it." She nodded thoughtfully. "We knew going into the convention that Walker had the nomination. That wasn't the point," she continued, living it over again in her mind. "The point was that we'd come closer than anyone thought we could. We wanted to do what Reagan did, back in . . . seventy-two or seventy-six — when Reagan lost to Ford: give a speech at the convention that no one can forget."

"So that four years later — after Ford, in this case Walker, lost — you start out running for the nomination as the odds-on favorite to win."

She was surprised, and even a little impressed. "Yes, exactly; except, of course," she went on rapidly, getting back to the central thread of her thought, "we did not have Reagan's appeal to hard-core conservatives. Walker had that. But we didn't want to show we had more support from conservatives; we wanted to show we had more support in the country. Walker had the nomination, but he did not have any realistic chance of winning the election. There wasn't any way he could get back to the middle after going so far to the right. He killed us in South Carolina on abortion, on prayer in schools. He practically insisted that everyone had not just a right, but a duty, to own a gun."

She threw me a sudden, anguished glance, like someone hurt trying hard not to cry. "We still might have won, if it had not been for that whispering campaign those liars claimed they didn't know anything about. Awful things, unbelievable things," she murmured. She shook her head at the unfairness of it all. They had done something despicable, and people who did things like that were supposed to lose.

"Walker was going to lose, and it was not going to be close. Everyone would finally understand that Browning was the Republicans' only chance. And then they came to him with that offer — if you want to call it that. More like a threat, if you ask me."

"A threat?" I asked, growing more intrigued.

"Connally did a poll. Different combinations: Walker paired with each of a dozen possible running mates. No matter whom he was paired with, Walker would lose by ten or fifteen points. Except when he was running with Thomas Browning. Then the race was dead even. They did another poll, measuring it state by state, to see if the same thing held in terms of the electoral vote."

I remembered the comment Browning had made. "And it came down to Michigan. With Browning they split the rest of the country and Michigan put them over the top."

She wondered if it was a shrewd guess or if I had heard it from another, better, source. The café was filling up. A young man in his thirties, dressed in a suit and tie, had taken the table next to us. Elizabeth gave him a quick, hostile glance, then turned her chair toward me and lowered her voice.

"They needed him to win, and they

135

hated him for that." Her eyebrows danced as her face came alive. "They hated him anyway," she explained. "This just made it worse. Connally told the senator that if he didn't agree to run as vice president, Walker's defeat would be his fault and that the conservative wing of the party would never forget it." She paused, pressing her lips together as she appeared to consider what she was going to say next. "I heard — I wasn't there, but I heard — that Connally said something about how the senator certainly couldn't be under any illusions about how far conservatives were willing to go for what they believed."

She looked at me to make sure I understood. "They were talking about what happened in South Carolina. They were telling him that if Walker didn't become president, Browning never would."

Elizabeth picked up the cup of coffee, brought it to her lips, hesitated for a moment, and then set it down.

"Of course, that wasn't the only thing that was said. They talked about the kind of close cooperation there would be: how as vice president he would be consulted on everything the president did. They promised that after the convention the two campaign staffs would be merged into one.

They promised that he would have a substantial say in the appointments made to the Executive Branch, including especially — they were quite explicit about this — the key appointments in the White House itself."

She picked up the cup, raised it halfway to her chin, and then put it down. There was a question in her eyes.

"He had to have known they were lying, saying whatever they had to so he would agree. He knew they would lie about anything. If he didn't know it before, he certainly knew it after the kind of things they said about him after he won in New Hampshire."

The puzzled expression in her eyes seemed to shift from an immediate object to something more remote. "I still don't understand why he did it. Without him, they would have lost. What was the point in settling for second when, if you just waited . . . ?"

"The threat?" I reminded her again. I wondered how she could have forgotten what just a few moments before had formed the core of her argument about why he had had to do what he did.

"I know," she replied. "I know what I said. I know what I've been told. It's just that it's never quite made sense to me. If he hadn't done it, if Walker had lost — what difference would it make if those right-wing fanatics didn't all come flocking to Browning? All the better! Browning is a conservative, a real one, not one of those Bible-quoting morons that pray to Jesus while they stab you in the back." Her blue eyes were hard, shrewd, unforgiving. "They would rather elect a liberal than a conservative who doesn't think that politics is just another path to Armageddon. The whole point was to let Walker lose, to show that the right wing would always lose, to show that only Browning could win when it came time for the whole country to vote. I don't understand why he did it — I just don't, and I guess I never will. And now those cutthroats want to get rid of him for good."

Two other young men joined the one at the table next to us. By now there was not a vacant table left. Swirling crowds came and went under the spacious dome.

"Let's walk," suggested Elizabeth. She pushed back from the table and got up. Straightening the light-colored trench coat that hung easily from her shoulders, she cast a cautious glance at the three faces at the table just behind her.

"I must be getting paranoid. I could almost swear one of those guys — the one who got there first — was sitting just a couple of tables away from me at the restaurant where I had dinner last night."

"Maybe it's just a coincidence," I suggested. She pretended to agree, but not before she threw another quick glance over her shoulder to see if he was still there.

When we were outside the station and clear of the throngs of people moving toward it, she again began to talk about the White House and Thomas Browning.

"It's an embarrassment to them to have him around," she remarked with a vindictive grin. "Every time he gives a speech, you can almost hear the gnashing of teeth. It makes them just crazy," she added as the grin gave way to a laugh. "Being shown up like that; knowing they can't do anything about it; knowing that Browning is brilliant and could give a better speech in his sleep than Walker could if he trained ten years. Browning speaks in whole paragraphs, sometimes from memory, and sometimes just off the cuff — and they sweat themselves into a coma worrying whether with all their polling and focus groups they've found the one word that will put the president on the side of whatever the public is supposedly waiting to hear."

We reached the middle of an open park, crisscrossed with sidewalks, a block behind the Russell Senate Office Building. She stopped and wheeled around.

"But they'd put up with that, put up with the fact that in any comparison between the two of them, the president will always come out second best. They'd put up with anything to win power and keep it. But now they have the power, and they think they don't need Browning anymore. They aren't worried about the next election; they're worried about the next one after that."

"The next one after that?" I asked, drawing out the words. I remembered where I had heard the phrase first, and from whom. "When the president has served his two terms, when someone else will be the Republican nominee?"

"Whoever is vice president in the second term — if there is a second term — has the nomination. I mean, it's never certain, but it's almost certain; and if Thomas Browning is the vice president the right wing can thump their hollow chests and threaten all they want: Browning wins and they know it. That's why they want someone else, why they want Browning off the ticket — why they'll do anything to get rid of him."

She turned and started to walk away, took three steps and stopped. "They haven't figured out a way to do it yet; but don't believe for a minute that those evil-minded bastards over there are thinking about anything else. They're trying to steal the country, and only Thomas Browning is standing in the way."

The burst of energy, the release that came with saying out loud what she really felt, gave a manic quality to her speech. Liberated from her own carefully imposed restraints, she became almost giddy. She took things to absurd extremes.

"Our own theory is that they'll use the hostages."

I was laughing without knowing why. "The hostages?"

She settled back into a more introspective mood. "The vice president was supposed to have a voice in who got hired at the White House. That got translated after the election into four or five positions for people who had worked with us. They're over there somewhere. They work during the day at some menial job, but they're locked up at night. And the only way to win their freedom is if Browning agrees to go quietly when they tell him he won't be on the ticket."

It pointed to an interesting dilemma. If it was true that Connally, and apparently Walker too, had threatened Browning with political extinction if he did not join the ticket, what could they use to make him suffer dismissal without complaint? As the nominee of his party, the president could name whomever he wished. There were precedents for replacing an incumbent vice president, but, as Elizabeth had adamantly insisted, Thomas Browning had a stature that made him into something of an independent force. He could not stop the president from choosing someone else, but he could turn it into the political equivalent of an ugly divorce. This was a possibility to which Elizabeth Hartley had devoted a great deal of thought. It had been the subject of heated conversations among the people who worked for the vice president.

"Take it to the convention," she explained as we walked along the sidewalk next to the Russell Senate Office Building. "First threaten it — then do it. Tell them you won't quit. Tell them they can pick someone else — announce it to the world, for all you care — but that you're the vice president, that you were nominated by a convention and you're going to the convention to seek the nomination again." A cunning smile on her lips, Elizabeth gave me a sidelong glance. "It's never been done before. Television would love it: a convention with something to watch. And it wouldn't matter what happened." She said this with a kind of forceful intensity, and I was fairly certain that it was an argument she had begun to make within that small circle of the vice president's advisors.

"It wouldn't matter what happened?" I asked. "You mean it wouldn't make any difference whether he won or lost?"

"None at all," she said with a cold, hard, determined look.

"If he loses, he's out — someone else is on the ticket."

"And the Democrats win the election and Browning runs next time as the Republican who tried to warn everyone about the dangers of a right-wing takeover," she replied without hesitation.

That was one possibility. There was another.

"He loses — and Walker is elected to a second term."

She tossed her head. "Browning's position isn't any worse than if he hadn't fought at all. Better, really," she added with a quick, shrewd glance. "He's set himself up as someone who will fight for what he believes — whatever the odds. He can run for the nomination as a way of continuing the fight. If he doesn't do it, if he lets Walker just pick whom he wants, how does he explain four years later that he didn't object to having some fanatic take his place?"

She was walking at a brisk clip, talking rapidly as we reached the corner and waited for the light to change. "And what if he wins?" she continued as the light changed and we started across. "Then he's shown such strength, he's such an independent force — no one will challenge him for the nomination at the end of Walker's second term."

"And if he wins, but Walker loses? Then what? Won't everyone blame Browning? Won't they say it's because he put up a fight that split the party and let the Democrats win?"

She was like a chess player who had spent hours, days, years, considering not only every possible move but also the way in which everything changed with each new move that was made. She knew it all by heart, knew it so well that the words were coming out of her mouth before the thoughts had time to formulate in her mind.

"Lost because Walker, not Browning, was at the top of the ticket. Lost because Walker tried to force Browning out, not because Browning fought back and won. Lost because no matter how much people trust and admire Browning, it's still just the vice presidency, and after four years the public has had enough of domestic disaster and narrow-minded sanctimony and want something else. So any way you look at it, by fighting for it at the convention, the vice president wins."

Even as she said this, her mood began to darken. There was something she did not know: a sense that other forces were at work. It was like a hint of danger: vague, disquieting and real. She could feel it. It had happened before.

"There's something — I don't know — like what they did in South Carolina. They might try that: a smear campaign. If they think it's the only way."

Elizabeth checked her watch. "Just got time to get you over to the embassy. That's where you're meeting the vice president — right?"

We were on Embassy Row, close to our destination, when I remembered something she had said, and the question I had wanted to ask.

"What happened in South Carolina?"

Elizabeth stopped at the curb. "They made up some awful stories, things that weren't true, but stories that you can't come out and deny without making it sound like there must be something to it."

"What kind of stories?" I persisted.

"Things about him, things about his wife; there were even some things about their children. The worst one, though, was a rumor."

"What rumor?"

"That years ago he killed someone, a woman — pushed her out a window in some hotel in New York." She shook her head. "These are dangerous people, Mr. Antonelli. If someone fell out a window now, you know what I would think? That they did it so they could start another terrible lie: that Thomas Browning must have done it because it was the kind of thing he had done before."

7

It was one of those countries known only to schoolchildren forced to memorize the names of countries on a map, one of those remote places that other than when an occasional earthquake of devastating proportions struck was never mentioned on the news, a place that exists without history or memory for thousands of years. The precise size of its population was a matter of hazy conjecture, and at least one of its borders followed certain of the tributaries of a vast swollen river that had never been entirely traced. The rain-rusted weaponry of its proud and vainglorious army, used on occasion against a few unarmed civilians, had never been fired in war. Insignificant and forgotten, it was still an independent country, and in the strange mathematics of international relations entitled to exchange ambassadors on terms of strict equality with the greatest power on earth. Like the famous equality of both the rich and the poor to sleep under the bridges of Paris, it was an equality that did nothing to change, or even conceal, the fact that no one in Washington paid the slightest attention to the ambassador or, with the possible exception of some junior clerk in the State Department, knew his name. His Excellency, the ambassador, the official representative of a sovereign nation that was only too eager to be a full partner in all relevant discussions about the great issues of war and peace, had finally convinced his government that the only way to be noticed by the colossus of the north was to build an embassy the like of which official Washington had never seen. The night it opened, everyone who was anyone lined up to get in.

Browning had not arrived, so I grabbed a glass of champagne from a waiter and got into the receiving line just ahead of the flowing robes of a sheikh from Bahrain. When I reached the ambassador, he was pointing toward an enormous weathered beam that ran under the glass ceiling from the wall of gold-filled mosaic to the opposite one of reddish beige marble.

"There were only two trees like it in the world," he said with evident pride at having cut the number in half. I gave my name to the ambassador's assistant whose job was to whisper the name of each new guest into his master's ear. The ambassador finished shaking hands with the statuesque woman in front of me. Because I was obviously of no importance, he bent his head toward the assistant, quickly memorizing the name of the sheikh from Bahrain, as he shook my hand.

I wandered around, through thick clusters of faces familiar to one another, conversing in a babble of languages that sounded more interesting than my own. Even the English sounded strange and foreign. A couple of Australians were laughing uproariously, taunting a hapless New Zealander with the outcome of a rugby match that had taken place ten thousand miles away at home. A slight, nervous-looking man, speaking in a clipped British accent, remarked that all the embassy lacked were the slot machines he had seen in the only other building that looked like this, "out in Las Vegas, where the American civilization has reached its peak."

"Do you always stand against a wall at these things, talking to yourself?"

I looked up into the laughing dark eyes of a woman in her midthirties with a mouth both intelligent and sad. Her hair was dark brown, the part of it in the shadows looked black. With thin shoulders and slim wrists, moving with a soft, lithe step, she was graceful and elegant and entirely self-possessed. She pronounced each English word as if she were trying it out for the first time, not certain how it would sound, with the effect that you found yourself sympathizing with her mistakes. Not only was she charming, she was the first person here I had seen who did not seem obsessed with having everyone see her. She was wearing a plain black dress. She held out her hand.

"I'm Gisela Hoffman."

"German?"

"Yes, German. And you are?"

I cringed at my bad manners. "Joseph Antonelli."

She laughed, teasing me with her eyes. "Italian? And what brings you here tonight? — A mission from your government — or did you simply fall in from the street to examine more fully — I think I mean 'more closely' — Yes? — the ugliest building in Washington and maybe the world?"

She held a glass of champagne at the level of her chin. She looked at me with a studious expression, as if she had passed a judgment of profound importance, the whole time daring me not to laugh.

"I wasn't invited, but I wouldn't have come on my own, either," I replied, watching the soft, easy way she moved.

"Then you're with someone," she remarked. There was a hint of disappointment, a hint so subtle that I could not be sure it had not been my own vanity imagining what was not there.

"In a manner of speaking, I guess I am."

She laughed, and then, as if we had been acquainted for a long time, placed her hand on my wrist and told me it was something she hoped no one would ever say about her. I was not quite clear what she meant. She laughed again, quieter, more intimate, than before. Her hand still rested on my arm.

"Be with me 'in a manner of speaking.' "

The sadness, that strange first impression of her mouth, turned into a bittersweet smile that a moment later died upon her lips. I did not know her — we had barely just met — and I was explaining myself as if I had done something wrong.

"No," I stammered, "all I meant was that I'm supposed to meet . . ." I started to say the vice president, but it sounded stuffy and pretentious and much too official. "I'm supposed to meet an old friend, my roommate from law school."

She raised her eyebrows as she sipped champagne, a kind of blank response that seemed to end a flirtation that had perhaps never begun. Her gaze roamed around the hot, crowded room. The friendly warmth in her eyes had been replaced with cold impatience. She was waiting for someone else as well.

"He's late," she said, turning quickly back to me. "He's always late." She plucked another glass of champagne from a silver tray that floated by. "Americans seem to think it doesn't matter — that you can come when you want, that everyone will wait." She checked her watch and stood tense and rigid, her eyes glittering with the severity of the judgment.

"You're the lawyer," she said suddenly. She seemed astonished that she had not known it before. "Joseph Antonelli. I thought you looked familiar. And of course the name . . . But what are you doing here? Yes, meeting your law school roommate. What an odd place to meet. We've met before," she said with a look that dared me to remember. "Last year — in Los Angeles — at the Stanley Roth trial."

I had met a lot of people in Los Angeles during that trial, but I was certain I had not met her. I would not have forgotten if I had.

"When you held that first press conference, the one outside the studio. I was there, one of the reporters writing down everything you said."

"You're a reporter? You covered the trial?"

"No, unfortunately not. I work for a German paper, and I was offered the chance to join the Washington bureau." She inclined her head, smiling to herself as she looked at me from a different angle and saw me in a different light. "Joseph Antonelli," she mused. "I saw the movie they made about the case. The actor who played you was very convincing."

She paused, searching for the exact words with which to make a strange observation. It was shrewd and subtle, and it went right to the heart of something that until I heard it from her I had not quite grasped.

"It must be difficult, though, to have become that famous and have everyone think you look like someone else."

"It may have been what saved me. What kept me from confusing who I was with what I saw on the screen." That was as far as I wanted to go. I did not want to talk

about me; I wanted to find out more about
her.

"You cover politics for a German paper?
That's why you're here — the opening of
the new embassy?"

She dismissed it out of hand.

"Browning. I cover the vice president
every chance I get."

With a casual gesture, she gently took
hold of my sleeve, pulling us a little closer.

"It's fascinating. The two of them, the
president and the vice president, represent
the two extremes in America: the best of
what you are and the worst. It's hard to believe — isn't it? You could have had
Browning and you chose Walker. It's fascinating. It really is. It's the best story in
town."

There was a sudden commotion. Then
all the noise stopped. Every pair of eyes
looked the same way at once.

"It's what I told you," whispered Gisela
Hoffman. "He always comes late."

The ambassador waited with open arms,
ready to embrace in the name of freedom
and equality the vice president of the
United States. Browning stopped a step
short and placed his left hand on the ambassador's shoulder, perhaps as part of his
greeting, or perhaps to hold him at bay. In

154

a distant gesture of formal goodwill, he offered his hand. The ambassador's smile froze on his face. Browning stepped forward to address the crowd, and the ambassador found himself alone and ignored.

Browning was gracious, but only to a point. He said he had wanted to see for himself the "very interesting" building that had caught everyone's attention, and that he was as mindful as anyone that there were countries in the world with rich cultures and traditions that were not given the attention they deserved. Then, under the towering walls of marble, gold and glass, he proceeded to remind them of how another country had once gone ignored.

"When the United States first became a country, we could not afford embassies of our own. The few ambassadors we sent to the great capitols of Europe, London, Paris, Saint Petersburg and Madrid, lived in boardinghouses or cheap hotels and waited sometimes for years before they were so much as granted an audience with the foreign secretaries of those great and powerful nations."

Browning looked around the crowd. His brown eyes danced with cheerful malice. When he spoke, his voice carried a cautionary tone.

"We made a very poor appearance among all the extravagance of a European court. We complied with all the forms of diplomatic usage in our formal relations, but that was as far as we could go. We were young, and perhaps unimportant, but we understood what we were and what we wanted to be. We had made a revolution in the name of freedom and we were not going to give that up. We were the New World, not because we were on one side of the Atlantic and Europe was on the other, but because we understood that republican government, that democracy, owned the future, whoever may have owned the past."

Raising his eyes, Browning stretched out his hand, a gesture meant to encompass all of his surroundings, from the timbered glass ceiling down to the elaborate hand-sculpted floor.

"Everything built eventually crumbles. Monuments made to last forever mock us with our vanity and turn to dust. The only thing that will be remembered is the example passed from one generation to the next, not so much of what we did, but of why we did it and who we were."

And with that, Browning turned quickly and took the ambassador by the hand. "Thank you for allowing me to come," he said with an air of finality. He stood for a moment, facing the cameras; and then, as quickly as he had arrived, he left.

The noise of the crowd again engulfed the room, everyone eager to make some remark, some observation that would be remembered and later repeated. Gisela Hoffman, who had moved in front of me to get a clearer view when Browning arrived, jotted something in a notebook and then turned around.

"Browning is an old friend?" she asked, certain she was right. "I read the speech and what he said about you. That's why you're here, isn't it? You're visiting the vice president. How long will you be in town?"

"Just a day or so."

Her eyes stayed on me as if she were waiting for the question she knew I was going to ask.

"Would you like to have dinner while I'm here?"

She started to smile, but before she could say anything I felt a hand on my shoulder. It was Powell from the Secret Service telling me it was time to go.

"Is there . . . ?"

Gisela wrote a number on a page of the small black notebook, tore it out and folded it in half. "You can reach me at home," she whispered into my ear.

I followed Agent Powell through the crowd. At the entrance, I looked back, hoping to catch a last glimpse of her before I left. She was talking to a tall blond man in a dark blue suit and she seemed quite upset. I reached inside my pocket and ran my finger across the surface of the paper on which she had written the number where she could be reached. I wondered if I should call.

I tumbled into the backseat of the waiting limousine. Under a reading lamp, Browning had his eyes on what looked like a briefing book. When the door shut behind me, he closed it on his lap and fixed me with a rueful, friendly smile.

"I haven't done any supermarket openings yet, but I wouldn't be surprised if that's next." He leaned his shoulders against the corner of the cushioned seat. "What did you think of that place? What did you think of him?"

Browning's chin sank onto his chest. That wistful look I had seen so often twist the shape of his mouth was there again, the promise of something he could not wait to tell.

"It's astonishing, the effect we have on others. We've become so powerful that it becomes enormously important just to be seen with us. This afternoon they sent over the text of the ambassador's remarks, what he was going to say by way of an introduction. Ten typed pages! And the language! It read like one of those speeches the conquistadors used to make when they claimed new lands for Spain! He would have pulled it out and read it if I had given him half a chance. I felt a little guilty doing it — stopping him like that — but not as bad as I would have felt if I had had to stand there for twenty minutes listening to him talk.

"Anyway, it's over." A sparkle came into his eyes. "I saw you talking to Gisela Hoffman. Be careful. She's a dangerous woman."

"Dangerous?"

"She's charming and beautiful. What could be more dangerous than that? She's married; but they're getting a divorce. He was there. He's also a journalist. Works for a different German paper. He saw the two of you together. He didn't seem to like it."

"You noticed all that?"

A bland expression, just this side of boredom, covered his face. "After you've said the same thing in court a couple of thousand times, do you really think about the words?"

The limousine crept along, the motor-cycle escort silent, all the lights dim, doing nothing that might attract attention. A few minutes later, we left the public street and headed up a private drive, passing through an iron gate where an armed sentry stood guard. There was silence everywhere, the hushed, anxious silence of people listening, watching, waiting for what might happen next. The house was close now, the covered porch caught in the headlights of the car. Browning turned away from the side window, but he did not look at me. He drew further into himself like someone rehearsing in his mind a scene that had been played more than once before, a scene that was never pleasant, but a scene that might with proper management be kept within tolerable bounds and, if not that, at least kept mercifully short. I began to feel a sense of panic, a wish to be anywhere but here. If it had been anyone else — some other former friend of mine I had not seen in years — if I had been anywhere else than in the vice president's official car hundreds of yards inside what for all intents and purposes was a military zone, I would have made my excuses — pled the press of other business or my own fatigue — and gone my separate way. I was becoming more uncomfortable, more ill at ease the closer we got. There was no mistaking that stern, set look in Browning's eyes. It told me all I needed to know, and far more than I wanted to learn, about what had happened, not just to Thomas Browning, but to his wife.

The limousine came to a halt. The door on Browning's side began to open. He hesitated, then pulled it nearly shut. He leaned toward me, clearly at odds with himself about what he should say.

"Joanna hasn't been well lately. Nothing serious," he added, sensing my reaction. "Nothing that can't be handled."

It seemed a strange way to describe an illness.

We entered the front hall of the Naval Observatory, the official residence of the vice president since Gerald Ford appointed Nelson Rockefeller to the job after Nixon resigned the presidency and Ford took his place. No one thought it either noteworthy or surprising that someone as rich as Rockefeller did not want to live in the modest circumstances of his predecessors in an office to which, it is safe to say, he had never aspired.

The first thing I noticed was an enormous dining room on the left with a table that could easily seat eight people on each side. Much of what happened in the vice president's office during the day was discussed and decided around this table at night. Opposite the dining room, on the other side of the spacious front hall, was the living room, with sofas and soft, comfortable chairs scattered all around. Through the open door I could see out the windows to the porch beyond. The lamps were still burning, and the few pieces of white wicker furniture that were visible were bathed in a ghostly yellow light.

"Your room is on the second floor. Your things have been brought over," Browning explained.

At the end of the hall, directly opposite the front door, a wide spiral staircase led to the two upstairs floors. Above the landing, three steps from the floor, on the wall next to the staircase, a series of ledges and shelves contained exact replicas of artillery pieces employed in some of the country's earliest wars. A mischievous grin crossed Browning's lips.

"When Gore was vice president, they were filled with shofras. You know what those are? Neither did anyone else — except the people by whom he wanted them noticed. A shofra is the ceremonial horn of a ram — what the Jews blow on to announce the high holidays. Gore picked them up in Israel." Browning sighed with weary resignation. "I think he must have spent every day he lived here thinking about money: how to get it, how to spend it, how to make it work."

On the second floor he walked me to the far end of the hallway and showed me my room. My suitcase was sitting in the corner. All my clothes had been hung up. Browning sat down on the edge of the bed, bouncing on it twice to test the mattress.

"Not bad," he said with the same grin I remember from the first day I met him, when he tried both beds before insisting I take the one he had found to be marginally better. "If you need anything," he added with a nod toward a telephone on the table next to the bed.

After I got out of my suit coat and removed my tie, I went over to the window and looked out. At the bottom of the long curve of the drive, I could see the iron gate and, beyond that, in the far distance along Embassy Row, the garish lights from the embassy still burning through the night.

I was supposed to meet Browning downstairs for a drink. I had just entered the hallway when I heard the first muffled shouts. I started to turn back, but I didn't feel like hiding in my room, trying to guess when it might be over. With rapid steps I made my way down the hallway to the stairs. With each step down the staircase, the sound of the noise subsided. The library, or study, was to the left of the staircase as I descended, behind the living room, facing onto the same yellow-lighted porch. Shutting the door behind me, I began to pass the time, examining the titles of books.

The white built-in bookshelves, circling around the fireplace and climbing halfway to the ceiling, were filled with volumes, some of them quite old.

"There is no other library like it in America."

I had not heard the door open. Browning's voice was calm, collected, with that same unblemished affability that made you feel so much at home. With a book in my hand, I looked at him over my shoulder. His manner was no more changed than his voice. Whatever had happened upstairs was over, forgotten, filed away with a kind of ruthless efficiency, the way he must have taught himself to move from one thing to the next. He had no time to question anything he had done, or to think too far into the future; he could not afford the luxury of feeling sorry for himself or, I imagine, for anyone else.

"Books on the vice presidency, on the men who have held the office — they're all here. Bad enough you have to be vice president; you have to read about it, too," he remarked with a jovial glance. He handed me a drink. "Scotch and soda — right?" He picked a book at random off a shelf near his desk and held it at arm's length, squinting for a moment before holding it toward me so I could see. "*Burr*, the novel by Gore Vidal. At least it's well written, even if he didn't get it right." A second thought, a kind of reconsideration, registered in his eyes. "Though he came a good deal closer than most of these . . ." He threw a disdainful glance at the shelves on the distant wall. "Most of this stuff was written by academics who never knew a public man, much less led a public life." It was an odd turn of speech. He caught the slight uncertainty in my eye. "It's the way the British used to talk — and write. Public men — wealthy aristocrats who took part in politics, who were elected to Parliament from districts they as good as owned, who formed governments — the men who ran the country. They used the phrase to distinguish themselves from the lazy bastards who only wanted to hang on to their country estates and indulge their taste for private pleasures."

He had not changed out of his dark suit, though he had unfastened the top button of his shirt and loosened his tie. He stood in the middle of the room, running his fingers through his thick reddish brown hair. A pensive expression spread across his mouth.

There was a clattering noise, growing louder, coming closer. The door flew open and a woman with hollow eyes and a desolate grin, a woman I barely recognized, burst into the room. Laughing wildly, she fell into my arms, repeating my name over and over again. I held her, listening to her tell me how glad she was to see me, how glad she was I had come, as I tried to pretend that she had not changed and that she was still the same Joanna I remembered and that she was not dead drunk.

Browning quickly pulled her away and led her back upstairs.

"It's the pressure," he explained when he returned. There was no trace of embarrassment, nothing even suggesting an apology for the way she had raged at him or the way he had answered back. He might have been describing a minor malady, something that cured itself with a good night's sleep.

"There's a lot in this business," he went on, attempting to shrug it away with indifference. He took a drink from a glass of something he had poured for himself. "Especially now.

"Joanna's had too much to drink," he said, determined that this would be the final word. He got up from behind the desk, stared for a moment down at the floor, and then, with a methodical look, slowly raised his eyes until his gaze met mine. "She does that. Fairly often, to tell you the whole, unvarnished truth. It keeps her company, I suppose," he said, his voice growing faint. "It's how she tries to cope." He bent his head, a wistful expression in his eyes. "It's better when we're in New York. She hates it here; hates the life — all the posturing, all the pretense. But she does what she has to, goes to all the things she's supposed to, says all the things she should. Tomorrow she'll be fine. It will be as if nothing happened."

He turned to the side, staring at something only he could see; something that was as real to him as anything he could touch.

"Everything would have been different if Annie had lived."

He lowered himself into the chair, grimaced with pain and immediately dismissed it as of no account.

"Twisted my ankle earlier tonight."

"The foot?"

He tossed his head and emitted a quiet, rueful laugh. "I forgot — you know. Yes, the damn foot." Annoyed with himself, he shook his head. "FDR — can you imagine what that must have been like? — Spends his life in a wheelchair, but every time you see him in public he's standing up, looking like the healthiest, most vigorous man alive, standing there — walking, for God's sake! — his hand on someone's arm, moving those dead legs inside those steel braces; standing at a podium, holding himself up, his head thrown back at that jaunty angle, giving everyone the confidence to go on — first the Depression, then the war. And then they build a monument and what do they do? After all the pain and suffering, after all that heroic effort to rise above that awful paralysis? — They put him in a wheelchair and make it look as if he had been proud to be there! God, what's happened to this country? Everyone wants to be a victim. You imagine anyone ever told Franklin Roosevelt they felt sorry for him?"

A knowing smile, a kind of secret, passed over Browning's mouth.

"That's what kept me going when I was a boy and they kept trying to fix my lame foot and, when they couldn't, made me wear those boxlike shoes so I could walk like everyone else and no one would know. I kept reminding myself what Roosevelt must have gone through. If he could do that, what right did I have to complain or feel sorry for myself because of a little handicap like this? What everyone should know about Roosevelt isn't that he was in a wheelchair, but that through sheer guts and determination he got out of it."

On the desk a lamp with a green parchment shade threw light on a book, marked toward the middle with what appeared to be a scrap of notepaper torn from a pad. Browning's hand strayed toward it, touched it, and then immediately drew away. A troubled expression came into his eyes.

"Do you remember Annie? How full of life she was? The way those dark eyes of hers were always laughing; the way you could hear the laughter in her voice? If she hadn't come that day — if she hadn't fallen — everything would have changed." He seemed to concentrate on each word, as if what he wanted to say had to be said exactly right. "Or could have changed, could have been different. I would have married her, and none of the rest of this would have happened."

I started to ask him what he meant, but he stopped me with an impatient glance.

"Maybe I wouldn't have married her; maybe she wouldn't have changed her mind about that. You remember Annie, what she was like. She always said she'd never get married, that if two people loved each other they should be together — but not forever, only 'till love died.'" Browning smiled to himself. "Not 'till death do us part,' but 'till love dies.' She said it always did — love always dies — and said it with all the worldly certainty of the vast experience of her twenty-some-odd years. I wonder what would have happened to her — how she would have changed; I wonder if she would have changed at all." He reached for the glass he had left on the far corner of the large mahogany desk. "I wonder if any of us really changes at all."

He took a drink, and then, with both

hands wrapped around the glass, held it in front of him, tipping it gently from side to side, watching the changing quality of the light reflected from the green-shaded lamp.

"Annie didn't really want to be a lawyer. She wanted to go off to Europe — to Paris, or Florence — and study art. She thought it would be exciting, a different way to live; and if it didn't work out . . . well, there would always be something else — become a rancher in New Zealand, or take up some religion in India or Tibet. You remember Annie. You remember what she was like."

Browning tapped his fingers lightly against the half-hollow glass. "I would have gone with her — anywhere she liked."

"You would have dropped out of law school with less than half a year left?"

"I didn't have your drive, your desire to become a lawyer. I went to Harvard because I could use it as an excuse."

"An excuse? From what?"

"From the company; from my grandfather; from the life that had been planned out for me from the day of my birth — an excuse from becoming the official guardian of the legend of the great Zachary Stern. Some people enrolled in law school because they didn't want to go to Vietnam; I

171

enrolled in law school because I didn't want to go back to Detroit.

"Annie made me see that I was just running away and that I'd always be doing that — running away — until I decided that it was my life and that I could do what I wanted with it and that it didn't matter what anyone else thought. Of course," added Browning with the shrewd self-appraisal that had come only much later, "what I wanted was to do exactly what she thought I should. But she didn't want me to do anything; she didn't want me to be anything. She wanted me to be myself, and all I wanted was to be with her." He put down the glass and stretched his arms high over his head. "I might have ended up on that ranch in New Zealand with a few thousand sheep and a dozen children, none of them born in wedlock because Annie — you remember Annie — did not believe in 'till death do us part.' Do you find that hard to believe?" he asked, placing his forearms on the desk as he turned and faced me. "That I would rather have wound up somewhere like that with Annie, living an anonymous life, than what's happened — become someone who was almost president, and still might, someone with more money than he can possibly use, someone married to a woman who has given him two fine children, a woman everyone admires, a woman who has never told anyone that in her heart of hearts she wishes that instead of me, she had married you?"

8

For what must have been hours I lay awake.
I saw Annie sliding through the Plaza suite,
that same wistful look upon her mouth and
eyes. I heard Thomas Browning in that low,
unhurried voice, doling out benign encouragement to someone tense with insecurity
about something — school, a girl —
somethings they thought would make or
break their life and that Browning somehow
knew would pass. I saw his eyes move toward
Annie, while she floated across the room,
looking back just long enough to catch his
glance, hold it, touch it . . . let it go. She was
in love with him. I seemed to know that now.
Perhaps not the way he must have been in
love with her, with that desperate all-or-
nothing feeling, willing to sacrifice every
hope, every ambition for the chance to be
with her; but as much as her free soul would
allow. He would have left, dropped out of
school, turned his back on the sworn duty of
his life. He would have gone with her anywhere and never thought he had sacrificed a

thing. He would have been that rancher with his own healthy brood. I knew that now, knew it in that way you sometimes do when you have known something all along, but have kept that knowledge a kind of secret from yourself. Perhaps it was Joanna; perhaps I had cared too much about her to think that she had ended up in a marriage in which she would always be in some sense second best.

Whenever it was I finally fell asleep, I slept like a dead man and did not awaken until the morning was half gone. I showered and shaved, and as I stared at myself in the mirror tried not to think too much about whether time had treated me with the same cruel indifference with which it had left the marks of its passage on Joanna's once young and beautiful face. I had seen pictures of her in the papers, and a few times on television I had heard her talk, but those had been staged appearances in the proper light, usually from a distance and seldom close up. If she had ever been anything but completely sober, it had never shown.

As I leaned closer to the mirror, I seemed to notice a slight increase in the number and depth of the lines about my eyes. I rubbed a dab of skin balm into my face and the color deepened into a healthy, reddish glow. I began to feel better. I slipped on a crisp, fresh white shirt and a clean blue suit and picked out a cheerful tie. On my way out, I stopped at the window. Buried under a large, floppy hat, a man mounted on a riding mower traced long, parallel paths across the rolling green lawn. The air was turgid, gray, hot and humid, threatening rain. I left the room not feeling quite so good.

The hallway was silent, but then, from somewhere in the distance, behind one of the closed doors, came the low humming noise of a vacuum cleaner. At the bottom of the long, spiral staircase I hesitated, not sure what to do. I listened, but except for the muted vacuum above, there was nothing to hear. I walked toward the front door, stopped at the living room and peered inside, then turned around and entered the dining room. A doorway led to the kitchen, but that seemed vacant as well. The study had the advantage of familiarity. I decided to wait in there.

Rooms, like people, have their moods. The midnight shadows on a lamp-lit wall create a different effect than the flat even dullness of a gray-covered sun. The massive dark desk that had gleamed hard and shiny like some late restored antiquity was old, worn, scarred, marked with years, decades, of pen strokes, left beneath the official important papers on which they had been made. It was the inadvertent record of the endless repetition of written and re-written words; words started, words stopped, words thrown away, a new sheet of paper placed where the old one had been, a second followed by a third, then a fourth, attempt.

There was a sudden commotion as the front door swung open and the house was drowned in a sea of voices. I moved away from the desk and began to examine more closely the photographs that I had barely noticed before. My eye had just settled on a picture of a man in his sixties with intelligent eyes and a firm, but forgiving, mouth.

"Phil Hart."

Startled, I turned around. Browning was standing in the doorway, his reddish brown hair windblown in a dozen different directions, his blue eyes curious and alert.

"Have a good sleep?" he asked, gently taunting me as he dropped into the chair behind the desk. "I had a seven-thirty meeting. Now there's a meeting here," he said, tossing his head toward the hallway through which he had just arrived. "Then

I'm off. I'm giving a speech at noon, another one at three. This evening I'm somewhere, and somewhere else later tonight." He let both arms fall from the sides of the chair and rolled his head to the side.

"Phil Hart." He spoke the name with a kind of eager exuberance, as if I had just mentioned some mutual long-lost friend. "Interesting face, don't you think? Served eighteen years in the Senate; died a week before the end of his last term. They named the third Senate office building after him; did it while he was still alive. First time a major public building in Washington was named after someone still alive. The vote to do it passed the Senate ninety-nine to zero; only Hart abstained."

A look of nostalgia swept across Browning's eyes. He sat forward in the chair.

"Hart was such a modest man, there were people who thought that when he heard what the Senate was going to do he might try to stop it. The night before the vote, someone on his staff suspected he might and put a note on his desk pleading with him not to do it. The next morning she found a note on her desk. He said he wasn't as modest as she thought and that he could not be more delighted at what the

Senate was going to do. He wouldn't vote for it himself, you understand . . . ," added Browning. He smiled hard to keep himself in check, and then, laughing at his own embarrassment, made an awkward gesture with his hand.

"They did that in the summer, and the day after Christmas he was dead. I went to the funeral. Half of Washington was there. Three of his closest friends in the Senate — Ted Kennedy, Ed Muskie, and Eugene McCarthy — were sitting together in the center section about a dozen rows ahead. Kennedy was on the aisle, and I could see him as plainly as I can see you. The tears were pouring out of his eyes, and his face was all red. I don't think I've ever seen anyone so distraught.

"Of all the tributes written, all the things people said, the most moving was a speech given on the Senate floor by — you simply won't believe this, but I swear it's true — Strom Thurmond. You could read for years through the *Congressional Record*, go down the list of five or ten thousand roll-call votes, and I don't know that you would ever find more than half a dozen on which they had ever voted the same way, and yet Thurmond revered him. Imagine! Strom Thurmond, who led the Dixiecrats out of the Democratic Party at the Democratic Convention in 1948; who promised segregation today, tomorrow, and forever before George Wallace was old enough to talk; who voted against every major piece of civil rights legislation for almost the next fifty years; and Phil Hart, the liberal's liberal, the floor manager for the Voting Rights Act of 1965, the act that put a federal guarantee behind the right to vote and changed the political complexion of the South. Impossible, isn't it? But true. Thurmond loved him. They all did, all those southern segregationists the rest of the country reviled. And do you know why? Because he treated all of them with unfailing courtesy and respect.

"There's a Hart story that you won't see written in any book. The Voting Rights Act was coming up. Richard Russell, the senator from Georgia — one of the other Senate office buildings is named for him — was presiding over a meeting of the southern leadership in the Senate, trying to figure out the legislative strategy of the other side. In the middle of the meeting, the telephone rings. It's Phil Hart. He's the floor leader for the bill, and he tells Russell exactly what he is going to do. Amazed — but perhaps not entirely surprised — Russell hangs up the phone, tells the other southern Senators what he's just been told, and then, in that ultimate southern compliment, looks around the room and remarks, 'And that was a gentleman.' "

Browning raised his head. A cunning look entered his eyes.

"Some people might think Hart had been naïve; others might think he was just trying to be fair. He was trying to be fair all right, but not just for the sake of fairness. This was not some game where it didn't matter if you won or lost, only that you played within the rules. This was going to change everything — and everyone knew it. Hart understood — I'm not sure how many others did; I doubt any of the liberals did — that even if you had the votes, it wasn't enough to win. You had to win in a way that left the other side some dignity in defeat. If the South was going to accept defeat, they had to know they had been given every reasonable consideration. It was exactly a hundred years since the end of the Civil War; it was not going to be another hundred years — not if Hart had anything to do with it — before the races treated each other with respect.

"There was another reason as well,"

added Browning. "The chairman of the Senate Judiciary Committee was James Eastland of Mississippi, and nothing got through that committee the chairman did not want. The real mystery is why Eastland, who could have stopped the Voting Rights Act with nothing more than a word, let it through. The answer, I think, is that Phil Hart asked him if he would. The bill got through the committee, and when it came to the floor, where all the southern senators would vote against it in what they knew, and had accepted, was a losing cause, one of them delivered a speech that attacked Hart by name. Someone started to rise in Hart's defense, but Hart held him back, explaining that it had all been prearranged. A little verbal abuse from a senator playing to the folks back home was a small enough price to pay for that same senator's quiet refusal to do anything more than cast a single useless vote to stop it."

Browning glanced at the black-and-white photograph. "It's the only picture of a public figure I keep in here. Hart kept only one picture as well. You know whose picture it was? James Eastland of Mississippi."

Browning got to his feet. "I keep that

picture because it reminds me of what people — even people in politics — can be." His eyes grew hard, calculating and even, I thought, vengeful. "I keep it to remind me that not everyone is like Connally and Walker and the rest of that crowd who think that government is the enemy and that the poor can take care of themselves."

His chest rumbled with laughter. "See? — Only one person in the room and I feel compelled to make a speech!" He started toward the door, glancing over his shoulder at Hart's picture. "Another story you'll never read about . . ."

He stopped, came back, sat down at the end of the leather sofa. He appeared to meditate on something grave.

"You remember Reynolds," he said presently. "What a miserable bastard he was." There was another pause, not so long, but in a way more profound. He raised his eyelids and revealed a scornful look. "You remember what he did."

It was not that I thought the offense less serious, or in some way more forgivable, but I had in what was perhaps the desperate comfort of a last illusion decided that if you did what Reynolds had done, you would always live with the knowledge that whatever you might later achieve was based on a fraud. Reynolds was a cheat, and because of that, his life was a lie. Reynolds did not matter. I had long ago dismissed him from my mind. I said this in no uncertain terms to Browning. In reply he gave me a look that told me he wished it were true.

"Unfortunately, that cheat, that liar, is the swing vote on a five-to-four Court. He hates me with a passion. He knows I fought his nomination, that when I heard what the president — it was Connally's idea — was thinking, I tried to get it killed."

"Did you tell them what he did at Harvard? How he cheated his way through?"

Browning broke into a broad, rueful smile. "That would have made them even more certain they'd found the right man for the job."

The smile faded from his lips. "What could I have done? Told them we all knew he cheated, but no one had ever proved it? Proved it? No one had ever accused him of it; not in a way that left an official record. All I could say — and I said this — was that there was some question whether during his long career he had always been honest in his methods. Of course, it all got back to him. He knows what I meant and he hates me for it. He hated me before, me and you and everyone else who knew. He hates us because we know, and I think he hates us even more because we've never told."

With a discouraged look, Browning got to his feet. He glanced again at the photograph.

"Years ago — it seems like forever now — Lyndon Johnson was president, and he put his great good friend Abe Fortas on the court. Earl Warren was going to retire. Johnson nominated Fortas to become chief justice." Browning looked at me. "You remember all this? Then it was revealed that Fortas had taken some money — not much, twenty thousand or so — as an honorarium, some kind of expense . . ." Browning was moving now, pacing slowly around the room, hair slipping down the right side of his high prominent forehead. "Fortas had to resign from the court. Johnson wasn't going to be beaten twice. He didn't have the strength he had once had — Vietnam had weakened him; almost destroyed him, really. He had probably already decided he wasn't going to seek a second full term. But he understood the Senate perhaps better than anyone ever had. He decided to give them a name they could not refuse. He was going to nominate Phil Hart to become chief justice of the United States Supreme Court."

Browning stood still and shook his head, baffled and amused that someone had really done something as remarkable, as unprecedented, as what he was about to tell me.

"Hart turned him down. He thought about it. He made at least one call I know about to ask someone's advice; but, yes — Hart turned him down. Chief justice of the United States Supreme Court and Hart said no. I don't know why he did that. The first chief justice, John Jay, didn't think the job worth having. He said as much when he quit. Then John Marshall took his place, and ever since then it's become the dream of every lawyer, the obsession of every judge, and Hart said no. I think he had a certain definite sense about the limitations of his own powers: He would not do something unless he thought he could do it well." Browning shook his head, sadly and with regret. "That of course is precisely the reason why he would have been a great chief justice, one of the best we've ever had. Strange when you think about it: In a city of such colossal egos, Hart wasn't sufficiently vain."

The glow of nostalgia in Browning's eyes vanished, replaced with a look cold, hard, intense. "And now exactly the opposite situation is playing out in front of my eyes, and there isn't anything I can do about it. Reynolds is on the court because Walker wanted him there, and Walker wanted him there because the chief justice is dying." With a stern look that swore me to secrecy, Browning added: "Only a few people know. Cancer. He has maybe a year."

I could not believe what I knew he was about to tell me. "Reynolds — chief justice?"

"Of course. They have the presidency; they want the court. Reynolds as chief justice is like having Arthur Connally over there. They'll tell him what they want, and he'll do it."

There was one hope left. As soon as I said it, I realized how ludicrous it must sound.

"Other presidents have thought that. They nominated people they thought would vote one way who voted another. Earl Warren didn't turn out to be the kind of chief justice Eisenhower thought he would."

Browning nearly laughed. "Reynolds? Even if he wanted to do the right thing, he'd never be able to figure out what it was. Remember what Teddy Roosevelt said about Oliver Wendell Holmes? — That he had the 'backbone of a banana.' Reynolds has the eyes of a beggar: craven, cowardly, eager to please. Watch him sometime, the greedy look in those nervous little eyes when he's introduced. His mouth starts to form the word *Justice* as if he has to hear it twice. His eyes light up like a match being struck. He loves the sound of it, the title, the fact that everyone has to call him 'Mr. Justice Reynolds.' He spent days training the woman who answered his phone to say it exactly right."

Browning caught the look of skepticism that flashed across my eyes. "Days, I tell you." A raised eyebrow acknowledged that if he had not known better he would have had the same reaction. " 'Mr . . . Justice . . . Reynolds.' That was crucial," Browning explained, suppressing a grin. "That pause — that pregnant pause — after each word." He cocked his head and gave me a puzzled, doubtful look. "The real mystery is why he did not add a flourish of coronets. I'm tempted to say it's because he didn't have the wit, but when it comes to advertising his own importance . . . No, it wouldn't be because he didn't think of it. He's probably saving it, keeping it for later, when he becomes chief justice and can reserve it for himself."

Certain he was right, he nodded once and then, vastly amused, shrugged his shoulders. "They play that flourish each time the president enters a room; why not the chief justice?"

He walked past me to the French doors that led out to the covered porch. He raised his arm and rested it against the corner of the bookcase as he stared through the glass. Seen in this attitude of repose, his hand was surprisingly graceful: a violinist's bow would have fit perfectly within the grasp of the smooth, round fingers. His hands were too small to have played the piano with more than passable skill, but I could see them moving with the blurlike speed of a virtuoso the short distance of a violin's strings. With a quarter turn, he leaned against the flat end of the bookcase and the casement of the door. He held his arms, loosely folded, across his chest, sunk in a single troubling and depressing thought.

"Reynolds has never been sick a day in his life. He could be chief justice for twenty, twenty-five years — maybe thirty. If that happens, and if I'm forced out — if they put the kind of man they want into the vice presidency, someone who can follow Walker with another eight years of welfare for the rich and laissez-faire economics for everyone else — there may not be anything that can put this country back together. With Reynolds chief justice, and with the additional vote they pick up by filling the vacancy, they'll have a permanent six-to-three majority. There won't be any constitutional restraints on what these people want to do."

"Abortion; the right to bear arms; prayer in schools," I said, beginning with the top of the list generally considered the conservative agenda. Staring down at the floor, Browning shoved one foot an inch or so ahead of the other.

"That's what they want everyone to think. It keeps everyone's attention away from what they really want," he muttered darkly. He pushed himself away from the side of the bookshelf and turned toward me, filling the space inside the frame of the French doors.

"Every time I hear Walker or one of his friends give a speech and mention Teddy Roosevelt, I want to throw up. Roosevelt understood what industrialization had done to the country and how it was going to change the world. There was no equivalency, no balance between the interest of business and the interest of the American government for Roosevelt. The government — the public interest — was what counted. The nation! — That's what mattered. You think these people believe that? They don't have the faintest idea what Teddy Roosevelt meant."

With a long, deep breath, Browning gathered himself, the look in his eyes urgent, serious, intense.

"We don't talk about ourselves as citizens, with a citizen's duties and obligations; we talk about ourselves as consumers, people whose basic function is to buy the things we make so we can keep making more. The country is attacked. What do we do? Call for great sacrifice? Call for a new dedication to what we believe as a country? Treat it as a second Pearl Harbor and ask everyone to join the military or in some other way help prosecute the war? Treat it as a great opportunity to change the way we live, to become a country with something more important to do than choose the latest amusement? No — Do the same thing you've done before: spend money, shop. The economy is the important thing. And patriotism — the willingness to sacrifice for freedom and for the country you love? It's become too expensive, something we can't any longer afford. If I had been president, things would have been different. I can assure you of that. The days of soft self-indulgence would have been gone forever."

"What would you have done?" I asked.

He did not seem to hear me, but then, as if the question had echoed somewhere in his mind, he looked at me hard and intense.

"I would have . . ." He caught himself. With his head bent forward, he made his way to the desk. He pulled open the second drawer down on the left and extracted a small, thin paperback volume. The cover was bent and broken, the purple color worn away.

"When you argue a case to a jury — when you know you're right — have you ever found yourself so swept up in the emotion, in the passion of the moment, that you say things that have an immediate effect; and it's exactly the effect you want, because it's the truth and you feel it; and because you feel it, everyone watching you, listening to you, feels it, too; and not only do they feel it, but they know they can trust you, believe you, believe that what you're telling them is true? And have you ever then gone back, after the trial is over, after all the heat of the moment is gone and read in the cold light of day a transcript of the trial; read what you said that day, read what you believed with such fervor, such conviction; and because the moment has passed, cringed just a little, wondering how you could have done it, how you could have said the things you did? And at the same time, didn't you know you had been right, that it was all true, and that while it might sound stilted, even fanatical, in the same circumstances, surrounded with the same sense of urgency, you would do it again? — That you would, in that old, timeworn phrase, 'seize the moment'?"

Browning glanced down at the book he held in his hands. When he looked up there was a trace of regret, a sense of having been close enough to touch, but not quite close enough to grasp, something he had wanted more than anything. It lasted only an instant, and if I had not known him as well as I did, or as well as I thought I did, I would have questioned whether I had seen it there at all.

"Here," he remarked, laughing at himself as he handed the book to me. He put his hand on my shoulder as we turned and I went with him toward the door. "Read this if you want. There is something in it that explains what I was going to say."

I glanced at the cover as he opened the door to the hallway. "Montesquieu, *The Greatness of the Romans and Their Decline.*" Puzzled, I looked at Browning, but he was walking quickly toward the dining room where behind the closed door could be heard a tumult of fierce, shouting noise. He put his hand on the door handle, but did not pull it open.

"Read especially the part about what happened, or rather what could have happened, after Julius Caesar was stabbed," he said, a distant, enigmatic smile on his lips. "Then there will be two of us who have."

He opened the door, and a dozen screaming voices were immediately dumb. Toward the far end of the table, Elizabeth Hartley opened the fist with which she had just struck the table and spread her fingers out.

"It's good to see that your deliberations are proceeding in such a calm, dignified manner," said Browning. "I'll be with you in a moment." He shut the door behind him and with his hand on my shoulder walked me a few steps away.

"Think about what I told you. I meant what I said: Someone is going to be indicted. You're the only one I trust."

"I still can't believe they would actually . . ."

"Mr. Vice President," said an urgent voice from the end of the hall. Browning waited as one of his assistants walked quickly toward him and handed him a telephone. Browning seemed to understand immediately that it was important. He held the phone to his ear, staring straight ahead, listening without the slightest change of expression until the end.

"Thank you. I understand."

After the assistant had taken the telephone and left us alone, Browning gave me an ominous look.

"Things are moving more quickly than I thought. The grand jury is meeting this morning in New York." He dropped his head and stared intently at the floor. A shudder passed through him. "They'll have an indictment by this afternoon."

I had the feeling that what was about to happen had happened a long time ago, and that I was somehow living it all over again, repeating it until I finally got it right.

Browning did not say who was going to be indicted, but I think he knew. Perhaps he was still hoping that it would not happen, that what he had just been told was wrong, or that if there were an indictment, it would name someone else. All he said was that we would know for certain before the day was out and that he was more certain than ever that I had to do what he had asked me to do the night before.

"Take the case. Call me as a witness; put me on the stand. I was there; I know what happened. I know how Annie died." He looked me straight in the eye. "When was the last time all you had to do to win a case was put a witness on the stand who told the truth?"

His eyes blazed with confidence. With his hand on my shoulder, we shook hands.

"I meant what I said two nights ago, at the dinner in New York: You're the best of them; and I knew it from the first day we met."

He had his hand on the door to the dining room when he remembered. "There's a telephone message for you," he said, gesturing toward an office on the other side of the stairs from the study. He looked away awkwardly. "And I'm afraid that Joanna won't be able to join you for lunch as she had planned. She isn't feeling very well today." He raised his head, glancing at me for an instant before he opened the door and disappeared inside. With that look he tried to apologize for the lie.

The message was from Gisela Hoffman. When I called her back, she answered on the second ring. The accent that made me start to laugh was gone. She was cold, aloof, severe. She said she had to see me. It was urgent.

In one of Browning's private limousines I was driven out the gate and onto the street below. We passed the embassy that had for a few brief hours been the center of Washington's attention the night before. People walked by without so much as a glance.

The driver pulled up in front of a narrow brick house on a leafy, tree-shaded Georgetown block filled with other houses of a similar look and nearly identical dimension. Most of them were three stories tall, with bay windows in the front; some of them had ornamental iron fences bulging with layers of lumpy black paint and shiny lacquered front doors; all of them had the dimly colonial look of lost elegance carefully restored. They were row houses, built originally to house the city's vast supply of what were then called Negro servants and menial workers, but who were then driven out when the housing shortage became desperate in the great expansion of government that came with the Second World War. During the heady days of the New Frontier they became the fashionable address of the Washington elite. They were still home to some of the most famous and powerful people in town.

Gisela answered the door with the face I remembered. The cold and peremptory voice on the telephone seemed to belong to someone else. Holding the edge of the door with both hands, she glanced quickly down both sides of the street as I slipped inside. Browning had told me about the angry confrontation that had taken place at the embassy the night before. I wondered if she was worried about what might happen if she was seen talking with me twice. There was something amusing, and in a strange way, thrilling, about the thought of a jealous husband waiting somewhere outside.

She was wearing a white blouse and a simple black skirt. Her hair was pulled up. She had on red lipstick and high-heeled shoes that left a sharp abrasive echo in the air as she led me through the marble entryway and onto the hardwood floor of the living room, really nothing more than a small parlor, past the steep staircase that seemed to rise straight up from the hallway to the towering ceiling on the third floor above, and from there through a mirrored, windowless dining room into a large kitchen in the back.

"Thank you for coming." She had that slightly embarrassed look I remembered from the night before, grinning like a schoolgirl at her best-intentioned failure at the right pronunciation of the words. "When you called me . . ." She hesitated, putting the sentence together in her mind. "When you called me back, I couldn't speak — talk. I was at the office," she explained. "I didn't want anyone to know. I'm afraid — I was worried — you must think me very rude."

We sat at a square table beneath the same high ceiling — at least ten, perhaps twelve feet — I had passed under in the rooms I had come through. Each floor must be like the first, one room wide, and with the sense, because the ceilings were so high, that the walls were pressing toward you, squeezing out the light.

Gisela looked at me with dark wide-open eyes, organizing her thoughts. She took a deep breath.

"I'm sorry," she said suddenly. Her long, fine lashes beat rapidly as she sprang to her feet. "Can I get you something?"

"You said you wanted to see me. You said it was urgent."

It was irresistible, that look of baffled embarrassment that swept across her face each time she remembered something she could not understand why she had forgotten. She shook her head and threw out her hands, then shrugged her shoulders, knit her brow, and tried hard to think.

"Well, *urgent* — perhaps that's not quite the word. *Important* might have been better." Slightly flustered, she blinked her eyes and glanced around the room as if she were a stranger, seeing it for the first time. "I asked you here, because I didn't know anywhere else that might be . . . safe? Yes, well, perhaps . . . where no one would know we talked."

With her fingernail she drew an invisible line on the table. By the time she stopped, she had become serious and strangely intent.

"You were in the same class in law school as Vice President Browning."

It was not a question; but then again, it was. Or rather it was the beginning of an interrogation: polite, civilized, friendly and, as I immediately understood, potentially dangerous. I was waiting for her when she raised her eyes.

"And there was also at the law school, though not in the same class, another student: a young woman named Anna Winifred Malreaux?"

All my hurried caution vanished. I started to smile.

"Annie's middle name was Winifred? I never knew that."

Gisela's expression did not change. She had not known Annie; she had not known any of us. She was interested only in what she had asked.

"Then, yes? Anna Malreaux was in law school at the same time?"

It was, I realized, a journalistic formality: the questions to which the answers were already known, before the other questions, the real questions, were asked.

"You already know that," I replied. "Why are you asking me what you already know?" I asked sharply. "If you want to know about the vice president, don't you think you ought to ask him?"

I was sorry that I had come. I started to get up. A wounded look entered her eyes, and without quite changing my mind, I paused, settled back in the chair and waited.

"I'm sorry. Perhaps I shouldn't have . . . but I thought you would want to know. There is a new investigation into her murder and . . ."

"Annie wasn't murdered," I objected. "It was an accident. She fell out a window — she wasn't pushed."

"There is a new investigation into her — death; and there is going to be an indict-ment."

I searched Gisela's serious eyes. "How do you know that? How could you know that?"

Gisela lowered her eyes, studying the backs of her fingers after she laid her right hand palm down on the table. Browning had only just learned of it — how did she know it so soon?

"When did you hear there was going to be an indictment?"

She raised her eyes. "I learned about it this morning, just before I called. I can't tell you any more than that." She held her-self with a rigid formality, like someone trying hard to be objective between the truth they cannot reveal and the lie they do not know how to tell.

"Someone in the New York district attorney's office told you this?"

She started to fidget with her hands, became aware of it and stopped. Her eyes stayed fastened on mine, afraid that by looking away she would tell me what she did not think she should. Instead of hiding the truth, it gave it away. She knew there was an investigation; she knew there might be an indictment — but she had not gotten that information from anyone in New York.

"Your source is someone here, someone in the White House."

She bent her head a little to the side. "You know I can't tell you that. But you can tell me — can't you? The vice president knew her — yes? It happened in his hotel room — yes?"

"No," I said almost angrily. "Not in his hotel room." It was odd the way that seemed to change the meaning, the way it gave a completely different interpretation to what had happened. "At a hotel suite — a suite at the Plaza — in New York." I laughed in frustration. "A suite! That scarcely does it justice. He may have had the whole floor: All the rooms connected one after the other. It was immense. There were people everywhere, milling all around."

She gazed at me steadily, refusing to let herself be drawn away from the central, all-important point. Behind that malleable self-deprecating manner, there was something firm and resolute.

"You were there, then. What happened?"

"Yes, I was there." I paused, hesitating; not about whether to tell the truth, but how much of it to share. "No, I wasn't there."

She stared at me in astonishment. "You were there — you were not there?"

"I was there at the Plaza in New York; I wasn't there where it happened, when she fell."

"Who was there?"

I looked away, glanced at my watch as if I thought it must be time for me to go. Scratching the side of my chin, I tried to sound indifferent and sounded instead like a fraud.

"It was a long time ago," I said, gazing into her unbelieving eyes. "It was an accident. It was an accident," I repeated. "There isn't any question about that."

"The vice president was in the room, wasn't he?" she asked in a calm, measured voice.

With anyone else, I would not have answered at all. I seldom spoke to reporters, and then only if I had known them for years and knew just how far I could go. But I was angry, angry at her for asking these questions, angry with myself for the foolish, awkward way I kept trying to avoid the truth.

"Why ask me something you already know? The White House must have told you he was there. It isn't any secret. There was a police report — perhaps they failed to mention that! Annie Malreaux's death was ruled an accident. Of course Browning was there. This is nothing more than a bad joke. The only reason there is an investigation is because the people who work for Walker — including, I imagine, the person you've been talking to — seem to have a talent for starting stories that help them get rid of people they couldn't otherwise beat!"

I was on my feet, mumbling an apology about the way I had just spoken, telling her I had to leave. She let me go on, rambling incoherence, while she sat there, calmly watching me with cool, lucid eyes.

"You also went to law school with someone named Jamison Scott Haviland?"

The long formality of the name struck me as odd, incongruous, as if Jimmy Haviland had become a distinguished jurist, a member of the United States Supreme Court, someone who might have sat in place of Reynolds, with folded hands and a dignified smile, when each October the nine justices sat together to have their photograph taken at the opening of another term; as if Jimmy Haviland had made something of himself, been what he once had every right to expect he could become, instead of . . . well, instead of what he had become.

"Yeah," I admitted, edging toward the kitchen counter. With my hands behind me, I leaned back, waiting for what came next. "Why?"

There was something strangely sympathetic in her eyes, as if she knew that Haviland's name brought back things I did not want to remember.

"What about Jamison Scott Haviland?" I asked with a sudden sense of foreboding.

"He's the one who is going to be indicted. He's the one they're going to charge with the murder of Anna Winifred Malreaux."

"It's impossible," I insisted. Jimmy Haviland seemed barely able to function as it was. Just going back to the Plaza had taken everything he had. An indictment, a formal, public accusation of murder —

Annie's murder — would destroy him.

"Haviland — he was a friend of yours?" At first I did not quite hear what she said. In a softer, more sympathetic voice, she asked again.

"We were — yes."

I could see him now, the way he had been, Jimmy Haviland, the one everyone liked, the one who, if you had had to guess which of the members of that class were most likely to go into politics and succeed, would have been right at the top of the list. Jimmy Haviland, who could always find time for someone who needed help; Jimmy Haviland, young and good-looking, who had gone out with too many girls to be serious about any of them, until he met Annie, and then did not know any other way to be.

"Then you'll help him — defend him? Take his case?"

"What?" I asked with an absent glance. "Would I do what? Help him?"

I was still thinking, still remembering, trying to see Annie's face, the way she looked, the effect she had, the way she changed the way other people — Jimmy, Browning, all of us — felt about themselves. I was nodding my head and did not know I was doing it.

"Yeah," I heard myself say in a vague, distant voice. "I'll do whatever I can."

"Because you are a friend of Jamison Scott Haviland, or because you are a friend of Thomas Browning?"

I barely heard the question, and I did not know the answer. My mind was on something else. Where had Jimmy Haviland's name come from? There was something troubling about it, something sinister and cruel that suggested an indefatigable resolve, a cold, iron will that would stop at nothing. And then there was the question, the question I was almost afraid to think about: that it was not just a rumor started out of nothing, that the people who were behind this knew something, that Annie Malreaux's death had not been an accident after all. But if that were true, what did Thomas Browning know and what was he holding back?

9

There is a kind of clarity that comes with the knowledge that, charged with the death of another, you may end up facing your own. The doubts, the fears, the haunted late-night regrets about the things you wish you had not done and the things you wish you had: All of it is pushed aside, dismissed as the vain imaginings of a life led too much in the past. Your only thought now is what lies ahead and how you are going to deal with it. The indictment for murder did not destroy Jimmy Haviland; it seemed to invigorate him, to give him a sense of confidence, or at least a sense of direction.

Jimmy Haviland had come to the alumni dinner in New York in a rented, threadbare tuxedo a size too large; Jamison Scott Haviland showed up for his arraignment on a charge of murder in a brand-new blue suit and a pair of black dress shoes polished to a hard, glossy shine. Surrounded by the successful and affluent members of his law school class, he had been nervous and ill at ease, with darting, furtive eyes and a rapid moving mouth that never stayed in position long enough to form a single, definable expression or give a coherent voice to a single well-considered thought. Amidst the lawyers, criminals and reporters that crowded the hallway outside the courtroom where he was scheduled to make his first appearance, his jaw was set in a firm, straight line, his gaze direct and impatient. He looked like a senior partner in one of those large downtown firms, a busy man a little short of time. I could not help but smile to myself as he came toward me down the hall.

"Browning said you wanted to represent me," said Haviland as we shook hands, "but I'm not sure I believed him."

He had never trusted Browning, but it still seemed an odd thing to say. "Why would he have lied about a thing like that?"

"There's always something else going on with Browning, something he won't tell you. Things are never quite the way he says they are."

It was all too cryptic for me. I put my arm around his shoulders and walked him down the hallway, away from the courtroom doors and the swirling crowd that had come to watch the arraignment of someone they had never seen because the case might involve, if only indirectly, someone everyone knew. We had only a few minutes of anonymity left.

"Listen to me. It was Browning's idea. He asked me to represent you. I didn't know if you would want me. That's why Browning called you — to let you know that I was willing to do it if that's what you wanted."

We were facing the wall, our heads bowed, my arm around his shoulders. He turned his eyes and gave me a skeptical glance. I tried to explain.

"This whole thing is an attempt to make it look like he covered up a crime, a murder. They're trying to destroy him politically."

Haviland's eyes flashed with anger. "It's always Browning. I'm going to be charged with murder, but the main thing is what they want to do to him!"

"He knows you're innocent," I began to protest.

"I know I'm innocent!" exclaimed Haviland, bristling. "I don't need him to tell me that."

"He's the witness whose testimony is going to prove it."

It had concentrated his mind, this

knowledge that he was about to be charged formally with a murder he did not commit. He had thought about it with an intensity I could not match and in ways I could not yet begin to imagine.

"Are you sure that's what he is going to testify? Are you sure he won't say that he can't be certain: that he was there, in the room, but that so were a lot of other people; that he did not actually see Annie fall; that he just assumed it was an accident?"

With a kind of knowing superiority, Haviland searched my eyes. "That gives him a way out, doesn't it? He wouldn't have to run the risk that a jury might not believe his testimony if he says Annie's death was an accident and that I wasn't even there. If he's so anxious to help, to clear my name, why hasn't he said anything? Why hasn't he issued a statement? Why is he waiting for the trial?"

Haviland paused, a strange, enigmatic look in his eyes, before he added, "Don't ever trust Browning. He doesn't tell the truth, the whole truth, even when he isn't telling a lie."

The case had not started, the first formal step in a process that would go on for months was only now about to begin; yet already there was a question about what someone else should have done. It is a marvel the way an accusation, especially a wrongful accusation, places everything in a new, more narrow perspective. The rituals of politeness, the decent concern for the feelings of others, the eager willingness to subordinate one's own desires to those of another, all the subtle arts of compromise and conciliation, the constant small adjustments by which we live with each other in a tolerable if imperfect peace, are forgotten, thrown aside, trampled upon by the urgent demand that what happens to us, our survival, our protection, come first. Marriages are destroyed, friendships ruined, because an innocent defendant begins to view as betrayal the failure to give him the kind of selfless devotion he thinks he deserves and knows he needs. There was no friendship here to ruin: Haviland already hated Browning. Nothing Browning could do would ever be enough, and there was nothing I could do to change Haviland's mind.

"You haven't been arraigned yet," I reminded him. "That's why we're here. How long have you known you were going to be indicted? When did Browning know? Just exactly when do you think he should have made a statement? Yesterday? What good would that have done?"

Haviland started to argue again that Browning should have done something. It was willful belligerence, stupid and short-sighted, and I had had enough. I turned him around, grabbed him by the shoulders and backed him against the wall.

"Listen to me!" I said, warning him with my eyes. "In about three minutes we're going to walk into that courtroom. We're going to act as if this whole thing is beneath contempt, that it's laughable, that we can't wait to go to trial because we can't wait to expose what's really behind this. And that means that starting in about three minutes, Thomas Browning is the best friend you've ever had!"

Haviland pulled his head to the side and tried to break free. "The best friend you've ever had," I repeated in a harsh whisper, holding him fast. "And you never use his name. If anyone asks, it's always 'the vice president.' Not only that, you speak of him with admiration and respect, as a great man, as someone who ought to be president. You voted for him, remember."

"I didn't. I didn't vote for . . ."

"You didn't vote for the witness for the defense? — For the witness who saw what happened — who saw Annie fall — who knows it was an accident? Are you sure you didn't? Are you sure you didn't vote for him?"

The look in his eyes changed from naked hostility to a reluctant, grudging acceptance of the necessity of things. He began to apologize, not for what he thought about Browning — he would never change that — but for taking it out on me. I let go of his shoulders. He raised his eyebrows in a gesture of resignation.

"I'll do whatever you say."

He was right in front of me, less than two feet away. Perhaps because my mind had been on other things, too caught up in the emotion of the moment, it was only now that I noticed. It was not quite ten o'clock in the morning and Jimmy Haviland — Jamison Scott Haviland — about to be arraigned on a charge of murder, had been drinking. I reached inside my suit coat pocket.

"Here, have one of these," I said as I handed him a roll of breath mints.

I did not say anything more about it as we made our way into the courtroom. I tried to tell myself that it was a one-time thing, that he had done it to fortify his courage on a morning that would have made a coward of us all. He had had a drink, that was all. You could not tell it from his speech; you certainly could not tell it from the easy, confident way he moved, with his head held high, his gaze steady, unwavering, as he walked just to my right as we entered the courtroom and went down the center aisle to the counsel table in front. He was so much better than he had been at the dinner at the Plaza; so much better than he had sounded on the one telephone call we had had; I was too grateful to be very much alarmed. But I knew about people who drank, and I knew about people who had just that one drink to get them started, that one drink to settle their nerves. I knew that without any more warning than this things could quickly get out of hand.

Haviland read my mind. As soon as we had taken our seats at the counsel table, he turned to me and with that brilliant bashful smile that had made him so likable in his first years at Harvard, assured me that it was not a problem.

"Just one. Just to make me good and alert."

Just one. It was funny how after a while that lie began to sound like the truth.

The arraignment was scheduled for ten

o'clock. I checked my watch. It was five minutes past the hour. An arraignment is a straightforward proceeding, perhaps the simplest thing that happens in a criminal case. The judge calls on the prosecutor to state the title of the case and present the formal document, usually an indictment returned by a grand jury. The prosecutor either reads the indictment, or, if the defense waives a formal reading, makes an abbreviated statement of the specific charges of which the defendant stands accused. The defendant is then asked how he pleads to those charges. There have been times when, if only to break the monotony, I would have gladly given up my fee if someone, acting on his own larcenous instinct, had replied: "Guilty as hell, Your Honor; but they'll never prove it!" Early in my career, an aging and incompetent thief shrugged his shoulders and remarked with a cagey smile, "Kind of depends on how you look at it, Your Honor," but that was as close as it ever got.

In the days when I was taking court-appointed cases, I might do eight or nine arraignments in the same morning, one right after the other. "Next case," the judge would order as the clerk passed up the next file. The assistant district attorney would grab the next one on the stack on the table next to him. If we were doing in-custody arraignments, the next shackled prisoner would be brought into court by a deputy sheriff. "*State* v. *Garcia*. Burglary in the First Degree." The judge would glance at me. The words were like a jingle in my head: "Acknowledge receipt of the indict-ment; waive a formal reading; enter a plea of not guilty, and ask that the matter be set for trial." The judge would hand the file back to the clerk and announce a trial date, which the clerk entered on the record as she handed another file up to the bench. The defendant, who had no idea what had just happened, was taken back to jail. That was it. If it took more than sixty seconds, it was only because the judge had taken a few moments to remind the defendant that he remembered him from the last time he had been arrested.

It was ten minutes past ten. Next to the door through which the judge would even-tually enter, a uniformed bailiff stood with his hands clasped in front of him. Well over six feet tall with broad shoulders and a short, thick neck, he had that same blank expression I had seen on the Secret Service agent who shadowed the vice president. The bailiff's eyes did not move from side to side in a constant unrelenting search for the first sign that something was not quite right, however; the eyes of the bailiff did not move at all. He might have been asleep for all they saw as he waited with the rest of us for the routine beginning of a perfectly ordinary event. After a while, he shifted one foot ahead of the other and crossed his arms over his chest. Pursing his lips, he dropped his head and stared at the reddish beige linoleum floor. He twitched his nose vigorously, driving his upper lip violently back and forth, like someone trying to stop a sneeze. He sniffed twice with such force that his head jolted up. Then, with his hands clasped again belt-buckle high, he stared straight ahead, resuming his dull, interminable watch.

Two minutes later, the door finally opened. The bailiff took one step forward and raised his head. His mouth had opened to announce that court was now in session when a woman's hand on his sleeve stopped him short. The court reporter carried her stenograph machine to her place on a raised platform a foot above the floor and directly below the witness stand. A woman in her late fifties or early sixties, with soft gray hair and modest, gentle eyes, she set the tripod on the floor and placed the machine on top of it. When she had everything the way she wanted it, she rose from the small leather stool and with a cursory but not unfriendly nod at the bailiff, left through the same door through which she had entered. We were going to start sometime, it just was not clear when. The district attorney had about run out of patience.

He started to rise from his place at the other counsel table. With a sulking, disgruntled expression he sank back in his chair, watching the court reporter with a kind of angry suspicion, as if it were somehow her fault that the arraignment had not started on time. When she left, he followed her with an evil stare, biting on his lower lip, trying to hold his wicked tongue. Out of the corner of his eye he saw me watching. Instead of turning away, ignoring me, he looked straight at me, a distant, grim, determined stare that reflected the narrow self-assurance of a man for whom life was a series of certainties, a closed circle that did not admit a moment's doubt or a moment's hesitation. Once he had decided you were an enemy, it was war to the end, war without mercy. That was what everyone I had talked to had told me, the observation that with uncanny regularity worked its way into every conversation: Bartholomew Caminetti took no prisoners.

Ruthless, cunning, relentless, Caminetti was in his second term as the New York district attorney. He wanted it to be his last. Whether he ran for governor or the United States Senate — or, as one rumor had it, became the United States attorney general when the current occupant of that office was nominated to fill the next vacancy on the United States Supreme Court — did not matter nearly so much as that he keep climbing, moving up, never stopping in one place, one office, long enough for anyone to think that that position, whatever it was, was as far as he could go. It was the single-minded ambition of the outsider, born without advantages, who had had to fight for everything he had, this refusal to tolerate even the suggestion that there might be any limit to what he could achieve.

Bartholomew Caminetti was born into a rigorously Catholic family, the youngest of eight children. Two of his sisters became nuns; his oldest brother became a priest. His favorite sister, Rosemary, the second-youngest child, went to Columbia on a full scholarship and was raped and murdered late one night in Morningside Heights on her way back from the library. Her death nearly destroyed her parents. Caminetti's mother, whom he apparently adored, would not come out of her room except to cook dinner, and would not leave the ramshackle house in Brooklyn except for that hour each day when she went to church and with covered head tried not to question too severely the inexplicable, and in her weakest moments, the unforgivable, negligence of God. Edward Caminetti, Bartholomew's father, buried his daughter in consecrated ground according to the rituals of the church, prayed for her soul in heaven, and never stepped inside the cathedral again.

The rapist and killer was caught. Though he had an extensive juvenile record of assault, he was only nineteen and too young to have an adult record of serious crime. The death of Rosemary Caminetti, a death that had such grievous consequences for her family, was simply another crime, another number to be added to what at the time was a murder rate of near-record proportions. An overworked assistant district attorney, trying to manage a caseload that was three times what it should have been, avoided the burden of a trial by negotiating a plea. Murder was reduced to manslaughter, and rape reduced to the lesser included crime of sexual assault. The young assistant district attorney took a certain satisfaction in knowing that with minimal time and expense a rapist and murderer was going to be off the streets for perhaps as long as ten years. Rosemary Caminetti's father kept his outrage to himself. He quietly bought a gun and probably would have used it if he had not died a few years before his daughter's killer was due to be released from prison.

Before his sister's death, Bartholomew Caminetti had wanted to become a lawyer; after her death he was intent on becoming a prosecutor. He graduated with honors from Fordham, and then, whether because, as some of his political enemies would later suggest, his scores on the law school aptitude test were not good enough to get into a more prestigious school like Harvard or Yale, or because, as he always insisted, he preferred to continue his Catholic education, he studied law at Georgetown. He worked summers on Capitol Hill in the offices of the congressman in whose district he had grown up.

It was quarter past ten. I watched the

bailiff's eyes, waiting for them to blink, wondering if he might be dead. Haviland nudged my shoulder.

"The judge probably decided to have a second," he remarked with a droll expression.

Caminetti stood up, glanced down at the file that lay open on the table in front of him, studied it for a moment, then pulled a long face, shook his head with weary exasperation, closed the file and sat down. Two more minutes passed. In a single, fluid motion, Caminetti got up again, walked over to where I sat and put out his hand.

"Bartholomew Caminetti," he said with the sharp accented voice of a native New Yorker. I stood up and shook his hand.

"Joseph Antonelli," I said, looking him straight in the eye.

"This is a little unusual," he said, nodding his forehead toward the closed door to chambers. "Lot of these guys get sloppy, don't respect other people's time. You know, make everybody wait because they're a judge and they can. You know, you must run into that kind of stuff, different places. But him — it's unusual. Well, give it another minute or so, then we'll see what's going on."

He turned away and without another

word sat down again. Slouching down in the chair, his elbows on the table in front of him, he spread open his hands and pressed his fingers together, waiting for the time to pass.

Caminetti's handshake had been firm, decisive, quick, the same way he spoke: short bursts of sincerity delivered as if he had just run into his oldest friend instead of a stranger or, in my case, an adversary whom a moment before he had looked at with open contempt. He had the kind of iron self-confidence that would allow him to praise you one moment, berate you the next, and never wonder that you might think him either inconsistent or cruel. It was, in a way, the secret of his success as a politician, the key to his apparent popularity. He said, or appeared to say — because I could not resist the thought that there was more than a little calculation in it — exactly what was on his mind. When he first ran for district attorney, a Republican in a decidedly Democratic electorate, he told every white working-class group he could get into that his sister had been raped and murdered and that he was determined nothing like that would ever happen to a sister of theirs, but that if it did, "the punk who did it is either going to die or he's going to spend the rest of his life in prison, not the ten years they gave my sister's killer."

If Caminetti had not been slow to exploit the tragedy of his own sister's death for political advantage, neither had he failed to recognize the public's preference for elected officials willing to put themselves in the line of fire. More than once, he had gone to the scene of a crime in progress — a robbery gone bad, hostages taken, the police in a standoff — and stood out in the open, completely exposed, issuing orders about what should be done next. It was great theater and he knew it. His opponents charged that that was the only reason he did it, and that all he accomplished was to impede the work of the police. But they could not fault his courage, and they were not so quick to criticize him once he suggested that he would be glad to invite them along the next time he tried to help the police prevent innocent people from getting hurt.

With an instinct for publicity, he seemed to be everywhere at once. When he was not on camera while the crime was taking place, he was standing behind a microphone describing with lavish praise the police investigation that had led to an arrest, or announcing with stricken, haunted eyes the awful crime that had been committed in the case that his office was about to prosecute with the utmost severity. Caminetti had been in office for six years, but this was only the second case he had decided to try himself. Once it was rumored that the vice president was somehow involved, no one asked why. Everyone knew that Bartholomew Caminetti had been among the first prominent New York Republicans to support the presidential candidacy of William Hobart Walker, and everyone knew what Walker might sometime soon do for his good friend Bartholomew Caminetti. It was another question what that did for the supposedly impartial administration of justice.

It was ten-twenty. Caminetti was out of patience. With a look of disgust, he rose from his chair and began to edge his way around the table, determined to find out why he was being made to wait. Grumbling to himself, he rapped his knuckles on the corner of the table as he made the turn.

"Hear ye, Hear ye," the bailiff, roused from a blank-eyed slumber by some sound only he could hear, began to cry. Caminetti froze in midstep, shook his head at the thoughtless waste of time, and retreated to his place behind the counsel table where, with the rest of us, he stood waiting while the Honorable Charles F. Scarborough bustled, or rather exploded, into the courtroom.

The end of his black robe flying behind him, Scarborough stalked across the front of the room, a bundle of books and papers clutched under his right arm. He held a large white handkerchief in his left hand, pressed against his nose and mouth. His eyes were red, his round face pallid. Reaching the bench, he dropped into his chair like someone shot dead with a bullet. The bundle of books and papers tumbled onto the flat surface of the space where he worked. He mopped the perspiration from his feverish brow with the white handkerchief and then covered his mouth with it and coughed. Raising his right hand in a weary gesture meant to apologize and surrender at the same time, he scowled. "Damn hay fever," he muttered. His face began to redden; his small round eyes became tiny slits; his short, slightly upturned nose wrinkled as his nostrils squeezed tight together. In the nick of time the handkerchief flew open like a bedsheet flapping in the wind. A tremendous wheezing noise was followed in an instant by a thunderous rush like a broken water main, as the judge buried his face in the wet white handkerchief.

"Welcome to New York, Mr. Antonelli," he mumbled. His eyes singled me out, held me fast, as he kept rubbing. "Pleasure to have you here. Don't you agree, Mr. Caminetti? Yes? Right," he said, stretching his eyebrows to their highest elevation as he set about methodically folding the handkerchief.

"You agree, Mr. Caminetti, that it's an honor — a great honor — to have someone of Mr. Antonelli's great gifts and splendid reputation in our courts — Yes?" His eyes watched his hand put the handkerchief securely out of sight. "I thought you might." He pulled his hand away and placed both hands together on the bench in front of him.

"I mean it, Mr. Antonelli. We're delighted to have you with us." A rather shy smile slipped almost unnoticed across his thoughtful mouth. "Whatever the court can do to make your stay with us more pleasant . . . ," he said in a soft, somewhat tentative voice.

Slowly, and a little reluctantly, he lowered his eyes. Brooding upon something, he stroked his chin. Slumped forward in that attitude of intense contemplation, he looked like one of those immensely learned English jurists with an encyclopedic knowledge of the law who can rattle off ancient cases the way other men can recite the results of last weekend's games; who can summarize the evidence at the end of a case without looking at a note or having to stop to remember a point; and who lies in wait for the first lawyer brave enough, or stupid enough, to try to cross swords. I did not like many judges, but I thought I was going to like him. He had not been in the courtroom two minutes, he had not yet done a thing, and I knew already that everything I had heard about him — all the stories about the legendary Charles F. Scarborough, said to be the greatest trial judge of his generation — were true.

One moment apparently lost in some private reverie, in the next he was all motion, his small smooth hands flying in eight different directions at once, his piercing eyes a firestorm of enthusiasm and excited incoherence. He smashed the flat of his hands on the bench and in a raucous voice bellowed at the tightly packed courtroom.

"And let me welcome all the public-spirited citizens who have decided to join me here this morning." He let the words echo through the high-ceilinged room. A grin, proud, defiant, demanding, stretched across his blunt mouth. "I have always thought that the needed formality of the law, the seriousness with which we are obligated to approach our duties, is only enhanced by being performed under the watchful eye of a vigilant citizenry." He paused. The smile etched farther along his lips. "You'll notice I said 'eye.' You are here to see, and never — never! — to speak. That is the one rule upon which I insist with the utmost rigor."

Scarborough had a habit, which I was now about to discover, of suddenly shifting his gaze to the side, as if he were turning to someone, an alter ego, with whom he frequently shared a confidence. The movement of his eyes was so abrupt, so definitive, that when he did it now I looked immediately to my right, toward the empty chairs in the jury box, wondering for just an instant where the person to whom he was talking could possibly have gone.

" 'Utmost rigor,' " he said, seeming to deprecate to his invisible auditor the slightly pompous way it may have sounded. His eyes flashed, caught the audience and held it fast. "By which I mean that if anyone so much as breathes a word during these or any other proceedings, I will by the power vested in me by the state of New York simply have you beaten to death. Are we clear on this point?" he asked as he bent his head to the side and drummed the fingers of his left hand.

Every face in the crowd wore a smile; no one made a sound. If he had told them to get down on the floor and do push-ups, they would have done it, grateful for the chance to share in some enterprise of which he had been the originating force.

"There is a reason we are here, Mr. Caminetti. Why don't you enlighten us as to what it is."

Bartholomew Caminetti was not part of the crowd. He was too busy thinking about what he had to do next to fall under the influence of anyone else. He had been standing at the counsel table, the charging document in his hand, waiting with blank-eyed indifference to get things started.

"Your Honor, we're here today in the matter of *People of the State of New York* v. *Jamison Scott Haviland*," said Caminetti in a dry, slightly nasal voice. "The defendant is charged with murder in the first degree." Caminetti took a step toward me. "Let the record reflect that I am handing to the defendant's attorney a certified true copy of the indictment returned by the grand jury."

I glanced briefly at the indictment before I placed it on the table in front of me.

"Your Honor, the defense acknowledges receipt of the indictment, waives a formal reading, and . . ."

Leaning forward on both arms, Scarborough darted a glance at his imaginary confidant. " 'Waives a formal reading.' " His eyebrows shot straight up. "The court appreciates learned counsel's efforts to proceed in an expeditious manner," said the judge as his gaze came swiftly around to me. "In a matter so grave as this, however, I think it worth our time to have the indictment read in full. Mr. Caminetti, if you would."

There was no exchange between the two of them. Caminetti did not so much as nod his acknowledgment that he understood what he had been asked to do. I had the feeling that there never was, that all those gestures by which we smooth out the rough edges of our spoken conversation and form a coherent whole out of the broken fragments of our everyday speech had been replaced by a stringent economy, dispensing with courtesy as a waste of energy and time. Caminetti began to read in a voice that, like the moment you turn on the radio to a program that has already started, seemed to have no beginning. Scarborough sat, trancelike, listening to every word.

"A moment," he said, raising the index finger of his right hand. "Again." He gave Caminetti an alert, inquisitive glance. " 'On December twenty-fourth, nineteen sixty-five'?"

Caminetti stared at him, without expression.

"Surely, that can't be right," remarked Scarborough in the tone of a gentle remonstrance. "You can't have had the grand jury return an indictment alleging that the crime took place with that specificity. Does it not in fact read: 'On or about December twenty-fourth, nineteen sixty-five?' " he asked in a voice as profoundly serious as if they were two law partners alone in a law library discussing the central point in the most important case of their careers. Caminetti looked back at the indictment.

"On or about December twenty-fourth, nineteen sixty-five," he read, continuing on without any break or alteration in his voice, as if he had read it exactly that way before and had not simply rushed past the once-omitted phrase.

"And how does the defendant plead?" inquired Judge Scarborough with an interested, searching glance when Caminetti had reached the end.

Haviland was standing next to me, on my left, his hands held in front of him. Under Scarborough's inquiring glance, he did not flinch or look away. He did not fidget with his fingers or suddenly gasp for air. He was as calm, as steady, not as any defendant, but as any attorney I had ever seen in a criminal court. He was a man who perhaps for the first time knew exactly what he was going to do.

"How do you plead, Mr. Haviland?" inquired Charles F. Scarborough in a kind, thoughtful voice. "Guilty, or not guilty?"

Haviland did not hesitate. The words came clear and strong, echoing through the paneled courtroom with the concise finality of something that instead of just beginning was about to end.

"Guilty, Your Honor. Annie Malreaux died because of me."

10

Jimmy Haviland was shaking like a leaf. A ghastly grin had taken hold of his mouth, pulling it, refusing to let go, twisting it into one bizarre contortion after another. I expected to hear hideous laughter come roaring out, pronouncing a verdict of insanity on himself, but he made no sound at all. He just stood there, trembling, that stupid look of what seemed almost like relief painted on his face. I was a fool not to have seen it coming. He had been too perfect, too much in command of himself, oblivious of the courtroom, the crowd, the formal ritual by which he was charged with the murder of the girl who in the half-imagined past of his memory was the only girl he had ever loved. He must have reached deep down inside himself to find the strength to produce that impression of outward calm.

It must have surprised him and, more than that, pleased him, to learn that he could stand there like that in open court, every eye on him, everyone, if not convinced, at least ready to believe, that he must be guilty of murder. At least for these few moments everything depended on him, on how he conducted himself under the kind of pressure that no one who has not faced it can possibly understand. He had done everything right, done it with the kind of noble reserve that when we were boys had been almost the definition of bravery: face the fire of the enemy without a thought for your own safety; look death in the eye with the laughing indifference of a man who would never think to complain about what fate might have in store.

Jimmy Haviland, broken by long years of disappointment and things worse, far worse, than disappointment, had pulled himself together, shaken the dust from the faded remnant of his own dignity and self-respect, and then, at the end, when he had only that one thing more to do — enter a simple plea of not guilty — everything fell apart. It was the proof of how hard he had tried, of how difficult and painful the effort to keep himself under control must have been. I put my arm around his shoulder to steady him and discovered that instead of feeling sorry for him, I admired him, for the courage that he had shown. Facing a firing squad a man grows weak in the knees at the order to shoot — Does that diminish the bravery he showed in walking under his own power to the place of his execution?

"Your Honor?" I responded to Judge Scarborough's worried glance. He smiled sympathetically, threw a meaningful look at the district attorney, and took matters into his own hands.

"There was a certain lack of precision, I'm afraid, in the way I asked the question. I did not mean to inquire into the reason why something may have happened. I did not mean to ask whether someone might feel some generalized sense of guilt because something happened to someone else. I mean to ask the much more narrow question whether the defendant wishes to plead guilty or not guilty to the specific charge in the indictment."

Scarborough's eyebrows were arched in high half circles, like the flying buttresses of a Gothic cathedral. It gave him the look of someone eternally curious, someone too intelligent for either anger or fear.

"Therefore, Mr. Antonelli," he said, looking quite deliberately at me and not at Haviland, "on the charge of murder in the first degree, how does the defendant plead — guilty or not guilty?"

I squeezed my left hand on Haviland's shoulder. The trembling stopped. He stared down at the floor, subdued, quiet, lost.

"Not guilty, Your Honor," I replied in a firm, confident voice. The words were barely out of my mouth when Caminetti was moving to the next order of business.

"Your Honor, the People ask defendant be remanded without bail," he said as he began to shove his papers back into the file folder. He seemed to think that what he had asked was routine and the response automatic. I turned my head and looked right at him. He did not appear to notice.

"This alleged crime took place more than thirty years ago. Before this morning, the defendant had never been charged with a crime — any crime."

Caminetti closed the folder. Pressing three fingers of his left hand against it, he kept his head bent, narrowing his eyes into a hostile stare. The muscles on the side of his face quivered with energy and tension. He was strung tight, ready to bolt out of that crouch and seize me, or at least my argument, by the throat.

"Never been charged with anything before now," I went on, becoming more intense as I watched Caminetti react. "The defendant has lived in the same town, practiced law in the same office, for years. He served his country in the armed forces of the United States. He's a decorated veteran. And Mr. Caminetti wants him sent to jail! — To wait for trial, charged with a crime that not only did the defendant not commit, but that never happened, a phantom crime, a death by accident that certain people have for purposes of their own decided to call murder. If there is anyone who should sit in jail waiting for trial, it ought to be . . ."

Caminetti's head jerked up. His face was red with anger; his small calculating eyes flashed with contempt and a kind of malice, a dark warning of things to come.

" 'It ought to be,' " he repeated in an ominous tone. "Let me tell you what ought to be . . ."

"Gentlemen, I believe the question at issue is whether the defendant should be remanded, granted bail, or released on his own recognizance," interjected Scarborough as he dragged the wrinkled white handkerchief out from beneath his robe.

His eyes began to water; his head raised up in small, abrupt movements; he spread the handkerchief over his face, veiling from his audience the regrettable explosion. With his mouth and nose still covered, he gestured with his free hand, picking up the thread of his remarks as if there had never been an interruption.

"Mr. Caminetti, precisely what are the grounds for the request that the defendant be remanded to custody?"

He finished wiping his nose, and with a look of mild disgust, folded the handkerchief and placed it back inside the black cotton robe. He inclined his head to the side and with the back of three fingers scratched his left cheek.

"Specifically, is there anything that Mr. Antonelli has just said — the absence of a criminal record, his background, his position in the community — that you care to challenge?"

As shrewd as the streets on which he had been raised, Caminetti knew better than to agree with things he could not deny. Everything I had said about Haviland was true; Caminetti ignored them as if they did not count.

"We ask for remand, Your Honor, because this heinous crime was not only committed by the defendant, but because for more than thirty years he has covered this heinous crime up."

Everything about Bartholomew Caminetti was tenacious; not just the way he looked, but the way he spoke, spitting out the words in short, staccatolike bursts, practiced words carefully chosen to express his indignation and rage. *Heinous* had always been a prosecutorial favorite. It was not easily mistaken for any other. It had the vaguely obscene suggestion of something twisted and perverse. Each time Caminetti used it, there was a flash of something furtive in his eyes, as if it conjured up some memory of his own of things he would rather forget, of temptations he had not quite been able to resist.

Resting his head in his left hand, Scarborough listened with a kind of amused astonishment as the district attorney described the cruel cowardice of a young man who had been allowed to live the life of a free man well into middle age instead of being locked up for life.

"This heinous crime has gone unpunished for too long," concluded Caminetti, drawing his eyes together in a piercing stare, as if he could through his own formidable powers of concentration force the ruling he wanted.

Scarborough stroked his chin. "The defendant will be released on his own recognizance. However, I will order that he surrender his passport to the court pending the outcome of the trial." He took a deep breath, pressed his lips together and wrinkled his nose. After a pensive moment, he let out his breath in a long sigh. "We have remaining the matter of a trial date." He looked toward the court clerk and was about to ask a question when he seemed to think better of it. "Before we do that, I wonder if I might see counsel in chambers." He rose from the bench, hesitated, sniffed to hold back a sneeze, and then looked out across the crowd that filled the courtroom. "Court will be adjourned," he said with a sly, mischievous smile before he disappeared through the side door.

I followed the district attorney through the same door through which the judge had vanished just moments before. A narrow corridor wound through stacks of cardboard boxes and metal file cabinets. A door on the right was wide open to the jury room. A table, double the width of a normal rectangular dining room table, caught my eye. It seemed strange to find it back here, in this warren of cubbyhole offices for court personnel, but then everything in the courthouse was like this: cramped, congested, things shoved into any place they would fit. Built before the war, the courthouse had grown dull, gray, dreary, with dead air and grimy walls, broken toilets and shattered sinks. When the corridors were crowded and the courtroom benches were packed — even then, if you stepped back from it a moment, let your gaze move slowly down past the elevators with their scratch-marked metal doors to the unwashed windows, or along the scuffed linoleum floors to the knicked-up wooden chairs and the splintered bottoms of the wooden doors, there was that nagging sense of a vast emptiness, a silent screaming loneliness, a sense that what was done here was a kind of charade, a secret no one wanted to admit, that what happened here was always too late.

The courtroom itself was a large rectangular room with wooden wainscoting as high as a man's head and, above it, dull grayish white plaster walls. At the top, where the walls joined the ceiling, square pieces with one-inch gaps between them formed a molding of faintly classical design. The wall on the right as you faced the bench contained four sets of double narrow windows that afforded a partial view of the Gothic exterior of the courthouse wing opposite. There were two sets of seven spectator benches, separated by a broad center aisle that led from the entrance, two sets of double doors at the back, to a raised wooden railing fastened on an eight-inch marble base, in front. There was no gate, nothing to push through, nothing to shove ahead with your hand as you made your way into that privileged place where only those who had business before the court were allowed to enter. There was a blue velvet rope hooked at each end to the side posts of the wooden railing. I half expected a maître d' to open it, and I wondered in my western ignorance whether, because it was New York, I was supposed to tip the bailiff.

Caminetti rapped lightly on an unmarked door and let himself in. I caught the door as it swung shut in my face. For an instant, I thought I had stumbled into a room somewhere in the Metropolitan Museum of Art, one of those period rooms done with the eye of an experienced and slightly demented collector willing to spend all the money in the world to achieve a single flawless representation of a long-vanished time and place. The walls, and not just the walls — the ceiling — were paneled in carved mahogany. The floors were carpeted wall to wall in a thick beige-colored rug on top of which were scattered in luxurious profusion oriental carpets in brilliant reds and blues. At the end of the room farthest from the door was a desk with elegant curved legs. It looked as if a medieval map of the partially known world should be spread out across it. The desk was set at an angle below the only window, situated in such a way that the light that passed through it would pass directly over the right shoulder of the judge when he sat, hunched over, reading from a law report or setting forth in writing a ruling he was about to make.

The walls that met in the corner near the window were lined with rows of oil paintings produced by the best-known of the Flemish and Florentine schools of the sixteenth and seventeenth centuries. The other two walls were filled with bookshelves painted to a hard finish, a kind of burnished reddish black. There was, so far as I could tell, not a single law book, not a single volume of reported appellate cases, not a treatise, not a compilation, not a digest; not one of the learned commentaries on the law, any law, that sit unread on the shelves of jurists everywhere. There was nothing but leather-bound books with gold lettering on the spines, grouped not by subject or author, or even by size, but by color: tan, red, green. However old the contents might have been — and on the volumes nearest my eye, I read the name of a Latin author — the leather bindings were shiny and new, not a line, not a crack, in them. It was the library of a man proud of his possessions, someone who wanted something to show for what he wanted others to think went on in his mind.

"Quintilian," said Scarborough as he saw my eye drift toward the title. "Have you read him?"

He greeted my admission that I had not with a benevolent sigh.

"I thought Quintilian's lectures on rhetoric were more for politicians," I remarked, as I threw a short glance at Caminetti. "I read Cicero because he tried cases in court," I added, looking back at Scarborough. "Not in Latin, however." I smiled and shook my head, disparaging my ignorance. "Though I probably would have understood as much of it that way as I'm afraid I did in English."

The civil expression on Scarborough's imperturbable face did not change. He smiled with his eyes, nodded wisely, and turned to Caminetti, waiting with bored impatience to find out why he was wasting his time here, listening to this, when he could be doing something important.

Scarborough stood next to a blue brocaded chair, resting his left arm on the top. He invited us to sit on the sofa just to the other side, but Caminetti, eager to make this visit as brief as possible, shook his head. Scarborough greeted the district attorney's refusal with a kind of amused neglect, shifting his attention to me in a way that suggested that his only concern was that we both be comfortable. His manner was polished, impeccable, adept at the subtle adjustments by which everyone is made to feel that they have been treated fairly, listened to with respect, their opinions taken into account, measured, considered and made a part of whatever settlement the issue requires. He had the brilliant temperament of a man who can make you think that only after agonizing over it for hours has he, reluctantly and with the greatest regret, concluded that he cannot do what you have asked; it was like the capacity of the courtier who never reveals a thing about himself and carries a stiletto inside a velvet glove.

"An interesting case, don't you think?" asked the judge, arching a single eyebrow.

"Interesting case," said Caminetti mechanically. Scarborough smiled and waited. Caminetti waited. "Interesting case," repeated Caminetti, wondering why he had to. Scarborough stroked his chin with his right hand and turned to me, a question in his eye. I had no idea what the question was. I waited. Scarborough raised both eyebrows, pursed his pink lips, turned and walked away, heading toward the desk on the other side of the enormous room. He took three steps and turned around, studying first Caminetti, then me, searching our eyes for something he obviously did not find. Shaking his head, he turned and, moving quickly, reached his desk. He picked up a newspaper and waved it in the air.

"Have you read this?" he asked calmly. "The column in this morning's paper that says this is a political trial? — That the only reason this case was brought — the only reason an indictment was sought in the first place — is to embarrass the vice president? That this whole thing has been orchestrated by people close to the president, people who want to get rid of Browning so someone else can be put into the vice presidency? That this . . . ?"

Scarborough placed the newspaper back on the desk and for a brief, reflective moment stared out the window. With a quick movement of his wrist, he unfastened the clasp on his black judicial robe. He slipped it off, hung it on a rack in the corner, and put on the coat of a Savile Row suit.

"I'm not concerned with anyone's motivations," he remarked in a casual tone of voice. He pulled each shirt cuff to the proper length beyond the suit coat sleeves. "I'm only concerned with questions of evidence and the orderly conduct of the trial."

His eyes were fixed on a cuff link that had slipped back beneath the outer slit in the French cuff sleeve. He tugged at it, pulling it through. When he had it in place, he rubbed the flat onyx surface with the side of his thumb, polishing away a tiny smudge mark. He looked up, but he could not yet let it go: He had to do it again, make sure that small, nearly invisible imperfection on the shiny surface of the stone was gone. Finally satisfied, he lifted his eyes and looked directly at the district attorney.

"Do you intend to call the vice president as a witness for the prosecution?"

Caminetti seemed to hesitate, but only for an instant. "Not at this time, Your Honor."

The answer did not please Scarborough.

His round, smooth face, blotched and irritated by sneezing one moment and blowing his nose the next, quivered with just the slightest impatience.

"We're not in court now," he reminded Caminetti with a frosty smile. "And the question wasn't what you were planning to do at the moment. What I want to know is whether the vice president is on the list of witnesses the prosecution intends to call at trial."

Bartholomew Caminetti listened carefully. Without moving a muscle, or blinking an eyelash, he concentrated on each word. He stood there, stiff as a board in a plain black suit that went a little too far straight across his shoulders, a suit with sleeves that covered his shirt cuffs and pants that sagged over the laces of his shoes. Without apology, he repeated the same answer.

"Not at this time, Your Honor."

The judge's head and eyebrows snapped up simultaneously. "I see." He came back across the room and sat down in the chair next to the sofa. "Sit down," he said in that practiced, untroubled voice, gesturing toward Caminetti with his hand while his eyes turned to me. He placed both wrists on the front edge of the arms of the solid upholstered chair and crossed his right leg over his left.

"Assume for the moment that the prosecution does not call the vice president. Will the defense?" Before I could answer, he added, "According to the stories — or perhaps I should say rumors — I've been reading, the vice president was there when it happened, when the girl fell from the window." He held up his hand as if to stave off an objection from Caminetti, who had dutifully taken a seat at the other end of the sofa. "However she happened to fall. If that's true, and if he was a witness to what happened, then I would assume . . . ?"

I had assumed that the prosecution would never call Browning as a witness. You do not put someone on the witness stand you know is going to testify for the other side. But then why would not Caminetti just say so? He had to give me a witness list; he could not keep it a secret. I was thinking as fast as I could, trying to figure out what might be behind his apparent reluctance to commit himself one way or the other. Whatever Caminetti knew, whatever his own involvement may have been, there was not any doubt that the newspaper column Scarborough had mentioned had it right: Jimmy Haviland was indicted for murder, but they were after Thomas Browning. That meant they had to show that Haviland had committed a murder and that Browning had helped cover it up. The best way to do that, the best way to make that accusation and make it stick, was to have Browning testify to something that you could prove was not true. It was a setup, a scheme to force Browning to testify for the defense so that he became fair game for the kind of lethal cross-examination that a cunning and relentless prosecutor dreamed about. It was the chance to destroy someone famous and powerful, the chance to strip naked someone who until that one decisive courtroom exchange had lived the life of privilege and immunity enjoyed by wealthy men of influence and prestige. Then why this reluctance? What was I missing? I decided not to give away anything. I turned it back on Caminetti.

"I haven't seen a witness list," I replied with a half glance at the district attorney. "I haven't seen anything, nothing except that piece of paper charging my client with murder."

"Discovery is ready," remarked Caminetti. He shoved himself forward, getting ready to rise from the sofa. "You can pick it up this afternoon." He paused, placed both hands on his knees, and leaned forward, a put-upon look of annoyance on his otherwise expressionless face.

Scarborough pulled his ankle across his knee and sank farther back into the overstuffed chair. "Quintilian is worth reading," he said as he bent his head toward me with the apparent intention of pursuing a subject that from the apologetic smile he darted briefly toward the district attorney he knew would not interest him at all. He let that utterly superfluous thought hang in the air, a delicate and malicious reminder that he would decide when things ended and when they did not. Pulling his hands from the arms of the chair into his lap, Scarborough appeared to study the back of his manicured nails, one after the other, a long slow march that went on without purpose or point until Caminetti's hands began to slide back from his knees. In a complete show of surrender, he pulled his knee up onto the sofa.

"Yes, the reason I ask about whether the vice president might be called as a witness is that, as perhaps you know, I am a longtime acquaintance of his. We were in law school together."

Scarborough caught the look of surprise

that shot across my eyes. He had been waiting for it.

"I was a year ahead." That was all he said, the only reason he offered to explain why he and I had never met. "We didn't know each other very well," he added. He looked across at Caminetti. "We got to know each other better later on, here, in New York. That is all I wanted to let both of you know: that I'm acquainted with someone who I thought might be called as a witness, but who neither one of you is apparently yet in a position to say will be called as a witness."

He paused, his eyes still on Caminetti, giving him a chance to amend his answer. Caminetti opened his palms in a gesture of puzzled indifference.

"I doubt very much that it would be grounds on which to recuse myself from hearing the case in any event, but I want it plainly understood by both of you," he added with a cursory, sidelong glance at me, "that once you leave this room you cannot decide that, yes, you are going to call the vice president as a witness, and that, because of my personal acquaintance with the witness, you would prefer that I step aside." He rose from the chair. "Do we understand one another on this point?

Good. Now, before you leave — one other thing."

Caminetti was on his feet, straightening his suit jacket, ready to turn toward the door.

"I'm not placing a gag order on anyone, yet; but the first time I hear anyone mention the vice president's name in connection with the issues in this case," he said with a stare that behind the surface of affable good manners was deadly serious, "the first time anyone connected with either the prosecution or the defense so much as speculates as to why or whether the vice president might be called as a witness; the first time this threatens to become anything more than a trial of an indicted defendant on a charge of murder, I won't hesitate for a moment to do so and to impose the most severe sanctions, including proceedings for disbarment, against any attorney who fails to comply."

Judge Scarborough placed his hand on my shoulder and walked me past Caminetti. "I hope you enjoy New York while you're here with us. If there is anything I can do . . . ?" He opened the door for me. I suppose I should have held it for Caminetti, but I let it shut behind me instead.

I was halfway down that narrow, bleak, crowded corridor, almost to the jury room, when I heard him coming up behind me.

"Antonelli," he called in that short, sharp New York voice. I stopped, twisted my head over my shoulder, waiting for him to catch up. He kept walking, did not even slow down, just kept moving, hurrying along to whatever he had to do next. Without wanting to, without really knowing why I was doing it except out of a kind of astonished curiosity to find out what he wanted and in the process perhaps learn something more about him, I followed, quickening my pace.

"Where are you staying?" he asked. I did not have the chance to answer or even decide if I wanted to. "You like Italian?" He did not wait for an answer this time either. " 'Course you do. Try Carmine's — Upper West Side. Don't take reservations. Always crowded. Use my name. You'll get a table. Really," he added with a slight, but decisive, nod as he glanced at me for the first time.

We were three steps from the door that led into the courtroom. I looked him in the eye and tossed my head, gesturing back toward the room we had just left. In a conversation with Bartholomew Caminetti words were a kind of fatal redundancy.

"That?" he remarked with a shrug. "Lot of money. Wife had money, too. Divorced couple years ago." He started to turn, realized that someone from out of town might require a more detailed explanation, and added, "New York money — finance, that kind of thing."

"New York money? Is that good?"

The question made no sense to him. "The money is good."

His mouth opened and his head bobbed up and down as his eyes glistened and his chest and shoulders shook. He was laughing, but he was not making a sound, or rather nothing more definable than a strange hissing gasp, a noise like that of air being let out of a bicycle tire.

"Good enough that he sits on every major charitable board in the city. Didn't know that? The Honorable Charles F. Scarborough is one of the wealthiest men in New York. You thought maybe that was taxpayer money that paid for all that stuff?" A grin full of cheerful malice rippled across the thin line of his mouth. "One of those paintings alone . . . Taxpayer money? I could indict someone for that," he said, shaking his head with regret that it was something he had not yet been able to do, if not Scarborough, then some other judge, some other official, someone he could take down, destroy, on behalf of a public always ready to revel in the chronicled corruption of judges and politicians and anyone else who had risen above the crowd. The thought of taking down the famous and formidable Thomas Browning must have come like the ecstatic vision of some cruel and ascetic saint.

"Remember: Carmine's. Use my name," he said as he opened the door and burst ahead of me into the courtroom where, as he must have expected, the same crowd of reporters who had come to cover the arraignment was waiting to see what provocative and inflammatory remarks the always reliable Bartholomew Caminetti would give them for the afternoon editions and the early evening news. I watched him sweep off the counsel table the few papers he had brought into court and march out of the courtroom, bristling with forced indignation as he responded to the shouting incoherence with assertions of "heinous crime" and "massive cover-up."

Jimmy Haviland was where I had left him, hunched over the counsel table, meditating on some distant and fugitive thought of his own, oblivious of the rising chorus that followed the district attorney out the doors behind him. The indictment was lying facedown on the place in front of my vacant chair. I picked it up, folded it lengthwise in half, and slipped it inside my coat pocket. I grabbed my briefcase from the floor next to the chair. Haviland did not move. He remained in that bent trance, a faint smile, weary, hopeless, and ineradicable, on his mouth. As gently as I could, I laid my hand on his shoulder and whispered that it was time to go. He nodded as if he were responding to some voice he heard, not now, in the present, and not my voice, but another voice, a voice that often kept him company when he lost himself in the remembered circling labyrinth of his mind.

"We have to go," I repeated, quietly insistent.

"Yeah, I know," he said, slowly, and as it were reluctantly, lifting his eyes until they met mine. His mouth twisted with regret. "I made a fool out of myself, didn't I?"

I peered into his eyes, measuring the depths of his unhappiness, and remembering as I did what he had been like when I first met him and there was nothing tragic about our lives. I laughed a little, and he caught the mood of it and let the mood catch him.

"Yeah, you did," I said, laughing a little more. "But don't worry about it. Everybody knows I'm a bigger fool than you."

Jimmy got to his feet, a glimmer of grateful irreverence shining in his eye. "Damn right. Only a fool would take a case like this."

The crowd of reporters that had swarmed around Bartholomew Caminetti had followed him out of the building, too intent on getting from him every ruthless, caustic comment they could to remember that in addition to a prosecution every trial had a defense. I might be the best-known defense lawyer in the country, but this was New York, and no one who did not live here could possibly be as interesting or important as someone who did. Until he moved here, Gatsby did not exist.

We walked down the gray deserted hallway and rode the elevator down to the ground floor. Two marshals were escorting a prisoner up the steps at the back of the building, moving in the methodical, practiced, stiff-jointed choreography of a city scene played every day. Across the street, we cut through Columbus Park, passing wooden tables of huddled Chinese watching with connoisseurs' eyes a board game played by everyone they ever knew. We were on the edge of Chinatown. Across the street on the other side, in a concession to the lawyers' trade, was an Irish bar.

Jimmy raised his eyes. "Just one?" he asked. "I'll buy."

We sat at the end of a long, shiny bar, two middle-aged men, each nursing a drink an hour before lunch.

"What time is your flight?" I asked for no other reason than to break the silence of Jimmy Haviland's blank forward stare.

"Don't have a flight," he said after he took another lifeless taste. I looked at him. "Didn't know whether I'd be held. Anyway, doesn't matter. I'm going to take the train. I used to do that, long time ago — take the train back and forth to New York. Haven't done it in years."

"How long does it take?"

"Doesn't matter. The longer the better. I'm in no hurry to get back. What about you? Your flight this afternoon?"

I was thinking about something else. "Are you sure you don't remember who was there — besides Browning, besides Annie? Someone who could testify that you left? That you weren't there when Annie fell?"

He shook his head in disgust. "Sometimes I wonder if I was there; whether I just dreamed I was." With both elbows on the bar, he stared down at the near-empty glass, trying to remember, to see it again, clearly, the way he must have seen it once.

"I wasn't interested in who was there. I went there to see Annie. There were dozens — hundreds — of people around. They were just faces. All I remember for sure is that when I walked into the room — the one right off the suite — they were alone, just the two of them, the way I told you before."

The bartender approached, ready to pour. Jimmy thought about it for a moment; then, smiling to himself, he covered the glass with both hands and shook his head no.

"Just one," he said, turning to me, reminding me that he had made a promise and that from now on at least, he would keep the promises he made.

"Let's get out of here," I said before that temporary sense of well-being was lost in the empty crying need for just one more before he quit.

We started walking, and the farther we went, the more crowded the sidewalk became until, finally, it was impossible to move without dodging out of someone's way.

"Listen, I've been thinking," I heard Jimmy say from somewhere behind my shoulder. "About what happened." With each struggling step his voice became harder to hear. "Maybe it wasn't an accident. Maybe Annie didn't fall. Maybe I was right all along: Maybe she was pushed; maybe she was murdered, not on purpose, exactly, but in a moment of rage."

I stopped and looked behind me. Jimmy was three or four feet away, just a face in the swirling crowd.

"She wasn't in love with him. She wouldn't have gone anywhere with him. Maybe he did it — got angry, hit at her, shoved her, pushed her back and she fell. If it wasn't an accident, if someone did it, it had to have been him."

"Who?" I shouted as he turned away, buried in the noisy, jostling crowd. "Who?" I asked, though I knew exactly whom he meant.

It was a strange sensation, something I had not experienced before: this hope that someone I was representing on a charge of murder was wrong when, beyond the vague insistence that someone else must have done it, he named the person who had. I wanted Browning to be right; I wanted to believe that the case against Jimmy Haviland was a made-up lie, part of a political conspiracy to drive Browning out of office. I had to believe that, not so much because of Thomas Browning, but because of his wife. If I had not quite realized that before, I understood it the moment I got back to the hotel and was told that there was a message from the vice president's office. Mrs. Browning wondered whether I might be able to join her for lunch the day after tomorrow in Washington, D.C.

11

When I was much younger I thought that everyone should fall in love in New York at least once and that probably everyone had. I did, or I almost did, once, a long time ago, that sweltering summer I spent in Manhattan, the summer before my last year in law school. I have been in love, seriously in love, only once; that is not to say that there have not been other occasions when I felt on the verge of it, felt that it could happen again, the way it had that one and only time before. I should have known it would never happen, that you only really fall in love once, but there is nothing quite so forgivable as hope and I had the excuse of my youth. There were times I was desperate to recapture that feeling, to find something that would last, times when it lasted all of a single half-drunken night, laughed off in the blue-gray haze of morning with more than a little regret. There were other times, however, when it was more serious and more lasting than that, when for a while at least all

I could think about was the girl, the new one I had found, and every thought of her was wrapped in bright ribbon inside a perfect golden glow. That was what it was like, that summer, when it happened in New York, when I met Joanna and began to think it could happen again, that I could for a second time fall in love.

Joanna had high cheekbones and soft brown hair and dark eyes that could fill with fire or ice, moving from one to the other with breathtaking speed. Always kind to strangers, she could sometimes be cruel to friends; though only, so far as I had occasion to observe, when they had misbehaved in a way that suggested they thought the rules that applied to everyone else did not apply to them. It was, or so I thought at the time, the reaction of girls from fine families who danced and rode horses and went to private shady tree schools, girls who had been bred so finely to the knowledge of what was always the right thing to do that by a second instinct — sharper, more natural than the first — they could give the appearance that they were doing it precisely when they were not. In the privileged circles in which Joanna moved with such comfortable ease, appearances were everything and respectability meant mainly not getting caught. It was, I suppose, part of the attraction, one of the things about her that made her irresistible: the sense that behind that façade of polished, irreproachable good manners, that look of studied indifference, someone was waiting to see if you were willing to take a chance.

I am sure it was that, or something like it, because the first time we met I did not like her at all. It was at a small gathering arranged by Thomas Browning for some reason that seemed important at the time, but perhaps had no importance at all and I only think it did because Browning was in New York and wanted me to attend.

We had spent a fair amount of time together in Cambridge while law school was in session, but that was pretty much all. Whether it had been Thanksgiving of my second, or my third, year; whether it was the year before, or the year after, Zachary Stern died, I had been invited to the fabled family estate in Grosse Pointe only once. The summer after our first year, Browning disappeared, to Europe mainly, but other places as well. I would sometimes get postcards from remote locations in Asia or Australia, and once, I think, from São Paulo, Brazil, with short, funny remarks about the burden of learning the foreign part of the auto business in languages he did not always understand. The next summer he was traveling again, but he had a week or two before he left and he was spending it at home, in New York.

When I arrived after work, everyone was already there, sitting around a large table in the back of Maxwell's Plum. Thomas Browning was telling them that the only thing worse than the prospect of having to go into the family business was the thought of practicing law.

"But here comes Antonelli, fashionably late," he announced with a languid grin as I finished twisting my way through crowded tables and settled into the last vacant chair. Browning was the only one I knew. The others were strangers, but obviously friends of his. I felt myself under the appraising glance of people, all about my age, who were clearly wondering exactly where I fit in. I had caught the tail end of his last remark. I returned his slightly irreverent smile.

"For those of us who don't have a family business to go into, it's called getting home from work."

They seemed to hold their collective breath, waiting for Browning's reaction before they made the hazard of their own.

Browning had an instinct for everything. Without a moment's delay, without that slight hesitation that would have suggested he was masking with politeness what he really felt, he made a grand sweeping gesture and threw back his head.

"Meet Joseph Antonelli, the only son of a bitch with guts enough always to tell me the truth! Somebody get him a drink."

And suddenly everyone wanted to be my friend. Or almost everyone. Sitting directly across from me, Joanna Van Renaessler, introduced by Browning as an old family friend, looked at me with a raised eyebrow and a skeptical smile. She did not believe for a minute what Browning had just said.

"I don't know that I've ever heard of anyone who always tells the truth."

A kind of hard shrewdness glittered in her eyes, like the look of a seasoned gambler who has lost too often not to calculate the odds. I was being patronized, but more than that, challenged to show if I had something of my own to stand on and was not just another one of Thomas Browning's temporary friends. That was the feeling I had, that she found something suspect about anyone she had not known for years — anyone who was not an "old family friend" — because anyone Browning met more recently was not someone he should trust. Though she did not know it, I had come to the same conclusion myself. I had seen the way people tried to get close to him because he was Thomas Stern Browning and he could do something for them.

There was noise everywhere, laughter and voices and tinkling glass. The others at the table were leaning one way and the other, starting conversations of their own. We were at the end of the table farthest from where Browning was carrying on what appeared to be separate conversations with the two well-dressed young women sitting on each side. His half-closed eyes kept coming back to us. I had the feeling he had arranged things this way, that I would be sitting across from Joanna and he could watch the fun. He would have done it without malice, without intending the slightest harm, just to see the way things worked when two people of such different backgrounds were thrown together in a situation where at least for a while they could not get apart. Perhaps it was more than curiosity that made him do it; perhaps his interest ran deeper than that; perhaps, though I did not know it then and would not suspect it until a long time later, he thought it held some lesson for himself.

I was going to law school on a scholarship and worked part-time and in the summer for the money I needed to get by. My family was not famous and could not trace itself back more than a generation or two. A hundred years ago we were politely called recent immigrants and, not so politely and rather more often, daigos, wops, and worse. Joanna Van Renaessler came from a family whose ancestors had practically invented America, a family that had been rich for so many generations that they could not quite remember how it had all started, whether from selling what had become Rhode Island or trading some part of New Jersey instead.

"I don't know if I've ever heard of anyone who always tells the truth," repeated Joanna, more amused than annoyed at my silence.

"You seem as though you'd be disappointed if you did. Why?" I asked as she got ready to say something in anger. "Because you're so certain they would have to be boring and uninteresting, without any secrets to hide — nothing they felt a need to conceal."

Her eyes flashed, then retreated behind a

cryptic smile. "Are you suggesting that the only way to hide a secret, the only way to conceal something you don't want to share, is with a lie?" She lifted her chin a bare fraction of an inch, just enough to invite me into the game. With a quick toss of her head, her eyes flashed once more. "Haven't you heard, young Mr. Antonelli, that 'silence speaks louder than words'?"

"Young Mr. Antonelli?" I was older than she, but the way she said it, the soft laughter in her voice, gave a hint of a feminine wisdom that made me feel she knew things about me I was still far from knowing myself.

"You mean the difference between lying and not telling the truth?" I bent farther across the table. "The lie that sounds more convincing because it's never spoken out loud?"

She lowered her eyes to the glass she was stirring, smiling quietly to herself.

"Is that a line you read somewhere in a book, some novel you read — one of those things you make a point of memorizing because you think it might be useful sometime?" Her eyes lingered over the glass. "Isn't that what young men do, the ones who are trying to make their way in the world — rising from humble beginnings to become something useful and important, famous, and of course rich?"

She raised her eyes. The smile had changed into something uncomfortably close to a smirk. An instant later it was gone, as if she had reconsidered, decided that she had made a mistake, said what she had not really meant. The color in her cheeks deepened. She bit the edge of her smooth polished lip.

"I didn't . . . I shouldn't . . ." She was not used to apologizing, and now, when she thought she should, she did not know how. Angry with herself, she turned toward the far end of the table. Browning, leaning first one way then the other while he carried on two conversations at once, was waiting for her, beaming at the disconcerted look in her eyes.

"Are we going somewhere for dinner?" she asked in a voice that immediately stilled the other conversations at the table.

Browning glanced at his watch and then, the smile still thick on his mouth, shook his head at how quickly the time had passed. He waved his arm for the waiter and pushed away from the table.

"That would be wonderful," he announced, gazing at each of his guests; "but I'm afraid the party has to end here. At least for us," he added, glancing at me for a moment before he turned his attention back to the others. "While the rest of you are here — or wherever else — having a good time, Antonelli and I are having dinner with a very dull man — a lawyer, wouldn't you know — to discuss a small legal matter that I'm sure I'll never be able to understand."

The look in Joanna's eyes suggested that she had expected something else, though it seemed less a question of disappointment than convenience: If she had known, she would have made other plans. As Browning and I were leaving, I heard her making her excuses when the others asked her to stay with them.

"She likes you," said Browning with an encouraging look as we left the restaurant and headed up the street. "I know her. I can tell."

There was a taste of something burning in the still, heavy summer air. The broiling heat rolled off the sidewalk, rising up in the shimmering diaphanous shadows of a desert mirage. My mouth was dry; my face had begun to glow under the throbbing light of an enormous reddish sun. All around me the brick buildings looked burned black. The sky had turned to ashes, colored by the fireball behind.

"She's working here in New York. At J. Walter Thompson — advertising. She has her own place." He chuckled as he began to walk faster, oblivious of the heat. "And she's gorgeous — don't you think?" he asked, aware that I had not said a word. He stopped and waited until I caught up. "Is something the matter? Why are you going so slow? She say something that depressed you?" asked Browning with that same knowing grin.

He returned my smile with one of injured innocence. "Sometimes I'm just not very good at getting out of things." He shook his head at his own announced incompetence. He seemed genuinely sorry. "I shouldn't have done that, but I did have to go. I had sort of said something about making a night of it, but then the other thing came up and . . ."

He was staring down at the sidewalk, thinking about what he had done. But it was over, and there was no use dwelling on what could not be changed. He straightened his shoulders and gave me a distant, friendly glance; letting me know, I suppose, that it was all right: that if I knew all the circumstances I would not think him guilty of anything more serious than a small, well-intentioned lie.

"Well, if we're not having dinner," I asked, hurrying to keep up as he renewed his rapid pace, "just where are we going?"

He stopped dead in his tracks. The reddish tint in his cheeks was suddenly redder still.

"God, how stupid of me. I . . . I have to meet someone in the Village. I didn't think . . ."

I put my hand on his shoulder and looked into his embarrassed eyes. "It's all right," I assured him, holding back a grin. "I'll have dinner with that lawyer by myself — just in case I ever see Joanna again and she asks."

He gave me a grateful look and turned to go.

"She hates me, by the way," I called after him. "And to tell you the truth, I don't much like her, either. Did you think I would?" I asked, laughing into the oppressive everywhere heat.

Browning tossed his head and twisted around without slowing a step. "No, you're wrong. About all of it," he added with a laugh as he quickly moved away.

I watched him for a while moving like an eager schoolboy down the street; moving faster, I thought, the farther away he got, as if he were afraid that whomever he was meeting might not wait. There was nothing for me to do but go home. I thought about taking a cab, and even stepped out into the street, ready to raise my hand to signal the first one I saw, but then I remembered the way she had looked at me, that trace of condescension I had been far too sensitive to miss, and I thought without reason or logic that I had something to prove, not to her, but to myself. I did not need anything, certainly nothing she could give. Let her go around with her fast, free-spending friends, riding in dark limousines, silent and aloof, and if they did take a cab ride felt proudly democratic. I did not need money; I could always walk.

The place I lived in in Manhattan had been arranged in a typical tortured New York way. The sister of a friend of mine, another member of our law school class, had a small one-bedroom on Twenty-sixth Street between Lexington and Third that she was willing to let me have for the two months of summer at half the rent she paid if I paid the cleaning lady who came once a week and if I promised to water the plants. My friend's sister had graduated from UCLA or USC — I was never sure which — and she had a job with one of the auction houses. She had a month's vacation, and she was taking an additional one, unpaid, so she could travel around Europe with an unhappily married artist who was searching for inspiration and thought he might find it with her.

I had been here only two weeks, and it felt like two years. I did not know anyone in New York, and after this evening I was reasonably certain I never would. Browning was leaving, or at least I thought he was; but even if he had changed his plans and decided to stay, I had the feeling I would not see him much. The days in the law firm where I was clerking were endless, a long pilgrimage into questions of law that had no answers other than the kind that were written by angels on the head of a pin. If I had ever had any doubt about becoming a criminal defense lawyer, a summer spent dealing with estates and conveyances was guaranteed to teach me the virtues of murder. The strange part was that the lawyers I worked for actually liked it, and thought I would too after I had spent enough eighty-hour weeks to see the logical precision with which things were properly done. Every day I slaved at the assignments they gave me, which meant, of course, that I was expected to spend nights and weekends, too.

I did not mind so much the brutal, sultry heat; it gave me something to think about beyond whatever I was going to have for dinner before I sat at the table and started to work on the brief that Mr. Dowling wanted by the end of the week. Moving slowly, each step an effort in the debilitating heat, my head bent low to avoid the white blinding glare, I did not notice her until I was half a block from the building.

She was standing in the shade of the awning, looking idly down the street the other way. By herself, without anyone to talk to, her face had lost that animation by which the mask we show the world changes with our need. She was lovely, pure and simple, with fine fresh skin and eyes that seemed vulnerable and even, I thought, a little lost. It was as if beneath the rapid glance and the sharp-eyed stare; beneath the quick, dismissive smile, the sudden toss of her head; beneath all the masks and gestures, it was all an act, an act that at least sometimes she wished she did not have to play. I crossed the street, hoping to take her by surprise.

Joanna saw me coming out of the corner of her eye. A smile crossed her mouth like a fugitive running away. She turned and faced me with a cool, appraising glance. My collar was wrung with sweat; my white dress shirt slithered around my chest. My eyes were tired and filled with harsh particles of dust; my hair, sopping wet, was crawling down my head. She started to laugh.

"Would not spend a dollar on a cab. Doesn't surprise me. Not after what I've heard," she said, leaning her shoulder against one of the black metal awning supports. She crossed her ankles and held her hands together in front of her, watching me with gentle, teasing eyes. "I've heard all about you, you know. How you work all the time; how you never go out; how the way to get you to do anything is to suggest that it's something that maybe, just maybe, you can't do. And so because it's too hot to breathe, you decided you had to walk." She bent her head to the side, a whimsical look of utter certainty in her eyes. "Is that about right? Is that what you decided to do and why? And remember," she added, lowering her chin in a way that told me she was about to invoke something from our very brief past, "the only allowable lie is the one you don't tell out loud."

I suddenly remembered where I was supposed to have gone. It must have shown, because when I started to speak, she placed her fingers over my mouth and said, "Better not."

" 'Better not'?"

She tossed her head, but not like before, with that lightning quick, measured contempt, but with an easy careless laugh. "Tell the first lie of your young life."

It was there again, that same suggestion of something somehow foretold, written out without my knowing, but already read from start to finish by her.

"I knew you weren't having dinner with Thomas and some lawyer; I know he was just using you as a convenient excuse. He does that — he's always done that: invented excuses that don't exist. He does it so well I think sometimes when he says it he actually believes it's true. It's not his fault, really. In a way, I suppose it's even nice. He has such trouble telling anyone something he thinks they don't want to hear. So who is he off with this time — some girl he met at school?"

She said it casually, but she could not quite conceal an interest and a hope that I might tell her what I knew. I did not know anything, really; but I did not tell her that. I did not tell her anything, and she seemed perfectly content to let the matter drop.

"And because I knew you weren't going to dinner with him, I thought you might like to go to dinner with me."

I wondered where I could take her. If I took her to the kind of place she was used to I would be broke for a month.

"I'm having dinner at home, and I thought you might like to join me," she went on as if she had an answer for each hesitation she read in my still-too-guileless eyes. "No, I'm not cooking," she added with a cautionary laugh. "My parents' place. I'm always expected," she explained with a deliberately enigmatic look. "Especially when they don't expect me at all."

She brushed a strand of light brown hair away from her eye and stepped away from the pole. She stood in front of me, her feet close together.

"Don't you think it's the proper thing to do — meet my parents — before you try to get me into bed?" She was laughing with her eyes, but at me or with me, I could not tell. "You know how awkward it can be when you wait and do it later — I mean meet the parents after you have already known the girl — that way, I mean. You know what I mean. Wouldn't you feel strange and guilty, as if you were lying about something, though of course that something would never come up?" She put her hand on my shoulder, teasing me, taunting me, trying to find that first sign of embarrassment as if it were some prize she had to win. "This way you meet them with a clear conscience, knowing that you never have, and maybe," she said, drawing back just enough so I could see the full extent of her proud, provocative smile, "just maybe, never will. Now why don't you shower and change and then we can go."

The Van Renaesslers lived in one of those fine old gray stone buildings somewhere in the sixties or seventies on Central Park West. They were older than I expected, in their mid to late fifties from what I gathered; though her mother looked younger, and her father older, than that. They had the look of people comfortably settled, without ambition for anything more than they had. The walls were covered with gold-framed paintings of artists famous and dead, going back from the French Impressionists to the Italian Renaissance, and even further back than that. There was the absence of pretension, an easy familiarity that made me feel like someone they had known for years, an invited guest, instead of a stranger brought unexpectedly to their door.

"I wanted you to meet him right away," said Joanna with a mischievous look in her eye. "I've fallen completely in love with him. We're going to be married day after tomorrow," she announced breezily as she plucked a piece of chocolate candy from a dish; "and we'd like you to be there if you can. City Hall at ten."

Her father nodded wisely, and then, shaking his head at this, her latest antic, turned to me. "I can say with a certain authority because I've known her all her life — which isn't to say I've ever understood her — that marriage to my daughter would be the greatest mistake of any man's life."

"You don't believe me!" she pretended to protest. "But I am in love, madly in love with Joseph — Do they call you Joe? — and I can't live without him and I'm going to marry him in two days whether he bothers to ask or not. Now, can we eat? I'm starving."

I was a frequent guest that summer in the spacious Central Park West apartment of Arthur and Millicent Van Renaessler. At least once a week, usually on the spur of the moment, Joanna would decide we ought to drop by. They were always glad to see us, and I think that after a while they began to assume that Joanna was actually serious, perhaps not about marriage, but about me. I had the odd sensation that not only did they not disapprove but that they felt for some reason a certain relief. Her father in particular seemed to go out of his way to offer encouragement by showing me that there were not any serious obstacles that would prevent his daughter and me from taking things as far as we wanted them to go. It was all very subtle, but even I could not fail to understand what he was driving at when he would remark in that wonderfully understated way of his that an old friend, someone with whom he had gone to school, had mentioned just the other day how difficult it was becoming to find any talented, eager young men. And, oh, yes, did he mention that this friend of his was one of the senior partners in one of the two or three most important law firms in town? When I told him finally that I was pretty certain I was going to return to Oregon when I finished law school and open a practice of my own, his gray eyes fairly glistened as he told me how much he had enjoyed his only visit to the Northwest years before and that he could not think of a better place to live.

"My father is always trying to marry me

off," remarked Joanna in her breezy fashion when I tried to kid her that her father seemed to think she would be much happier in Portland than she had ever been in New York. She watched me with a teasing smile that was less teasing than it looked. "I told them the first night we met — remember? — that I had fallen madly in love with you. I didn't tell them — and I still haven't told them — that you've fallen madly in love with me."

If we had been in a restaurant, or sitting on one of the benches in the park, somewhere quiet where time belonged to us and questions came with answers and the only thing spoken was the truth, I am not sure what would have happened, what I would have said, but I would have said something and our lives might have turned out much differently than they did. It was the end of August and we had spent some part of every day together, and every time we said good-bye I could not wait until I saw her again. I did not know if I was in love with her, and for that I was a fool; because the only reason I did not know was that I had been in love before. It did not feel the same way: It was not nearly so all-pervasive, so all-consuming. I thought of her, looked forward to her, but I thought of other things as well. I was not smart enough to understand that what I felt about Joanna was closer to what you should, and that it was different when you were grown up than what it was like when you were still really just a boy. If I had had to tell her what I thought, things might have surfaced that, because I had not had to talk my way through them, were not yet clear in my mind. I started to say something, though I am not sure what it was, when Joanna's eyes grew wide with excitement and she grabbed me by the arm.

"There he is!" she shouted into the deafening noise that had suddenly taken possession of the room. Moving through the crowd of the basement ballroom of the Roosevelt Hotel like some shining golden eagle, John Lindsay, running for mayor, was on his way to the podium to greet a thousand new volunteers.

"Isn't he gorgeous!" cried Joanna with a starstruck look. "Isn't it wonderful! Isn't New York the greatest place there is?" She was clutching my arm, smiling into my eyes. "Tell me you'll come. Tell me that after next year, after you graduate, you'll come here, to New York, to Manhattan. You'll love it here — I know you will. It's the only place there is."

And then she turned and shouted with the others, her eyes sparkling and alive, cheering for the next great new beginning for the city that lived not just all around you but inside you, part of who you were. I stood there, watching all of them chanting, knowing as well as I had ever known anything that Joanna would never leave.

It was one of the last times I saw her, in the middle of September, before I left to go back to school, that Mr. Van Renaessler explained, or tried to explain — because he was, after all, only guessing — the relationship between Joanna and Thomas Browning. They were, as Browning had told me that evening I first met her, old friends, connected through certain family ties. That was the phrase he used: "certain family ties." He said it with the thoughtful precision of someone who, when he had to, could be very careful in his speech.

It was a bright, clean day, one of those days that seem to carry with them something of fall and summer both. Joanna was helping her mother with something and at his suggestion we had gone across the street, wandering for a while in the park until we found an empty bench.

"The families were never friends, never as close as that. It was business, mainly.

For Stern, of course — the old man — that was his whole life, that company of his. The only reason he talked to us — maybe the only reason he talked to anyone — was that we had something he needed. In the years when things did not go well — he needed a source of money. That's why he came to us — because of the bank. A lot of banks went under back then, but there was never any danger of that for us. Whatever we loaned him, Stern always paid it back, right on time if not earlier. But I must say, he did it with as much ill grace as I've ever seen."

Mr. Van Renaessler wrinkled his nose. A moment later, he emitted a slight chuckle.

"In all the years he did business with us, first with my father, then with me, he never once said thank you. We carried him through the Depression. Without us, all those plants of his would have closed — and never once could he bring himself to thank us for what we had done. We got our money back. He seemed to think we ought to have thanked him. And who knows? Perhaps we should have. It took more than money," he said, quick to acknowledge merit where he saw it, even, or perhaps especially, in someone it was plain he could barely tolerate. "It took a kind of ruthless genius to keep something going that was that big, that complex, with hundreds of thousands of people doing hundreds of thousands of things."

Mr. Van Renaessler sniffed the air. He pulled his far shoulder forward and grasped one hand with the other. As he stared down at the bench, the lines in his forehead deepened.

"I want to be very careful about the way I say this. Thomas Browning is as fine, and as intelligent, a young man as I've ever known. But he's all wrong for my daughter." He studied me for a moment with a strange intensity, as if he were searching for an answer to a question he knew he could not ask. "There is a point at which a father can't get involved in his daughter's life. That doesn't mean, you understand, that he isn't — it just means he has to wrestle with things alone and never to any real purpose, because, in the end, all he can do is hope that things turn out for the best." He paused, and with as kind a smile as I have ever seen, said with a sadness that surprised and touched me, "I understand that next spring, when you finish Harvard, you won't be coming back."

I started to mumble something, and I think if he had not stopped me I would have changed my mind about what I was planning to do.

"No," he said, shaking his head. "You're right to do what you think you have to. It's the only way to live. Believe me: If I haven't learned anything else in my life, I've learned that. You'd be the best thing that could happen to her for the same reason Thomas would be the worst.

"They've known each other since they were children. Joanna couldn't have been more than eight or nine when Stern started bringing his grandson with him when he made his trips to New York. Thomas has two fine parents, but you wouldn't have known he had any from the way that old man took over his life. Thomas didn't have a childhood — perhaps he's told you some of that himself — but you had to see it to believe it: the way Stern took away all the spontaneity, all the life, and burdened him with a sense of responsibility that men my age would find too much to bear. He had no friends; he did not go to school — he had nothing but private tutors until the day he left for Princeton; he did not know how to talk to anyone who wasn't dressed in a suit. That's why from I think the first time he saw her, Joanna became the one person with whom he thought he could ever be himself.

"It's gone on for years now. They're like brother and sister; except, of course, they're not. Whenever he has a problem, whenever something has gone wrong, he turns to her because she's the only one he trusts. And that's what worries me: They're too close — and they're not close enough. When she's with you, Joanna is natural and alive; around Thomas it's as if she thinks she has to protect him not only from the world, but also in some sense from himself. There's something else. Something I really should not say. He has spent so much time trying to get away from his grandfather's influence, trying to be something different than what the old man wanted him to be, that sometimes I think that underneath all his outward charm he has become, not what Zachary Stern wanted, but what Zachary Stern was: a man driven to do something no one has done before."

The sun had sunk below the horizon. There was a chill in the air. Joanna's father stood up, buttoned his gray cardigan sweater and plunged his hands deep into his pants pockets. In the distance, a child cried out as she tumbled down a grass embankment into her mother's arms.

"When the old man died two weeks ago,

the first call Thomas made was to Joanna. He's coming here next week. Did you know?"

Joanna had not told me.

12

The driver turned a corner in Georgetown and suddenly we were there, the shabby side entrance to a two-story building of broken mortared bricks and weathered paint-chipped wood. In front, two steps down from street level, the solid door to the restaurant gleamed with a hard black varnish. There was no menu, nothing pasted inside a glass enclosure to tell an interested passerby what was served or at what price; there was no telephone number someone might call. The name itself, five words in French, was enough to give it the impression of a place too expensive to just drop in. Climbing the back wooden stairs, surrounded by the mongrel scent of a dozen different dishes, rapid-fire muffled shouted voices, beaten pots and pans, lent a different perspective to what privilege really meant. The splintered stairs creaked beneath my feet; the hand railing, attached to posts with nails that in a century of weather had rusted and worked themselves loose, wobbled at my touch. Under the broken glass of a dented outdoor lamp, a screen door hung at a crooked angle from a broken hinge. A hand from inside pushed it open.

His heavy-knuckled hand still on the door, a Secret Service agent, dressed in a tightly buttoned suit, nodded silently toward another door less than three steps away. Another agent stood next to it, his hands clasped in front of him, his feet spread shoulder width apart. I reached for the doorknob, but his hand was there first. I entered a private dining room, and the door behind me shut.

There were eight small tables in the room, each of them covered with a white linen tablecloth. Only one was set. In the far corner, the light slanted through shutters closed three-quarters tight, across a pair of hands that rested on the table. In the shadows, Joanna sat watching as I came toward her.

"Hello, Joseph Antonelli."

The teasing laughter in her voice brought me back to what she had been, when I first knew her, that summer in New York, that summer when I almost fell in love with her and maybe really had. She was still quite beautiful, not as she had been before, but with that look that usually comes only with breeding and wealth: that look of youthful beauty that has faded but not disappeared. Her looks had always depended on something subtle, something you did not notice so much when she was young. It was the way she held herself — a little distant, a little aloof — the easy way she moved; but beyond everything else, it was the way she looked at you: as if she knew everything there was to know about you and liked everything she knew. I sat down at the table with the vague wish that I had never left New York.

Joanna offered me her hand. "I'm afraid I made something of a fool of myself last week. I hope you can forgive me."

Her voice was more measured, more controlled — the sweet fullness of it was gone; measured, controlled — the way, I tried to remind myself, it had to be when every word that came out of her mouth was taken down, transcribed, given a meaning that if she was not careful might not have been her intent. Her voice was drier, more circumspect; the eager enthusiasm of it had vanished, gone. Measured, controlled, a distant empty echo of something lost; a pale imitation of the voice I had loved and that, for a few brief months, had played over and over again in my young and foolish mind.

"There's nothing to forgive. You didn't do anything wrong."

With her back perfectly straight, she leaned forward, her elbows on the table. Her chin rested lightly on her folded hands. Her eyes glittered with rueful malice.

"A woman my age can be forgiven a lot of things, perhaps even getting a little drunk. But to stumble into a room where you know you'll find the boy with whom you were once madly, desperately, in love — not only drunk but without makeup — is worse than unforgivable; it's stupid." Joanna paused, then added: "But I couldn't wait to see you. Strange the way we think. All those years, and suddenly I can't stand to wait another night."

She reached across the table and squeezed my wrist. A strange, bittersweet smile flickered candlelike over her lips. I covered her hand with my own and smiled back. A door opened behind us. Her hand slipped away. Moving like a shadow, silent and without effort, a waiter brought a bottle of wine, filled our glasses and left.

"You never married, did you?" she asked, watching me over the glass she raised to her mouth. I waited while she drank and, because I knew she knew the answer, waited for what she wanted to say next. "I suppose I'm not surprised, though I don't quite know why. Maybe it was that girl you told me about — the one you were so much in love with, the one in Oregon, the one you wanted to marry." She thought a moment. "Jennifer. That was her name, wasn't it? Jennifer. Whatever happened to her?"

We had not seen each other in years, but however much we had changed, the memory we had of each other had not. It gave us, I think, a sense of safety, a sense that we could talk to each other as if instead of years since our last meeting, only a few days had passed. And so I told her the truth, or as much of it as I could bear. I told her that Jennifer and I were going to get married, and that something had happened and that now she was gone forever, lost in a place no one could find her, trapped inside a mind that had shut off the lights and closed down for good.

"I used to go see her; I don't anymore. She didn't know who I was; she never will. It's one of the reasons I left Portland; one of the reasons I stayed in San Francisco: I don't feel quite so much guilt."

Joanna did not ask me to explain. It's

impossible to live past forty and not know what it means to feel guilty about things over which you have no control. It is a fact of existence, as tangible, as real, as hunger or thirst or carnal desire: this vague, troubling suspicion that never quite goes away, that there must have been something we could have done to change things, something we were too stupid or too selfish, too caught up in our own ambitions, to find out. And so we try to run away, try to put what distance we can between ourselves and the memory of things that can never be changed at all.

"But you married," I said, turning us away from things too unbearable to expect, or to want, anyone to share.

She leaned closer, searching my eyes. She was about to speak when the door opened again. A second waiter, older than the first, with gray wire-bent hair and thin, sharp-edged shoulders, entered the room. He never once raised his eyes, never once looked at either one of us, as he served a Caesar salad first to Joanna, then to me. The silence was inscrutable, profound. Joanna watched him until he had finished, and then followed him with her eyes until the door whispered shut behind him. As if the waiter had been a chimera, a figment of her own imagination, and the food had always been there, waiting on her pleasure, she lifted her fork and turned to me with a pleasant smile.

"This is my favorite restaurant," she announced without enthusiasm. "Not as good as the ones I like in New York." She took a bite of the salad and with her eyes passed a judgment of partial approval. She took another bite, put down the fork, and gently pushed aside the gold-embossed plate.

"You weren't surprised I married? Or you weren't surprised I married Thomas?"

It caught me off guard. I tried to remember what I had thought about it at the time, but all I could really remember was that I had not heard about their marriage until after it happened. I think I must have read about it in the papers.

"You didn't come to the wedding." She said it as a simple statement of fact; but from the way she turned her head, looking at me now from a watchful angle, there was more to it than that. "Thomas said you wouldn't come." She was still watching me in that intensely interested way. "He didn't know if it was because of him — or me."

She was waiting for something: some response, some reply; but I didn't know what it was.

"Thomas said you wouldn't come; he said it was better not to invite you: you wouldn't feel you had to make some excuse."

Her expression changed. A lost, wistful look settled in her eyes. She stared at me, bravely, in defiance of her own lost control, determined to say what she wanted to say.

"Why couldn't you have stayed in New York — come back to New York after law school? Why would that have been so bad?"

I wanted to tell her the truth, or what after all the things that had happened seemed like the truth; because, after all, there was nothing to judge it against: no hard, incontrovertible fact — nothing more than the futile thought of what might have been.

"Why couldn't you have lived in New York?" Her voice echoed quietly in the silence of the room and in the silence of the long journey we had in our separate ways both traveled.

"I wish I had," I answered honestly, or as honestly as I knew how.

I leaned against the cane-backed chair, gazing down at the carpeted floor. It was as if we had gone through our lives in some parallel fashion: I still had the feeling that she had always been out of my reach, beyond my grasp, a woman who lived in a world I could never really know.

"I thought about it a lot the first few years after that summer. I'd remember what it was like, what it felt like, that summer in New York; and I'd wonder what would have happened if I hadn't left, if I'd finished law school and gone back to work in that Wall Street firm." Raising my eyes, I looked at her looking at me, and for a while I remembered how things had been. "I started thinking about it again when I knew I was coming to New York, when I thought I was going to see you."

I lowered my eyes and bent forward, my arm on the table, trying to think of how to say what I thought was true and wished was not. It was too late; it had always been too late. That was the truth of it. I knew that, and yet, there was something, a kind of second knowledge, a doubt that cast a shadow over the bright shining certainty in which I had once buried the past, a sense that perhaps I had been wrong after all.

"But how would I have ever fit in there?" I asked, glancing up. "I was a kid from Oregon. My father was a doctor, a GP; we were never poor, but we were never rich. You didn't want to leave New York, not just because you loved the city, but because you owned it, were part of it, had always been a part of it. You were always going to wind up with someone else, someone from your own background and class. I think it was inevitable that it was going to be Thomas Browning. I should have seen it at the time, the way the two of you always looked after each other, that you would end up married to him."

With a deft movement of her hand, Joanna wiped away a single tear. She waited with a blank expression while a third waiter led in two others, one of whom removed the salad plates while the other arranged new silverware around new plates. The two left immediately after they had completed their tasks; the third one, with a worried smile, spooned out portions, pausing with an upturned glance to see when he should stop. Joanna would not look at him. She nodded once, briefly; and then, walking backward the first few steps, he was gone. As if she had been holding it all the while, she let out her breath.

"I hate being who I am," said Joanna with a poisonous glance directed, not at me, but at the world of intruders she could not manage to keep away.

She had not looked at anyone who had come into the room while they were looking at her. I wondered if it was a way she had of protecting herself against the constant violation of prying, eager eyes. She tossed her head back and with a helpless look apologized, not for what she had said, but for the circumstances under which she was forced to live her life. She turned toward the cream-colored shutters on the window a little ahead of where she sat. With a tentative motion, she reached forward, adjusting them to let in more light.

"The weather here is awful," she said, stealing a glance outside. "Hot, humid, debilitating: It drains you of energy, makes everything slow down. It's why southerners talk so slow; why they drink so much: The sheer effort of speech brings on the thirst." She laughed softly and with a certain pleasure at her own affected drawl. The laughter lingered for a while in her eyes and then slowly, reluctantly, faded away.

"I would have married you — if you had asked." She raised her head to forestall any interruption. "And if you didn't want to live in New York, I would have gone wherever you wanted. But you never asked me;

you never asked me to go with you. So I asked you to come back to New York because that's where I was, where I lived, where — if you had been there — we could have been the way we had been that summer, that summer in New York."

She had not touched anything on her plate. She shoved it aside and picked up her glass.

"And I think it was my fault: for not telling you how I felt; for just imagining that you must have understood that the reason I talked that way — about New York — was because I thought that if you loved it too, you'd come back and wouldn't go somewhere I couldn't be."

It is the habit of unhappiness to rewrite our lives and from a different beginning come to a different ending. We cling to the past and what it could have been: what we wanted, or thought we wanted, before we were taught by a broken heart that our own good intentions have little effect on the way things are.

Joanna held up her head. Her eyes were bright, eager, wistful.

"My father was devastated when we broke up. He . . ."

"Your father: Is he . . . ?"

"He died three years ago. My mother

died a year before. He was fine for a while, not depressed. He put up a good front: He never showed his emotions — or almost never. His generation was like that. In my whole life I never once heard him raise his voice. If he disapproved of something you'd done, he would just look at you, not speaking a word; and you'd know how disappointed he was in you and you'd swear to yourself you'd never let that happen again." Pausing, she looked away, shaking her head at the memory of what had happened. "I never saw him look more disappointed than the day I told him you were going back to Harvard and wouldn't be coming back to New York. Unless it was the day I told him I was going to become Thomas Browning's wife."

She had placed her hands on the table. She examined them with a strange, intense fascination.

"I used to have lovely hands," she said, spreading apart her fingers. With a scornful expression she pulled her hands off the table and buried them out of sight in her lap. Sitting at an angle, she stared quietly out the shuttered glass, thinking back.

"My father was terribly disappointed," she said presently. "He didn't want me to marry Thomas; he wanted me to marry you." A smile edged its way along the corner of her lower lip. "He told me about that conversation he had with you, that afternoon in the park. That wasn't like him; that wasn't like him at all — which made the fact that he did it make me love him even more. He thought the world of you: In his own way I think he loved you as much as I did. He did not love Thomas. He respected him, admired him in a way; but you were the one he could have thought of — did think of — as a son."

I could hear her father's voice; I could see him sitting on the park bench next to me, telling me his fear.

"He thought he might turn out too much like his grandfather — old Zachary Stern," I said.

Joanna's eyes did not move from the window. She sat there with that look of rigid elegance, the smile that had crawled across her mouth now bitter, filled with unconcealed contempt.

"My father was always a shrewd judge of men." She kept staring out the window, lapsed into a silence that became drowsy and immense.

"Thomas is using you. You know that, don't you?" she asked presently, moving her head in a level arc until her eyes, inquisitive and relentless, met mine. "He didn't ask you to come to New York for that dinner — he did not agree to speak at that dinner — for old times' sake. He might have done it because he wanted to use you to make a point — I read what he said about you. He meant it, too. That is what he thinks about the lawyer — the kind of lawyer — you've become. But that wasn't the reason. He brought you here, to Washington, and it wasn't because he wanted you to have the chance to see me. I wanted to see you in New York. He had his office schedule me for some idiotic event somewhere else."

She laughed a little, a mild rebuke to her own intensity; an apology for appearing to act as if she could demand explanations, or anything else, from me.

"Isn't that a wonderfully convenient power to have? Anytime you don't want your wife around, schedule her to go off somewhere and give a speech? I'm always being told what to do and where I have to be. Even today, instead of being able to take all the time I want, they're whisking me off somewhere after lunch."

Joanna started to take a drink. Aware that I was watching her, she put down the glass. She seemed to watch herself with a kind of brooding irony as she pushed the tips of three fingers against the base of the glass, sliding it at least metaphorically beyond her reach.

"It's Annie, it's always Annie," she remarked with a tired, discouraged look in her eyes. She kept staring at the tips of her fingernails, stretched toward the glass. Her mouth twisted into a knot; her chin, rigid and tense, began to tremble. With a slight shudder, she took a long slow breath and then let it go.

"She wasn't what you thought she was," said Joanna. She put her hand back in her lap and moved away from the window. She sat directly in front of me, her head slightly inclined, speaking calmly, quietly, completely self-assured. She told me things about herself, and about Thomas Browning, that changed what I remembered into something new and made me wonder how much of the rest of what I thought might also be wrong.

"Thomas and I were more like brother and sister. We were children when we met. His mother — Penelope Stern — was beautiful, vapid and vain. His father, Warren Browning, was almost as bad: weak, vacillating, handsome as the devil and more charming than that. They used to remind me of the Duke and Duchess of Windsor: polished, polite, all dressed up in their expensive clothes; people you could imagine complimenting each other on how they looked while they were stealing a sidelong glimpse of themselves in the nearest mirror. It was everything: the clothes, the jewelry, the perfect good manners; and between them, not a thought in their heads. They traveled everywhere; they knew everyone: They were too busy to worry about anything except the next party, the next place they had to go, and of course about themselves. They would have left Thomas in the care of a nanny while they traveled around the world; but they didn't have to: Zachary Stern took care of all that.

"I came from a wealthy, privileged background. I know that. But my parents wanted me to have a normal life, to be like other kids. I think they must have succeeded, because when I first met Thomas Browning I thought he was a freak. He was twelve years old, with a pudgy face and pudgy little hands, and he talked to me like I was the hired help, ordering me about, telling me what to do. I ignored him, and when he kept it up, I laughed at him; and when he still didn't stop, I left him standing there while I walked into the room where my father was meeting with Zachary Stern and told him that if he left me in that room a minute longer I was going to slap that awful boy's face.

"We became friends, and the more I learned about the way he was treated, the way he was raised — the expectations, the demands, the way his whole life was being planned for him in advance — the more I tried to help, to show him that there was another world out there, that he didn't have to become what his grandfather or anyone else thought he should be."

Joanna tossed her head and then, at the memory of something distasteful, wrinkled her nose. "It was already too late, of course."

"Too late? He was still just a boy!"

"A boy shaped in the mold of Zachary Stern himself! He had not been to school; he had not made any friends — and he never would."

"Never would?"

"How could he, after a private education provided by a dozen different experts paid small fortunes for their time. He had the mind of someone twice his age and the emotions of a spoiled, willful child. There was never anyone to resist, to fight back, to insist on getting their own way when the only way they could get it was if Thomas did not get his. All the rough edges that get knocked off on the playgrounds, that get smoothed away in the civilized competition of the classroom — he never had any of that."

"But he wasn't like that when I knew him. There wasn't any of that kind of arrogance, that kind of selfish attitude toward things. He was probably the least self-absorbed person I knew."

She gave me an odd look, but appeared to concede the point.

"Yes, later . . . on the surface at least. But didn't you notice how he always seemed to be looking at things from the outside? Sitting there with that amiable smile, talking quietly — or more likely just listening — and all the time watching, watching the way other people behaved, as if he were a stranger trying to learn the customs of a place he had never been."

Joanna shook her head, angry with herself that she was not getting it quite right. "It wasn't arrogance; it was more than that. He did not go around bragging that he was one day going to run the world, or at least the 'largest industrial organization' the world had ever seen. That was just a fact, a terrific, overwhelming fact no one would let him ignore. And that is what Zachary Stern never understood: that what would have been the dream of any other man's ambition — what had been the dream of his own ambition — was where his grandson's ambition began."

Joanna looked at me with a kind of puzzled, questioning intensity, searching my eyes to see if she had explained it properly, to see if I understood.

"It was like being born into a religion — being born Catholic, for instance. It's who you are; it's what you start with; it's the way you look at the world. Thomas, Thomas Browning, grandson of Zachary Stern, was for all practical purposes born believing that the company — that astonishing industrial organization — was his. Don't you see the incredible irony? Zachary Stern, a man my father truly hated, had spent his entire life building that company, destroying anything and anyone who got in his way, so he could leave it in the hands of someone whose only thought when he got it would be: 'What next?'

"They say that certain traits skip a generation. Thomas is every bit as ambitious as Zachary Stern ever was. Zachary Stern

314

wanted to found an industrial empire; I think Thomas wanted to be president from the first day he realized it was the only way he could escape the shadow of his grandfather. That was one of the reasons why I tried to stop him from getting involved with that girl, Annie Malreaux."

Joanna repeated what she had said before, determined for some reason to convince me that I had been wrong, as if it still made some difference what anyone thought.

"She wasn't what you thought she was. She wasn't what she seemed: all poetry and verse, different from the rest of us because she appeared to float on the surface of things, refusing to take seriously what others thought important. Thomas thought it was real, that the only thing she did not like about him was his position, his wealth; that she thought those things were obstacles to being who you really were and living free." Joanna gave me a knowing, cynical look. "She said she came to Harvard because she thought it would be interesting to learn a little about the law. That was a matter of convenience, that dismissive attitude she had. It gave her a certain protection against having to face up to the fact that while she was good enough to get into Harvard, she might not be good enough to be among the very best. It's what some people do, isn't it? If you can't win, disparage the game. So she lived this little lie of hers, playing the part of the ethereal free spirit floating above the common run of ambition, deriding with a superior smile the prevalent materialism, while the whole time what she really wanted was to marry Thomas Browning and find herself suddenly quite rich."

"Do you really think so?" I asked quickly, wondering if she could possibly be right. It was hard for me to think of Annie as anything like as calculating as Joanna had thought. "Perhaps you were just being protective, given the way you felt about him then," I suggested.

Joanna gave me a strange look, as if I had forgotten my place. Too late to hide the irritation, she tried to cover it with a thoughtful smile.

"Perhaps I was. One thing I know for certain is that it would have been better if he had run off with her and found out for himself whether she was everything he thought she was." With a bitter glance she shook her head. "More than anything, I wish she hadn't died. What happened that day changed everything. It's why I married

Thomas; it's why he married me: because she died that day. She was gone — so were you. He married me, but he's never gotten over her. And now we get to live it all over again; and worse yet, so do you. It isn't fair! It isn't right! It was an accident, but there isn't anything these people won't do."

She looked at me with a kind of pleading intensity, as if she wanted me to understand something she did not quite understand herself. I thought that at any moment she might burst into tears.

"I told him what these people — Walker and the rest of them — were like. I told him they only wanted to use him for the election and that after that it didn't matter what they promised: They wouldn't do anything they said. He could have stayed in the Senate, but he's so mesmerized by the presidency he couldn't stop himself. And now this! Someone is charged with murder, and he's tricked you into taking the case."

"Tricked me? What do you mean?"

"If you ever loved me, please — please promise me that you won't do this, that you won't be involved in this trial."

"But I am involved: I'm Jimmy Haviland's lawyer."

"Find someone else to do it. Make some excuse. You don't understand!"

"What don't I understand?"

She did not answer; she kept staring at me, a frantic look in her eyes.

"What don't I understand?" I repeated, mystified by the sudden urgent sense that something terrible was about to happen and that I should have known what it was.

The door suddenly swung open. The Secret Service agent let her know it was time to go. Quickly gathering herself, Joanna got to her feet. She stood next to me for a moment, saying nothing. Then she put her hand on the side of my face and forced a smile.

"I would have married you, if you had asked, that summer in New York."

I started to say something. She put her hand on my lips.

"No, don't. I don't want to change the way I remember it. I want to keep believing that you would have asked me to marry you if you had thought I'd ever leave New York."

Then she was gone.

13

Why did Joanna want me off the case? Jimmy Haviland might think that Thomas Browning was responsible for the death of Annie Malreaux, but surely Joanna did not believe that. Or did she? It seemed impossible, but then, the more I learned about what had happened in the lives of these people with whom I had once been so close, the less I knew. Perhaps she was only trying to warn me about the people who were out to destroy her husband, the people around the president who were ready to convict an innocent man of murder because it would help them force out of office a vice president they did not want. If they were willing to do that, it was not likely they would hesitate to go after a defense attorney who got in their way.

The more I thought about it, the more certain I was right: Joanna could not stop Thomas Browning from putting himself in danger's way, but she could try to stop me. She must have known it was futile, that

Browning had his part to play, but that so did I. Browning may have wanted me to take the case, defend whoever was charged in Annie's death, but I was the one who had decided to do it. Jimmy Haviland was my responsibility. Even had I wanted to, I could not walk away from that.

Bartholomew Caminetti did not have any regrets or reservations; he certainly was not wondering about what had happened to former friends of his, people he had not seen in years. He was getting ready to make the case for murder, and I had seen enough of him to know that there was not anything that would be left to chance. I was going to have to be as well prepared for this as for any case I had ever tried, and that meant that I had to know everything there was to know about the victim, about Annie Malreaux; not just how she died, but how she lived. Every way I turned, I was face-to-face with the past.

I had known Annie Malreaux at Harvard for one short year, and I had known some of her friends; I did not know anything about what she had been like before she got there, and I did not know anything about what had happened to the people with whom she had once been so close. I was looking for something — anything —

that would teach me who she had really been and why her death had to have been the accident Thomas Browning had always said it had been. At least I knew where to start.

I found her on her hands and knees pulling weeds out of a small garden behind a narrow gray stone house where she had lived since long before her daughter died. She knew I was coming, but she was a woman in her eighties, and I could not be sure she would remember the time. When no one answered the door, I opened the gate at the side and let myself into the backyard.

"Mr. Antonelli!" She sat up on her knees and pushed a floppy hat back from her eyes. "Right on time." She got to her feet, dusting the dirt from the long sleeves of her shirt. With a graceful movement, she swept the hat from her head and tossed it onto a wooden stake around which a tomato plant had begun to climb. Her fine brown hair had only the slightest tinge of gray. Her eyes were large, inquisitive and proud. She had high cheekbones, a long, straight nose and a large animated mouth. She had the look of a woman who would not hesitate to speak her mind.

"Hot as hell, isn't it, Mr. Antonelli," she

said in a voice that quavered, but only slightly and only at the end. With the back of her hand she wiped away the perspiration that had run from her high forehead into her eyes. Squinting into the sultry haze, she seemed to hesitate, uncertain of what she wanted to do next. She crooked her head and tried to think.

"People used to come here," she remarked with a generous, thoughtful smile as she walked toward me. "In the summer, to stay at the lake. Just a few blocks away," she added, twisting her long and still-elegant neck, until her eyes, turned away from the sun, fell under the shadow of the eastern sky. "That's why they built all the big hotels, the ones with closets as big as bedrooms — for the summer trade. No one had air-conditioning then, and as long as you had to be miserable anyway, why not come to the beach and enjoy the water."

She put a frail-looking hand on my sleeve and with unexpected strength held on to my arm as we made our way to the back door.

"They use a couple of them now for dormitories, student housing. There isn't much call anymore for summer resorts on the south side of Chicago. It's too bad, really." She opened a rickety dark brown screen door. "Some of the hotels were quite wonderful: I lost my virginity in one of them. The Windemere, I think it was." She said this in a slightly puzzled voice, as if she wished she could remember, but could not really be sure. Her wintry eyes were full of mischief, and I knew that she had not forgotten a thing.

"You're from New York?" she asked as she removed a pitcher of lemonade from the refrigerator and poured us each a glass.

I followed her out of the kitchen into the dining room, where we sat at a ponderous dark wooden table with round thick legs. There were only two chairs, one at the end and one just around the corner at what would normally have been the first place on the left. Scholarly books with long and obscure titles, writing paper covered with a precise and calibrated longhand flourish, pages of double-spaced and frequently corrected typescript were strewn across it in the careless haphazard fashion of a work in progress.

"Just shove that aside," she said as if the stack of handwritten notes in front of me had no more value than last week's newspaper. "My lecture," she remarked. Closing her eyes, she held the icy glass against the side of her taut, wrinkled cheek. It seemed to relax her. A languid, almost sensuous smile crossed her parchment mouth. "Yes, at my age," she said as she opened her eyes and set down the glass. "How exactly can I help you, Mr. Antonelli? You're from New York?" she asked again, looking at me with extreme interest. "That's where I'm from — originally. New York — there's no place quite like it. Wouldn't you agree? Is that where you're from?"

She reached for the typed manuscript, ten pages or so that, following her instruction, I had pushed toward the center of the table, away from my glass. As she held it in her hands, I noticed a slight tremble. Then I realized that it was always there, and that the constant barely discernible motion of her head, which at first I had attributed to an intense interest, was symptomatic of the same palsied condition, the same decline, gradual, irreversible, and cruel.

" 'Tolstoy's Unacknowledged Indebtedness to Rousseau.' " She raised her eyes, certain I would understand the daring significance of it. Or was that what she wanted me to think? That she assumed she could talk to me about her work as an equal when she assumed nothing of the sort. There was something comfortable, assuring and not entirely honest about the way she enveloped you with that look of hers, as if she understood a part of you that until you saw that look you had not quite known was there. It was uncanny, the way she made you feel that you were discovering something about yourself, but only by seeing it first through another person's eyes. It had happened to me before, a long time ago. I had forgotten about it, forgotten that serious and at the same time strangely whimsical look. Now, when I saw it again, I remembered more than the look, I remembered the eyes; and it seemed to me that I was seeing them again, the same eyes a second time, this time in the woman who had had them first.

"I suppose I might call it 'Plagiarism Pure and Simple,' but that loses a little of the precision, a little of the subtlety, don't you think?"

She sat perfectly erect, an indulgent smile on her dry, desiccated lips. There was something about the way she held herself: the high neck, the loose-limbed broad shoulders, the light-filled eyes, the strong yet somehow vulnerable mouth, the ever-trembling hands; the way her voice seemed to quiver into a kind of breathless silence at the end; the way each question she asked sounded like a personal appeal, that reminded me of the way I had remembered an aging and majestic Katharine Hepburn. It was impossible not to like her; impossible not to fall under her spell.

"Do you think I'm too old to keep doing this, Mr. Antonelli?" She held her head back at an angle. "No one here seems to think so. It's one of the things that make this place different; one of the reasons some of us — the ones who have been here the longest — love it so much. The University of Chicago has the peculiar idea that it just might be possible that the mind is worth more than the body; and that the gradual decline of the one may not be inconsistent with the continuing, and perhaps even increasing, power of the other. You may die here, Mr. Antonelli; but you don't retire here: because at the point when you can't work, can't do what you were put here to do, you should die. Or, rather, your body should die. The mind never dies; not if it has been part of the conversation."

She smiled at my dense, puzzled expression. "The conversation that goes on over the centuries with the minds that knew how to think. Do you think Aristotle is really dead? Open the *Metaphysics* and see if you don't find yourself talking to him, questioning him, finding answers. Anyway, that's what we do here: ask questions of people like Rousseau who once wrote — Why did he write? — 'If you want to live beyond your century.' "

"How long have you been here, at the University of Chicago, Mrs. Malreaux?"

A thin smile creased the corner of her mouth. Leaning forward, her back arched straight, she placed her right elbow on the table. With her middle and index fingers spread along the side of her face, she joined her thumb and two remaining fingers at the apex of her chin. The smile began to float, slip sideways across her mouth.

"The university was founded in 1892. Sometime after that." She tilted her head to an angle a little more acute. "It isn't 'Mrs. Malreaux.' I never married. Call me Vivian. How can I help you, Mr. Antonelli? Why did you want to see me?"

It seemed impossible that she did not know, but it was clear that she had no idea why I had come.

"I knew your daughter, Ms. Malreaux. We were in law school together, and . . ."

Her gaze became curious, intense and alert; but there was also a sense of confusion and an instinctive reserve. Why would someone who had known her daughter in law school want to see her now, after all this time?

"You knew Anna at Harvard. You were in the same class?"

"No, she was a year behind me. I was Thomas Browning's roommate."

This seemed to put her again at her ease. "Ah, yes — Thomas." She searched my eyes, waiting for me to explain.

"I'm representing Jimmy Haviland."

The name produced the same look of recognition in her eyes; but this time there was more than the acknowledgment of a fact: There was a feeling of sympathy and understanding that had been absent at the mention of Browning's name.

"Why would Jimmy need representation?" she asked with a worried glance. "He can't have done anything wrong. Not the Jimmy Haviland I remember."

How could she not have heard? The rumored involvement of the vice president of the United States in a criminal cover-up had made it one of the most widely covered stories in the country. She must have read about it, and then, with the faltering memory of age, simply forgot.

"It's been in all the papers, all over the

television," I began to explain, looking down at my hands with a growing sense of embarrassment.

Instead of the blank look of forgetfulness I expected, I looked up to find her half laughing at what I had said.

"I'm afraid I don't read the papers, Mr. Antonelli." She threw me a glance terrific in its cheerful indifference to what the world thought important. "I'm eighty-two years old: What new thing do you think I should follow with interest? And as for television . . . Why would I? Why would anyone? But, please," she went on, anxious to get back to the question she had raised, "tell me about Jimmy Haviland. What's happened?"

"He's been indicted for murder."

With stoic reserve she kept hidden whatever reaction she had. She knew there was more to it, and she waited for me to tell her what it was.

"They claim that Annie's death wasn't an accident; that it was murder; that Jimmy pushed her out the window."

Vivian Malreaux threw up her hands. "In a long life in which I have seen stupidities of every description, that is unquestionably the single stupidest thing I've ever heard suggested. I would have pushed her out a window before Jimmy ever could have. Why are they doing this? They can't possibly believe it's true."

Vivian Malreaux stared straight ahead, bleak, disconsolate, angry. She lifted her chin and, as if she were trying to hide them, folded her palsied hands in her lap. A brief shudder passed through her. She clenched her hands into fists and beat them in soft despair against the hard wooden table. With her mouth twisted into a knot, she slowly shook her head.

"I used to tell Anna she was going to ruin Jimmy Haviland's life," she said in a bitter, anguished voice. "He was so in love with her, it was almost painful to watch. It was not her fault, of course — a lot of young men were in love with her, or thought they were. But Jimmy was different. He loved her too much. I saw it right away, the first time I met him: the way he looked at her, trying so hard to figure out what she wanted, how he could please her. He loved her too much. If he had loved her less, he would have known that he was doing all the wrong things, that he should have kept a certain distance, made her think he wasn't spending all his time thinking about her."

Vivian Malreaux threw me a significant

look. She wanted me to understand that the judgment she was about to pass was not quite so cruel as it might at first sound.

"In the end, of course, it would not have changed things. Jimmy Haviland was in love with something he could not have. Anna was never going to be in love with him. But it would have made him depend less on how she felt and left him something of himself."

A smile, strange, mysterious and profound, flashed through her eyes. "I imagine something like that happened to you once, Mr. Antonelli. Something tragic," she remarked, lowering her eyes to spare me the embarrassment of a reply.

"In some people, tragedy deepens the soul, makes them see things in a different light. It makes sense out of the world, this terrible knowledge that terrible things happen, that there are no happy endings, that we can't know — not really know — what fate has waiting for us. But other people — people like Jimmy Haviland — never recover from it. They can never quite believe it really happened, that the world could be that unfair, that life can be that unjust. I knew it when I saw him, saw the way Anna had become his whole world. I knew it was going to end badly; I knew that he was going to have his heart broken. What I didn't know was that it was going to happen twice."

She held her head high, rigid, yielding as little as she could to the palsied tremors that laid siege to her mouth. Her face was like a raw winter wind, cold, desolate, unforgiving. Her eyes searched relentlessly through the layered past to that moment when, once she had it, she could recall as easily, as clearly, as if she were reciting it from the written page of a well-written book.

"Jimmy called. That's how I learned Anna was dead. Jimmy called." There was a long, stringent pause. Her eyes half closed, she rubbed the palm of her right hand with the thumb of her left. "I think I knew it before he said anything; I knew it from the sobbing gasp in his voice when he tried to speak my name; I knew it when he tried to say Anna's name and broke down completely. He came here; he helped me with all the arrangements; he was quite brave. He came here because he thought he should try to help me; he came here, and I did what I could to try to help him."

A sad and wistful smile floated over the straight, fragile, trembling ruins of the mouth of Vivian Malreaux. Her voice was hesitant, sympathetic, the echo of vanished things that linger forever, clear and vivid, in the quiet and aching memory of the mind.

"He asked her to marry him. She broke his heart when she said no. But Jimmy Haviland was one of those rare, decent beings that I think you don't find so often anymore, someone who believed — really believed — that it wasn't quite possible to love anyone as much as he loved her and not have her love him back."

The wistful smile, become more hopeful, hovered a moment longer, began to dim, and then, sadly and irretrievably, died out. Her remarkable eyes appeared to pull back from some fixed point in front of her and cast about for something else to hold, some other place from which to begin.

"He was right: Love is never unrequited, not entirely. That's the rub, of course — that 'not entirely.' Jimmy loved her with all his heart, and Anna loved him because of it." She turned her head suddenly and gave me a sharp, searching look. "Anna did love him. She loved him because of how much he loved her — not because he was in love with her, but because he was capable of it, of being that much in love with someone. She envied that a little, that capacity to feel like that about someone; it was not a capacity she had. She was too much a woman for that."

" 'Too much a woman for that'?" I blurted out, astonished at what she had said. "What do you mean? — 'too much a woman for that.' "

With a kind of luxurious self-indulgence, an enigmatic smile curled along the corner of her mouth. With two fingers of her left hand she gently touched her chin.

"Anna understood the changeable nature of things; that what you feel today you may not feel tomorrow, and you almost certainly won't feel next year or the year after that. She understood, not that love doesn't last, but that love changes what it means. Jimmy Haviland was in love with her — Thomas Browning was in love with her — there were a lot of young men in love with her — and they all wanted to marry her; but marriage, if it means anything, means possession, and she was not able to do that, be possessed by someone. She understood herself too well for that; understood herself too well as a woman for that."

I was still confused, but not so much that I did not see the flaw, the error she had made. Vivian Malreaux said she had never married. Annie had been born out of wedlock when that sort of thing did not pass unnoticed or always go unpunished. Vivian Malreaux's objections to marriage had undoubtedly been based on a serious conviction, but what may once have been a reasonable analysis of the oppression of women seemed as dated as the Victorian furniture that filled the house in which she lived.

"Do you really think marriage is about possession?" I asked, hiding my incredulity behind a mask of polite interest. To my further astonishment, she laughed.

"Only when it works," she said, her eyes shining at my shocked and helpless stare. "It's why marriage has become an impossibility; why it isn't anything more than a temporary arrangement by which two parties agree to have sex and make money." She looked at me with a kind of gleeful mischief. "Marriage ended sometime in the nineteenth century. It did not just end because the economic situation of women changed and they became more independent, more self-sufficient; and it did not just end because it became easier — a lot easier — to get a divorce. Why did divorce become easier? Because women acquired an equal status in the law. But once women had an equal right to all the protections of the law, and all the economic opportunities of the marketplace, a woman was no longer an object, no longer dependent for her existence, her livelihood, her happiness on anyone but herself. She was not an object: She could not be possessed. But if she could not be possessed — if she could only belong to herself — how could a man believe that she belonged to him? And if she didn't belong to him — if she was not a part, an ineradicable part, of himself — how could he ever protect her with the same fierce passion with which he would protect his own life? How could he have about her the same kind of instinct of possession and responsibility that she — that any woman — has about her child?

"It is the vanity of our age, Mr. Antonelli: We keep thinking we can change the very nature of things and that there won't be anything lost. Marriage died a hundred years ago when women were set free to do what they liked, because then of course men were free to do the same thing. Now everyone has their rights and, it seems to me, not much else. I did not marry, Mr. Antonelli. I was not about to belong to someone else; and because, to be quite frank about it, the kind of man who would have settled for anything less simply did not interest me very much."

"But you had a . . ."

"A child?" With a slight movement of her head she acknowledged the force of this entirely conventional objection. "You assume I was asked." She rested her chin on top of her fingers, closed partway into a crippled, arthritic fist. A restless smile moved along the shadow of her mouth. "You assume Anna's father knew he was Anna's father. You assume . . ."

She gave a start like someone suddenly aware of her own bad habit, smiled a silent apology and rose from the table. She stood behind the chair, both hands on top of it, looking down at me.

"I might have married Anna's father, if he had survived the war. Perhaps he did. I don't know. I don't know what happened to them, any of them, the boys who went off to the war that summer, the summer of nineteen forty-two, the summer I lived in New York. It was the war, Mr. Antonelli — the war. Young men . . . going off to fight and die in a war. A look, a glance, a touch . . . an hour, a night . . . and no regrets. There were half a dozen young men who could have been Anna's father, young men with whom I slept during the time she had to have been conceived. By the time I realized I was pregnant, there had been other young men. I didn't even try to guess who it might have been, or even what he must have looked like. I didn't care. It didn't matter. I wanted it to be every young man I had been with, every young man to whom I had said good-bye and sent off to war."

Brave, defiant, indomitable, the fire in her wintry eyes lit up the room.

"Who was Anna's father? A boy I knew one wonderful summer night in 1942 in a small walkup apartment in Greenwich Village not far from Washington Square. I think that's why she turned out so well: born to love and bravery in the middle of a war."

A faint smile on her mouth, she left me alone and went into the kitchen. A few minutes later she brought out a wooden tray with tea and cookies. The air-conditioned house was comfortable, but not so cool that I would have been tempted to put on my jacket. She had thrown a sweater over her shoulders to stop a chill. The teacups rattled as she placed them as carefully as she could on the saucers. She nibbled on the edge of a chocolate cookie.

"I'm an old woman," she said with an impish glow. "Not so old that I could have danced with Isadora Duncan — but frankly, not so stupid that I would have wanted to. I did not want to be something men desired; I wanted to be someone who had a value in my own eyes. And that's what I wanted for Anna: to be herself, to be what she was — not what she thought someone wanted her to be." Her head came up sharply. "The last thing I wanted was for her to try to be like a man. Isn't it pathetic? These raging demands for equality between the sexes. Equal with respect to what? Work? Letting someone else tell you how to live? That's what I wanted for Anna: to live!"

She stared at me for a moment, then looked away. With a pensive expression, Vivian Malreaux sipped on her tea.

"It's strange what we remember, isn't it? I see the things Anna did, the things she accomplished, and I think I see what would have happened, how she would have lived, what she would — or could — have become, but of course . . ."

Pulling the sweater closer around her throat, she huddled beneath it as if the cold had reached down to her bones.

"When is the trial?" she asked in a

calm, dispassionate voice.

"The first week in October."

"How is he? How is Jimmy holding up? It must be tearing him apart. I haven't seen him in years. He used to come, once in a while, when he could; and then, for a long time, he'd write. Every year at Christmas I would get a card, but then it stopped. I hoped that maybe it meant that he had stopped believing that part of him had died that day, too. He believed that, you know. From the look in your eyes, Mr. Antonelli, I can see he still believes that, that his life ended, too; that from the moment Anna died every hope and dream he had died, too; and that whatever happened after that, it was always going to be judged with that kind of bittersweet nostalgia that tells you that nothing is ever going to be that good again. We all do that, I suppose — have something in our lives that makes other things seem not so good as they would have been if we had not had those other things first. It was worse for Jimmy Haviland, though; because what Jimmy had — what he remembers — was not anything that ever happened. What Jimmy had was that hope, that almost sacred hope, of what might have happened, what in his mind was bound to happen, once Anna understood — really under-stood — how impossibly and desperately serious he was; once she understood that no one would ever — could ever — love her as much as he did, as much as he al-ways would. Jimmy was the exception that proves the rule: He would have loved her forever; and, good God, he still does — doesn't he?"

Vivian Malreaux faced forward, her long thin arms stretched in front of her on the space cleared in the mountain of books and papers scattered over the heavy-legged dining-room table. With the tip of her left index finger, she beat insistently on the hard dull surface, her eyes narrowed into a penetrating stare.

"No," she announced abruptly as that incessant drumming echoed into silence. "It isn't reasonable; it isn't fair. There isn't any way in the world Jimmy Haviland could have done anything like what they say. Not in a thousand years. He was hurt, disappointed — I'm sure of it; but he was always a gentleman. The last thing he would have done was allow himself to get angry over the way Anna felt. Anna loved him, you know — in that way she had. She was not going to marry him, or take him to bed — Anna didn't love him like that. She didn't love anyone like that — until . . . That's why it's so incredibly sad."

"Didn't love anyone like that until — whom? Thomas Browning?"

Vivian Malreaux was thinking of Jimmy Haviland. At first she did not quite understand what I had asked. She blinked her eyes, a puzzled expression on her face. It was gone in an instant.

"Yes. She brought him here once: that fall, a few months before the accident, a few months before she died. I don't know if she was in love with him: She was intrigued by him. Who wouldn't have been?"

I knew what she meant. "He was different from the others," I started to agree. "He always seemed older, more intelligent . . ."

"More intelligent?" She gave me a skeptical glance. "Yes, I suppose he was, more than most," she remarked, her glance subdued, thoughtful, measured. "Intelligent, charming, considerate; but those aren't such rare qualities in the world that Anna would have had the same reaction, the same interest, to someone else who had them. No, Thomas — Thomas Browning — had another quality, a quality that set him apart from every other young man she had known, and from every other young man she was ever likely to know."

I scratched my ear, trying to think of what quality she meant. She peered at me from behind those defiantly intelligent eyes as if I already knew the answer and would, once she told me, wonder why I had had to wait to hear it from her.

"He was going to become one of the richest men in the world. She would have married a man like that."

It was said without the trace of a suggestion that there was anything heartless or mercenary about it. She kept looking at me, daring me, I think, not to laugh, not to admit that what she had said about her daughter reflected not the tragedy, but the great comedy, of the human condition. She lifted her proud head, holding it at a confident angle, someone who can see not just to the heart of things, but to the best in things. She was what I think Anna would have become, and what, all those years ago, I had thought Joanna had been: a woman with qualities of her own, qualities that made her immune to the ill-informed judgments of the world.

"She might have married him for that, for having that much money, in the same way she might eventually have decided to marry Jimmy Haviland for having that much love. Don't you see why? Because she did not need either of the things they had — love or money. Because she would not have taken what they had to give, they would each of them have become astonishingly generous men."

Laughing with her eyes, she patted my hand. Then she twisted her head to the side as if she were about to share with me the secret that explained everything.

"There is no equality between the sexes, Mr. Antonelli. There never has been, there never will be. Everything interesting or important a man has ever done was done for a woman. Men create religions, but only so they can worship women in a different form. Men are only what women let them think they are. It's not my fault that so many women seem to have forgotten that rather important fact of life."

Through the open sliding door that divided the dining from the living room, she glanced at the clock on the fireplace mantel.

"I have to be over at my office," she said as she rose from the table and began to clear the dishes. "I have a doctoral candidate coming by. It won't take me a minute to get ready. If you have time, walk over with me. We can talk on the way."

Under a white relentless sky, we made our way along the Midway. The August heat was oppressive, inescapable; the air left a bitter burned taste in the mouth. We passed the Rockefeller Chapel, and then, a block or so later, walked next to the iron spiked fence behind which a grass schoolyard ran the length of a gray stone Gothic building. It was, she explained in a brief reference, the Lab School, where Anna had gone to grade school. Two blocks later we crossed the street and passed through a narrow opening between two larger Gothic structures into one of the quadrangles.

"Anna went to school here, from the Lab School when she started, all the way through college. The university was really her home. She graduated when she was nineteen."

"You must have been very proud of her," I remarked, breathing slowly the heavy, humid air. I followed her through a leaded-glass wooden door.

"This is Harper," she explained as we waited for an elevator in a building that had the look of something that, instead of a hundred, had stood there for a thousand, years.

Her office was on the top floor with a ceiling that sloped under the roofline toward the outer wall.

The doctoral student had not yet arrived. I stood in the doorway, watching her.

"There's just one more thing I wanted to ask. Annie had a friend, a young woman. They were in law school together, but I think she had known her before. I can't remember her name, and I don't know where she might be now."

"You must mean Helen, Helen Thatcher." She came around the desk, staring down at the uneven gray stone tiles, trying to remember. "Yes, they were good friends. I don't know what's happened to her. I used to hear from her. The last time — and that must have been years ago — she was living somewhere out west. California, I think; but, as I say, years ago. I don't know if she would still be there or not. I might still have that address — I kept most of the letters and cards I was sent by Anna's friends. Would you like me to try to find it? I'll be glad to send it along."

Down the hallway, the small elevator clunked to a halt and the narrow metal doors cranked open. With tousled brown hair and dark moody eyes, the young man whose dissertation awaited what he still thought an uncertain fate came slouching toward us.

"Would you mind waiting, Evan?" she asked him. She put her liver-spotted hand on my sleeve and started to walk me down the hall. Her heart was too gentle, and her respect for good work too great — too much a part of who she was — to make him wait in suspense. "It's quite good, Evan," she said over her shoulder.

I had to look back; I had to see for myself the reaction, the inexpressible sense of relief that comes with the knowledge that something to which you have given years of your life, something that has an importance that no one who has not tried it can ever understand, has come out as good — no, better — than you had ever dared hope.

"It's better than good, Evan. It's one of the best things I've read."

His eyes lit up with a youthful, bashful enthusiasm. I remembered what that felt like, when the future — your future — suddenly seems to stretch out forever and there is nothing in it except all the things you thought you could ever want. It had been like that once for all of us, for Anna, and Joanna, and for Thomas Browning, and for no one more than Jimmy Haviland, who, more than the rest of us were capable of, had loved something — someone — more than he had ever cared about himself.

"Poor Jimmy," said Annie's remarkable mother while she stood with me, waiting for the elevator to come back. "You know what he did — after?"

I was not quite sure what she meant. "After he quit school? After he came back and finished?"

Her eyes acknowledged the fact. "Yes, that's right. He did quit. I made him go back."

"You?"

"I told him that it was the last thing Anna would want — that he should quit and not finish. So he went back, that next fall. But after he graduated, that summer? He enlisted, went into the army. He went to Vietnam. He tried to get himself killed, if you ask me. How many others signed up for a second tour? Jimmy! He thinks he's a failure because he didn't die. Jimmy did everything right, and everything always went wrong. He should never have met Anna," she said with a short, decisive motion of her head. "If he had not known her, none of this would ever have happened. He would have had a good life."

I wondered if that was true, or whether, if it had not been Anna, it would have been someone else, and though the dream would have been different, the end would have been the same. Some of us seem born to unhappiness.

The elevator jerked to a stop; the doors creaked open. She held my sleeve a moment longer.

"He really did love her; maybe more than anyone ever loved anyone. He did everything for me after it happened. I never saw him shed a tear after that first awful phone call, he was so determined to see me through it." A wistful smile crossed her mouth. "Thomas Browning loved her, too; but I never heard from him, not once, not even a card."

14

Thomas Browning had been right when he said that I had wanted from the beginning to be a defense lawyer and that I did not care what it paid. But he was also right when he said that I ended up making more than most of the attorneys who had started out with only money in mind. I had come to San Francisco to try the case that first made me famous; I stayed because I did not want to lose the woman with whom I had lived for a while in the autumn warmth of a middle-aged romance. Always restless and discontent, looking for something I could not define, I lost her anyway, but by then San Francisco had become the only place I had ever felt at home. I bought an apartment on Nob Hill for a price that was utterly obscene. And each evening as I watched the sun slip down the sky, turning into a ball of liquid fire that spread out along the purple edge of the Pacific; each evening as I watched it pull down behind it the black, impenetrable night, I knew it was worth the price.

It was odd to think that Helen Thatcher, Annie Malreaux's law school friend, lived in San Francisco as well. If we had not been close enough to be called friends, we had been something more than strangers; and yet I might have passed her on the street a dozen different times and not recognized her. She was married, or at least had been when she sent that last letter to Annie's mother. Her name was now Helen Thatcher Quinn, and she lived less than ten minutes away.

Vivian Malreaux also sent some photographs, all but one of them pictures of Annie taken while she was a student at Harvard. They seemed to have been arranged in a chronological order. In the first one, Annie is standing next to another young woman in front of the law library.

I had not been able to draw a picture of Helen Thatcher in my mind, nothing beyond a vague, shadowy image of a girl in her early twenties, smart and pleasant, with the passable plain looks of a bookish existence. The photograph showed her to be better-looking than I remembered, with brave, cheerful eyes, and a rather sad and vulnerable mouth. If I had not noticed her much at the time it was because, as the photograph showed again, there was something magnificent and proud, something almost electric about Annie Malreaux. Her large, laughing eyes drew you toward her, promising to make even the most ordinary, everyday things seem the most interesting, exciting things you had ever seen. Annie drew you toward her, but now, old enough to remember how plain girls had turned into beautiful women, Helen Thatcher's face drew me back. She had about her a sensibility, an understated confidence that allowed her not to mind so much that everyone would notice Annie first, the girl with the stunning smile and the mysterious eyes, the girl Jimmy Haviland still loved and Thomas Browning could never forget. It was hard to look at that photograph — two young women, their arms full of thick law books, laughing at themselves and at each other as they stood on the law library steps, trying to strike a comic pose — picture taken so they could remember later what their lives had been like when the best part of the future was that they did not yet know what it might be.

There was a photograph of Annie with Jimmy Haviland, holding hands beneath the spreading branches of an elm tree somewhere on campus. She was smiling at the camera; Jimmy was smiling at her. I looked at it for a long time, trying to remember him the way I had known him then, when he was still a young man looking forward to things, before he had lost Annie not once but twice and could only look back with anger and regret. Someone must have said something funny, probably Annie. A smile had just started across his mouth, and a moment later he must have started to laugh; but the camera caught the beginning and not the end, and the smile, innocent and well-meaning, became because of what I knew the sad, unfinished prologue to a haunted, tortured past.

In a photograph taken with Thomas Browning, Annie Malreaux seemed, if not less certain of herself, more concerned with conveying the impression of a woman who knew what she was about. She was standing next to Browning, but they did not touch; whatever feeling they may have had toward each other, their eyes stayed straight on the camera. She was smiling, but there was none of the teasing laughing gaiety, none of the casual, friendly ease that had been there in the photograph with Jimmy Haviland. That photograph was the kind you laugh over later; the kind that reminds you of how much fun you had; the kind that when you go back to them years later make you wonder what happened to the other people in them and hope that all of it has been good. This photograph was too formal, too serious, for that: It seemed to announce a fact of some weight and importance, a change in the way things would be. It was the kind of photograph a young woman might send home to her parents, or a young man show his best friends; not an engagement, not yet, but an expectation, an implied promise that unless things went terribly wrong, an engagement was only a matter of time.

I could imagine the same picture, that same look of affectionate reserve, taken later on, after the engagement, after the marriage, brought together, and held together, not by impulse or passion but by a certain sympathetic recognition of a mutual interest, of what they could do for each other. Browning, however genuine his declared willingness to run off with her to the other side of the world and live an anonymous life, had that same look of quiet self-assurance he always had, waiting for things to come to him, certain that they would. It was strange, really, how much different Jimmy Haviland looked, and how little Thomas Browning had changed. I held the photograph up to the light, examining it more closely. It reminded me of that painting by Modigliani, the one I had stared at for such a long time in the Metropolitan Museum of Art. It was the same small, protuberant mouth; the same half-circle eyes. Browning had always looked older than the rest of us; perhaps that was the reason he now looked so much younger.

The fourth and last picture was a photograph Jimmy Haviland had sent to Vivian Malreaux from Vietnam. He was standing in front of a sandbagged bunker, grim faced and unshaven, bent dog tags hanging around his neck on a thin chain. His shirt-sleeves were hanging out; a thin T-shirt, dark with sweat and dirt, clung to his chest. A cartridge belt was slung loosely over his right shoulder. The butt of his rifle resting on the ground, he gripped the dull metal barrel with his hand. His eyes belonged to someone I did not know, someone waiting to die, his only wish that he would not have too long to wait. I wondered — anyone who saw that picture would have wondered — why he had sent it to her, why he would have sent it to anyone he did not want to hurt. Then I remembered that if there was anyone who could look at things straight on, it was Vivian Malreaux. They had shared the death of her daughter, her only child. Is that what he was doing — inviting her to share his death as well? Not because he wanted to add another injury, another wound; but because she was the only one he could trust, the only one who could understand and, by understanding, give some meaning to the death he must have thought might be only days, or even hours, away. It was the only way he had not to die alone; it was a way to have in death what he had not had in life: Annie, the girl he loved, joined forever in the living memory of the one person who had known and loved them both. The few lines he wrote her, the short letter he sent with the picture, seemed to suggest it was true.

"We lost three men on patrol last night; two more the night before that. No one says too much about it. There isn't too much you can say. We're losing, and even if we wanted to win, I'm not sure we would know how. Put a flower on Annie's grave for me. I don't think I'm coming back."

The letter was written on the narrow lined paper of a tablet, a few words scribbled late one night while the tracer bullets flew like fireflies in the restless jungle heat.

When he wrote it, Jimmy Haviland must have thought he was already dead. I folded the letter along the well-worn crease and put it, with the photographs, inside the envelope.

From the window of my office, down the narrow, busy street, I watched the bay glistening silver gray. It was a soft, hazy, sunlit afternoon, one of those days between summer and fall when you remember things with nostalgia and without bitterness or regret, and when even the things you wish had turned out differently do not seem to matter very much. I remembered as a boy — or perhaps I remembered what others had told me — the ships that came home from the war in the Pacific, the sailors flinging white caps into the bay, soldiers shouting and laughing and waving, as they sailed under the Golden Gate, home for good. Jimmy Haviland's war had a different ending. There had been no cheering crowds waiting on the San Francisco docks, no jubilant Market Street parades for him. He landed at an air force base forty miles north, put on civilian clothes and disappeared, an unwelcome stranger, home from a war that had not even done him the favor of letting him die.

Of the three of us, Haviland, Browning,

and myself, he was the only one who had answered the call of his country and gone to war. I used to think it mattered that the war was unpopular and that so many people opposed it. I do not think so anymore. Browning never thought so. He used to argue — or rather, suggest in that understated way of his — that there was something terrifically obscure in the reasoning of all those spoiled and affluent children of the white upper middle class, protesting a war from the safety of their college deferments while other young men — young men who could not get into college, or could not afford it, young men who instead of being born rich had been born black — were being killed in their places. Of course, Browning did not go either, and knew there was not any chance he would: He was 4-F, or would have been had he ever gone for an army physical and his lame foot been discovered. That did not happen because he had the same student deferment as the rest of us; and because, though no one ever spoke about it, everyone knew that in that war at least, the sons of prominent and powerful families did not serve. Every draft board met its quota; how they did it was largely up to them.

I took my deferment with the rest of them, but I agreed with Browning: There was something wrong about insisting too loudly that a war was immoral when you were safe at home and others were dying in your place. So I waited my turn, knowing full well that my turn would probably never come. When I finished law school I had only a year or two left before I would be too old to be drafted; I was already of an age where I would have been taken only as a last resort. If Browning had been drafted, I think he would have gone, if not eagerly, then without hesitation. If I had been drafted, I would have gone too, but I would have wished I did not have to, and I would have been scared to death.

Jimmy Haviland did not have to go either. Unlike Browning, and unlike me, he opposed the war and did it with the kind of passion that did not leave room for argument. He agreed with Browning on one point, however. He agreed that it was wrong and unfair that if you did not go someone else would go instead. He had come to that conclusion on his own. He did not need Browning or anyone else to point out the moral tension in which he was placed by his own argument. So he protested the war, and mentioned to only a few of his friends that beyond his student deferment he would do nothing to avoid the draft. Then Annie died and he did not care so much about the war, and he did not care anything at all about what happened to him. He finished law school, but I think only because, with the best of intentions, Vivian Malreaux had told him that she was certain it was what Annie would have wanted him to do. Then he joined the army and went to Vietnam, which meant that there was someone else who did not have to go.

It's been a long time since Vietnam, but whenever someone remarks on the courage I have supposedly shown by taking the case of a defendant no one wanted to represent, or by standing my ground under a barrage of invective from some vain and arrogant judge, I remember a few people I knew like Jimmy Haviland, not all of whom came back, and I cringe a little that I was once so willing to let someone else take my place and risk his life for mine.

The day was drawing down to a listless close. Nothing seemed very important; there was nothing I had to do, nowhere I had to be. High above the clattering noise of the narrow city streets, I sat in the quiet stillness of my office, feeling a little sorry for myself. The room had the look of a private club, one of those rooms with thick carpets and thick wood-paneled walls, with overstuffed chairs into which you sank so deep that someone on first entering could not easily tell if anyone was there or not. There were a gray marble fireplace and two tall windows covered with heavy, velvet drapes that let in a discreet and measured light. On the mantel of the fireplace, off to the side, three leather-bound books with pages that, so far as I knew, had never been cut, stood between two white marble bookends. My eye wandered along the rich, gleaming paneled walls, the shining reddish hue of the antique rosewood desk, the whole, entire quiet opulence of the room. Other than those three unread leather volumes on the mantel, there was not a book in the room.

Every morning, I sat in a wing-back chair, wearing one of my tailored suits, holding the newspaper open in front of me, pausing occasionally to lift from the table next to me the cup of fine china filled with coffee made the way my secretary knew I liked it. The newspaper was the only thing to read. There was not a bookcase in the room, none of those shelves that used to line my law office walls, groaning under the weight of each new addition to the reported cases of the appellate courts. The firm had a complete and up-to-date law library. When I needed something, the law librarian, or one of his several assistants, would find it for me. If I needed a book, they would get it; if I needed a citation, they would find it. If I needed more than a citation, if I needed to know the current state of the law on a legal issue that might decide a case on which I was working, there were law clerks, eager to make an impression; there were associates, anxious to make partner; there were even junior partners, hoping to learn something from me about criminal law, to take care of it.

There were no bookshelves on the walls; there was no paper on my desk. Everyone fluttered around me, making certain that everything was done that needed to be done: that all the messy, annoying details — the sweating, swearing effort required to get ready for trial — were handled by someone else. It was simply assumed that I was much too busy for work. All I had to do was speak a word and the whole machinery of the firm rumbled into motion with the same heartless efficiency, the same narrow and specialized division of labor, that had been Zachary

Browning's industrial dream.

I had everything I once thought I wanted and yet I felt sorry for myself, because it did not measure up to what others had done. Thomas Browning had almost become president, and there was still a chance that he would. But it was not Browning who mattered; it was not Browning who made me feel uncomfortable. It was Jimmy Haviland. He was a wreck, his life a shambles, accused of a crime he did not commit, and yet . . . and yet there was a sense in which I envied him for what he had done, and for what he had tried to do. He had had his heart broken and he never recovered from it, but when you got right down to it, when you summed it all up, what that really meant was that unlike so many of us with our changeable lives and replaceable dreams, Jimmy Haviland had at least had a heart that could be broken. More than that, he did what he could to make things come out right: He fought in a war he did not think should be fought because he thought his own life was over and that he ought to take the place of someone who still had a reason to live. And what at the end would be listed among my accomplishments? That I had kept countless evil people from suffering the punishment they deserved? Perhaps my only hope left was to do everything I could to keep Jimmy Haviland from being punished for something he did not do.

It was time to leave. The letter from Vivian Malreaux, the photographs and the letter Jimmy Haviland had written were on the desk, enclosed in the envelope in which she had sent them. It occurred to me that I ought to take them with me, that the photographs might bring back the memory of something important, something that might help Jimmy Haviland.

The car picked me up in front of the building; the driver had been told where to take me. Ten minutes later, when he pulled up in front of the address he had been given, I had that strange feeling, almost a form of precognition, of knowing something without quite knowing what it was. I had seen this house before. I had walked past it — I do not know how often, perhaps once a week — on my irregular wandering jaunts down from Nob Hill and through Pacific Heights. And all this time I had, without knowing it, known the woman who owned it, the woman who had lived there for years.

The dark brown shingle-sided house was on a corner, the street in front straight and flat, the other one, like a picture postcard of San Francisco, so steep that it seemed to fall right into the bay. I crossed the brick courtyard, went up the steps and rang the bell. A Chinese houseboy answered the door. I gave him my name; he stepped back from the door, gestured toward a large, brocaded chair with dark curved wooden arms, and disappeared.

There was a heavy scent of jasmine in the air. The furniture, the rugs, the silk tapestries on the walls, the vases with their intricate and colorful designs, all of it was Chinese; all of it, I was certain, old, ancient, authentic, and not just expensive, but priceless. Minutes passed and the silence was so profound you could hear it, that thin, distant hum, the sound in your ear like the sound trapped in a seashell. More time passed. I began to feel ill at ease, as if I had stumbled into a place where I was not supposed to be. The chair was taller than my head, so narrow that my elbows were forced onto the wooden arms. I felt like one of those full-size toy soldiers displayed in store windows at Christmas. I got up and began to look around the long rectangular living room.

There was a grand piano at the far end of the room, and bookshelves on the wall across from the windows that gave an un-obstructed view of the Golden Gate. The books were neither very old nor very new. They all had dust jackets, and the titles suggested a comfortable middle-class taste. They were the sort of things that were discussed in reading groups of well-intentioned people and then, within a year or so, put away and forgotten, something worth keeping even if they were never going to be read twice. I suddenly became aware that I was not alone.

"You have some interesting books," I said as I turned around, ready to say hello to a woman I had not seen in half a life-time, the woman who had once been Annie Malreaux's best friend.

My first thought was that I had made a mistake, that I had either come to the wrong address or that Helen Thatcher and Helen Thatcher Quinn were not the same person after all. The woman who was standing at the entrance to the living room was older — I do not mean older than she had been — older than she should have been, twenty years older. She was dressed impeccably — too impeccably — in a black knit suit and black high-heeled shoes, with a gold necklace and gold earrings, like a woman with a luncheon engagement at a private club that only let in a new member when an old one died. Her hair, shiny black and as stiff as if it had been lacquered into place, had the look of something kept at night on a mannequin. Her eyelashes had the same hard brittle look as they beat in a false even rhythm across her cold, distant eyes. She was as heavily made up as an actress onstage, with blushing cheeks and a red painted mouth. Everything about her was a costume and you had the feeling that each night, when she went to bed, she slipped out of the whole thing, the clothes, the hair, the makeup, and left it hanging, like a clown's suit, on a hook on the bathroom door. There was something strangely familiar about her. I had seen her somewhere before, sometime in the last few years; but I could not remember where.

"Mr. Antonelli," she said with a civil smile as she extended her manicured and painted hand. "Please," she added, inclining her head ever so slightly toward the sofa a few steps away.

She sat at the opposite end, perched on the edge, her knees pressed tight together and her small hands in her lap. She looked at me without recognition and without any apparent interest.

"It's nice to see you again," I said, watching her eyes for a sign that she remembered. There was nothing. "We knew each other at Harvard, not very well, I know; but you were a friend of Annie Malreaux's and I was Thomas Browning's roommate. I was also a friend of Jimmy Haviland."

There was a slight movement in her eyes, a slight tremor at the corner of her mouth.

"I knew Annie Malreaux, yes." She said this with a kind of caution, an admission she was forced somewhat reluctantly to make, afraid perhaps that it would lead to something with which she did not want to be involved.

"You were her best friend," I insisted.

"She was a friend of mine," she replied as if it were a barely remembered fact of no importance.

I began to be irritated, and I let it show. I reached inside my jacket pocket for the envelope. I found the picture I wanted and handed it to her.

"You were her best friend; you went everywhere together. You were in New York the day she died, the day she fell out of a window at the Plaza Hotel. You knew Thomas Browning; you knew Jimmy Haviland; and if I'm not mistaken, you knew me."

She glanced at the photograph. A thin smile started onto her mouth and then stopped. She looked at me.

"I knew Annie Malreaux. We were friends."

I handed her the next photograph, the one taken of Jimmy and Annie holding hands. "And you remember Jimmy Haviland, too, don't you?"

She glanced at it and gave it back. "Yes, I remember Jimmy Haviland."

I handed her the next one and asked her as she looked at Thomas Browning standing next to Annie Malreaux if she remembered him as well.

"Yes, of course. I remember. But I don't know anything that could possibly help you, Mr. Antonelli."

"Then you know that I'm representing Jimmy Haviland and that Jimmy has been charged with Annie's murder?"

"Yes, I know that."

It was stunning how indifferent she seemed, stunning and inexplicable. She had changed — we had all changed — but was it possible to forget entirely someone with whom you had once been as close as she had been to Annie Malreaux?

"You don't seem to be much bothered by it," I remarked, running out of patience.

Her made-up eyes flashed with contempt, as if I had forgotten my proper place. She got to her feet. I did not budge.

"You were in New York the day she died?"

"Yes," she said with a rigid glance.

"You were at the hotel?"

"No, not when it happened. I had left hours before that. I left that morning. I went home. It was Christmas Eve. I really can't help you, Mr. Antonelli. I tried to explain that. Now, if you'll forgive me, I have other things I have to do."

Embarrassed, I got to my feet and tried to apologize. "I'm sorry, Mrs. Quinn. I didn't mean to suggest that you didn't care about what happened to Annie, or what might happen to Jimmy. I know it was a long time ago, and that a lot has changed."

She acknowledged, and at least in a formal sense accepted, my apology, but she did nothing to suggest that she wanted me to stay. She started to walk me to the door when she suddenly stopped, told me to wait and went across the room to the piano. There was a picture on it, a framed photograph. She brought it over and showed it to me.

"This is my daughter, my only child."

I looked at a photograph of a quite beautiful woman in her late twenties or early thirties and somehow I knew. "Annie?" I asked, as I gave it back to her.

"Yes, Annie. It was the only name I wanted to give her. I suppose I hoped she would have something of that same bright intelligence, that same amused detachment that Annie had." She paused, pondering some thought that had come to her, some reason that might explain why she had not wanted to talk about it. "Some things are too painful to remember very clearly, or to think about too often. I thought about Annie all the time after she died; I could not get it out of my mind — the way it happened, on that day of all days, Christmas Eve nineteen sixty-five. I did not really stop thinking about it until I wrote about it, in that first novel of mine, the one that started everything."

She saw the look of puzzled astonishment in my eyes. She smiled, laughing a little at herself.

"You didn't know. And here I assumed that was the reason, or part of the reason, you wanted to see me — to see if my name could be of some use. I write under a pen name, Joseph Antonelli — and yes, I remember you, and of course I've read all about you in the papers. I have even from time to time thought about giving you a call to see if just by chance you might have remembered me, Annie Malreaux's shy and quiet friend." She had her hand on my wrist, holding it like an old friend. "Here," she said as she drew me with her to the bookcase. "I'll give you a signed copy and then, if you ever read it, you can tell me what you think, and whether I got at all close to what Annie was really like."

A shadow fell over her eyes as we started again to walk toward the door.

"It's fiction, of course. I could not write the whole truth: that Annie fell out a window on the very day she became engaged."

I was moving toward the door, caught in the confusion of memories of my own, wondering why I had not remembered that I had once been told that the woman who lived in this house was Rebecca Long, one of the most critically acclaimed authors in the country.

" 'Became engaged'?" I asked without comprehension, repeating a meaningless phrase.

"Yes. Didn't you know? She was going to marry Thomas Browning."

15

Annie Malreaux was going to marry Thomas Browning. She had told Helen Thatcher, but — and this was the tragedy of it — she had not told him. Browning was desperate to have her stay longer, desperate to find someplace where they could talk, away from all the other people who had crowded onto the eighth floor of the Plaza Hotel. He wanted to tell her that he would do anything — give up everything, run off to the other side of the world, if she liked, anything — if only she would go with him, be with him, marry him. He was desperate for her to stay and she kept telling him she had to leave, and he never knew that it was because she did not want to tell him — not with all those other people around — that she wanted to marry him, too. And then, when he finally had her alone, Jimmy Haviland walked in, angry and demanding, and ruined it all.

I remembered Annie Malreaux. That light, fleeting, ethereal, take-nothing-too-seriously attitude was a mask, a pose, a way of watching the world, the amused spectator of the awkward follies of people around her, a way of making sure no one could see too closely into what was important to her. Who knows how many times Browning may have asked her to marry him, but this time, the last time, sometime that Christmas, she had made up her mind to say yes, to marry Thomas Browning. That was something far too important, far too serious, to be announced in the middle of a party that had gone on so long no one could quite remember when it began.

I wondered if I should tell him, or whether that would only make a bad thing worse. Still, it was the truth, and that carried a weight of its own. Perhaps it might put things in a different perspective, changing the way he remembered Annie Malreaux from the girl always just beyond his grasp, the woman too young, too elusive ever to belong to anyone, to the woman who had changed her mind, given up the antic possibilities of moving breathlessly and irresponsibly through the world, and said yes without condition to living her life with him.

It was nearly six o'clock. The temperature was dropping, the air chilly and damp.

The fog had run in from the ocean, billowing up against the Golden Gate Bridge, drawing a gray curtain around the city and the bay, everything in front of it colorful and bright, full of action and life. Three blocks from Helen Thatcher's Pacific Heights home, famous because it was owned by San Francisco's best-known writer, the world-famous Rebecca Long, I stopped at a corner, watching through the narrow aperture of a steep twisting street the sunlit sky turn purple, lavender and pink, as the fog swirling around the towers of the bridge changed from a dull, amorphous gray to a deep, mysterious rose. I could see the traffic heading out of the city, crossing over to the other side; the traffic coming the other way, toward the city, was buried in the fog and could not be seen. It was like watching a memory at work, some things indelible and clear; other things almost more real because they never quite come back the way you think they should.

I shoved my hands into my pockets and began to walk in a deliberate, purposeful stride, bracing myself against the gathering cold. Keeping to the same brisk, steady pace, I went another block before I began to slow down, wondering why I thought I had to hurry. No one was waiting for me at home; no one would worry about me if I were late. I had dinner when I felt like it, and went to whatever restaurant I chose. I did not need to consult the desires, or try to anticipate the wishes, of anyone else. There were a number of places I went, and if there were not quite so many as there had been when I first started dining alone, it was only because it was easier to go somewhere close. There were two or three restaurants I went to with some regularity, and one where I suppose I dined more often than the others combined. It was an Italian restaurant, a quiet, neighborhood place, not at all like the crowded, noisy restaurant in New York where I might still be waiting for a table if I had not used Bartholomew Caminetti's instantly influential name.

I ate in the same restaurant, but there were other places I could have gone. I dropped my clothes at the same dry cleaners, but only because it was convenient. I bought groceries, when I bought them, at the same market, and I stopped at the same café for a cup of coffee every Saturday afternoon I was in town. I walked past the same store windows and browsed in the same small musty bookstores. It may have had all the outward appearance of a dull-as-dust middle-aged, middle-class life, but that was not how it felt. I was in love with the city. I could sit in that same restaurant for hours, watching the way the waiter made friends with a couple who had never been there before, watching the way the two of them seemed to become more interested in each other, watch them linger late into the night, sometimes until the restaurant closed. I had a nodding acquaintance with some of the bookstore clerks and with a few other shop people as well, part of that circle of anonymous friends that makes city life more comfortable than life in a small town. It is the surface of things, not the illusion that things are what they look like, but the more interesting, the more mysterious illusion that things are as heartbreakingly beautiful, as tragically romantic, as you ever imagined they could be. New York was energy and excitement, ambition, power and wealth; San Francisco was the end of the rainbow, the place you kept dreaming about because it was the place where you never stopped dreaming.

It had been a mistake to let Thomas Browning talk me into going back to New York; it had been a mistake to get involved in the lives of people I had not seen in years and only thought I knew. Because I did not know them; I did not know them at all. I would have known them better — Browning, Joanna, Jimmy Haviland, all of them — if I had not known them years before, if we had never met. Then I would have begun with simple ignorance, writing what I learned on a blank page. Instead, I saw them through the distorted lens of what I thought I remembered about how they had been before. When I lived there in my twenties, that summer in New York, I thought I knew it, what made it work, why everyone thought it was the only place to be. I could have stayed there — I would have stayed there if I had understood what Joanna had been trying to say — and become a New Yorker and tried to fight my way to the top. It was too late for me now; I had been away too long: They were all strangers to me. I wanted to stay here, in San Francisco, where I never felt like a stranger even among people I did not know.

Nob Hill was a few blocks away. The fog had swallowed the bridge, taken the avenues — the long, straight streets that stretched flat on both sides of Golden Gate Park — and begun to roll up the hills. Across the bay, on the eastern shore, Berkeley glowed a shiny scarlet gold under the dying light of a bloodred sun. The sunlight was warm against my face; the mist, moving ahead of the fog, was damp against my skin. The seasons were a scandal, always changing what they were, and never the same thing twice; but each new thing something that made you wish you could see and feel it again. I did not want to go back to New York.

The doorman was not at his usual place under the green awning in front; he was not anywhere in view behind the glass-paned wooden door. As I reached for my key, he suddenly appeared and with a backward movement of his long, bulky left arm pushed open the door.

"How are you this evening, Mr. Antonelli?" he said with his usual husky grunt.

"Fine, George," I replied as I headed toward the elevator, a few feet across the dark tile floor. He was right behind me. His thick-fingered hand reached in front of me and pressed the button to summon the elevator.

"Might get pretty thick out there a little later tonight, don't you think?"

"It might," I replied, staring down at my shoes, waiting for the elevator door to open. It was George's habit to wait with you, then reach inside and without looking press the button for your floor. Old women seemed to like it; I was still trying to think of a polite way to ask him to stop. The door opened and I stepped inside.

"What do you think about the news, Mr. Antonelli?" he asked. Whatever the news was, it made him forget what he normally did next. With a certain satisfaction, I pushed the number of my floor. Smiling, I raised my head.

"What news is that, George?" I asked as the door began to slide shut. He stepped back, a dull, puzzled look on his thick, square face.

"About the vice president. You really haven't heard?" The door shut tight and the elevator began its smooth, methodical ascent.

What about the vice president? I wondered with a growing sense of urgency as the elevator stopped on the second floor. A prim well-dressed octogenarian with a snide-looking Pomeranian in her arms got in. She was talking to it, scratching it under the chin, apologizing that they had to wait while the elevator went up before they could go down, the whole time looking at me as if it were my fault, that if it had not been for me they would not have had to wait. "Sorry," I said when the elevator finally reached my floor. She raised a single white eyebrow, lifted her minor chin and pressed her wrinkled mouth. It was as close to forgiveness as she was prepared to go.

What about the vice president? I asked myself as I unlocked the door and let myself in. I turned on the television, but the last time I had it on I had been watching one of the old movie channels. Before I could change it, the telephone started to ring. It was Gisela Hoffman.

"It's nice to hear your voice," I said. "I thought I might see you in New York."

I slouched against the back of the sofa, sank into the cushions, my feet against the edge of the coffee table in front of me, listening to her funny, girlish voice. I could see her face in front of me, that blushing, puzzled expression each time she mispronounced a word.

"I saw you at the arraignment, but I . . ."

"You were there — in court? Why didn't you tell me you were going to be there? We could have had dinner; we could have talked."

"I just came up for the arraignment. I could not stay. I need to ask you — on the record," she added in an awkward voice, a little embarrassed that she had to strike a note of formality. "What is your reaction to what happened today? Will it make any difference in how you plan to conduct the Haviland defense?"

I pulled my feet down from the table and sat up. "What happened today?" I asked, finally alert to the fact that something of profound importance had taken place and I seemed to be the only person who did not know about it. "What about the vice president?"

There was a dead silence. She could not believe I did not know. "Your friend, Thomas Browning, did something no one expected — something no one imagined. He resigned. Three hours ago."

"He resigned the vice presidency? He quit?" I was incredulous, but then I realized that I was not incredulous at all. There was always a reason for the things Thomas Browning did. There was a reason for this as well.

"Why did he quit?" I asked, intensely interested. My mind raced from one thing to the next. Did it have something to do with the trial? Was there something I did not know — something he had never told me? "What reason did he give?"

"He did not give one," replied Gisela in

a baffled tone. "It's what has Washington on its . . . What is the phrase? Yes, 'on its ear.' Browning resigned the office — the letter he sent, the letter his office released to the press, says only, 'I hereby resign the office of vice president of the United States.' He doesn't give a reason; he doesn't say anything."

"But he has a reason, doesn't he?" I asked, thinking out loud.

"Yes, I think so. He must."

A chill ran up my spine. The president's people had wanted him off the ticket. They were the same people who had beaten him for the nomination by using those ugly anonymous rumors about Browning and a murder in New York. I was defending a man accused of that murder, a case Browning was convinced had been started for no other reason than to make sure he would never have a chance to run for the presidency again. And now he had simply quit, handed in his resignation, given up? Why? Unless it was the only way to save himself from something worse than political defeat. With a gnawing sense of panic, I asked Gisela what she thought.

"I don't know. He could have resigned anytime he wanted: He chose to do it today, on a Friday afternoon, just in time for the evening news. It's what everyone will talk about — speculate about — all weekend. It's what they'll be talking about on the Sunday shows. Browning resigns and no one knows why. Everyone will be waiting for next Friday to find out."

"Friday? Why, what happens then?"

"Browning scheduled a press conference for next Friday afternoon."

She paused, and when she spoke again her voice had a different quality about it. She was not a reporter anymore.

"When are you coming back to New York?"

"Tomorrow. The trial starts Monday. Will you be there?"

"Yes. Can we see each other? There is something I have to tell you, something I think I better not tell you on the phone."

We said good-bye and I sat in the lengthening shadows of the fog-shrouded sun, trying to concentrate on what she had told me; trying, and failing, not to think too much about her. There was something elusive about her, something I could not quite put my finger on. She was married, but she was going through a divorce; she was a European who stumbled over English words, but knew more about American politics than I ever had; she was shy and at times withdrawn, with fine, delicate features and beautiful dark eyes, but she could put herself forward and demand answers to questions she thought should be asked. But more than any of that, more than the fact that she showed different sides of herself at different times, there was a sense, profound, haunting, and irresistible, that I knew her and that she knew me, and that, in the way that sometimes happens, we had known each other from the first moment we met.

An hour later, I was still thinking about how much I liked her voice and how much I wanted to hear it again. When the phone began to ring, I hoped it was she, calling back to tell me she just wanted to talk.

"How are you, Joseph?" asked Thomas Browning in a calm, considerate voice. "I know I should have called you before I made the announcement. You must have thought when you heard it that they'd forced me out. You must have thought that I had to resign because Annie's death wasn't an accident."

Browning waited for me to answer, to admit that I had at least wondered if it might be true, that Annie's death had not been an accident and that he had known it all along.

"No, that never occurred to me." It was not entirely a lie. I had thought about it, as I had before, but I could not bring myself to believe that Thomas Browning had anything to do with the death of Annie Malreaux. Browning would never have allowed someone else to be blamed for something he had done. I was certain of that, or as certain as I could be.

"Do you know why I did it? Why I resigned?"

It is remarkable how one suddenly remembers something. "Because you had already carved your initials in that drawer?" There was a quick, breath-catching silence, and then he started to laugh, and then I knew why he had done it. I remembered the look on his face, that look of disdain directed as much against himself, his own weakness, his own vanity, his own failure of imagination, as against William Walker and the other people who had talked him into accepting the nomination for vice president. He had carved his initials in that drawer where they had all left their marks, the men who had settled for second place; had broken the tradition by doing it the first, instead of the last, day he was in office. He was going after the only thing he wanted, the only thing besides Annie

Malreaux he had ever dreamed of having.

"You're running for president. That's what you're going to announce next week — that you resigned the vice presidency because you've decided to challenge the President for the Republican nomination. You wouldn't have resigned if you had wanted to stay on the ticket with Walker." I paused, and then I guessed. "You were never going to do that; you were always going to go after the presidential nomination, weren't you?"

He denied it, in a fashion. "No, that's not quite true. If they had wanted me to stay on as vice president for a second term, then of course I would have been a fool to do anything else. No one could have challenged me for the nomination at the end of Walker's second term. And when I first started talking — publicly — about refusing to quit, about running in the primaries, letting the convention decide, I thought that might make them change their minds, decide that it was not worth the fight. But then, the more I thought about it, the more convinced I became that if I was going to have to fight them anyway, I might as well fight them for the whole thing. Walker should never have been president, and if I have anything to do with it, he won't be president again."

With the portable phone pressed against my ear, I got up from the sofa and wandered over to the windows and stared out at the city burning pale yellow under a thick blanket of fog. I could not see the Golden Gate, and there was nothing on the farther shore.

"You're going to announce next Friday? You don't want to wait until after the trial?"

There was a kind of caution, a kind of hesitancy — not in his voice — that was still the same: calm, quiet, confident, almost too confident, as if he knew in advance, not just everything that was going to happen, but when it was going to happen and how it would affect everyone else who had an interest in the game that was being played. No, not in his voice, but in the silence that filled the space between the end of my question and the beginning of his answer.

"Nothing will happen at the trial," said Browning presently. "Nothing. You'll win; you'll show them for the liars they are."

"Jimmy made some statements," I said with a certain reluctance. "He said some things that could be taken as admissions." I had not told anyone this; I had not even discussed it yet with Haviland. "He made them a long time ago, while he was in therapy — for alcoholism."

Browning dismissed it with almost brutal contempt. "Haviland is a drunk. It doesn't matter what he said. None of it matters. Don't let it bother you. It doesn't mean anything," he said impatiently.

"The prosecution will argue that it means a great deal," I retorted, showing a little impatience of my own.

"These are statements he made to other people, statements that they now remember he made all those years ago! You mean that someone asked these people, not just what they might remember about Haviland, but if they remembered whether he ever said anything about some girl he knew in law school; not just had known in law school, but a girl he might have pushed out a window! That's what they would have asked, isn't it? That they were investigating a murder, a murder that happened back in the winter of nineteen sixty-five; a murder in which a girl Haviland had been involved with was pushed out a window at the Plaza Hotel in New York. And then they would ask whether they ever heard Haviland say anything about it. Isn't that what they would have done, and doesn't that suggest something about the difference between what someone remembered and what he now starts to think that maybe he remembers? And besides, isn't it perfectly obvious that Haviland must have said things that, looking back on it, start to sound as though he had admitted doing something? Good God, you were there — what he said in court at his own arraignment: tried to plead guilty because he's 'responsible' for Annie's death. My God, Antonelli, he's just a mess, isn't he?"

He had not told me anything I did not already know, and I rather resented him for thinking he could. Browning had not argued a case in his life, and so far as I knew had never spent a moment inside a court of law. I did not pretend to know anything about politics, yet he was explaining to me how to try a case. I was getting a little angry, but Browning, always a step ahead, understood immediately what he had done. He knew before I had said a word what I felt.

"You know that a lot better than I do. You're the best there is. You aren't going to have any trouble showing a jury all the problems in the way someone remembers what he thinks someone else meant."

There was fog everywhere. All I saw in

the window was my own reflection, drifting in space, an image as insubstantial as the gray mist on which it floated. Browning was talking about the trial that had not started, encouraging me; but I was not thinking about any of that.

"I saw Vivian Malreaux, Annie's mother."

There was a sudden, immediate silence. "She's still alive?" inquired Browning after a long pause.

"I'm not sure I've ever met anyone more alive," I replied, watching in the window the way my eyes, staring back at me, seemed to acknowledge the truth of it. "She's still at Chicago, still teaching, still writing out lectures months in advance. Do you remember her? She sent me a couple of photographs, one of them of you and Annie. You both look very serious."

Browning lapsed into a long, brooding silence. Finally, he asked, "Do you think I could have it?" There was a pleading, bittersweet quality in his voice, a sentimentality, a vulnerability, I had not heard before. It had the same effect as if in my presence he had begun to cry. I lowered my eyes and stared down at the floor.

"Yes, of course," I mumbled. "Consider it done."

It was then, after I understood far better

than I had before how much she still meant to him, that I knew I had to tell him.

"Annie was going to marry you. She was going to tell you that day — Christmas Eve, the day she died."

Words can lie, but silence almost always tells the truth, at least that part of the truth it is given to us to know. I had the feeling that he was not completely surprised; that, despite what he had told me before, he had in some sense known it all along.

"Did her mother tell you that?" he asked in a voice devoid of emotion.

"No, she never knew. Helen Thatcher. Remember Helen — Annie's friend? She told me. She lives here — in San Francisco. I saw her today. Annie told her that you had asked her to marry you, and that she had decided to say yes."

There was no reply, nothing, not a word; only a prolonged silence that started to become awkward.

"Helen turns out to be a famous writer," I said in the hope of getting some kind of response. "She writes under the name Rebecca Long. I had no idea. She . . ."

"It isn't true," said Browning. He sounded almost angry. "She's lying. No," he added immediately, "I shouldn't say that. She may think it's true, but it isn't. She doesn't remember it right. Maybe Annie told her that I'd asked her to marry me — I think I told you that; I know I told you I would have married her. Maybe Annie even told her that she might think about it, but she never told her that she was going to say yes."

How could he be so certain? And why had he felt the need to be so emphatic?

"I believed her. I think she remembers it perfectly. Annie was going to say yes. She wanted to marry you. Why don't you want to believe that?"

The silence was palpable. I had the feeling that he could barely control himself, that he was right on the edge, ready to abandon all restraint; that he would have given anything to be able to tell someone all the things that he had kept private. But that was one thing he could never do. It was a form of weakness to which he would never yield; a point of honor, like that malformed foot he had with such constant, excruciating pain kept hidden from public view.

"Why don't you believe that?" I asked again, insisting on a reply, not because I needed one, but because I thought he needed to say it, to get it out.

"Because that makes what happened hurt even more," he said in a distant voice. "You won't forget that picture?" he asked, suddenly tired and subdued. "Bring it with you, if you would. I'll see you next week in New York."

16

Five minutes, ten minutes, fifteen. For at least the third time, Bartholomew Caminetti glanced at his watch, grimaced with disgust, leaned back in his chair and tapped on the counsel table an impatient lament. Seconds later, he stopped drumming his fingers. He crossed one leg over the other; with a sullen sigh he threw his arm across the back of the wooden chair. His foot picked up the left-off rhythm of his hand. He started biting the inside of his lip, gave it up, placed both arms on the table below him and both feet solidly on the ground. Hunching forward, he narrowed his eyes into a murderous stare.

The bailiff stood with his arms crossed, listening half consciously for the sound that would start him talking before he knew he had opened his mouth. The court reporter sat in front of the blank abbreviated keyboard of the stenotype machine, her mouth set at a dreamy angle, gazing into the distance through half-closed eyes. The courtroom was packed, a silent, breathless audience, as eager as a Broadway crowd waiting for the show to begin.

It was only the second time I had been in Room 1530 on the fifteenth floor of the courthouse, the courtroom with the narrow high windows through which, like one of those forward-looking drawings of the 1930s, a steep-angled shaft of light caught the witness stand and seemed to bring it closer to the eye. Only the second time I had been here, and I felt as if I had never left. That was the serious side of what I did, this feeling that the case, the trial, no matter how much time might pass between the next proceeding and the last, was all of a piece: with a beginning, a middle and an end. Each trial is like a life reconsidered, when everything has a meaning after all, because each thing that happened shaped and changed everything else.

The bailiff's eyes shot wide open, his head snapped up, his arms flew down to his sides. He stepped forward, the words, sharp as brass as he cried into the brittle silence, "Hear ye, Hear ye. The Superior Court in and for the city and county of New York is now in session, the Honorable Charles F. Scarborough presiding."

Split asunder, the silence echoed back,

followed an instant later by a single voluminous shudder as a hundred people stood
straight up, rigid and attentive, as the door
on the left swung open and Charles F.
Scarborough came wheeling into court.

He took three quick steps, paused, and
sneezed. "Hay fever, colds, flu," he began,
shaking his head in misery. He raised the
handkerchief to his nose, held it there a
moment, and then, as a wry grin began to
make its way onto his mouth, put it away.
He cast a cheerful glance around the
crowded courtroom. "Last week I had to
sentence a man to prison for a very long
period of time. The whole time, he kept
coughing. He was sick; now I am. I think it
was deliberate." He stroked his chin,
laughing silently as he led his audience on,
winning them over by the open insincerity
of what he claimed. "They do that, you
know — try to get even," he insisted, nodding his head in agreement with the charge
while he held back another sneeze.

"Yes, well, the reason we are here —
other than to make Mr. Caminetti a little
crazy with what I am sorry to report was
an unavoidable delay — is to begin the
trial in the matter of *People of the State of
New York* v. *Jamison Scott Haviland*. The
charge is murder; the plea is not guilty;

trial is scheduled for today. Mr. Bartholomew Caminetti, I am delighted to say, is here on behalf of the state of New York. And Mr. Joseph Antonelli, I am equally delighted to say, is here on behalf of the defendant.

"Before we begin — before we begin jury selection — there are a few things I wish to say about the somewhat unusual circumstances of this case and the rather extraordinary measures that must be taken because of them. I find it regrettable that a number of people have decided for reasons of their own to parade back and forth in front of the courthouse, waving placards demanding a verdict before the trial has begun; I find it astonishing that some of these same people think to further their cause by shouting insults and invective at court personnel. They have of course the right to assemble peaceably and make their views known, but three persons were arrested this morning for assault, and I can assure you that anyone who attempts to interfere with what goes on in this courthouse will find themselves prosecuted to the full extent of the law."

Scarborough dragged his handkerchief across his nose as he took a long look at the crowd.

"I understand of course the great public interest in this trial; I certainly understand how eager those of you are whose business it is to report on these proceedings to get as much information as you possibly can. You need to understand that the court will not tolerate even the slightest breach of the integrity of this trial. I have already denied the request to televise the trial. This morning I have issued a further order banning all cameras from the courthouse. This is not a television show, ladies and gentlemen. This is a trial, a trial in which the defendant has been accused of a homicide. This is a serious, solemn event; not some sideshow to which you can sell tickets, or commercials."

With his elbows planted on the bench, Scarborough bent forward and with a severe expression began to shake his forefinger.

"Let me be extremely clear about this. Until the trial is over, until the jury has rendered its verdict and been dismissed, the jurors are not allowed to discuss the case with anyone, not even among themselves, until the evidence has been submitted, all the witnesses called, closing arguments have been given and they have retired to the jury room to begin their formal deliberations. And if they are not allowed to discuss it with each other, they are certainly not allowed to discuss it with the members of the press. If, despite that, some venturesome reporter attempts to talk to a juror while the trial is still in progress, that reporter will not only be barred from this courtroom, but should expect to face criminal charges for jury tampering."

The judge glanced around the courtroom. The look on his face suggested that he would not mind at all the chance to show them that he meant what he said.

"There is an important public right at issue here: not that doubtful and imaginary thing, the self-serving invention of the people who exploit it for their own commercial purposes — the public's supposed right to know — but the real and substantial public right to the impartial administration of justice. And that, ladies and gentlemen, is a right upon which this court insists."

Having said what he had to, Scarborough became again the soul of affability, the generous host whose only concern is for the comfort and well-being of his guests.

"I'll hang you if I have to," he said, breaking into a smile of profound and cheerful regret, "but I'm sure you won't let it come to that. I'm sure that you'll find the trial itself sufficiently interesting not to have to go asking questions where you should not. I think we can depend upon Mr. Caminetti and Mr. Antonelli to keep things lively."

With a formal nod to the crowd, he turned to the bailiff and asked him to bring in the jurors.

Until they walked into Room 1530 and saw the crowd, all they knew was that their names had been drawn from among the much larger number waiting in the dull silence of the assembly room; that they were being taken upstairs for a trial; that they would sit in the courtroom while twelve of their names were called to sit in the jury box where they would be asked questions; that some of them would be dismissed and others called to take their place until the lawyers were satisfied or had no challenges left and had to take what they had. There was a chance, of course, that they might end up on the jury in the trial that involved Thomas Browning — that was how, before it began, the trial was generally known: the murder trial that involved one of New York's most famous citizens — but there were perhaps a dozen other trials scheduled to begin that week, and the odds were much better that their names had been called for one of them.

You could see it in their eyes, an immediate recognition that this was different, that this was not some minor civil case, an accident victim seeking damages, or one of those criminal cases which, no matter how grievous the crime, were tried routinely and without publicity every week of the year. This was important. They knew that, and they knew it right away. This was something that those who served on the jury, the people who decided the case, would be talking about for the rest of their lives. They filed into the two rows of spectator benches that had been kept empty for them in front. They sat there, bunched together, while the court clerk, a wiry, middle-aged man in a gray suit, pulled at random a dozen of their names and sent them, one by one, into the jury box.

Bartholomew Caminetti sat at the counsel table closest to the jury box, directly in front of the witness stand. Lawyers tend to like that position, as close as possible to the jury, closer than the other lawyer, the close physical proximity of a friend, someone who wants you to see him for who he is: someone who has nothing to hide, someone you can trust. When I first started practicing, I would come early to get that table for my own; now I came to court not much sooner than I was supposed to and took the table that was left. Perhaps I had gotten lazy, or perhaps I wanted the other side to think that I was too confident of what I could do with a jury to have to depend on small tactics and cheap tricks. Caminetti understood the game. When I arrived and settled into my chair, he asked if I would rather have the one he had taken first. If there had ever been a danger that I might underestimate Bartholomew Caminetti, that single gesture taught me that that would be a fatal mistake. I returned his smile with one of my own and told him that, no, it did not matter to me where I sat, this table was fine.

"I don't mind," he said; in part, I think, so we could lie to each other again.

With each juror called into the box, Caminetti, hunched over with angled intensity, scribbled a brief note to himself, the name, and perhaps something that caught his eye from the jury questionnaire he consulted with each person summoned. I sat at the other counsel table, with Jimmy Haviland sitting on my right, watching from across the room the faces of the dozen prospective jurors, wondering which of them I wanted to keep and which to let go.

As I examined those waiting, watchful faces, darting glances not at each other but around the room, at all the faces watching them, I worried about their age. I did not know if I wanted them older, or younger, or somewhere in between. There was a kind of shock, almost a warning of mortality, of time running out, when I stared into the faces of those twelve jurors and suddenly grasped the otherwise prosaic fact that Annie Malreaux had died before four of them had been born. They had no memory, no memory of their own, that reached that far back; nothing to remember in their own lives that would establish a connection between what had happened in the Plaza Hotel that Christmas Eve afternoon and themselves.

"There are certain — what shall I say? — novel aspects about this case," said Judge Scarborough with a courtly bow after the last of the twelve jurors had taken her chair. "The defendant is charged with the crime of murder in the first degree." Holding the indictment in his hand, he twitched his nose, stifling a sneeze. "It is alleged that 'on or about December twenty-fourth, nineteen sixty-five, Jamison Scott Haviland did knowingly and with malice aforethought' take the life of Anna Winifred Malreaux by causing her to fall to her death from a window in the Plaza Hotel in New York City."

Resting his weight on his right elbow, Scarborough bent forward. Two parallel vertical lines creased his forehead as he drew his eyes together in a stare of concentrated intensity.

"If you do not understand anything else I tell you today, I beg you to understand this: This charge, this indictment, this allegation is not worth the paper on which it is printed in terms of what it proves. It proves nothing whatsoever. It has no evidentiary value. It is nothing more than a formal notice of an intention, an intention to bring the matter to trial, to begin a proceeding in which you — the twelve people finally chosen to serve — will decide whether this accusation has merit. It is as simple as that. There is another piece of paper. I have it right here."

Lowering his eyes, Scarborough reached for the file folder on the bench in front of him. He held up another sheet of paper.

"This document is a court record of a

court appearance, an arraignment," announced Scarborough, glancing from one juror to the next. "An arraignment is that proceeding in which a defendant is told in open court and on the record that a charge has been brought against him and what the nature of that charge is. The defendant is then asked whether he wishes to plead guilty or not guilty to the charge. The defendant in this case — Jamison Scott Haviland — entered a plea of not guilty. That simple denial of wrongdoing, that plea of not guilty to the charge brought against him, must stand — unless and until there is evidence so clear and convincing to the contrary that no reasonable person could possibly doubt that the defendant is in fact guilty of the crime charged. Anything else is a dereliction of your duty as jurors, sworn on your oath, to render an impartial verdict in this case."

Scarborough lifted his elbow from the bench, sat back against the hard black leather chair, and for a few brief moments stroked his chin. His eyes never left the jury. With an audible sigh, he moved slowly forward again, dropped both elbows on the bench and rested his chin on top of his folded hands.

"This is a murder trial. The defendant,

Jamison Scott Haviland, is accused of the murder of Anna Malreaux. You would think, however, from all the coverage the case has already received, that this trial has nothing to do with the defendant, and really, nothing to do, at least directly, with the crime; that this was really a trial about the credibility of a certain well-known public figure. There is a very good chance that Thomas Browning will be called as a witness in this case. It seems almost certain that he will. Whether any of us happens to be personally acquainted with Mr. Browning, all of us, or certainly most of us, have the feeling that we know him. Is this not correct?

"The question is not whether you can banish from your mind everything you have ever thought about Thomas Browning — that would be an impossible thing to ask — the question is whether you can weigh his testimony with the same impartial judgment with which you weigh the testimony of any other witness. The task of the jury in this case is to decide a single question: whether or not the prosecution has beyond a reasonable doubt proven that Jamison Scott Haviland murdered Anna Malreaux. The effect of that decision on Thomas Browning, or on anyone else, must not even enter your minds. It is irrelevant; worse than irrelevant, it is an exercise of precisely that prejudice and bias that have no place in an American court of law."

He watched them carefully, studied their reaction to what he had said, teaching them by the intense scrutiny with which he examined their faces that the burden of their responsibility was as serious and profound as anything they had ever done in their lives.

"We'll take a short recess. When we return, we will begin voir dire."

"Almost makes you proud to be a lawyer, doesn't he?" remarked Jimmy Haviland as the door to chambers swung shut.

I had not quite heard what he said. I was thinking ahead to what I was going to ask on voir dire. The question of how old I wanted jurors to be, what I wanted them to remember, kept taunting me. I did not know what I wanted, and, worse yet, I did not know why.

"He's the best I've ever seen," said Haviland, marveling at what Scarborough had done. "Of course, I never practiced in courts where I was likely to run into someone like him. It's what happens when you're a sole practitioner in a small town: petty crimes, an occasional, friendly, divorce, real estate sales — everything pretty much cut-and-dried."

"Do you think we should try to have jurors old enough to remember nineteen sixty-five, or do you think it's better if they don't know anything about it except what they've heard or what they've read? I can't make up my mind," I admitted, turning toward him with a puzzled look.

"You're asking me?" replied Haviland. When he saw I was serious, he nodded and thought hard.

"Older, I suppose; better than younger. They'll have more of a feel for what things were like." He shook his head. It was not quite what he meant. "If they're older, there is a better chance they know what it's like to lose someone you love."

I did not ask him whether he meant lose someone because she died, or lose someone because she loved another man. I was more uncertain than ever about what kind of juror I wanted to have.

I tried to tell myself that it did not matter, that I did not have to make a decision in advance, that it was a mistake even to try. I had done this for so many years, I knew better than to formulate some hard-

and-fast rule about which jurors to take and which to let go. Jury selection was an art, not a science. It was not until you talked to them, looked them straight in the eye — made them look straight back at you — listened to what they said and how they said it, that you got a sense of what kind of people they were and whether you could trust them to at least try to do the right thing, to follow the law, to assume without any doubt or reservation the strange and illogical obligation to acquit someone they were convinced must be guilty of a crime the prosecution had not quite been able to prove. I sank back into the chair, and tried to concentrate on the first juror and the question I wanted to ask her.

Ten minutes after Judge Scarborough called a recess, he returned to the court-room. His step was quicker, his gaze more intense. He perched on the front edge of his chair, erect and alert, as if he were just waiting to spring back up again.

"Now we begin voir dire," he announced in an eager, vibrant voice. "Because it is masked in those two foreign words, it sounds like something difficult, complex, something mere mortals could never understand. What it means in plain English is that an inquiry is made into the qualifications of those who have been summoned for jury duty to see if each of them is in a position to be fair and impartial. That's all it is, nothing more."

Smiling to himself, Scarborough tapped his fingers together under his chin. Wrinkling his nose, twisting it tight, then quickly moving his lips, pressed firmly together, first one way, then the other, he held back a sneeze.

"It is our habit to think we all know this, that we all know what a jury is and how the rules apply. But a habit — shall I tell you? — was described by the great Blackstone hundreds of years ago as a thing which has been done the same way for so long that 'the memory of man runneth not to the contrary.' "

His eyes suddenly shot up to the windows high above the jury box. " 'Runneth not to the contrary!' " he repeated, jubilant, to whichever one of his fictional friends he now imagined. He placed his right arm on the bench, hunched his shoulders over it, and gave the jury a sharp look.

"In the beginning only the defense could challenge a juror's capacity to serve. This was in England, not here. The defense was given thirty-five challenges, and the prosecution got none. Thirty-five, not thirty-six, because if the defendant threw out three full juries he was not sufficiently serious about going to trial and they might just as well hang him as go to all the bother."

With a glance to the side, he remarked, "I see Mr. Antonelli grinning, while Mr. Caminetti looks quite put out. That's how they always react — defense lawyers and prosecutors — when I tell them how things used to be. Juries, on the other hand, just look terrified when I tell them that in one of the first jury trials that ever took place, the king did not like the verdict and put the entire jury in prison in the Tower of England until they came to their senses and changed their minds."

He held up his hand as if to parry an objection. "Yes, yes, I know: It sounds quite tyrannical. But the king only did it because the jury had been corrupted, and it was the only way to make sure justice was done. Believe me, whatever happens, you won't be thrown in prison . . ." Scarborough's smallish head began to bounce; his eyes filled with mischief. "Assuming of course that you listen carefully during the trial and follow all my instructions at the end."

The eyes of the jury had stayed on him

the whole time; not once did a juror look toward the crowd of spectators and reporters, or steal a glance at either Caminetti or me. The courtroom belonged to Charles F. Scarborough. He knew it, and, as I was about to find out, he would not have it any other way.

"Voir dire is often conducted by the lawyers. They ask the questions and they decide who should stay and who should go."

At the word *often* I was suddenly alert. He was going to do something I did not like, take over at least some of the questioning himself.

"Rather than have the lawyers ask each juror what often amounts to the same thing, it will save considerable time if I simply ask you as a panel certain basic questions. Let me begin by asking if any of you are acquainted with the defendant, Mr. Haviland, or with either of the lawyers, Mr. Caminetti for the prosecution, or Mr. Antonelli for the defense."

He waited for a response, and when there was none, nodded his satisfaction.

"Very good. No one is acquainted with the defendant or with either of the attorneys. My next question has to do with witnesses. Let me read you the list of witnesses the prosecution intends to call; and please, if I read the name of someone with whom you are acquainted — or someone with whom you think you might be acquainted — simply raise your hand."

None of the twelve knew any of the witnesses on Caminetti's list. Scarborough glanced at the list submitted by the defense. Pursing his lips, he raised his eyebrows. His head began to nod up and down, a silent acknowledgment of the difficulty he faced.

"Are any of you personally acquainted with Thomas Browning. And I emphasize the word *personally*. Anyone? No? Good. The next question I want you to think about quite carefully. Is there anything about Thomas Browning — anything about the way you feel about him — that would make you view the testimony he gives either more credible or less credible than that of any other witness called to testify in this case?"

No one raised a hand, but Scarborough sensed a reservation. "This is very important. If you have any doubt at all, even the slightest hesitation about whether you might be inclined to treat the testimony of one witness differently than you would that of a witness you did not know, then you have an absolute duty to say so and to say so now."

A woman's bare arm rose slowly from the far corner of the back row of the jury box. Scarborough raised his eyebrows, then lowered his eyes briefly to a chart on which he had written each of the juror's names.

"Yes, Mrs. Warfield?"

"I think I would tend to find Mr. Browning more credible. I like him. I like what he stands for."

"But I assume you would not, for that reason, believe him on a point you knew, or that was shown to be, false?"

She agreed immediately that she would not. He asked her several more questions and then turned to the district attorney.

"Is there anything you wish to add, Mr. Caminetti? Any question you think I may have left out?"

Caminetti jerked to attention. "No, Your Honor," he said with an abrupt, emphatic shake of his head. Scarborough turned back to the jury.

"Your Honor?" I insisted as I rose from my chair.

Scarborough's head turned just a shade farther than it had before. "Yes, Mr. Antonelli?"

"I have just a few questions . . ."

"Are you sure, Mr. Antonelli?" asked Scarborough. His head came all the way around. There was no mistaking the look of profound disappointment in his eyes. "You can, of course — if you wish; but I had hoped to finish with all of mine first. The reason I invited Mr. Caminetti to add something if he wished was only because the witness under discussion is one of yours and not one of his."

It was a point of procedure, a way to achieve a desired result: a fair and impartial jury to decide the case. I was free to disagree with it, to insist on my right to take the juror up and make my own inquiry. All I had to risk was the enmity of a jury that now looked to the judge as the source, not only of counsel and guidance on how they should conduct themselves, but of the standard by which they should measure everyone else. Whoever controls the courtroom controls the case, and I knew that this time it was not going to be me.

"Yes, of course, Your Honor. I did not understand."

The disappointment vanished from Scarborough's eyes, replaced by something close to gratitude. It was almost as if he believed he owed me a favor for yielding to what on this occasion he thought best.

He asked several more questions of the panel concerning their knowledge of Thomas Browning and whether any of the things they knew about him might influence their judgment about either his credibility or, depending on his testimony, the ultimate issue in the case: the guilt or innocence of Jamison Scott Haviland. Finally finished, he made the strange remark that it might be better if jurors were selected only if they had some knowledge of witnesses, and not just them, but of the defendant as well.

"It is one of the peculiarities of the present arrangement that one of the few phrases we all remember about trial by jury has a meaning completely different than it had at the start."

Reaching across his chest, Scarborough rubbed his right shoulder. The creases in his forehead deepened; a bemused expression entered his tranquil eyes.

"You know the phrase; you remember it well. Everyone has the right to a trial by a 'jury of their peers.' That used to mean a jury made up of people that knew the defendant and knew the witnesses: people who would know if they were lying or telling the truth. I mention this in part because I do not want you to feel too much the burden of knowing something about a famous man who happens to be a witness in this case. It seems to me that it can only help to know that someone who comes into court is more, or less, likely to tell the truth."

With that, he began to ask more questions: whether any of them were related to anyone in law enforcement; whether any of them had been the victim of a crime. There were several women, married early, who had never worked; there were several others who supported their children by holding whatever low-paying jobs they could get. There was a retired postal clerk, a black man who had never been outside New York except for the years when he fought as a foot soldier in the Second World War. Three of them had graduated from college; the rest had a high school education, if they had that. Scarborough talked to them as if they were all as smart as he.

If I had just been a courtroom spectator who had dropped in to watch, I would have marveled at Charles Scarborough's capacity to bring others up to a level higher than they had known before. But I was not some disinterested observer, and the only feeling I had was the gnawing sense of an opportunity lost. I had won cases on voire dire by leading a jury to see things the way I wanted them to see them. That was not going to happen here. Judge Scarborough had seen to that.

"Does counsel wish to challenge any of these jurors for cause?" he asked in a calm, friendly voice.

Caminetti sprang to his feet. "No, Your Honor."

"Mr. Antonelli?"

I still did not know what I wanted, and now I knew that I was not going to have the chance to find out. Only after I said it did I began to think that it might carry the advantage of a show of confidence.

"No, Your Honor, the defense will not challenge any of these jurors for cause. Nor will the defense exercise any of its peremptory challenges. We're satisfied that this is a fair and impartial jury. We accept the panel as it stands."

Hunched over the table, jotting a note to himself about the jurors he wanted to excuse, Caminetti froze. His head came up, slowly, methodically; his eyes narrowed into a shrewd, calculating stare. He had to decide right then, and I knew before he did what that decision would be. It was the one thing I knew I could count on, this belief that was as much a part of him as the city itself, that if you ever ran away from a challenge you would be running all your life.

"The People are satisfied," he reported with a brief, emphatic nod. He tried to make it sound as if it had been his idea all along.

17

It was like a street scene from Manhattan, the quick, abrupt, sharp-angled movements; the sudden way he turned his head, looking one way, then the next; the eyes that stared right at you while his mind was racing through a dozen different thoughts. Bartholomew Caminetti insisted that the evidence the prosecution would introduce at trial would be sufficient — no, more than sufficient — to prove the guilt of the defendant in the murder of Anna Malreaux. It was, he remarked as he paused in his breathless pacing and lowered his voice to a solemn tone, "a heinous crime, a crime that has to be punished."

With his right hand resting on the railing in front of the jury box, Caminetti rolled both shoulders forward and with whispered gravity reminded them of what they had been told before.

"It makes no difference that Anna Malreaux was murdered in nineteen sixty-five. It would not change anything if she had been murdered just last week. As Judge Scarborough told you yesterday, there is no statute of limitations on murder. Murder is the one crime we can never forgive. It is the one crime that we prosecute however long it takes to catch whoever is responsible for another person's death. Life is precious," continued Caminetti as he let go of the railing and with his head bowed again began to pace the floor. "Life — it's the one thing no one has a right to take away." He came to a stop, his left foot a full stride ahead of his right. His face swiftly turned. "We have laws against suicide: You're not allowed to take your own life; you're certainly not allowed to take the life of someone else."

With a stern glance, he turned away, resuming that endless back-and-forth half-circle march. He did not say another word until he reached the far end of the jury box. Below the raised platform of the witness stand, he turned back, squared his shoulders and spread his feet.

"The People will call a number of witnesses to establish first the manner and cause of the victim's death, and then the defendant's motive for committing the crime."

Caminetti could not stay still for long.

He pulled his feet closer together. With the hands that had been held behind his back, he began to gesture first with one, then the other, as he entered upon a brief recitation of who each witness was and what the jury could expect that witness to say. The sleeves of his suit coat, a size too large, slapped against his wrists, as he waved his arms in short bursts of enthusiasm for every piece of evidence, every word of testimony, he was going to marshal against the defense.

"Anna Malreaux was in her second year of law school. She was here, in New York, during the Christmas break that year. She was at a party on Christmas Eve, a party held on the eighth floor of the Plaza Hotel."

Caminetti wrapped his arms across his chest and took a step forward. His eyes narrowed, pinched together, creasing the bridge of his nose.

"She was pushed out a window, pushed to her death from the eighth floor. Pushed by the defendant, Jamison Scott Haviland."

Caminetti's head jerked up. His eyes flared open.

"Why? Why did he do that? Why did he push her through that window? Why did he push her to her death?"

Caminetti's head moved like a ratchet from one end of the jury box to the other, looking at each juror, waiting while they each in turn wondered about what he had asked.

"Jealousy — jealousy and pain," he said finally in a hard, dry voice that insisted there could not be any doubt. "Maybe some people die when their own heart is broken, but a lot more die because they broke the heart of someone else. Anna Malreaux broke Haviland's heart. He wanted to marry her; she said no. He was hurt, he was angry; he could not stand the pain. He came to New York because he knew she would be here. He went to the Plaza Hotel. Maybe he was going to give her one more chance, one more chance to say yes. He was in love with her, obsessed with her: He could not leave her alone. He went to the Plaza Hotel, he found her at that party up on the eighth floor. He was hurt, he was angry; he was not going to let her get away. If she would not belong to him, she was not going to belong to anyone. If she would not live with him, Anna Malreaux was going to die."

His head bent in a thoughtful pose, Caminetti moved in small, slow steps halfway across the front of the jury box. He looked at the jury, shaking his head at the foolish weakness to which the flesh is heir.

"And so he killed her, shoved her out that window, watched her fall eight stories to her death on the sidewalk below. He could not have her, and now no one ever would."

For a moment longer, Caminetti shook his head in that same mournful way. Then, with a sudden step forward, he seized the jury box railing with both hands.

"Someone must have seen it happen, seen the whole thing; seen him shove her out the window, push her through it to her death! Why didn't they say anything about it? Why didn't anyone tell the truth about what happened that day? Why did they let it get reported as an accident when they knew it was murder and not an accident at all?"

Caminetti pulled his hands out of his pockets and folded his arms across his chest. He stood straight, sliding one foot cautiously ahead of the other, as if he were testing the ground to see how solid it was before deciding whether to go any farther than he had. His eyes darted back and forth around the jury box; then he looked back over his shoulder, taking in with a single glance Haviland and the courtroom crowd as it sat watching, waiting to hear what he was going to say next.

Something started echoing in my mind, and I could not get it to stop. Someone must have seen it happen. That is what he had said. He was talking about Thomas Browning. But then why had he kept asking why they had not told the truth about what they had seen? Was it just a figure of speech, something said in that abbreviated manner of his? Was it just my own nervous suspicion that there was more to the prosecution's case than what I had been able to learn, more than what I had been told? He was not supposed to keep anything concealed, but I did not trust him not to hold anything back.

Caminetti eyed the jury with knowing confidence. "Before this trial is over, you will know how that happened and why."

Judge Scarborough, sitting sideways to the bench as he followed the prosecution's opening statement to the jury, waited until Caminetti returned to the counsel table and took his chair. From underneath his robe, he pulled out his handkerchief and blew his nose. Waving his right hand in a languid, desultory fashion, he moved his head barely an inch or so in my direction, inviting me to give the opening for the defense. I did not move; I did not say a word. Perplexed, he put the handkerchief away, and then turned his head, or rather let it fall to the side.

"Do you wish to reserve your opening, Mr. Antonelli? To deliver it at the conclusion of the state's case and at the beginning of yours? The court will permit that, should that be your preference," he said in his rich, cultured voice, coarsened by the residual effects of what I had begun to suspect were the habitual symptoms of a largely imaginary disease. The handkerchief was a prop, begun as an affectation, done for show, become with time and habit a necessary, if only dimly conscious, part of the drama by which to make the courtroom the interesting place he wanted it to be. It was just a bit of cloth, but in its own way as effective as the silk gown and white wig by which a British magistrate holds the attention of the crowd.

"No, Your Honor," I replied in a voice that suggested a vague and continuing uncertainty. I stayed where I was, sitting in that chair, my right hand resting on the edge of the table, three fingers tapping soundlessly against it, the counterpoint to the quiet emptiness of my mind.

With growing amusement, Scarborough let the handkerchief dangle from his hand as he bent closer across the bench.

"That would seem to narrow the choice to making an opening statement now, before the prosecution calls its first witness, or, as is your right, not making one at all."

"Yes," I replied. Caught up by his manner, I began to smile.

"Yes?" Scarborough's thick gray eyebrows shot straight up. He turned to the jury box, a cheerful expression glowing on his face, but instead of looking at any of the jurors, he looked just above them. "Yes?" he repeated, speaking to that imaginary alter ego of his that had, once the jury was impaneled, been moved to another place. "Yes?" he repeated for the third time, gazing now right at me with an irrepressible grin. "Yes, what, Mr. Antonelli? Yes, an opening? Or yes, you agree that, in a way like Hamlet, to give one or not to give one, exhausts the known alternatives?"

As quick as one of Caminetti's sudden moves, I was on my feet, walking toward the jury box, nodding briefly toward the judge.

"That was the line — that line from Hamlet — on which all the action of the play depends: 'To be or not to be.' If we know no other line of Shakespeare's, we have all heard of that. To be — being — to be part of what is, part of the chain of being that connects the generations, the chain that stretches back to the beginning, the very beginning, the first humans, Adam and Eve; and from them down to us, the present time; down to us, and after our brief turn, to the next generation and all the generations that come after that. Annie Malreaux was part of my generation, or perhaps I was part of hers: a generation that came into being during the war, the Second World War, and that lived through wars of its own. Some of you were not alive when Annie Malreaux fell to her death from a window at the Plaza Hotel, late one snow-filled winter afternoon. You had not yet come into being. She died before you were born. You never breathed the same air she did; you never, without knowing it, passed each other on a crowded New York street; you never stood on a corner together, waiting for a light, exchanging a few brief anonymous words."

I searched their faces, faces that were almost anonymous to me. "And those of you who were born sometime before Annie Malreaux died, how much do you remember about what it was like, that December, all those years ago? How much do you remember about what you did — or even where you were — not just that Christmas, but anytime that year? Memories fade and disappear, vanish forever because so much of the little time we have is taken up by the current necessities of our lives. We forget everything, and what we do remember, we may not always or even very often remember the way we once did, a few hours, a few days, a few weeks after it happened."

With my hands in my pockets, I gazed for a moment down at the floor in front of the jury box, smiling to myself. When I raised my eyes, I looked at each of them with a kind of innocent curiosity, the way you do when you are first introduced.

"I remember where I was that day, the day Annie Malreaux died. There are some things you never forget. I remember that day because I was there, at the Plaza Hotel, when it happened, when Annie Malreaux fell to her death. I knew her," I said, placing a hand on the jury box railing. "I knew Annie Malreaux, and not just her: I knew them all." I looked back at the counsel table on the far side of the courtroom. "I knew Jamison Scott Haviland —

Jimmy Haviland — and I knew Thomas Browning as well. We were friends, or at least we knew each other. We were in school together: That is where we all met, Jimmy Haviland, Thomas Browning, Annie Malreaux and I — where it all began, years ago, when we were young and just starting out, eager to make our mark and certain that we would. We were at the Harvard Law School when we met — Jimmy and Thomas and Annie and I — and we took ourselves very seriously indeed."

I took them back, as best I could, to that time when things were so much closer to the beginning than they were to the end, and tried to make them see what we had been instead of what we had become. The time raced past, moving more quickly the more I talked about what had happened in the past. I told them what I remembered, how bright and beautiful, how strange and different, Annie Malreaux had been. I told them about her mother and the remarkable way her daughter had been raised. I told them what Jimmy Haviland had done, when he learned what happened, the sobbing, choking phone call in which Vivian Malreaux first heard that her daughter, her only child, was dead, and how he had gone to Chicago and tried to do what he could to help and how she had done what she could to take care of him.

"Does that sound like someone who had pushed the girl he loved to her death?" I asked and then hurried on, turning to Thomas Browning and how, like Jimmy Haviland, he had been in love with Annie Malreaux and what her death had done.

I spoke for an hour, two, remembering with each thing I said something I had forgotten, something that made more vivid what had happened and why it had now been tortured into something it had never been. Two hours, three, I talked to those twelve jurors as if they were the only friends I had ever had.

"I knew them all, Browning, Haviland, Annie Malreaux — and in their different ways they of course knew each other. If they had not known each other, none of this would have happened. If Annie Malreaux had not gone to Harvard, had not met Jimmy Haviland, never known Thomas Browning, she would not have been in New York, she would not have gone to that party at the Plaza, she would not have gone looking out that window and there would not have been that accident, that fall."

Pausing, I searched their eyes, measuring their willingness to believe me when I told them what I believed.

"And if Jimmy Haviland had not known Thomas Browning, if they had never met, he would not be sitting here today, a middle-aged man dressed in a suit, accused of a crime that not only did he not commit, but that never took place. He knew Thomas Browning; they knew each other at school. That is the reason — the only reason — he has been accused of a murder: not because of what happened to Annie Malreaux, but because of what happened to Thomas Browning instead."

With a quarter turn, I looked long and hard at Bartholomew Caminetti. His face was a blank sheet, the only expression the quiet calculation in his eyes. He was listening to what I said, thinking about how he could use it, how he could take it apart, bend it to his own advantage. I turned back to the jury.

"If Thomas Browning had been just another law student, another young man of that generation who later, like Jimmy Haviland, went off to war; or, like me and others we knew, stayed out of it and, safe from the violence, made careers in the law, there never would have been a prosecution, because there never would have been a crime. The only reason Jamison Scott Haviland is on trial for murder is that Thomas Browning ran for president in the last election and may be about to do it again. Yes, I remember," I said, waving my hand with impatience, "I remember what Judge Scarborough said at the beginning, that this is a trial on the single question of whether the defendant, Jamison Scott Haviland, did or did not take the life of Annie Malreaux, and that you are not to be influenced by what effect your verdict might have on Thomas Browning or anyone else. But I'm not talking about the effect: I am talking about the cause. Remember what Judge Scarborough told you? Not about your obligation to decide the case on the evidence, but what that evidence was going to be, the witnesses that were going to be called. One of those witnesses is Thomas Browning, but who is going to call him? Not the prosecution. Mr. Caminetti told us who his witnesses are, and Thomas Browning's name is not among them."

I paused long enough to direct an interrogating glance at the district attorney. He returned the look with a blank stare, a show of unflappable indifference.

"Why isn't it there? Why isn't Thomas Browning on the prosecution's list? Why isn't Thomas Browning the first name — the only name — on that list?" I asked, my voice charged with emotion. "Thomas Browning was there — he was in the room! Thomas Browning saw what happened. Thomas Browning alone could convict the defendant — if the defendant had done anything wrong. But the prosecution is not going to call him, this witness who saw Annie Malreaux fall."

Knitting my brow, I tried to puzzle it out. "Why? Because Thomas Browning is a liar. That's what the prosecution now insists; that is what you were told earlier today: that Thomas Browning did not 'tell the truth about what happened that day.' Those are the words that Mr. Caminetti used. He charged — you remember — that what happened to Annie Malreaux was reported as an accident when Thomas Browning 'knew it was not.' It doesn't matter that Thomas Browning's name was not used; Thomas Browning was there. The whole world must know that by now. The prosecution knows it, too. But they are not calling him as a witness, and it is because they cannot. It is extraordinary, inexplicable, that the only witness to the death — the accidental death — of Annie Malreaux has to be called by the defense."

I began to pace, a few short steps; then I stopped. I narrowed my eyes and clenched my teeth, angrily shaking my head. Throwing out my hand, I began to jab the air, emphasizing over and over again that single, solitary, all-important point.

"The defense is calling Thomas Browning so that Thomas Browning can take the oath, swear to tell the truth, and tell you and tell everyone what he saw that terrible day, Christmas Eve, nineteen sixty-five. The prosecution won't call him as a witness. In its complete and thorough investigation, in its exhaustive and painstaking reexamination of the evidence in a case officially ruled an accident when it happened," I went on, becoming more sarcastic with each word, "with all the witnesses they must have interviewed, all the people they had to track down and find, all the enormous resources expended on this massive effort to solve a crime, it was, I suppose, nothing more than a minor oversight, a small failure, an understandable mistake, that no one — no police officer, no detective, no investigator, no assistant district attorney, no, not even Mr. Caminetti himself, ever so much as asked to speak to Thomas Browning. They took no statement; they asked no questions. They did not invite him to appear before the grand jury; they did not even give him the courtesy of a telephone call to inquire whether he might have anything to say. And now, the district attorney, in open court, makes his opening statement to the jury and with what I must confess was theatrical brilliance tells you, and through all the reporters gathered in this courtroom, tells the world — what was it? — oh, yes, 'Someone must have seen it happen, seen the whole thing. Seen him push her out the window, push her through it to her death.'

"The prosecution's entire case rests upon the proposition that Thomas Browning is a liar, a conspirator in a crime. That is why it is not quite right — why I must in some manner dissent from the view so ably espoused by Judge Scarborough. This case is not only about the guilt or innocence of the defendant. The defendant is being used: He is a pawn in a dangerous game, a game played by powerful and ambitious people out to destroy Thomas Browning, people who do not mind for a minute that they might in the process destroy Jamison Scott Haviland as well."

I had been talking for hours. It was the

longest opening statement I had ever made. There was sweat on my forehead, some of it rolling into my eyes, burning them with salt. My hair was damp; my shirt was drenched.

"The prosecution promised to tell you who covered up the murder of Annie Malreaux and the reason it was done. 'Before this trial is over you will know how that happened and why.' Remember? I will make you a promise as well," I said, turning slowly until I was looking Caminetti squarely in the eye. "Before this trial is over, you will know who the people are who have conspired together to use the judicial system of the United States to knowingly bring about a wrongful conviction for murder out of a desperate need to hang on to political power and their own political careers. It is a conspiracy, ladies and gentlemen, that reaches inside the White House and before this case is over I am going to prove it!"

With a last glance at the jury, I walked to the counsel table. Utterly exhausted, I sank into my chair, glad I had made that promise and too tired to worry about whether I could keep it.

An immense stillness, a profound silence, filled the courtroom. No one moved, no one spoke; no one knew what to think. They had come to witness a trial in which the vice president might be implicated in a crime, or at least involved in a scandal, and found themselves confronted with an accusation that Browning was the victim of a criminal conspiracy directed perhaps by the president himself. Judge Scarborough looked suddenly tired and drawn.

"I think this might be an appropriate place to adjourn for the day," he said in a voice that seemed both reflective and subdued. "We'll begin in the morning at ten. We have finished now with opening statements. Tomorrow the prosecution will call its first witness and begin its case."

I managed to get Jimmy Haviland out of the courthouse the back way. We crossed the street into Columbus Park, and before we said good-bye I cautioned him against the Irish bar.

"There will be people in there — reporters, and not just reporters, some of those crazy bastards who think Browning ought to be dead — and the only story will be about the defendant drinking himself stupid instead of thinking about his trial. Go back to the hotel. If you need a drink, do it in your room, and do it alone."

Jimmy broke into a chastened grin. "I

promised you I wouldn't do that. Don't you think I can keep my word?" Embarrassed, I started to apologize. "No, it's all right," he said. The grin softened into a vague, distant smile. He kicked at the sidewalk with the tip of his shoe. He raised his eyes and gave me a rueful glance. "If I hadn't made that promise, that's exactly where I would be — heading toward that bar, probably staying there until I couldn't remember why I didn't want to leave." A grim expression of self-inflicted doubt creased the corners of his aging eyes. "It's always been such a stupid thing to do."

I felt so sorry for him; I wanted so much to say something that might help take away just a little of the pain. I remembered what Vivian Malreaux had said, not just about what Jimmy had believed, but what because of her strange and generous nature her daughter might have done.

"She might have married you. After a while, after she figured out what she really wanted to do, Annie might have married you. She knew how much you loved her, and that meant a lot."

A faint smile, tragic and nostalgic, bitter and forgiving, crossed Jimmy Haviland's straight, narrow mouth. There was a kind of hard-won clarity in his eyes, as if he had finally realized what his weaknesses were. It was the look of someone who understands that it is too late, and that it probably always was; that the things that changed our lives, that made us who we are, that left us damaged and half destroyed, the walking wounded with our shattered dreams and our lost illusions, our bent ambitions and our broken souls, had been written from the beginning next to our names. Jimmy Haviland looked at me, tired and quietly triumphant, willing finally to accept the hand he had been dealt.

"It was never about Annie; it was always about me. If she had married me, it would have been for all the wrong reasons — because she felt sorry for me, I suppose — and it would have ended badly, and that would have been worse; not worse than the fact that she died, but worse than if she had lived and married someone else, someone she loved a little the way I loved her. No, it wasn't about Annie. If I hadn't met her — the way you said in there today — if I hadn't met Annie, do you really think my life would have been all that much different? That I would have led a normal, happy life — whatever that might be? If it hadn't been Annie, it would have been someone else."

Jimmy shook his head, and I thought there was just a slight suggestion of something close to pride, a sense that he had not been willing to settle for second best, that he had not been afraid to risk staking everything on the way he felt.

"I was a lot like you that way," he remarked with a sympathetic glance that caught me completely off guard. "Always wanting something I knew I could never have. What's that old line — 'your reach should exceed your grasp, else what's a heaven for?'" Haviland laughed. "And they wonder why the Irish drink."

He said good-bye and started to walk away, heading up the street. He stopped, turned around and came toward me again.

"Browning was right about one thing. He was right about you. What you did in there today — that opening of yours . . ." He smiled, and in a gesture that meant more than words, nodded his approval. Then he quickly turned on his heel and vanished in the swarming crowd marching endlessly up and down the narrow, noisy, shouting street.

I turned around, ready to go the other way, when I saw her standing there, waiting right in front of me. I tried to hide my surprise.

"Are you here as a reporter, or as the woman I tried to invite to dinner but who did not return my call?"

The cool, dark eyes of Gisela Hoffman had that slightly baffled expression they had each time she tried to translate into English something she thought important. An embarrassed smile started onto her mouth, and then, embarrassed even more, tried to turn back. With a helpless laugh, she gripped the strap of the large leather purse slung over her shoulder, plunged her other hand into the deep pocket of the camel-hair coat she wore, and bent her head at a delicate angle to the side.

"I don't know why I'm like this around you, a tongue-tied adolescent, a stammering fool. Yes, that's the reason," said Gisela as her eyes shot wide open into a shining accusatory glance. "It's what you do — the way you do that . . . Tease me with your eyes, make fun of me like that!"

I took her by the arm, turning her around, moving her with me through the jostling crowd. The air was cold, clear, crisp; the sky a hard brittle blue. The delicate white skin on her cheeks was glowing red like the spots on a child's painted doll.

"It's too early for dinner," I remarked as we turned the corner at the end of the park. "But I haven't eaten all day. Let's find someplace quiet, where we can talk."

In the back of a dimly lit café, I devoured a sandwich while Gisela sipped on a cappuccino and tried to explain why we kept missing each other.

"There is so much going on in Washington. I couldn't leave until the trial started." She wrinkled her nose, a puzzled expression in her night-colored eyes. "The way you start . . ." She shook her head. "No, I mean the questions they ask . . ."

"Voir dire? Jury selection?" I suggested between hungry bites.

Her eyes lit up. "Yes; voire dire. I assumed that would go on for quite a while — until the end of the week. Yes?"

My mouth was full. I nodded.

"But then it's over, all in one day. So when I heard that, that today you and the prosecutor would make your opening speeches . . . Speeches? Opening statements. I didn't have time to do anything except pack a bag and catch an early-morning flight."

A smile, tentative, intelligent and shy, slipped across her fine, graceful mouth.

"When I heard your voice on the machine last night, I . . ."

Shoving the plate to the side, I leaned forward on my arms. "I looked for you the other day, when the trial started. I thought you would be there, and I was disappointed when you were not. So last night I thought I'd call, and find out what happened and whether you were going to be in New York or not."

"I didn't call back because it was late, and because I think I wanted to sneak up on you the way I did and surprise you." She frowned and shook her head, scolding herself, as it seemed, for telling less than the truth. "I was scared; I wasn't sure I should. I wasn't sure it was safe to call you back."

"Safe?"

Gisela reached into the purse she had placed next to her in the booth. It was nearly the size of an attaché case, large enough for the unmarked manila envelope she pushed across the table.

"This is for you."

"What is it?"

"I'm not sure. The man who gave me the documents would not tell me what they meant. He asked me to give them to you, to make sure you got them before the prosecution called its first witness. He said he thought you would know what they meant."

" 'The man'?"

"A friend of mine." She paused, and then with a serious look added: "Someone I used to know."

A former lover who was now a friend, someone who knew she knew me.

"Someone you used to know," I remarked with a pensive stare.

"We've become good friends. He trusts me. He wanted you to have this." She nodded toward the manila envelope that I had begun to open. "He knows I won't tell anyone who he is."

I did not know who he was, but I thought I knew where he worked.

"Your White House source? The one who told you about the investigation and about the indictment?"

She threw me a glance of disapproval. I mumbled an apology and emptied the envelope. There were a half dozen sheets of paper inside, printed copies of messages downloaded from someone's computer. The same e-mail address was plainly visible across the top.

"WH.EOP.GOV." I looked at Gisela. "EOP?"

"Executive Office of the President."

"WH . . . White House? And GOV . . . government?"

"Yes," she replied, leaning forward, bursting with curiosity. "It comes from someone's computer inside the White House. But I checked the name — Lincoln Edwards. No one by that name is listed in the White House directory."

I began to examine the documents, reading through each one and then checking them against each other, comparing both the dates and the sequence of the transactions recorded.

"Do you know what they are?" asked Gisela, anxious and intense.

I put the documents back in the envelope and placed the envelope next to me on the seat. "I think so."

I glanced around the restaurant to see if there was someone I had seen before. If this was what I thought it was, I knew I had to be careful.

"I know you're not going to tell me who your friend is, but it has to be someone inside the White House. Only someone who worked there could get something off a White House computer. Why would someone on the White House staff, someone who works for the president, want to give me this?"

"What is it? What do those numbers mean?"

"Numbers and names," I reminded her. "You were there today when Caminetti talked about his witnesses and what they were going to say. Didn't two of those names sound familiar?"

"I didn't understand the numbers; I didn't pay much attention to the names," she said, shaking her head. Then, suddenly, she looked at me with intense curiosity. "You mean, two of the witnesses for the prosecution . . . What do the numbers mean?"

"It's a record of a routing sequence, money moved from one bank to another, moved through offshore accounts to make the source of it virtually untraceable. It's a record of money paid to six different people, two of them key witnesses in a murder trial."

"Who are the other four?"

"I don't know," I admitted. "But I still want to know why your friend gave this to me. Why is someone inside the White House — one of the president's own men — giving me information which, if it's true, could bring down the president? I want to talk to your friend; I want to talk to him right away. Can you arrange it?"

"I don't know. I'll ask."

We lingered in the café until well after dark, gradually talking less about the trial and more about ourselves. Gisela told me about growing up in Germany, in divided Berlin, and how, after university, she got a job at a Munich newspaper where she met the man she eventually married and from whom she was now officially divorced.

"He had an affair with a woman before we had been married a year. So then I had one, too. Just some man I knew," she said with bland indifference, as if she were explaining the opening gambit in a well-practiced game.

A soft, enigmatic smile floated over her mouth. She looked at me with a hard, glittering stare. It was like the suggestion of innocence drawn toward, and then addicted to, sin.

"Women enjoy it as much as men," she announced, the smile now open, certain of itself. She seemed almost to dare me to disagree. "Sometimes more than men," she added, mocking me with her eyes. "He thought he could sleep with every woman he wanted, but that I would stay faithful, inventing some perfect little world where, when he was home, he could play the perfect faithful husband attended by his perfect wife. Imagine his disappointment when he discovered that while he was involved in his various infidelities, I was engaged in some random promiscuity of my own. He thought I had betrayed him, that what he did was one thing, but that I didn't have the right. He was very German about it; I was more — how shall I say? — European: willing to be married, but eager to be in love."

The second half, that other side of her, closed in on the first: The soft vulnerability that made you want to help her, and then this sudden and unexpected eroticism that made you want to have her, completed the circle that now enclosed me, unable to think about anything but her and what it would be like to be with her, naked and alone.

"There is a certain charm in having an affair, being with someone when the only motive, the only reason, is that you want to be. There aren't any of those prosaic calculations about how you are going to live, or where, or what you can look forward to when you get older. You don't worry about things like that: You just worry about how you can arrange the next time you can steal a few hours for what makes you feel so alive."

I felt myself drawing closer, losing myself in her, taken over by a grasping need, a whirlpool that the faster it spun me the faster I wanted to go. I watched her, teasing me with her eyes; watched her, naked and in bed; I watched her, making love with me in my mind.

"You were never married — yes? So you wouldn't know what that was like, except perhaps that halfway thing for which there seems to be no word, when a man who is single is sleeping with a woman who is not. You have done that, haven't you? Been with married women who wanted to be with you?"

Her dark eyes held mine close and fast. In the silky silence I could almost hear the laughter I saw dancing at the gentle, teasing corners of her mouth.

"Now we're just two single people, a man and a woman, wondering what it's going to be like, a little while from now, when we start making love and make love all through the night. Would you like to do that with me, Joseph Antonelli? Would you like to take me back to where you're staying . . . take me to bed . . . take me? I wanted to the first night we met; but then, you knew that, didn't you?" she asked, certain she was right.

We left the restaurant, and I put my arm around her against the chilly New York night. We got into a cab and she huddled close and then looked up at me, waiting, knowing that I had only been waiting for her. With her arm around my neck, I kissed her and lost myself in her even more. Her breath against my face was warm, willing, the whispered scent of every girl I had ever known. We did not speak a word; there was nothing to say, nothing that would not spoil the mood. There were lights everywhere, and I could not see a thing, just her face, what she looked like and how she moved. I watched her step out of the cab, smiling up at me, holding on to my hand, and for an instant I remembered another cab ride, one that had brought me a few blocks farther up the street, and what it had been like, at the beginning, that first time in New York, when I was still young and so was everyone else.

She was in my arms before I had shut the door, and we were both half undressed by the time we stumbled, frantic and impassioned, across the bedroom floor. We made love, and then we made love again; we made love in ways I had not imagined, and we did it as if instead of this being our first time together, we had been making love all our lives. She taught me things I did not know; and because it all seemed so right, I knew nothing of that jealous desire to ask when she had learned. We seldom slept and almost never talked; her eyes, her touch, said all I wanted. We knew each other through the passing brevity of the night, until morning came.

Lying in the shadowed silence of the room, her thin arms each spread across a rumpled pillow, she looked at me through barely opened eyes.

"You're dressed? You're going?" she asked in a drowsy, peaceful voice.

I pulled the white sheet from the back of her knees up to her shoulder. Turning on her side, she tugged it under her chin.

"What time is it?" she asked, rubbing her eyes. Clutching the sheet, she sat up, looking around the room she had seen only in the darkness. "You live very well, Mr. Joseph Antonelli." With a dreamy smile, she slid down until her head was below the pillows. "Do you mind if I stay a while longer? If I slept all day, perhaps you could tell me later what happened at the trial."

I suggested she stay longer than that. "I have this place for the duration: until the trial is over, and, if I want it, longer than that. Why don't you stay here, too? As long as you like." She rolled her head to the side and without any other expression stared at me with trusting, childlike eyes. "It's nicer than a hotel; and if you're here, I won't have to worry so much. I'll know you're safe."

"Safe?" she asked as if she had not any idea what I meant. "Will we have dinner tonight?" She closed her eyes and a moment later was back asleep.

18

It was better than any novel Rebecca Long ever wrote; better than any mystery written by an author who appealed to the popular taste; better by far than the dull biographies constructed from the lying memories of politicians trying to hide their mistakes. It was not like a book at all: more like a play, a play between acts, the audience left waiting in breathless suspense for what the curtain might reveal. Thomas Browning had resigned the vice presidency, but for a full week that was all that anyone had known. The White House, always full of rumor, had retreated into an uneasy silence, no one willing to speak even off the record; all the anonymous sources unwilling to be even that well known.

It was the reaction of people who feared the worst and did not know what the worst might turn out to be. The lights burned through the night; no one dared to leave. Arthur Connally and the other close advisors to the president huddled together, making plans and changing them, wondering what Browning was going to do next and what they would then be forced to do. The reporters who reported this did not claim it as a fact, but rather that it seemed almost certain that this was what must be going on. Secrecy bred speculation, and speculation became that kind of temporary what-if set of facts that led to more speculation still. Members of the Senate, members of the House, governors, mayors, the chairmen of the Democratic and Republican parties — anyone who held an office or had ever aspired to hold one — were asked what they thought of the vice president's resignation and what they thought it meant. Opinions flew as fast and furious as snowballs in a schoolyard fight, did what damage they could to the angry, flabbergasted faces of those who had, almost at random, found themselves on the other side, and then melted into what from any distance was a swirling white unintelligible haze. Up to the very moment Thomas Browning stepped in front of the cameras, the country was still debating what he was going to say and what he was going to do.

The news conference scheduled for Friday morning at ten was postponed until five-thirty in the afternoon, and instead of Washington it was now going to be held in New York. With no reason given for the change, anyone who wanted to was free to invent one of his own. By midafternoon there was a growing suspicion that the change of location might have something to do with the trial in which Thomas Browning was alleged to have been a witness to a young woman's murder. At five o'clock, a half hour before Browning was scheduled to appear, the network reporters who had gathered on the sidewalk across the street from his East Side apartment began live coverage by reporting the most recent rumors from unnamed sources. Browning was going to reveal what he knew about the murder and why he had kept it secret so long; Browning was going to tell everything and ask forgiveness from the family of the girl. Browning, in those familiar and meaningless phrases, was going to "try to put this behind him" and "move forward with his life."

I laughed out loud when I heard it, this solemn invocation of blank stupidity, this mild-tempered superficiality that thinks comfort the only thing worth having and the kind of tragic sense of loss that stays with you forever, a constant affliction in your anguished soul, the unhealthy reaction of someone in need of help. I could almost see the pained expression on Browning's face, the gesture of contempt with which he had always dismissed the mawkish sentimentality that dwells so much on what it feels because what it feels is always on the surface and the surface is all there is.

At five-thirty, Thomas Browning walked out of the apartment building on Fifth Avenue, crossed the street, and with his back to Central Park stood in front of a battery of microphones and made the short announcement that changed everything.

"Last week I resigned the office of vice president of the United States. I did this so that I could today stand before you and announce my candidacy for the office of president of the United States."

Browning's eyes sparkled with cheerful belligerence. A smile started onto his mouth. He placed his hands into the jacket pockets of his gray double-breasted suit and bent forward, peering at the crowd of reporters pressing toward him. His head suddenly snapped up and he threw out his right hand, waving in response to the shouted cheering madness that had begun to roll in, engulfing him in the noise.

Thousands of people, brought by the news that Browning was going to be there, had come out, filling the streets, stopping traffic on Fifth Avenue for several blocks in each direction. The announcement that he was running for president, that he was running against Walker for the nomination, had excited the crowd, turning all those single faint voices into a tremendous, cavernous roar. At first it was encouragement, the crowd telling him that it was behind him, that it approved of what he wanted to do; but the noise of it kept growing, becoming more intense, building to the point of a demand, an insistence that he do what had now become their idea, that he run, that he win, and that he do it for all of them. It went on and on, a new generation of enthusiasm bred every second, expanding in every direction at once, as if the crowd itself was growing, spreading through the narrow crosstown streets, filling up the avenues, taking the city by storm. Browning stood in the middle of it, without a thought of trying to make it stop; drawing strength from it, staring back at it, smiling at it, waving at it; acknowledging its power and accepting the truth of what it said and what it wanted. I remembered the last time I had seen a crowd, a New York crowd, react like that, the last time I had seen one man draw that much single-minded, devoted attention to himself. I remembered the look on Joanna's face that first moment she caught sight of John Lindsay that day I was with her in the basement ballroom of the Roosevelt Hotel.

I think Browning had meant to make that short, two-sentence statement, announce that he was going to run against Walker for the Republican nomination, and then take questions from the press. The time had been changed from mid-morning to late afternoon because, with the network news coming on live, it was the perfect time to talk in a calm, measured voice about what he had done and why. He had not anticipated the crowd and the astonishing intensity with which it had taken up his announcement and made his cause its own. He had meant to have a conversation, and now he had to make a speech.

Thomas Browning stood in the reddish gold autumn light and with nothing written out, not even a note to remind him of what he wanted to say, gave a speech that no one who heard it would ever forget. He had not had a moment to prepare, but in another sense he had been preparing all his life. Browning lived in the company of words. He used them, thought about them, weighed them, measured them; listening as much to how they sounded as what they meant, because it was the sound of them that captured the attention of an audience and held it, fascinated, as if the voice it heard was coming from somewhere deep inside itself. He had trained himself to it, memorizing long passages from famous speeches, or, as he had with Lincoln's Second Inaugural, the speech in its entirety; pages of fine flowing prose from Gibbon and Macaulay and others of the great historians. Name a poet, and he could immediately recite at least some of the best-known lines; mention a character in one of Shakespeare's plays, and he would begin a soliloquy as if he had for years been acting the part on the New York stage. It seemed, at least to my ignorant ear, that nothing important had been written that he had not only read but remembered, word for word. And yet, this prodigious memory of his he thought nothing like as good as it should have been. He told me once that he had read somewhere that Macaulay could recite from memory the entire Old Testament. "In Hebrew," he added, shaking his head

461

with the stunned disbelief of a man forced to confess a serious limitation to what he can do.

Perhaps it was because of who he was, what he had been born to; perhaps it was this desire he had to go back to the beginning of things as the best or only way to understand what had happened and what might be done about it. Whatever the reason, he had spent years training himself to do things that others thought unimportant and a grievous waste of time. There were so many things going on, they argued; so many things to know something about, so many things to do. You hired people to write speeches; you did not write them yourself. Let the speechwriters struggle with the dull necessities of finding words or phrases that send the right signal to the group or constituency you want to please. Lincoln? Churchill? Famous people of the past who wrote their own? Those were different times, and things were more complicated now. Browning never believed any of it; there was no reason he should. The people who said these things, the people who prided themselves on how busy they were staying up to date, could only look as far forward as they could look back. Browning wanted to make history; they had forgotten what history meant.

He was becoming more confident as he spoke, more at ease, talking as if this were some private conversation instead of a public speech. He had that gift of making you think that you were the only one he cared about. He could do it when there were just the two of you in the room, and he could do it when you were a part of the crowd, because Browning never talked about himself, he talked about you, or rather about what you and he could do together.

"We live in perilous times. What shall we do about it?" That was how he began one part of that remarkable speech. "Shall we — as some keep insisting — turn our back on the freedoms so many of us have fought for and died for? Shall we, in order to defeat those who would destroy us, become just like them? Shall we become a country in which no one is allowed to speak his or her mind because someone might disagree, because it might not be what someone in the government wants to hear? Have we become so unsure of ourselves that the only way we can defend ourselves is to lock up those with a different point of view? Shall we become the land of cowards and informants, spying on others in the dismal hope that it will prove there is no reason to spy on us? Shall we do this — turn our back on two hundred — more than two hundred — years of sacrifice and trial, give up the promise we once made to the world to be the 'last best hope of freedom' and go sniveling into the night, traitors to ourselves?"

He went on, challenging them, the crowd that filled the streets and the millions more watching it in their homes, to take themselves seriously, free citizens who would never yield to fear. There were those who could turn a crowd into a mob, seething with anger and ready to do violence to anyone who stood between it and what in its throbbing blood-blinded impulse it had to have. Browning had taken a crowd and taught it to rise above itself, become better than what each of those who stood there in the dying autumn light would have been on their own. He had given them something important in which to believe.

When it was over, when that vast, street-filling crowd began gradually to disperse, what was left was a sense of inevitability, a feeling that the future had become a well-established fact; not just that Thomas Browning would become a candidate for the presidency, but that the presidency was all but his: his by right, because no one else came close to having the courage and grace, the nerve and intelligence, the strength and foresight the presidency required. I had seen it once before, a long time ago, before I was old enough to vote, my freshman year in college, one cold dark night in Ann Arbor when John F. Kennedy stood on the steps of the student union and talked about the Peace Corps and how America could again bring hope to the world.

After giving that speech that afternoon, Browning gave another one that night in Chicago. The next day, Saturday, he visited three more cities and gave three more speeches, arguing with cheerful intensity for the kind of active vigorous government that made some Republicans wonder why he was not a Democrat and a great many Democrats wish he were. Relieved of the restraints of office, no longer required to lend his support to policies in which he did not fully believe, he seemed to look for the chance to be controversial, to say the things that, according to the traditional rules, the conventions that had come to dominate and to limit political thought, would destroy any political career.

"The president is preparing a new round of tax cuts, Mr. Vice President, and I . . ."

Browning bent forward, laid his hand gently on the moderator's arm and with a gleam in his eye suggested that he might want to address him in another way. "I'm no longer vice president. Perhaps you've heard: I retired."

This was one of the Sunday shows. Always pugnacious, sometimes argumentative, but only on rare occasions openly hostile, the moderator took the correction in stride. With a quick smile, he went on.

"The president is proposing new tax cuts. Tell us, Mr. Browning, as someone who hopes to take the Republican nomination away from the president, do you disagree with the administration on this very important question?"

"Yes," he said finally.

" 'Yes'?" repeated the moderator, breaking into a grin. He shrugged his shoulders and shook his head, peering intently at Browning, certain that he must want to add some modification, some cautionary condition that would leave him room for maneuver. "Yes?"

Browning stared right back at him. "Yes."

"You're against any more tax cuts?"

"That's correct. And not only that, certain taxes need to be raised."

"You're proposing to increase taxes?"

Browning's head came forward. His amused detachment was replaced by a look of serious engagement.

"We have schools to build; we have roads to repair; we need airports, railroads, public transportation of all descriptions; the entire infrastructure of the country needs to be rebuilt. We need police officers, firefighters; we need hospitals, doctors, nurses — a new health-care system that takes care of everyone and not just the steadily diminishing number of those who can afford to pay for it on their own. We have to pay for it — all of us; especially those who, as I have said before, owe the most because they have been given the most."

The moderator nodded, and then lowered his eyes in a way that suggested he was getting himself ready for a particularly unpleasant task.

"There is a trial going on in New York. Your college classmate Jamison Scott Haviland is charged with the murder of a young woman, Anna Malreaux, with whom you were at that time involved. This took place a long time ago, Christmas Eve way back in nineteen sixty-five, while you were still in law school. As you know, there have been endless rumors. Some have even suggested that you knew what happened and that, for whatever reason, you have all these years kept it covered up, lied about it in fact; called it an accident when you knew it was not."

He looked hard at Browning before he asked, "Are you worried that this trial will distract attention from everything you are trying to do — make people forget that you resigned the vice presidency to challenge the president for the nomination — make them wonder what really happened and why it has taken so long for it finally to come out?"

I was watching it on television in an apartment on the other side of the park from where Browning was now a resident instead of an occasional visitor. I had more than an ordinary interest in what Browning would say.

"There has never been anything to come out," insisted Browning. "The death of Anna Malreaux was a tragedy, a terrible tragedy. She was a remarkable young woman, one of the most remarkable people I have ever known. She fell out a window at the Plaza Hotel. It was an accident.

Haviland didn't murder her, and everyone knows it."

" 'And everyone knows it'? But then — if everyone knows it, Mr. Browning — how do you explain the fact that your former law school classmate is now on trial for the murder you say everyone knows did not happen?"

Browning slouched forward, his gaze riveted on the moderator. "They had to indict someone. They had to put someone on trial. You can't have a cover-up without a crime, and they have to have a cover-up, because without that they can't get me out of the race. They're not fools. It worked for them before."

The moderator gave Browning a searching look. "You're referring to those rumors in the last presidential primaries?"

"Yes, of course: the rumors that I had been involved in a murder," he said with open contempt. "And now that I'm again a candidate, here comes that same rumor all dressed up as a formal judicial proceeding, a trial for murder. I couldn't do anything about the rumor, but I can do something about this."

"You're going to testify — at the trial?"

The color in Browning's soft round cheeks deepened and spread. His eyes were focused straight ahead, angry and intense. His mouth took on the aspect of open belligerence.

"Of course I'm going to testify." There was a short, meaningful pause, before he added, "And after I do, I'm going to insist that there be an investigation into how and why this case was brought in the first place. Who do these people think they are? Do they really think they can do anything they like? Condemn an innocent man for a crime that not only did he not commit, but a crime that never happened? And all because they want to get me out of the way so I can't threaten what they are trying to do to this country?"

The moderator fixed Browning with a solemn, rigid stare. "Are you saying that the president of the United States is behind this? Are you saying that the president is involved in an attempt to convict an innocent man for a murder that never took place?"

"Just how far inside the White House this goes, I'm not prepared to say. Whether the people who did this were acting on specific instructions; whether they were acting with the knowledge of others; or whether they were acting entirely on their own, are all questions that need to be answered."

A strange expression, a kind of angry certainty, crossed Browning's mouth.

"The people who thought that the trial of Jamison Scott Haviland was going to be about me were wrong. It is going to be a trial about them, about what they have done, about the way they have abused the power they were given."

Half an hour after I turned off the television, half an hour after I began to wonder about how I was supposed to conduct a trial in which nothing less than the future of the presidency, and perhaps the country, hung in the balance, there was a knock on the door. It seemed strange, not that someone would come by on a Sunday morning, but that the doorman had not called first.

"Well, did you see it?" asked an ebullient Thomas Browning as he marched past me and took up a position in the middle of the marble foyer. He bent his head first one way, then the other, as if he were there to inspect the premises.

"It isn't too bad, is it?" he asked with a hopeful glance as he took a half step to the side. With a vague gesture of his small, babylike hand, he included the enormous living room that looked out onto the park.

"I'm not sure I needed all fourteen

rooms," I remarked as we took a couple of chairs on either side of the French doors that led to a small balcony. "And I don't have any idea what I'm supposed to do with the cook."

Browning sat with his elbows on the arms of the chair, both feet planted on the floor. A wry smile tugged at the corners of his mouth.

"I just thought that while you were here you ought to live as other people do in New York. Now," he went on with an eager look, "what did you think? You saw it, didn't you — what I said about the trial? Haviland can't fault me for that, can he? I said he didn't do it; I said that Annie's death was an accident."

His eyes were excited, intense, as if he could not wait to hear what I was going to say, what my reaction had been. A moment later his expression changed. He bolted out of the chair and with his hands behind his back began to pace rapidly around the room, weaving along in a series of consecutive half circles, starting, stopping, going first in one direction, then another.

"Everything depends on you now." He stopped abruptly, looked up from beneath his brow, searching my eyes to make sure I understood the importance, the monumental importance, of what I had to do. "Everything," he repeated, drawing his eyes inward. "Haviland will be a hero at the end of this: the innocent victim of a malevolent conspiracy."

He said this with such certainty, such confidence, that for a moment I almost thought he believed that Jimmy Haviland should be grateful for what had happened to him; that he was not a victim at all, but in some manner a beneficiary, of the attempt to discredit Thomas Browning.

"It's a terrible thing, of course; to go through something like this: to be accused of something you did not do. But it will turn out in the end. You'll see."

His eyes swept past the French doors, and then came back, caught by something he had seen, or something he had remembered.

"Were you there?" he asked with sudden interest. "Or were you still in court?"

"No, I wasn't there. I wish I had been," I admitted.

Browning nodded. "I wish you had been, too. I thought about that, about you being there. You told me once that you had been in Ann Arbor, that night in October, just weeks before the election, when Kennedy spoke. You told me how 'electric' it felt.

That was the word you used. That was what it felt like — over there — at the edge of the park, thousands of people in the streets: electric. All the energy from the crowd, the way it starts to belong to you, and then you know you can do anything you want with it, take it in any direction you choose; but you don't — unless you're one of those two-bit demagogues that only know to get the blood up, turn the crowd into some senseless mob. No, you feel the force of it, all those people waiting to be told something that will let them become better than they have been, better than they have been allowed to be; and it makes you better than you were, that demand that you give them the best of what you have, that you appeal to what is best in them. That is really what they are waiting for, you know — the chance to do something brave and noble and worth remembering; something important, something of value, something that will last."

Browning leaned against the door, and for a moment he appeared to be listening to himself, caught in the tumultuous noise of the vanished crowd. When his eyes came back around to mine, his look was sober, restrained.

"There is a chance I won't survive this,"

he said in a very matter-of-fact way. "There are people out there who think that Walker and all his right-wing friends are doing the work of God. In their demented minds I've become the Antichrist. You should see some of the letters. Makes your skin crawl."

"The Secret Service?" I asked, referring to the security detail assigned to protect him.

Browning shrugged. "Some. Not as much as when I was vice president, but some. I'm not worried about it. You can't be. You do what you have to. You certainly don't run off and hide somewhere because some mindless fanatic thinks that God came to him in the night and told him he had to put a bullet in the devil. But at the same time, you can't pretend that it could never happen. That's the reason why I want you to have this."

He reached inside his jacket for a sealed envelope that had my name typed on the front.

"If something happens to me, if they stop me, use what you find inside this any way you choose. But," he added with a cautionary glance, "it's only to be opened in the event of my death. Are we agreed?"

Browning shook my hand and started for the door. "I'm going to be quite busy," he remarked in a voice now filled with brisk efficiency. "Barely a moment to spare from here on out. But I'm always available for you. Anytime you like." With his hand on the door, he paused. "I assume you'll want to go over my testimony," he remarked, nodding gravely. "Just let me know."

He thought of something.

"You remember Elizabeth Hartley? You can always find me through her. She's involved in the campaign. You should have seen her face when I told her and the rest of them that I was going to resign. It took everything she had to hide her astonishment." He slowly shook his head, a glint of nostalgia in his eyes. "I suppose it's important when you're that age to believe that you have all the experience you need and that you have nothing important left to learn." He placed his hand on my shoulder. "Is that what we were like then, always so certain of ourselves?"

He seemed genuinely interested, as if he could not quite remember. Before I could answer, or think what it was I could answer, he shrugged his shoulders. A look of weary resignation burdened his eyes.

"I suppose we had to be. If you wait long enough, you discover that you can't really be certain of anything, can you?"

19

Outside the building, waiting for the private car that picked me up each morning so I would not run the danger of being late, I felt a sudden foreboding, a kind of panic. The prosecution was about to call its first witness and I still did not have a sense of the case, a sense of what Caminetti thought he could prove. More than that, I could not stop wondering what was inside that sealed envelope I had promised not to open except in the event of Thomas Browning's death.

The car, a large four-door Mercedes, a somber, understated black, pulled up to the curb. Despite the crushing traffic, it was right on time. With the engine running, the driver, an African from Namibia, bolted out the front and hurried around to open the door.

" 'Morning, Mr. Antonelli," he said in a husky, even-cadenced voice. He bounced on the balls of his feet while I got in, drawing a deep breath of the autumn air as if he were out in the country instead of parked at the edge of a congested, slow-crawling city street.

In the quiet luxury of the leather-cushioned ride, I asked a few listless questions and then let him tell me for the third or fourth time the great mysterious secret of American finance and how capitalism would eventually conquer the world. I liked hearing him talk, the strong, assertive way he made his point; the way his eyes flashed with the shrewd enthusiasm of a man who believed he had found the promised land, and that it was not America, but the idea America had put inside his mind.

"All my business is here in Manhattan, because Manhattan is where the rich people are. I don't live in Manhattan; I live in the Bronx because its cheaper there than Queens. I have a wife and a couple of kids. Two-bedroom place; it's pretty nice. I work where things are expensive; I live where things are cheap. Maybe I could live a little better — live over in Queens; but I need to save money so I can go back home and have a business of my own. There is a big difference between my country and here." He caught my eye in the rearview mirror. "Borrowed money."

He said it as if that two-word phrase was a talisman, a magic chant that, repeated with the proper gesture and the proper respect, would produce all of what you could ever want.

"Borrowed money — that's the reason you're rich and we're poor. I want a business: buy things made in China and sell them in a store. Costs thirty, maybe forty thousand to start. But no one has anything — I don't have anything — and with no collateral, no loan. But here I drive around in this expensive car and make a lot more money than I could at home. How do I have the car? I borrow the money! How do I borrow the money without collateral? The car. I make the payments, I pay the interest, and if I don't, the bank takes back the car. Same thing with a house. They loan you money here because they can always take back the house. Borrowed money, it's the best thing there is."

"But you're going to go back?" I asked, fascinated by the way he saw the world. "When you have enough to start that other business?"

With a huge white glittering smile, he threw back his head and laughed. "Too damn crowded here; too damn cold in the winter; everything costs too much. In my country, fifty cents buys you a good meal.

A dollar? A rich man's feast! It's all a question of finance," he added in the confidential tone of a man used to giving advice.

The street in front of the courthouse had been cordoned off. Police in riot gear, nightsticks at the ready, had formed a double line along the bottom of the courthouse steps. Protesters marched back and forth, shouting and waving placards, denouncing with self-righteous fury the blatant immorality of the things, whether gay rights or abortion, Thomas Browning refused to oppose.

"I'll take you 'round to Columbus Park," said the driver with a worried glance. "You can go in the back."

"No, it's all right," I said with false bravado. "I'll get out here."

He stopped the car and turned around. "Look at those people. Look at their faces; look at their eyes. People like that, doesn't take much to get the blood up. I'm taking you around back."

Pushed back by the police, the crowd surged into the street, bodies flying everywhere. Twisted faces pressed against the glass; fists began pounding against the doors. Ducking his head down between his shoulders, the driver hit the gas. The car shot forward, straight to the corner where, with tires squealing, we turned up the street.

"Call me when you're finished," he said when he dropped me across the street from the courthouse, in front of Columbus Park. With a tremendous grin, he added, "Don't worry, I'll give you a very good rate."

In contrast to the violent commotion outside, the courtroom on the fifteenth floor was all civility and quiet. Sitting next to Jimmy Haviland, I tried not to daydream through the tedious and mechanical testimony of the prosecution's first witness, a woman who knew nothing about the crime. A man was on trial for murder; the prosecution had the burden of proving that the woman he was accused of killing was actually dead. Dr. Alice Barnham worked in the coroner's office. She had reviewed the files.

"And as determined by the coroner's office, Dr. Barnham, what was the cause of death?" Caminetti turned away from the witness and looked at the jury.

Alice Barnham was a heavyset woman in her early fifties. She was not fat or round; there was no extraneous flesh hanging from her arms or wattled around her neck. She was simply large, with broad shoulders, wide hips and thick, muscular hands.

Her eyes were cold and gray. She was all business.

"Massive injuries to the head."

Caminetti's eyes stayed on the jury. "Consistent with a fall?"

"Yes," replied Alice Barnham in the gravelly voice of a woman who had once smoked several packs of cigarettes a day. She could not sit demurely on the witness stand, one leg crossed over the other; she bent forward, her elbows, wedged close to her sides, resting on the arms of the chair. "There is no question that the decedent, Anna Malreaux, died from the fall. None whatsoever."

Stern and implacable, his eyes fixed on the jury, Caminetti asked whether there had been any wound or injury on the body that might have been sustained before the fall. Barnham answered that there had been no stab wounds, no gunshot wounds, nothing to suggest that there had been a violent fight.

"And was anything found on the victim's body — skin under her fingernails — anything that suggested that there had been any kind of struggle before she fell?"

"No, there was not."

Caminetti looked away from the jury. With a cursory thin-lipped smile, he signaled to the witness that he was through.

"Were you in the coroner's office when the autopsy was done on Anna Malreaux?" I asked as I rose from my chair.

Caminetti leaped to his feet. "Your Honor, she already testified she's been in the office for eight years." A jackal-like smile cut across his mouth. "I don't know about Mr. Antonelli, but I think the rest of us can do the math."

"This is cross-examination, Your Honor . . ." I gave Caminetti an evil smile of my own. "I don't know about Mr. Caminetti, but I think the rest of us know what that means."

Judge Scarborough rolled his eyes, drew the ever-present handkerchief swiftly across his nose, and grinned at the jury as if he had been called upon to referee a fight between two overgrown, unruly boys.

"If you wish to make an objection, Mr. Caminetti, rise and make one. If you wish to comment on the way the other side is conducting its examination of a wit-ness . . . Try not to, or we will be here all year. Now, do you wish to make an objec-tion, Mr. Caminetti? Or were you simply, with your usual goodwill, trying to help Mr. Antonelli move things along?"

Plunging his hands into his pants

pockets, Caminetti moved his closed mouth back and forth across his teeth. His eyes narrowed into a pensive stare.

"Mr. Caminetti?" the judge insisted.

Caminetti shrugged his shoulders. "I can't decide."

Scarborough's right eyebrow shot up. "You can't decide?"

Caminetti's hands came out of his pockets; he began to wave them in the air as he took one quick step forward and then, just as quickly, one step back. "I can't decide. I'd like to be helpful, but I think I have to object."

"Then you wish to object?"

"Yes, Your Honor."

"You object to Mr. Antonelli's question?"

"Yes, Your Honor."

"On what grounds, Mr. Caminetti?"

"The question was already asked, already answered."

"But that objection can only be raised when the question has been asked by the same party who asked it before. The party asking it is compelled to take the answer given. But here . . ."

"Are you overruling my objection, Your Honor?" asked Caminetti, shifting his weight from one foot to the other.

Astonished, then amused by the sheer temerity of the district attorney's impatient demand that he, the judge, get to the point, Scarborough eyed him with suspicion.

"Yes, Mr. Caminetti, I am indeed. Objection overruled."

"In that case, Your Honor, I've changed my mind."

"You've changed your mind?" asked Scarborough, more than puzzled, intrigued. "About what, Mr. Caminetti?"

"About what I want to do. I don't want to object; I want to be helpful. Thank you, Your Honor." Caminetti smiled to himself as he sat down and waited for what I was going to ask next.

The jury seemed to enjoy Caminetti's little show. They liked the good-natured banter, the way he took center stage; they liked the fact that he was not the least intimidated by the judge, the other lawyer, or anything else that went on in court. Then, before they could decide that on second thought he had gone too far, he again got to his feet.

"Sorry, Your Honor. I got a little carried away. No disrespect intended. Not to the court, certainly not to Mr. Antonelli."

One innocent insignificant question, and

Caminetti had turned everything upside down; one stupid question had become one short step to a trapdoor. I tried to ignore it. With earnest curiosity, I repeated the question.

"No, I was not with the coroner's office then."

"Your testimony concerning the cause of death is based on your review of the records kept by the coroner's office in that case?"

"Yes."

"In the years during which you have been with the coroner's office, have you conducted autopsies of your own?"

"Yes, of course." Her square chin came up a bare fraction of an inch. She conducted a kind of inquisition with her eyes, searching for the first hint that I might be about to question her competence.

"Have any of those autopsies included deaths like this one, where someone died from a fall?"

"Yes."

I was standing directly behind my empty chair. The morning light fell through the window high above the jury box and lit the gray floor between us, making the distance from the counsel table to the witness stand seem even greater than it was.

"I assume some of these were victims of homicide, pushed, or thrown, from some lethal height, murdered as surely as if the killer had used a gun or a knife?"

"Yes," she replied in a tentative voice. She was too intelligent not to suspect that I had something else in mind, that I had a reason to ask this otherwise trivial question.

"Should I also assume that some of these deaths were suicides: someone jumped off a bridge, or a building perhaps?"

She nodded silently, then remembered she had to answer out loud. "Yes."

"May I further assume that some of these deaths were accidental? No one pushed them or threw them, and they certainly did not do it on purpose themselves. They fell, they tripped, they stumbled, they blacked out, they had a coronary. In other words, Dr. Barnham, they fell to their death by accident. You have had occasion to examine their bodies as well, correct?"

"Yes, that's true; and yes, I have — conducted autopsies on accident victims, I mean."

I lowered my eyes, pausing, as if to consider quite carefully what I was going to ask next. When I raised my eyes, I cocked my head and studied her closely.

"According to the reports you mentioned — by the way, did you also review for your testimony here today the police report that was filed at the time?" I asked this so quickly she did not have time to think.

"Yes, I did."

"Good. Now, as I was about to ask, you testified there were no indications that Anna Malreaux had suffered any injuries except those caused by the fall?"

"Yes."

"And there was no evidence to indicate that immediately prior to her fall she had been involved in a struggle — a struggle that you might expect if someone were trying to shove you out a window and you were trying to resist — is that correct?"

"Yes, that's correct."

"In other words, Dr. Barnham, according to the evidence discovered by the coroner's office, there is nothing to distinguish the death of Anna Malreaux from the death of any other person who has fallen accidentally out a window, isn't that correct?"

Caminetti was on his feet, objecting. Scarborough overruled him and instructed the witness to answer.

"The coroner's report of Anna Malreaux's death is entirely consistent with death by accident, correct?"

"Consistent with an accident, consistent with a homicide. She died by a fall, whatever the cause of that fall might have been," replied Alice Barnham with a grim, satisfied smile.

"Consistent with an accident," I repeated forcefully. "And consistent with that other report you read as well, isn't it? Isn't that what the police concluded, in nineteen sixty-five, when it happened: that the death of Anna Malreaux was an accident, not a homicide?"

Caminetti was again on his feet, but before he could open his mouth to object, I waved my arm and after a last withering glance at the imperturbable Dr. Barnham, announced that I was finished with the prosecution's first witness.

Barnham's testimony had taken all morning. During the lunch recess I wondered whom Caminetti would call next and whether it might be one of the names on that list that had been given to Gisela to give to me. The list was tantalizing, but there was nothing on it I could use. It was no more than an anonymous record of transactions that had no more value as evidence than an anonymous call claiming that someone had committed a crime.

Only if I was desperate, convinced that it was the one chance left not to lose, could I confront a witness with something like this, insist it proved bribery and demand that he confess. There had to be corroboration, a way to prove that it was real, that it meant what it said. Gisela's friend, whoever he was, had to give me more.

When trial started again in the afternoon, Caminetti called his second witness. It was not one of those mentioned on the list, and I breathed a little easier knowing that I still had time.

"The People call Albert Cohn," announced Caminetti without looking up from the file folder that lay open on the table below him.

I glanced over my shoulder to get a look at Cohn as he came striding down the center aisle. The door had swung shut behind him, and I started to turn away. Out of the corner of my eye, I saw Gisela sitting in the audience in back. She smiled at me, and before I knew what was happening I felt my cheeks begin to burn. Like an awkward, hot-blooded adolescent, afraid that someone watching might discover what was going on, I had begun to blush. It struck me as so incongruous, so wild and outlandish, such a stark departure from my worldly, sometimes cynical life, that the slight smile that had started onto my mouth broke to pieces in a gawky grin. Embarrassed twice over, I began inexplicably to laugh.

Albert Cohn stopped in his tracks, two steps short of the clerk who was waiting to administer the oath. He looked across at me, wondering what he had done. Caminetti gave me a puzzled, impatient glance. Judge Scarborough did not miss anything that went on in his courtroom. By his amused expression I knew that he had seen what had happened and understood what he saw.

The witness took the oath, and Caminetti went right to work.

"Name for the record," he said, nodding quickly to set the tempo of the question and, if he could, the reply.

Albert Cohn was not the kind of man to be rushed. In his early sixties, he was just under six feet tall, with round shoulders and a head that was partially bald. His nose was long and straight, and his eyes had a definite intelligence and were evenly spaced. His mouth was generous, quick to smile, but though he might do it often, he gave the impression he never did it for very long. Albert Cohn, always civil, would not be caught playing the fool.

"How are you employed, Mr. Cohn?"

Cohn sat on the witness chair, one leg crossed over the other, both hands in his lap. He wore an expensive tan-colored suit and an understated tie.

"I am general counsel for the Stern Motor Company."

"Your office is here, in New York?"

"That's correct."

"How long have you been employed by Stern Motors?"

Caminetti stood midway between the counsel table and the witness stand. Twisting his jaw a little to the side, he clicked his teeth together. It was a nervous habit, barely noticeable except for the monotonous frequency with which it was done.

"How long as general counsel, or how long with Stern Motors?" Cohn wanted to know.

Caminetti gave him a sharp glance. "Both."

"Nearly twenty-five years with the company; almost twenty as general counsel."

"You were hired by Thomas Browning?"

"Yes, Mr. Browning hired me."

"Hired you, then made you general counsel?"

"Yes."

Caminetti spread his feet apart, lowered

his head into his shoulders and fixed the witness with a bellicose stare. "In your capacity as general counsel — or, as I believe you were before, assistant general counsel — did you hire the defendant, Jamison Scott Haviland, to a position with Stern Motors?"

Under the bare shadow of a smile, Albert Cohn stared back. "No."

Caminetti's jaw dropped. "No?" He took a step forward, an aggressive, instinctive act. "You didn't hire Mr. Haviland to do any work for the company?"

Pushing out his chin, Cohn snapped back, "That was not your question. You asked if I had given him a position. I did not. Then you asked if I had hired him to do some work. I did."

Caminetti threw up his hands. "Didn't hire for a position, but hired for work." His eyes lit up. "I see," he said, nodding. "Because he was put on retainer. He was not an employee, so he didn't have a position. Explain that."

"Explain what?"

"Having someone on retainer. What does it mean? You're at Stern Motors. Haviland is a lawyer in private practice. Stern Motors has him on retainer. What does it mean?"

Caminetti lowered his eyes and began to pace back and forth, three steps one way, three steps back. Cohn watched him for a moment, and then looked at the jury.

"At Stern Motors we have, like many large corporations, a general counsel's office that takes care of any legal matter affecting the company. We have a staff of attorneys that do most of the work in-house; but, again like many large companies, we have attorneys all over the country, and in our case, all over the world, who from time to time represent the interests of the company in legal proceedings that take place within their respective jurisdictions."

Cohn, the seasoned professional, leaned across the arm of the chair, addressing the jury with the relaxed familiarity of one who has spent a lifetime describing complicated things in the simple, easy-to-understand language of the uninstructed. Several of the jurors leaned forward; all of them listened intently.

"To give you just one example. We recently had a case in which a woman, whose husband had unfortunately died when his car — one of ours — plunged down a hillside, sued the company for defective design. It was a rather unusual case," he went on, a look of amusement in his eyes.

Caminetti had stopped pacing. With his hands clutched behind his back, he looked up.

"The man — the woman's husband — was in the front seat of the car with a woman, not his wife. It was late at night. It was dark. The car was parked in a remote area at the edge of a steep ravine." Caminetti blinked his eyes. "The two of them, the man and the woman not his wife, were apparently so engrossed in whatever they were doing that they did not notice that they had somehow managed to disengage the handbrake. On that particular model it is located directly between the two bucket seats. It was the woman's claim — it is the wife we are now talking about — that had the handbrake been located under the dashboard to the left of the steering column, the way it is on many other models, including many of our own, none of this would have happened; and that, moreover, infidelity — that was the word her lawyer used in her complaint — being a common event and therefore a foreseeable use of the front seat of a car, the manufacturer should be liable for the damage suffered by this woman because of the loss of her husband."

A droll smile on his lips, Cohn raised his head to a jaunty angle. "We frankly don't have much experience of this sort of thing. But we do have a firm on retainer in Los Angeles, where this happened, and I suppose because everyone out there spends so much time in their cars, they did not seem to think it that unusual at all."

"That's enough!" cried Caminetti in pure frustration. "I think we understand. You have lawyers — in private practice — on retainer. You pay them a certain amount, and then they bill against that amount — correct? But they get the money whether they do any work or not — correct?"

Clasping his hands together, Cohn faced straight ahead. "That's correct."

"And the defendant was one of those lawyers?"

"Yes."

"Did you hire him on your own, or were you asked to do so by Thomas Browning?"

"Mr. Browning was the president of the company. He was also a highly trained lawyer. He approved every decision to put someone on retainer."

Caminetti was beside himself. He looked up at the bench, then over at the jury; he stood for a moment balanced on the balls of his feet, peering out at the crowd. He shut his eyes and grit his teeth so hard his head began to vibrate. When he finally turned and faced the witness, his voice came out like a hushed high-pitched scream.

"Did Mr. Browning ask you to hire — to put on retainer — the defendant, or did he not?"

Cohn looked at him with studied indifference. "Yes, I believe he did."

"You believe he did," mumbled Caminetti to himself as he started all over that endless, relentless march back and forth in front of the jury box. "How many years ago? Twenty-five, or nearly that — right?" he asked, pulling himself up short.

"Yes, I believe . . ."

"And for all those years he's been paid — what? — forty, fifty, sixty thousand a year?"

"Yes, I believe . . ."

"Whether he did anything or not?" A sly grin eased its way onto Caminetti's angry mouth.

"There were years he did quite a lot, years in which he took on a number of cases . . ."

"And got paid at an hourly rate for everything that went beyond the normal retainer he received?"

Cohn bent his head sharply, raking Caminetti with his eyes. "That's the way a retainer works."

"I understand." The grin became a little broader, a little more sure of itself. "The years he did quite a lot — years in which he represented Stern Motors as defense counsel in cases in which the company was being sued — cars with defective brakes that went off cliffs, that sort of thing?"

There was a titter of laughter in the courtroom. The jurors tried not to smile. Cohn did not change expression. Serious and alert, he took the question straight on.

"Mr. Haviland was the defense counsel in a number of cases for Stern Motors. He did quite well."

"I didn't ask you how he did," Caminetti snapped. "But so long as you brought it up, didn't he lose more than he won?"

"I'm afraid I wouldn't be able to quantify it in that way. And besides, Mr. Caminetti, you and I both know that whether the case is won or lost isn't always the best method of deciding who the best attorney was."

Caminetti sneered. "The loser can call himself anything he likes. Back to why Mr. Haviland was hired. He and Browning were in law school together — right?"

"Yes."

Caminetti stood at the end of the jury box, his right hand on the railing. A combative look creased his sharp-angled face.

"You know why we're here — the defendant is charged with murder. Anna Malreaux fell from a window during a party, a party that had gone on for days, a party in which the quantity of alcohol was more than what gets used in a typical bar on New Year's Eve, a party . . ."

"Objection!" I thundered as I sprang to my feet. "There has been no evidence offered to support that assertion."

Caminetti turned on me with a vengeance. "You saying there wasn't any liquor there, that no one drank?"

Scarborough quickly intervened. "The issue, Mr. Caminetti, is whether the prosecution has yet introduced any evidence that anyone did. You have not, and until you do you may not ask the witness a question that assumes such evidence."

Caminetti took it in silence and proceeded as if he had never been stopped.

"You've been in the company a long time, Mr. Cohn. Isn't this the kind of thing — a girl getting killed — that would have done incalculable harm to the company, to the reputation of the young man — the heir apparent — who threw the party, who was in charge of it, who let it get out of control? And wouldn't that explain all those payments, payments made for years in which there really wasn't any work, payments made even for cases he lost? Wasn't that the reason, the real reason for those payments? To make sure that Jamison Scott Haviland would never do something stupid and start admitting what he had done — killed a woman with whom they had both been involved during some drunken orgy that Thomas Browning should have stopped?"

I was shouting my objection while Caminetti shouted all the way to the end, putting before the jury and the world the motive that had presumably made Thomas Browning first a witness to a murder and then a conspirator and a liar. He had done it despite my objection and despite the rules. The jury had heard it and so had everyone else, and nothing, not the fury of the judge who threatened sanctions for a repetition of what he did not hesitate to call "a cheap prosecutorial trick," nor the measured instruction to the jury to ignore every word of what the prosecutor had said, was going to clear it from their minds.

It was there, burning hot and deep in their collective memory, an ineradicable, permanent scar, a double badge of guilt worn not just by Thomas Browning, but by Jimmy Haviland as well.

20

I lay in bed, gazing across the room, the memory of what had happened in court that day vivid in my mind.

"That was what was always missing," I mused out loud. "The motive, the reason why Browning would cover it up. Why would he protect someone who killed the girl he loved? If Haviland pushed Annie out the window, why would Browning let him get away with it? I did not think it through; I did not try to imagine what motive Browning might have had to keep quiet about it. Caminetti is no fool. By giving Browning a motive for the cover-up, everyone jumps to the conclusion that there was a cover-up and that there must have been a crime. If Browning is guilty, then Haviland must be, too.

"Caminetti is smart, as shrewd as they come. Nothing gets to him; nothing bothers him. He does what he has to and doesn't think about it twice. Today, when it was over — after that screaming match

502

we had at the end, when you would have thought we were ready to go after each other with our bare hands — I was closing my briefcase, getting ready to leave, when he comes over and asks me if I'd had the chance to try Carmine's and what I thought about the food."

Sitting on an armless chair, Gisela pulled her stockings up. Then she rose and with both hands carefully smoothed out the front of her dress. She had not heard a word I had said.

"Are you going to stay in bed all evening?"

A lush, provocative smile, a promise of more pleasure to come, slipped as easily across her mouth as the stockings had onto her long slim legs. She stood in front of the floor-length mirror, tossing her head to one side and then the other, giving herself a cool, appraising glance. The smile, suspended while she studied herself in the mirror, was back on her face when she turned around and began to laugh.

"You promised me dinner, but I think all you wanted was sex."

My head propped up on two pillows, I felt like I was floating, caught in the slow-flowing current of a wide-awake dream. All the energy I had lost seemed to have been given to her. She stooped and gathered up my clothes and then dumped them unceremoniously on top of me.

"Get dressed," she insisted, glancing over her shoulder as she left the room.

We had dinner at a French restaurant a few blocks away. Our table was one in a long row of tables the same size, where we were one of a dozen couples having an intimate dinner, touching elbows with strangers on each side. With the sensitive looks of an aspiring young actor, the waiter, wedged sideways between the curved wooden chairs, scribbled down our order and vanished into the noisy crowd.

"The answer is yes," said Gisela, bending forward, her hands, folded on the table, touching mine. Her dark lashes fluttered as she looked down and then, having collected her thoughts, looked up. "If you still want me to."

In the dim yellow-gray light, her eyes looked more burgundy than black, and she looked less like a full-grown woman than a young girl, a girl who spoke in such low modest tones that I had to strain to catch each word. It seemed impossible that this was the same woman who just an hour earlier had behaved in my bed like a courtesan of vast experience and not an ounce of shame. I had known many women, perhaps more than I should, but Gisela was the first European. She had made me feel like an innocent with inhibitions I had not realized I had. I was still so mesmerized, so captivated by everything about her — the way she looked, the way she moved, the funny way she spoke and the earthy way she laughed — that I did not immediately remember what I had asked.

"If you still want me to stay with you, at the apartment, until the end of the trial."

"Only until the end of the trial?" I asked, wondering in my American way why anything had to end. If the present was good, the future could only be better. When she looked at me with that dark-eyed stare, I was already hearing the words that would tell me that she wanted that too. Instead, she talked about the practical limits of what we should expect.

"You're not going to stay in New York, and neither am I. You'll go back to San Francisco, and I'll go back to Washington; or perhaps, at a time not too far away, I'll go back to Berlin."

My romantic irresponsibility was still intact. I wanted her as much — no, more! — than I had wanted anyone before. I could not remember anyone but her; my memory had stopped, shut out everything, the moment we had started taking off our clothes.

"You could come to San Francisco; I could stay in New York. Why rule out anything at the beginning? Why not let things just take their course? Why not wait and see?"

"Why not see things the way they are?"

I started to object, but she stopped me with a smile. "Yes, all right; if you wish. See how things are when the trial is over and it's time to leave. But in the meantime, spend your days in court, and your nights with me. It's better to live in the present, I think; not worry too much about what might happen next. It's a problem with you Americans, you know: always worried so much about the future that by the time you get there you don't have a past."

We finished dinner close to ten and started walking back to the apartment. The temperature had fallen, and a bitter wind blew down the avenues and howled through the crosstown streets. It lashed my face and whipped against my eyes. Without an overcoat I was freezing half to death. I pulled Gisela close to protect her with my arm. With her face buried against my chest, we moved bent against the wind. Gisela could not see anything and laughed as she stumbled backwards up the street. We passed a newsstand that was shutting down for the night. I barely saw it, the headline screaming across the front page of every paper, stacked in a bundle held in place by a metal weight. Gisela's muffled laughter went an octave higher as I stopped and, my eyes fixed on what I had only half seen, drew her forward as I started back.

The vendor had a fleshy, whiskered face and a red, bulbous nose. His eyes were narrow, without expression except for the tough dull glimmer that reflected the hard-paid price of staying alive. I gave him twice what the paper cost and turned away before he could make change.

"What is it?" asked Gisela in a girlish voice, clinging to me as if she were afraid she would be blown away if she let go.

"The chief justice. He's in Bethesda. They think he might die."

We reached the apartment building. Inside the lobby, Gisela stamped her feet, took off her leather gloves and rubbed her hands against her frozen cheeks.

"May I see?" I gave her the newspaper, which she read until the elevator opened on my floor. "There must be something on the news. Can we turn it on?"

The facts, though fragmentary, painted a bleak picture. The chief justice had collapsed during a session of the court. He had started to challenge some assertion made by one of the lawyers during the last oral argument of the day when, according to those who were there, he stopped in midsentence, forced a smile, explained that he was not feeling well, turned to the associate justice who sat on his left, and then fell to the floor. He was taken by ambulance to the Bethesda Naval Hospital where, in a carefully worded statement, it was announced that "the chief justice is resting comfortably." Nothing was said about what caused the collapse or how life-threatening his condition might be. It was understood — and this was how every physician asked by the various news media to comment prefaced what they said — that because the chief justice was eighty-three, whatever had happened was serious.

"Cancer," I said out loud. Gisela, sitting next to me on the sofa, looked up. "He's dying of cancer."

"You know this?"

Too late, I remembered how I had heard it. For a moment I was afraid that she might feel compelled to use it. We exchanged a glance, and I knew that anything I told her would stay between us.

"Browning?" she asked, just to be sure. "Do you think the White House knows?" The question answered itself. "Yes, of course they must. So then, if that happens — if there is a vacancy . . ." Her eyes, quick and alert, caught a glimpse of the truth. "Reynolds. With Reynolds as chief justice, and with another conservative like Reynolds to take his place, the court becomes . . ."

Gisela got to her feet, a determined look on her face. I had seen it before, that look. Once she decided there was something she had to do, there was a forcefulness, an almost brittle stiffness, in her manner.

"I have to go back to Washington."

"Tonight? To cover that?" I asked, gesturing toward the flickering images on the television screen. "Go in the morning if you have to go. Take an early flight. There isn't anything you can do about it now. And what about the trial? Who is going to cover that?"

Gisela had moved next to a window that looked out over Central Park. She glanced at her watch, calculating the time it would take to get to the airport and what time a late-night flight would get her in.

"Stay tonight; go early in the morning," I

said, thinking about what I would miss if she was not here.

Her mind was still on the story she had to cover and what it meant. "The trial and what's happened are both connected," she remarked with a preoccupied look as she again checked the time.

She caught herself. The taut, concentrated expression on her mouth fell away, replaced by an embarrassed, apologetic grin. She came over to the sofa and perched on the edge of it, her legs pressed closed together and her hands resting in her lap.

"You're right. I'll go in the morning. I can get an early flight."

"What did you mean — just now, when you said they were connected, the trial and what's happened to the chief justice?"

There was a slight, sideways movement of her head. She looked at me with a baffled expression.

"I forgot," she said, breaking into a smile. "You have been spending all your time either in court or in bed." I laughed and started to reach for her, but she shook her head. "They're connected — *intertwined* might be a better word. If Haviland is convicted, Browning is finished." She gave me a searching glance. "If Haviland is guilty, then Browning covered it up. It's what you said to me a few minutes ago, only the other way around. And if Browning can't go on, then Walker will control the court — yes?"

She had left something out. "But if the chief justice dies before the election, it doesn't matter what happens to Browning. Walker can name whom he wants."

She shook her head vigorously. "No, that's not true — or it might not be true. That's part of the story I want to find out. There are people in the Senate — Republicans — who won't vote to confirm Reynolds, or anyone like him, while there is a chance Browning might win. They'll make sure the Senate doesn't do anything. They won't take Reynolds unless they have to; they certainly won't take Reynolds while there is still a chance Walker might lose. That's the story I need to write about: what will happen if the chief justice doesn't survive this term of the court."

She suddenly thought of something. She looked at me with a different interest than she had before.

"You could say that not only the presidency, but also what happens to the Supreme Court now depends almost entirely on you."

When Gisela left in the still-dark morning, she woke me long enough to say goodbye with a kiss.

"I'll be back Monday at the latest. Call me tonight and tell me everything that happens today."

That gentle request that I tell her what went on that day at Jimmy Haviland's trial stayed with me. As I listened to each witness testify, I found myself thinking of how I could later describe it to her.

Dressed in another of his dark, ill-fitting suits, Bartholomew Caminetti jerked to his feet when the honorable Charles F. Scarborough entered the hushed and crowded courtroom. Caminetti's head bounced from side to side, as if without some gesture of impatience on his part, things would never speed up. He opened his mouth and held it there, waiting for the judge to take his place on the bench, ready to announce in a rapid-fire dull monotone the name of the next witness for the prosecution.

"Mary Beth Chandler."

Scarborough seemed to take a certain twisted pleasure in slowing him down. "Mr. Caminetti?"

Caminetti catapulted out of the chair almost before he had sat down again. "Your Honor?"

"I assume you mean to call this person as a witness?"

Caminetti glanced toward the double doors through which a middle-aged woman, tall and pampered, with a thin mouth and razor-sharp eyes, had just entered the courtroom. She was here, she was on her way to the stand. Caminetti looked up at the bench and shrugged.

"You failed to mention that," said Scarborough with a wry grin. "You said the name, nothing more."

"Why else would I . . . ?" An explanation would only waste more time. "The People call Mary Beth Chandler," said Caminetti, staring in blank-eyed disbelief.

A cursory nod and an occasional slight inflection of her voice the only gestures she allowed herself, Mary Beth Chandler answered each question with an economy of words that, by the end of her testimony, had even Caminetti in awe. She held herself with a cold reserve. She was not here because she wanted to be; she had no interest in what was going on. She answered each question and never once looked either at the jury or at the courtroom crowd. She had been at the party at the Plaza that Christmas Eve, and she had seen the defendant, Jamison Scott Haviland, talking with Anna Malreaux.

"That was on the eighth floor of the Plaza Hotel, Christmas Eve — December twenty-fourth — nineteen sixty-five?" Caminetti had to establish the fact that Haviland was there.

"Yes."

"Did you also see Thomas Browning there as well?"

"Yes."

"The three of them — Haviland, Browning, Anna Malreaux — were in the same room at the same time?"

"Yes."

I knew that she was married to a well-known senior partner in one of the large investment houses, the private institutions that manage much of the world's wealth; I knew that she was one of the women no one who wanted to make a mark in New York society would ever dare cross; I knew all that, but seeing her in person, sitting a few short steps away, I began to wonder if there was not something else I knew as well.

"We've met before, haven't we?" I asked as I rose in response to Judge Scarborough's invitation to take the witness on cross. I buttoned my jacket and centered my tie. "The summer before Annie

Malreaux's tragic death."

She was not willing to admit the possibility. She looked right through me, as if I were invisible; the way, I imagine, she looked at anyone she did not know, or did not like. Smiling to myself, I insisted that I was right.

"Sometime in June, I think it was; one evening at Maxwell's Plum. Yes, I'm sure of it now. There were about a dozen people, all friends of Thomas Browning. He was sitting at the end of the table. I was the last to arrive. I was clerking that summer at a Wall Street firm. Browning was sitting there at the end of the table, and you were sitting either just to his right or just to his left — I don't remember which. All I remember is that he spent most of his time talking to you."

She did not answer; she did not say a word. With bored indifference she waited for a question that had something to do with the case. I raised my head and with a thin smile let her wonder what I was going to do next.

"You didn't know Thomas Browning at Harvard, did you? You didn't go to law school?"

"No, I . . ."

"And you didn't know Anna Malreaux,

did you?" I was guessing, but I would have been surprised had I been wrong. Browning had a talent for segregating his friends. "She was at Harvard; you weren't there. That's correct, isn't it?" I asked with a degree of indifference to rival her own.

"Yes, I . . ."

"Yes, you knew him before that. You've known him, if I'm not mistaken, from sometime before he went to Harvard Law. You met him, if I'm not mistaken, when he was an undergraduate, or perhaps even before that." I was leaning against the corner railing of the jury box, my right foot crossed casually over my left. "You were living in New York, isn't that right?"

"Yes, that's . . ."

"Well, it doesn't really matter when you met him," I remarked as I walked away from the jury. "The only reason you're here today is to tell us that you saw Thomas Browning and Anna Malreaux and . . ." I stopped at a point equidistant from the witness stand and the counsel table where Jimmy Haviland sat alone. "Have you ever met the defendant, Jamison Scott Haviland? Let me rephrase that," I said, suppressing a smile as I shot a sidelong glance at the jury. "Do you remember ever having met him?"

"No," she replied, decidedly unamused.

"But you remember, after all these years, seeing two people you did not know, that you never met, talking to each other during a party at which there must have been — how many? — a hundred, two hundred people, going in and out." Before she could answer, I made a quarter turn and looked straight at her. "Are you sure we never met?"

She was not going to answer this time, either; but I did not give her the choice. "Your Honor, if you would instruct the witness."

"No, I don't recall that we've ever met," she said, her eyes cold and impenetrable.

"Not at Maxwell's Plum, that day in June?"

"No."

I stared right at her, a small, triumphant smile slanting across my mouth. "And not on December twenty-fourth of that same year, at that party given by Thomas Browning, where I was as well?"

It had no effect on her, none at all. It had become second nature to her, that look that shielded her from everything and everyone she did not want to know.

"You testified that you saw the defendant and Anna Malreaux 'talking.' Did you hear what they were saying?"

"No," she said in a vacant, almost disembodied voice.

"You testified that you saw Thomas Browning in the same room. Mr. Caminetti did not ask you if, when you saw them, the three of them were alone. So I will. Were there other people in the room at the time?"

"I'm not sure."

"You're not sure. I see," I said, shaking my head at her proud defiance, at the way she limited each answer to the bare minimum of what it should be. "Humor us, Mrs. Chandler; indulge us in the perhaps vain belief that you don't really think a court of law, in which a man is on trial for his life, is a complete waste of your time, better spent, no doubt, shopping for a new bracelet or a new pair of shoes!"

It worked. She came unglued.

"How dare you!" she cried, bending forward as if she wanted to come after me with her long, sharp nails. "Who do you think you are to talk to me like that? Who do you . . ."

"I think I'm the attorney for the defense, entitled to whatever limited attention you might deign to pay the questions I ask!" I shot back, doing everything I could to drive her mad. "You walk in here, wearing clothes that cost more than half these jurors make in a year, and you act like you're making some kind of sacrifice. So the question, Mrs. Chandler, isn't who do I think I am, but who do you think you are? Other than spend money you never earned, what have you ever done that makes you think you can treat with this kind of condescension, not just other people, but the law?"

If she had had something close at hand — a rock, a purse, anything — I think she would have thrown it at me, so great was the rage that had taken possession of her, twisting her mouth into an ugly, hateful knot. With an angry glance, I made a dismissive gesture with my hand and walked away. At the counsel table, I turned around. She was struggling to hide her embarrassment at having for one of the few times in her life lost control.

"There were a great many people there that day, weren't there?" I asked in a voice, quiet and subdued.

"Yes, there were," she agreed without hesitation.

"And from the absence of any suggestion to the contrary in your direct testimony, I take it that you, yourself, were not in the room — the suite — when Anna Malreaux fell from the window to her death."

She was sitting in the witness chair the way she had been before, but without the same air of annoyance and contempt. She answered the questions as if she had decided that they were important after all, and that she should do everything she could to make her meaning clear.

"No, I wasn't there when it happened. I had only come by to say hello to Thomas — Thomas Browning, that is. We were very old friends. That was the first time I met Anna Malreaux. I knew that she and Thomas were involved. I did not know how serious it was, of course. That's not something Thomas would have confided in me about. That is also how I happen to remember Mr. Haviland. As soon as I walked in and saw the look on their faces, I could tell they did not much like each other. Thomas walked me outside, into the outer suite. He told me that he — Mr. Haviland — was in love with Ms. Malreaux, but that she was not in love with him."

For the first time, she glanced at Haviland. She smiled sympathetically, as if she understood how much that must have hurt, and then she looked back at me.

"You said you could not hear what was said between the defendant and Anna Malreaux. Was there anything about the way they were talking that made you think that Mr. Haviland was angry, ready to do her harm?"

"No, but he did seem quite upset with Thomas," she said quickly.

"Did Mr. Browning appear to be concerned for his safety?"

"No, not at all. I think he was just waiting for Mr. Haviland to leave."

I was standing in the middle of the shaft of light that cut through the windows above the jury box. My arms folded across my chest, I stared down at the floor. At her answer, my head snapped up.

"And so far as you know, he did. Isn't that correct, Mrs. Chandler? So far as you know, he left right after you did, and — what was it you testified before? — that you left a long time before Anna Malreaux fell from that window to her death."

"I wouldn't know anything about what happened after I left the hotel that afternoon."

I asked a few more questions, all to the same point: She did not know what happened, but Haviland had not done anything to make her think he was angry with Anna Malreaux.

"When you heard that Anna Malreaux had died, you must have been shocked?"

"Yes, of course I was."

The light that fell from the window struck my eyes. All that was visible on the witness stand was a gray hazy outline, and for the moment it lasted I saw Mary Beth Chandler the way she had looked that evening at Maxwell's Plum.

"You were sitting on Browning's right," I said before I knew it. I bent my head a little to the side until the light was out of my eyes. She did not say anything, but a slight movement of her mouth acknowledged it as a fact. I went back to my question.

"You were shocked, of course. And did you at the time, or at any time until this case was brought against Jamison Haviland, ever have reason to think that Anna Malreaux's death had been anything but what the police said it was at the time — an accident?"

"No, absolutely not," she said emphatically. A worried look came into her eyes. There was something she wanted to add, something she thought everyone should know. She turned to the jury, an earnest expression on her face. "Thomas was devastated, inconsolable. If it hadn't been for Joanna — Mrs. Browning . . ." she started to explain. She realized that having explained that, she had to explain something else as well. "Thomas and Joanna had been close friends for years. Their families — the Brownings and the Van Renaesslers — were very close. Thomas always turned to her for comfort and advice. After the tragedy — after what happened — they were inseparable. He probably would have gotten through it on his own," she said, biting her lip as she speculated about the past. "We were young, and the young are resilient; but I can't believe it would have been the same without her. A year or so later, they were married. It's strange, isn't it?" she asked, turning her attention back to me. "What happens to us and why."

I started back to the counsel table, cross-examination at an end. I raised my eyes to the bench to announce that I was through; but then I remembered. I stopped and wheeled around.

"You've known Thomas Browning nearly as long as that yourself — since you were still a girl in your teens, isn't that correct?"

She had her hands on the arms of the witness chair, just about to stand up. Her eyes swung across the room.

"Yes, like the Van Renaesslers, our families were acquainted."

"And from what you testified, Thomas Browning was in love with Anna Malreaux — you said he was 'devastated' by her death, 'inconsolable.' "

"Yes, that's true."

"You know Thomas Browning as well as anyone does. Is it possible that he could have watched someone murder this girl he loved and then told the police that it was an accident? And then spend the rest of his life covering up the crime?"

"Objection!" thundered Caminetti as he came out of his chair. "Calls for speculation, it's irrelevant, immaterial. It's . . ."

Scarborough struck his gavel hard. "Sustained!" He leaned forward on both arms and peered down at me with a worldly smile. Raising both eyebrows, he used his middle finger to scratch the underside of his chin. "I'm sure I do not have to explain the reason why Mr. Antonelli's question — or should I say his rather lengthy commentary — has been ruled impermissible." The smile grew a little larger, tickling the corners of his mouth. "Which of course raises the question why, when counsel both understand the rules so well, they seem to get broken so often."

Scarborough darted a glance at Caminetti, and then, sliding over until he was leaning on his hip, he stared at a point just beyond the jury box and finished with a private remark to his imaginary friend.

"Unless — and I would hate to think this was true — they believe the only rule is whatever they can get away with."

His eyes came down to the jury, his face animated, eager, alive. He could not wait to let them share in the subtle pleasure of putting lawyers in their rightful place.

"With that mild admonition, Mr. Antonelli," he announced with a graceful nod, "please continue."

"No," said Mary Beth Chandler before I could open my mouth. "He never would have done that. The Thomas Browning I know would never let someone get away with murder. It's absurd."

Caminetti had automatically bounced back on his feet. Speechless, he could only roll his eyes. In what was almost a slow-motion gesture of helpless frustration, Scarborough threw up his hands. As if I had not noticed anything wrong, I made a slight bow toward Mrs. Chandler, thanked her for her testimony and announced that my cross-examination had now ended.

"The witness's last statement will be stricken from the record," announced Scarborough in an even-tempered voice. "The jury is instructed to ignore it. You may call your next witness."

I could scarcely wait to tell Gisela what I had done.

One more witness that morning and two more in the afternoon took the stand to testify on behalf of the prosecution that Jimmy Haviland had not only been at the Plaza the day Anna Malreaux died, but that he had been in love with her, obsessed with her, unwilling to accept the fact that she was not in love with him.

"He had asked her to marry him. She had said no," testified one of her law school friends, a plump moonfaced woman who seemed to radiate goodwill. She was that rare phenomenon: a lawyer who loved her work.

"You specialize in the legal rights of women, is that not correct, Ms. Dell?"

She burst into a confident, pudgy-cheeked smile. "And proud of it, Mr. Antonelli!"

Clover Dell — that was her actual given name — was a legend, the groundbreaking advocate on nearly every major feminist issue in the last twenty years. Despite themselves, people who hated what she stood for could not hate her: They could not quite resist the power of the unblemished enthusiasm that never came close to fanaticism. She had walked into Scarborough's courtroom, both arms swinging at her sides, like an owner coming home, glad to find that instead of an empty house there was a party going on, one that could only get better now that she had arrived. The moment she settled into the witness chair she looked up at Scarborough and to his immense amusement greeted him like a long-lost friend: "How are you, Judge? Keeping these two straight?" she asked with a quick glance first at Caminetti, then at me.

"You testified that the defendant asked Anna Malreaux to marry him, but she did not want to marry him."

"I did."

I had to be careful: I did not know how much she knew. "Were you aware that there were other young men interested in her?"

"Sure, but she wasn't interested in them. I don't mean she wasn't interested in men. No, but she certainly didn't have any interest in marriage. Not that she had anything against marriage, but it wasn't something she was going to do before she had established herself in her own career. That's what we were about, Mr. Antonelli — becoming independent women who could choose the lives we wanted." She squared her shoulders and faced the jury with a look that suggested that they all had to agree that there could be nothing more important than that. "Anna Malreaux was one of the most independent-minded women I ever had the good fortune to know. It's a tragedy that she didn't live. She would have been an enormous success. Huge."

I wondered whether she would have thought the same thing if she had known that Annie Malreaux had decided to become Thomas Browning's wife.

"So she wasn't going to marry anyone, at least not right away. In addition to her independence, would you also describe her as thoughtful and kind, perhaps unusually so?" I asked the question as if it were nothing more than innocent curiosity, and when she immediately agreed, I suggested what seemed the only logical, the only fair conclusion.

"So when she said no, told Jimmy

Haviland that she would not marry him, don't you think it possible that she might have told him that? What you just said — that she wasn't ready for marriage, that there were a lot of things she wanted to do first? Wouldn't she have done something like that, both to let him down easy and because — as you yourself have just told us — it was true?"

Out of the corner of my eye I saw Caminetti coming out of his chair.

"Isn't that what she told you? I know it was a long time ago, but you remember everything else so distinctly, perhaps you remember that as well: what Anna Malreaux told you she told Jimmy Haviland when he proposed."

Did she remember? I do not know. But she thought she did, and she had no doubt what, knowing Annie, Annie would have done.

"Yes, I'm almost positive she told me that. I can't remember her exact words, but they were words to that effect."

"So Jimmy Haviland would still have been left with some reason to hope." I glanced briefly at the judge, turning away before he turned his gaze on me. "No more questions, Your Honor."

Jimmy Haviland had not been charged

with manslaughter; he had been charged with murder. The prosecution had to show, not that he caused her death through negligence, but with deliberate intent. It was not enough to argue that in a moment of anger he had shoved her and that, as a result he should have foreseen, she had fallen to her death. Caminetti had to show that when Haviland pushed her it was because he wanted her to die. That meant he had to show that that thought had been in Haviland's mind. In the afternoon, he called two witnesses who, at least on first impression, seemed to make the case that it had. The first, Clarence Armitage, whom I vaguely remembered from school, testified that Haviland had been so upset when "Annie turned him down" that he stopped going to class, refused to eat, and seldom left his room. Caminetti pounced upon it.

"So he spent all his time brooding on it, letting it eat away at him?"

Armitage shook his head. "He was despondent."

Caminetti took the answer as if it only confirmed the worst. "In other words, depressed."

I was not sure I needed to, but given Caminetti's penchant for answering his own questions when he did not like the answers he got, I decided to underscore the obvious.

"He was despondent — I think that was the word you used — not *depressed?*"

"Despondent; yes, that's what I said."

"You were good friends; you were rooming together at the time, isn't that correct?"

"Yes," replied Armitage, bending forward as he glanced across to where Haviland sat watching. "We were good friends."

"He told you what happened with Annie, and you could see for yourself how he felt — Is that correct?"

Armitage ran his fingers through gray-streaked hair. He was dressed in the fastidious fashion that was still expected among the senior partners in a Wall Street firm. It occurred to me when I first saw him on the stand that it could have been me sitting there, calm and correct, had I accepted the offer to come back to the firm where I had clerked that summer I spent in New York.

"In other words, you knew him rather well, didn't you? Well enough to anticipate his moods, to know what he was thinking. My question is this: During that whole period, after he proposed to Anna Malreaux and she refused, did he ever, even once, suggest that he might want to do her any harm?"

The answer was plain, emphatic, without either hesitation or doubt. "Never."

With his next witness, Caminetti came at the same issue from the other side. Haviland's friend and roommate had testified that he had been distraught, a fact that Caminetti would use to suggest that the pressure and the pain had finally built to the breaking point, and that the death of Anna Malreaux had come to be seen as the only way out. Abigail, or, as we had all known her, Abby, Sinclair testified that Anna Malreaux had been afraid of what Jimmy Haviland might do.

"They had been going together?" asked Caminetti in his energetic, abbreviated way.

Abby Sinclair had been sworn in, and Caminetti was standing in front of her, not more than six feet away. She sat on the edge of the chair, raising herself up until she could see over Caminetti's shoulder. Her brown eyes sparkled with recognition the instant they caught my own. We had been friends once, and Abby was one of those people, rare enough, who never forget a friend, no matter how many years had passed. She had wanted to become a lawyer so that she could do something to help the poor; she was now the head of a large foundation that did just that. She looked at Caminetti and let him know that she was not someone he could rush.

" 'Going together' would not be right. They had started going out sometime in the spring — the early spring, I think — of our first year. But Annie went out with other young men as well. That summer — the summer between our first and second years — Annie lived in New York, but Jimmy wasn't here."

Is that when it started — that summer in New York? I had forgotten, if I had ever known, that Annie had been there, too.

"She saw him a few times early in the fall, after school started, in Cambridge."

Abby had large, generous eyes, offering comfort to whoever was fortunate enough to come under their gaze. She had that kind of gawky, bucktoothed look that made you want to laugh with sadness at how much more beauty shined out of that plain, unaltered face than you were ever likely to see in the flashing eyes of high-fashion women used to turning every head they passed.

"But then she told him she could not see him anymore. I don't know why," she admitted. "I was a friend of hers, but she had other, closer friends, and perhaps she told one of them. That's when he asked her to marry him, when she said she couldn't see him anymore. I think he was desperate not to lose her, and maybe thought that if she knew he was that serious about her, she would think about him in a different way."

Caminetti was pacing the floor. "But she said no," he interjected the moment she stopped.

"Yes, that's right."

Caminetti straightened his shoulders and looked directly at her. "And after she said no, she was worried what he might do?"

"Very worried."

Ready with the next question, Caminetti took a step toward her. He stopped, and with a miser's stare, reconsidered.

"No, never mind." He darted a glance at the bench. "No more questions, Your Honor," he said, his hands trailing in the air behind him as he turned and moved steadily toward his chair.

It was too easy, and I should have known it.

"Annie — Anna — Malreaux was worried what he might do?" I asked this with a cautious expression, as if I were only trying to clarify a point. With my back to the jury, I looked at Abby and smiled. Then I stepped away, giving to the jury an unobstructed view. "Worried about what he might do to her, or what he might do to himself?"

With a quick shake of her head, she dismissed any possibility that Annie had been afraid for herself. "She was worried about him."

Without thinking, I had given Caminetti everything he needed. On redirect, he stood in front of the counsel table and gave Abby a serious, searching glance.

"In other words, Anna Malreaux, who knew him well, thought him quite capable of doing something violent!"

Whether he had been born with it or learned it from the Jesuits, this instinct for changing the plain meaning of things, Caminetti could do anything with words.

It was nearly four-thirty and I thought we were through, but as soon as Abby Sinclair had been excused, Caminetti immediately called someone else. He stood at the side of the counsel table, tapping on it impatiently with the fingers of his left hand.

"State your name."

"Gordon Fitzgerald."

"Do you know the defendant?"

"Yes, I do."

"Where do you know him from?"

"We were in a rehabilitation center together."

"For the treatment of alcoholism?"

"Yes."

"During the time you knew him, did the defendant say anything about a woman by the name of Anna Malreaux?"

"Yes. He said he killed her; he said he was responsible for her death."

Tall, thin, all legs and arms, in a sweat suit
stretched so tight she looked as if she had
been painted naked, the first runner streaked
by me in a blaze of grimaced pain. Seconds
later, two more women grunted past, trailing
bursts of vapored breath. A few yards ahead,
an old man, bundled up against the morning
chill, stood at the edge of the asphalt path,
watching two squirrels chase each other
through the yellow wind-scattered leaves.
The park was coming awake. Rising above
the buildings that lined Fifth Avenue, the
sun hung in the hazy overcast sky, a pale
silver disc barely bright enough to see.

Thomas Browning was waiting for me
when I stepped out of the private elevator
onto his floor. Though it was only seven-
thirty, he looked as if he had been up for
hours, rested, perfectly relaxed, as if he did
not have a care in the world. Dressed in a
V-neck sweater slipped over a tan shirt and
a pair of pleated gray checked slacks, he
might have been holding a golf club in his

hand, one of those weekend players who was not very good but loved the game. He greeted me with the indulgent attitude of someone welcoming home a stray.

We reached the study, that small, private room with the awning-covered balcony that gave a view of the park and the city beyond. Browning settled into the chair behind his desk. His eyes sparkled as if he had been looking forward to something that was just about to start. I tried to remind myself that all he knew about the trial was what he had read in the paper, or what he had been told. He could be forgiven for thinking things had been going better than they were. I sat down on the only other chair in the room, held my briefcase on my lap and snapped open the lock. Browning gave me a puzzled glance.

"I brought something I want you to look at. I'm hoping you can help explain it to me, because . . ."

He shook his head. There was something more important, more interesting, on his mind. He picked up the telephone from the corner of his desk, held his hand over the receiver, and asked me what I wanted for breakfast.

"Nothing," I replied, anxious to get back to what I wanted to talk to him about.

"You must," he insisted. "I'd feel like a fool sitting here having breakfast while you sit there twiddling your thumbs."

"Coffee, eggs," I said without enthusiasm.

Browning laughed at my sullen reply, turned away and spoke for a moment into the phone.

"I've been trying to reach you for days," I complained.

"They have me going everywhere. The West Coast, the East Coast, the North, the South," he said, as a grin grew wider on his mouth, mocking the formal sound of his voice. For some reason I did not understand, he was having an enormously good time. His left arm was thrown carelessly over the corner of the chair, his right leg was crossed over the left. He raised his chin and studied me with the clean, decent benevolence of a friend.

"You've been killing yourself working on this trial. I know that. And I know that I promised I'd be available anytime you wanted. That's why I asked if you could come by this morning: so we could talk. I got back last night, and I'm going out again at noon."

I had one more complaint. "So I did what you told me I should: When I couldn't reach you, I tried to reach Elizabeth Hartley — the one you said I should reach because she could always reach you."

It seemed to strike him like some private joke, one he was willing to share, but just not quite yet.

"Elizabeth is the reason I asked you to come this early."

There was a soft, polite knock on the door. A maid wheeled in a cart with platters stacked with food: eggs and ham and bacon, kippers and potatoes, biscuits, muffins, toast and scones, jams and jellies and seven different kinds of fruit, coffee, tea, orange juice, tomato juice, juices I had never seen or heard of before, and finally, fluted glasses and two bottles of champagne. With each thing I took Browning kept repeating that I needed to take more, that I looked a wreck, that he was worried about my health. When I had my plate fully loaded, wondering how I was going to get through half of it, he helped himself to a single slice of buttered toast, a cup of black coffee, and ignored the rest.

"Eat!" he cried eagerly. "You don't have to watch your weight."

I was not hungry, but to placate Browning I took a few bites before I tried again to get him to talk about the documents I wanted him to see. He stopped me before I could start, told me I needed to eat some more, then glanced at the clock and muttered something about not wanting to miss the beginning. With a remote control he turned on a television set in the corner of the room.

"Have something to drink," he urged, waving his hand toward the bottles of champagne in two ice buckets standing together on the cart. "This will be worth celebrating, just to see the look on that poor bastard's face." Browning was hunched forward, his arms resting on his knees, peering intently at the images flickering on the screen. "This is the reason I asked you to come this early, to see this," he said, turning his head briefly toward me. "I wanted you to watch this with me," he added, turning his attention back to the set. "Then you can tell me what you think."

It was one of the Sunday talk shows. There were two guests: Arthur Connally, the president's chief of staff, and Elizabeth Hartley, introduced as "the communications director for the Browning for President campaign."

"He doesn't look happy, does he?" asked Browning with a sidelong glance. He sat up, folded his arms across his chest and crossed his ankle over his knee. "Thought he was going to be on with me; that he and I were going to have some little debate. Arthur has always suffered from a strange form of megalomania. He spends so much time telling Walker what to think and what to do that he tends to forget that he doesn't actually hold the office himself." A harsh look of disdain raced through Browning's eyes. "He's a staffer, for Christ's sake!"

The look in his eyes changed. A sly grin flickered over his mouth as the face of Elizabeth Hartley appeared on the screen.

"He's a staffer — so I sent one of my own, younger, smarter, infinitely more telegenic." He looked at me for confirmation. "And with an ambition, I'm afraid, every bit as great as his own."

The show had two moderators, Martha Riles, a White House correspondent for the network, and Gilbert Graham, the legal affairs reporter for the *Wall Street Journal*. Both of them wanted to know about the trial. Riles insisted that the prosecution seemed to be getting the better of things at trial, while Graham claimed that none of it was doing the political prospects of Thomas Browning any good. Riles challenged Elizabeth Hartley to disagree with her assertion that the trial, and particularly the prosecution's last witness, had raised serious questions about the credibility of what in a rather strident voice she called "the whole Browning defense."

Elizabeth Hartley smiled. "The 'Browning defense'? I'm afraid you're confused. Vice President Browning isn't on trial; a man named Jamison Scott Haviland is."

Staring in practiced disbelief, Graham asked her not to disregard the obvious. "Everyone knows the trial is ultimately all about Thomas Browning," he said in an unctuous, pontificating voice. "If Haviland is guilty, so is Browning; and he can't possibly stay in the race for the presidency if he is. Isn't that right, Ms. Hartley?"

The two guests sat next to each other, facing their two interrogators across an oblong table. Hartley held herself erect, a firm, determined look in her hard blue eyes. Instead of rushing to a reply, the instinct of most people suddenly cast into the national eye, she gave herself time.

"Your question has no point. Jamison Scott Haviland isn't guilty." She said this in a calm but quite emphatic voice. "Mr. Browning has already stated publicly that Mr. Haviland is innocent."

"What else could he say?" interjected Connally as he turned on Hartley with a venomous glance. "He was there. Only now it looks like his story is — what shall I say? — a little less than convincing. Haviland admitted that he killed her and . . ."

"He admitted no such thing," Hartley fired back, raising her chin a belligerent half inch. "There is a distinction between what someone says and what someone else tells you he said. I realize that with your penchant for rumor and hearsay that distinction may be a little lost on you, but it's a distinction that won't be lost on the court."

She had pulled herself around, clutching with her hand the corner of the chair. She fixed Connally with a relentless stare.

"The witness, the witness called by the prosecution, the witness who claimed that Jamison Haviland told him that he killed Anna Malreaux, is a liar, and everyone who was in that courtroom, everyone who saw what Joseph Antonelli did to him on cross-examination, knows it."

Connally started to reply, to argue the point, but Elizabeth was not through. She talked right over him, growing more confident with each word she spoke.

"Don't you remember that part? It was only a couple of days ago, Mr. Connally; it was in all the papers." A mocking smile flashed across her mouth, the kind that, if you have to suffer it, drives you half mad with its assumption of a vast, illimitable superiority. "The confession you just referred to — that was the one supposedly made while both Mr. Haviland and Mr. . . . What was his name? — Fitzgerald — were in a rehabilitation center together? Mr. Haviland was there because of a dependence on pain medication, if I recall correctly; pain medication that had originally been prescribed for injuries sustained in the war. Mr. Fitzgerald, on the other hand, had an addiction to alcohol, and also cocaine — or was it heroin — or was it both? It was hard to know because — don't you remember? — in the course of Mr. Antonelli's cross-examination he was forced to admit that he had been in treatment not only before, but several times after, the time he met Mr. Haviland. Drugs, alcohol — he seemed to have experienced about every kind of addiction there is, except perhaps to telling the truth. And when he wasn't using some mind-altering drug, he . . . You remember this, don't you, Mr. Connally? When Antonelli asked him about the time he served in prison for fraud, the dozens of elderly people whose life savings he had supposedly invested but had instead actually spent."

Elizabeth turned away from Connally with contempt. "That's the witness — the only witness — they've got," she said with an air of quiet triumph as she looked across at the two reporters.

Stunned by the ease with which the relatively young communications director of the Browning campaign had taken apart the president's feared and inflexible chief of staff, the best either Riles or Graham could do was to look at Arthur Connally and wait for his response.

Connally tried to hide his anger, but the smile that started onto his mouth was strained, awkward, artificial, and died halfway across.

"You take your witnesses as they come. How many convictions do you think there would be of organized-crime figures if you could not use the testimony of informants who had been with the mob?"

Elizabeth was leaning in, ready with a reply. With a thrust of his forehead and an evil stare, Connally cut her off.

"But if you're so convinced that the witness was lying, that for some strange reason he made the whole thing up, then why refuse to answer the question Gilbert just asked you? If Haviland didn't kill that girl, then Browning doesn't have anything to worry about, does he? So there wouldn't be any reason — would there? — not to agree that if Haviland is found guilty — of this crime he did not commit and that Browning did not cover up — Browning will immediately withdraw. He'd have to anyway, wouldn't he? The American people are never going to elect someone who helped cover up a murder — no matter how long ago that murder took place."

"Now, Elizabeth; do it now."

I looked across the room. Browning was hunched forward, his eyes narrow, intense.

A smile ran like vengeance across Elizabeth Hartley's taut, fine-featured face. "You think Thomas Browning should give up the fight for the Republican nomination if Jamison Haviland is found guilty at trial? Is that the question? A better question would be what President Walker will do if he is not."

Connally had been upstaged by this junior staffer long enough. Slapping his open palm on the table, he turned on her.

"Are you suggesting . . . ?"

That was all he got out. "Not suggesting anything," Elizabeth shot back. "But if Haviland isn't guilty, then someone is — not of murder, but of something worse. Who suddenly decided that there was a murder? And not only a murder, but that the vice president was somehow involved? Was it just a coincidence that it's the same thing — the very same thing — that was done to Thomas Browning in the last election, the last time he had the courage to challenge you and William Walker and all that you and all the people like you represent?"

Connally looked at the two moderators, expecting them to intervene, to caution this out-of-control young woman about her behavior and her tone of voice.

"So the answer, Mr. Connally," said Elizabeth Hartley in a voice that was suddenly all reason and light, "is yes, absolutely: If Jamison Scott Haviland is found guilty of murder, Thomas Browning will withdraw. And now that I have answered your question, why don't you answer mine? If Mr. Haviland is acquitted, found innocent, will the president quit as well?"

Arthur Connally looked at her as if she had lost her mind. The show went to commercial. Browning turned off the television set, sat back in the chair and began to stroke his chin. There was a look of immense satisfaction in his eyes.

"She's a quick study, that one. I talked to her barely ten minutes before she went on. That had to come out — that business about whether if Haviland was found guilty I would quit; and it had to come out just like that: something that can't possibly happen because Haviland is innocent and the only reason there is a trial is because of them. Don't you think that was something we had to do," he asked, "make them talk not just about me, but about them? Make it — what it really is — an issue about who can be trusted and who cannot? If Haviland is guilty, Browning quits! But if Haviland is innocent, then, Mr. President, where does that leave you?"

Browning sprang out of his chair and for a moment stood perfectly still, his hands locked behind his back, brooding on what he had just said. "It had to be done," he said emphatically. His hand gripped the corner of the desk. He looked at me with a sense of urgency in his eyes. "The chief justice is in the hospital."

"Yes, I know that, but . . ."

"He isn't coming out. A matter of days, I should think; a week, two at the most. I have to make everyone think that Walker may not last." He gestured toward the darkened screen. "That's what they're talking about now, what those people want to know: Whom the president is going to nominate if the position of chief justice should suddenly become vacant. That's all anyone wants to talk about, that and the trial." A rueful expression deepened the lines around his eyes and mouth. "Death and political destruction, the wheels on which Washington — at least Washington rumor — runs."

He shook his head as if to banish everything irrelevant from the narrow focus of his mind. "Walker wants Reynolds. We both know that. I have enough support in the Senate to stop it, but only for as long as there is reason to think Walker is in trouble and that I have a chance." He gave me a sharp, searching glance. "Do you understand all this? Do you see that so long as I'm in this thing, Walker and Connally won't dare move on the Reynolds nomination? Because once he does that — nominates him — no one can kid themselves anymore; no one can pretend Walker isn't every bit as radical as the rest of them, all those moralistic know-nothings, those religious zealots who think they're the chosen instruments of God.

"I told you at the beginning that it would come to this, that they had to destroy me, that I was the only one in their way. They have the White House, they have the Senate and the House, and now they're just one dying old man away from having the Court as well. I can stop them, but only if you win. If Haviland is found guilty, Connally is right: I'm finished, and those people will own the country for as far into the future as you and I can see. God knows what will happen then," he added, shaking his head as a worried look passed briefly over his eyes.

Browning went back to his desk. "I'm afraid it's all on your shoulders now. What can I do to help?"

Pushing aside the cart with all its wasted food, I pulled my chair up to the desk.

"I did what I could the other day on cross-examination, but it wasn't enough, not half as effective as Elizabeth Hartley made it sound. I didn't break Fitzgerald; he held his own."

Browning twisted his head to the side, gave me a questioning look and waited.

"I made sure the jury knew that he had a criminal record and that he used narcotics; but I could not show that he had any reason to lie. I asked him, right at the end, whether anyone had talked to him, offered him anything in exchange for his testimony. I knew he was going to say no; but I had to have it on the record so I could use it against him, show that he is a liar, when I confront him with the evidence that he has taken money, that he was bribed."

I reached into the briefcase and handed Browning the list of names and numbers that I had not been able to use. He ran his eye down the first page and then the second; then he looked up at me and in a somber gesture nodded twice. He guessed their significance at once.

"Money paid out, but first moved around — is that what you think this is? And Fitzgerald's name — his testimony was bought?"

"Two names on that list are on the list of witnesses Caminetti intends to call. He called Fitzgerald, and now, this week, he'll call the other."

"Then you've won," insisted Browning. Grabbing the sheets of paper in his fist, he raised them high in the air. "This proves it! It's what I said from the beginning! The White House is behind it, all of it!" Springing up from his chair, he spread the sheets out on the desk. "Look! There's no mistake. See what it says, where it comes from? It's the White House. There isn't any question."

"But it's just names and numbers — they could mean anything! And Gordon Fitzgerald? There's no proof that it's the same Gordon Fitzgerald who testified at the trial. It isn't a particularly unusual name," I added, frustrated by Browning's obstinate insistence that I was making up a problem where none existed. But Browning had passed beyond his own impatience. He settled into his chair, clasped his hands under his chin and tapped his index fingers, pressed close together, against his mouth.

"Yes, I see your point," he said presently. "And that is the reason you did not use this against the witness — after you asked him if anyone had 'talked to him, offered anything in exchange for his testimony'?" He repeated the phrase that had come off the top of my head as if it were something he had read in a book and then memorized. "How did you get this? It has to be someone in the White House. Who?"

"I don't know," I admitted.

"You don't know who gave it to you?"

I started to tell him that Gisela had given it to me, and that it had been given to her by a friend. I changed my mind. What Gisela had done was between her and me.

"It came from an anonymous source. I don't know who it is."

"But this is all they gave you," he said, glancing at the sheets of paper scattered over his desk, "and you obviously don't think it is enough."

I shook my head in discouragement. "Even if it really did come from inside the White House, the name at the top, the person who supposedly put together the list . . . No one with that name works at the White House."

With the tips of two fingers, Browning dragged one of the sheets of paper closer to get a better look. " 'Lincoln' — sounds like what one of those pretentious fools would use for a cover."

Pausing, he seemed to look at me from a different perspective, as if he were reminding himself that there were things he took for granted that I did not know.

"Everything in the White House," he explained, "everything that anyone sends to the president — everything anyone sends to anyone — goes through the staff secretary. The office of the staff secretary is in the West Wing, directly below the office that, before my arrival, had been used by the vice-president. You remember: I took you over there. The office is set up to provide some discipline, some organization to what gets to the president. If a cabinet officer wants to send a proposal to the president, the staff secretary makes certain that everyone the president would want to comment on it does so before it's sent on to the president. The system stores everything. Every e-mail — all of it — is kept forever. The law requires it; there are millions of these things on the database. There is something else. The system works only inside the Executive Office of the President: EOP. That's what the rest of that means," he said, pointing toward the top of one of the pages on the desk. "The address: 'So-and-so at EOP.' Nothing sent from a White House computer can escape the system. It's all stored; it's all kept; it's all still there, including the originals of these," he explained. "All you have to do is produce them. That will prove where they came from; that will prove that all of this was done by someone inside the White House."

"But it still would not prove what they mean," I replied with a hopeless gesture.

Browning had his mind on something

else: a fact that suddenly seemed the key to everything else.

"All those millions of messages — it doesn't matter what names were used — every one of them can be traced back to its source. That's how you get the name; that's how you'll know. That's how you can show that if this whole business didn't go right into the Oval Office, it went close enough. Call the staff secretary as a witness." His eyes were eager, intense, alert.

He was adamant about it, determined that I see it his way. He was too close to it; he had too much at stake. It was almost willful, this refusal to acknowledge that nothing that he had said, nothing about the way the White House system worked, proved what those names and numbers really meant.

"I have to have more; and whoever gave me this knows it, too. He's following the trial: He knew Fitzgerald was going to be a witness." I looked straight at Browning. "I know you're right about what Connally and those people have done. This person — whoever he is — knows that, too. He knows I didn't use what he gave me; he knows there is something wrong."

Browning sank back into his chair. His eyes moved back and forth in small, measured half circles as he gazed about the room. He began to rub the knuckles of his index finger along the slope of his upper lip.

"And if he has gone as far as he can? If he won't run the risk of making direct contact with you; if he can't run the risk of getting you more than he has given you already — what then? What will you do if you can't get proof that those records mean what you think they mean?"

He watched me closely, gauging my confidence, trying to see how much I believed that whatever might still happen, we were going to win. Not whether Haviland was going to win, not whether I was going to win, but we — Haviland and Browning, Browning and I, whichever way you wanted to put it, so long as you understood that he played the crucial part in the drama that was fast approaching its final act. As much as any defendant — more than Haviland himself — Browning seemed to need the assurance that everything was going to turn out all right.

"What will I do?" A broad, automatic smile cut across my mouth, the instinctive accompaniment of the lie I had told so often that I was no longer quite certain it was not true. "I'll invent something; I'll make something up. I haven't been in a trial yet where something unexpected did not happen, something that changes everything — if you're quick enough to see it and know how to use it."

Browning smiled back, but it was a pale imitation, mocking by deliberate understatement the empty sincerity of my own.

"In other words, you have no idea what you might do."

The smile on my mouth grew smaller, and more honest. "That would be a fair summary."

There was one thing more I needed to ask. Why had he never bothered to tell me that Jimmy Haviland had been on retainer with the company for years?

Browning lowered his eyes. "Is it important?"

"Caminetti made it sound like it was a payoff; a way to keep Haviland quiet; to make sure he would never confess to what he had done — because of the damage that could do to you. And I didn't know anything about it. Haviland had not said a word."

Browning continued to study his hands. "I knew a little bit about what Haviland had gone through: Annie . . . the war. I thought I should do something." He looked at me with a guarded expression. "He's a good lawyer," he said, his voice solemn, subdued. "And he's a good man. Why shouldn't I have?"

"He thinks you did it out of guilt."

Browning did not say a word.

"That's why he did not tell me," I continued. "He's embarrassed by the fact that he took it. He tried to tell himself that he was only doing what any lawyer would: agree to a retainer from a major client. But he knows he did it because he needed the money, and he hates himself for that. He thinks it was blood money. He doesn't think Annie's death was an accident; he thinks you killed her. He thinks you were angry because Annie went after him, that you argued, that you pushed her, and that's why she fell."

There was something sad and distant in Browning's eyes. He nodded slowly, as if he not only understood but also sympathized with what Jimmy Haviland believed.

"I know that's what he must think."

He saw the question in my eyes, the question that no matter how many times I thought I had answered it, kept coming back.

"I didn't do it. That's the last thing I would have done."

He looked as if he was watching in the darkness of his mind the scene with which he must have tortured himself for years: the moment that Annie fell.

"It was an accident; it wasn't anyone's fault," he said, turning to me with a look that brought the matter to an end.

I got up to go, but Browning waved me back to the chair. "Don't go just yet; I have a little more time." There was an awkward pause before he added, as if in passing, that Joanna had asked him to say hello. "She wanted to see you," he remarked in a voice that had become formal and even a little forced. His eyes drifted toward the sliding glass door as if they wanted a place to hide. "She was with me in California; we got back only late last night. I thought it best not to wake her."

It was a decent, civilized lie; a polite reminder that what may have happened in the past had no bearing on the way things were now. After that lunch in Georgetown I had had the feeling that I would not see her again, that what had been said that day was a kind of second good-bye. I was sure of it now, sure that Joanna was gone; almost as sure as I was that after the trial I would never hear from Thomas Browning again. Browning wanted to change things, to bend the future to his will, no doubt to make things better, but better according to him. He lived with the vision of what, if only he had the power, he could do. I had nothing like that kind of ambition, and the older I got the less I thought about what might happen next year or the year after that. I wondered instead about the past and the way things that had happened had shaped and sometimes destroyed so many lives.

"Mary Beth Chandler testified the other day. Caminetti called her because she had seen Jimmy and Annie talking together that day. . . ."

"Who?" asked Browning with a blank expression.

"Mary Beth Chandler. She's an old friend of yours. She's married to that investment banker."

Browning did not seem to remember, and then, when he did, he did not seem to care.

"I recognized her. There was something about her, that cutting look in her eyes; I knew I had seen her before — that night, at Maxwell's Plum, that summer I was in New York."

There was a look of annoyance in Browning's eyes, as if he could not understand where any of this could lead; but I was caught in the growing enthusiasm of what I was watching in my mind: the avid, determined look on Mary Beth Chandler's much younger face as she tried to get Browning to pay all his attention to her.

"She was sitting right next to you — you remember! It was that night you used me as an excuse to leave. . . ." I almost said Joanna, but I held back just in time. ". . . to leave everyone there because you were meeting someone in the Village."

Nothing registered. He had no idea what I was talking about. But then his eyes lit up and his whole expression changed. Then color flooded his cheeks.

"That's when I started seeing Annie: early that summer in New York. You're right. I'd forgotten all about it. I didn't want Joanna to know," he began to explain. His eyes left mine and raced into the distance, searching for what now seemed immediate and real. "That night. Yes, I remember all about it now. You and I sneak out of there like a couple of thieves, going off to have dinner with some lawyer on some dull business I supposedly had to take care of."

"She testified, and so did Clover Dell — remember her? And Abigail — Abby —

Sinclair. It's surprising how much both of them are just the way you would have thought they would be. Maybe no one really changes, after all; maybe we just get older."

The names meant nothing to him. He gave me a puzzled glance, wondering, I think, whether there was some reason they should. Annie he would never forget, but the rest of the people he had known then he did not seem to remember at all.

The sun was shining through the glass. The gray morning mist had burned away and Central Park glowed clean and dark and elegant under a blue, unbroken sky.

"They all remember you," I remarked as I rose and extended my hand. "Even Judge Scarborough considers you a friend."

Browning gave me an uncomprehending look.

"I used to know a lot of people when I ran the company, and a lot of people knew me. Now everyone knows me, and I don't know anyone. Except you, of course, my old friend," he said as he gripped my hand.

There was something warm and consoling in the way he looked at me, as if he knew all the things I had ever done wrong and all the things I wished had never happened, and instead of thinking less of me because of it, only regretted that he had not been there to help. It was what I had always felt under his intelligent, benevolent gaze: the sense that he saw things I could not see and that I could trust him with my life. He kept looking at me, but the past slowly vanished and he began to talk eagerly about what might happen next. I think I had always known Thomas Browning was destined to become a very great man.

"It's going to be an interesting few weeks, don't you think?" said Browning, resuming an exuberance that made you feel he was unstoppable, that no matter what the odds he would always find a way to win.

"Come on, I'll walk you out. I'll do better than that. It's such a gorgeous day, I'll walk you partway across the park."

He slapped me on the shoulder, took two steps and then, remembering what he had to do, shook his head.

"Better let them know," he said, mainly to himself. He picked up the telephone and said he was going out. "A little walk in the park with my old friend."

The Secret Service agent was waiting for us when the elevator opened on the lobby floor. His eyes began to move ahead of us as we made our way toward the front door.

"You remember Mr. Antonelli, don't you?" asked Browning with an impish grin. "The fellow who turned us down when we offered him a ride after that dinner over at the Plaza, the one you had to go get later and bring back here."

Agent Powell nodded politely. "Yes, sir; I remember."

"Good to see you, Agent Powell," I replied, nodding back.

The doorman held open the glass door. Agent Powell went ahead, holding his arm behind him to keep Browning close. Out on the sidewalk, Browning raised his head and squinted into the sun. Then he turned to Powell.

"We'll just cross the street and walk a little ways. I'm sure that will be all right."

Powell looked worried. He turned to Browning and said something. That is when I saw him: a man with his hands shoved into the pockets of a tan windbreaker, coming right at us — fifteen, or maybe twenty, feet away — moving quickly, faster than a walk, not quite a run. There was a strange, determined look in his eyes. His hand was coming out of his pocket. I knew before I saw it that he had a gun and that he was there to murder

Thomas Browning. "Watch out!" I cried as I threw myself at the man as hard as I could. He fired just before I hit him. I felt a searing pain in my shoulder and then I heard the second shot. I looked behind me and saw Browning sprawled on the sidewalk, thrown there by agent Powell, who lay on top of him. Blood was pouring out of Powell's head, and I knew immediately that he was dead.

22

The Secret Service tried to pull Thomas Browning away, but he refused to leave. With a look of utter desolation, he watched Powell's body being placed inside a black bag. He walked next to the gurney and waited while it was loaded into the coroner's van. When the doors were shut, he came over to the ambulance, where a paramedic was wrapping a bandage around my shoulder and upper arm.

"It wasn't anything," I said. "The bullet passed through my arm. I'm sorry about Powell. If I'd been just a second faster . . ."

Browning shook his head. "You saved my life, and so did he." He shifted his gaze to the paramedic, a Hispanic woman in her late twenties. "Is he going to be all right?"

Her hands kept moving. "He'll be fine," she said as she tore another piece of tape. "He shouldn't be in the hospital more than a couple of hours."

"You saved my life," Browning repeated in a solemn, whispered voice. "Now I have to call Harold Powell's wife and tell her that her husband was one of the two bravest men I ever knew."

A crowd had begun to gather, filling the street and stretching out across the sidewalk next to the park. Television had begun to broadcast live coverage from the scene, and reporters shouted questions above the noise. No one knew what had happened to the shooter, only that in all the confusion he had managed to get away. More insistent than before, the Secret Service told Browning that they had to get him inside. With the siren wailing, the ambulance started to move.

The doctors told me that I had been lucky, that the bullet had not hit bone and had not done any damage to the nerves. "It will just hurt like hell," said one of them with a physician's practiced touch. They gave me something for the pain, scheduled an appointment to change the dressing on the wound and sent me home.

Released from the hospital, a little before two in the afternoon, I took a cab to the apartment on Central Park West. I tried not to think too much about what had happened, but I could not think about anything else. It is a strange feeling: the sad euphoria of surviving a shooting in which someone else is killed. I had not thought about Browning or Powell or doing something heroic when I threw myself at the gunman. If I thought about anything, it was only about myself. I saw the look in the killer's eyes; I knew what he was going to do. I thought I was close enough to stop him before he fired, that I could take away the gun, but Harold Powell put himself in the line of fire. That was bravery, something worth remembering, something worthy of honor; all I could claim for myself was that I had not been a coward.

The telephone was ringing when I walked in the door. With my hand on my bandaged shoulder, I hobbled across the room, hoping to reach it in time. I thought it was Gisela calling to make sure I was safe. It was Jimmy Haviland, and he sounded depressed.

"Are you all right? That agent — he was the one I saw that night after the dinner, wasn't he? I recognized the picture they showed on television."

I dropped onto the sofa and kicked off my shoes. The sunlight through the French doors barely reached the edge of the blue Kerman rug that covered part of the polished parquet floor.

"Maybe we should make a deal, plead to

something, get this over with before someone else gets killed. They missed Browning; that doesn't mean they won't try again."

"There's nothing you can plead to," I reminded him. "You didn't do anything."

He knew that as well as I did. Browning was the only witness who could testify that Annie Malreaux's death was an accident and that Jimmy Haviland had not been in the room. If Harold Powell had not taken the bullet meant for Thomas Browning; if Browning had died instead — Haviland would have had no defense. When the first confused reports started coming in, when he first heard that there had been an assassination attempt and that someone had died, he could be forgiven if he had started to wonder what it might mean for him.

I wanted to get off the telephone: There were calls I wanted to make; but Haviland was desperate to talk. Everyone else might be thinking about what had happened that morning, but none of them were facing Jimmy Haviland's long ordeal. When you are accused of murder, put on trial for your life, there is nothing else you can think about. It is as if the day the police came to arrest you they ordered every other thought out of your head.

"What did you think about Abby Sinclair?" he asked. "She hasn't changed a bit, has she? Have you ever met anyone more genuine in your life?"

Haviland paused for a moment. When he started talking again his voice seemed to come from somewhere far away.

"I guess that was the difference, the reason you couldn't help liking Abby Sinclair and couldn't help wanting Annie Malreaux: Abby was always the same; Annie was always becoming someone else. You could see it behind her eyes."

We talked for a long time, or rather he talked and I listened. I wanted him to talk, to purge himself of the doubt and uncertainty that had built up inside him. He had a gift for description. I marveled at the shrewd perception with which he could single out the dominant trait that defined who and what someone was.

"If Cesare Borgia had married Mary Beth Chandler," he remarked, full of his own narrative, "he would have stopped killing others and poisoned himself."

Our muted laughter faded into a long silence as we came back to the bleak and solemn reality of our lives.

"I don't want a plea."

"I know."

"I'm glad Browning is all right; I'm sorry about Agent Powell."

In my stocking feet, I padded across the thick, luxurious carpet and pushed open the narrow French door. Down below, the pathways twisting through the park were filled with people moving under the pale November sun, each of them thinking thoughts of their own.

"You coming back tonight?" I asked quietly. I leaned my shoulder against the casement, overcome with nostalgia for the days when Central Park was a place I went to spend time instead of a place I cut across.

"I haven't left; I'm still in New York."

"Why?" I asked vaguely. I followed the crenellated line made by the stone buildings on the other side of the park. In an odd way, it reminded me of what it must be like, coming back from a long voyage and catching sight of New York, waiting, still unchanged, on the farther shore.

"Why didn't you go home? It's just a couple of hours by train."

"It's easier to stay in New York. I don't have to answer any questions, and no one looks at me twice." There was a slight hesitation: I could hear it in the silence between the words. "It isn't because I wanted to drink. I haven't had a thing." He knew I believed him and that that was the reason I made no reply.

When I hung up, I checked the messages. Gisela had called while I was on the phone. I called her back, but she had already left. The White House had scheduled a press conference in which the president, after expressing outrage at the attempt on the life of his friend and former vice president, was expected to announce the formation of a federal task force to track down the assassin. In her message Gisela said she was glad I was all right and that she would call later that night.

The pain in my arm and shoulder began to throb. I took a dose of the medication I had been given and stretched out on the sofa. I must have lain there for an hour, trying to sleep, my mind racing from the shooting to the trial, from how much zealous hatred there was in the country to how important it was that Haviland be acquitted and that Browning go on. Restless, tired of being alone, I changed my clothes and went outside, across the street to the park.

The shots fired that morning had left no visible traces on the faces of the people I passed, but all the voices I heard were quiet and remote, and, except among the smallest children, there were no sounds of laughter. My eye caught sight of an older man bent down on one knee, helping a small boy launch a toy sailboat on the pond below. A woman in her early thirties, tall, gorgeous and proud, stood a few feet off to the side. From the look in her eyes, I knew she was the boy's mother and that she had married a man her father's age. It was a scene I had witnessed before. It was all part of New York: beauty and money and the lovely, eager-eyed children their merger made. I decided that life in Manhattan had not changed at all.

The boy's father looked up at his wife with a sad, pensive smile, as if to tell her that she and the boy were the two most important things in his life. If he had looked up the path and seen me, Charles F. Scarborough would not have remembered who I was. He was used to seeing me only in court; and after what had happened this morning to his friend Thomas Browning, he had doubtless other, more troubling thoughts on his mind.

Seeing him there with his young wife and child changed my mood again. It gave Scarborough a life outside of being a judge, and seemed to give me less of one. A lawyer, a trial lawyer, was all I was.

Other than the few antic evenings I had spent with Gisela Hoffman, it was the only life I had. With my hands plunged into my pants pockets I trudged back across the park, restless and depressed. The wind kicked up, and the autumn leaves swirled around my legs and ankles and crunched beneath my feet. I pulled my jacket close around my throat. Winter was coming, and I could not remember where the summer had gone.

I stayed up late, waiting for Gisela to call. I wanted to talk to her, to hear her voice; but more than that I needed to tell her that I had to talk to her anonymous friend. After what happened this morning, I could not take the chance of waiting any longer to get whatever he had. Sometime after midnight, I turned out the lamp and tried to sleep. Hours later I was still awake.

This would be the critical week at trial. Caminetti had two more witnesses, and then it was all up to me. I planned to lead with Annie's mother, Vivian Malreaux. I wanted the jury to know what Jimmy Haviland had done after her daughter had died. I wanted them to wonder whether he could have committed a murder and then become such a source of comfort and support. I wanted them to hear from Vivian

Malreaux what Jimmy Haviland had done in the war. But mainly I wanted that jury to see her, to see through the mother something of what the daughter must have been.

I lay in the dark, staring at the ceiling, watching the trial unfold. Vivian Malreaux first, Jimmy Haviland next. Normally, I would put him on last and let the jury begin deliberations with the defendant's adamant denials still fresh in their minds; but as everyone knew, this was not a normal trial. I was aware that there was a certain cruel irony in what I was going to do, that even at Jimmy Haviland's trial for murder, Thomas Browning would have the last word. There was no choice. Browning was the witness to what really happened to Annie Malreaux and that it happened only after Jimmy Haviland had left.

Those were my witnesses. I had one surprise. Whether I could get anything more from Gisela's mysterious source, I had to do something with what I had. If I could not prove what those names and numbers meant, I could still force someone who worked for the President to explain to a skeptical jury why two witnesses for the prosecution appeared together on a White House list. There was the chance that it was false information; that Gisela's friend, working for the White House, had taken advantage of her — or that someone inside the White House had taken advantage of him — that it had been given to me so that I would accuse two witnesses of taking White House bribes and then have it shown that they were just names and numbers and nothing close to proof. But I could play that game as well. I did not have to accuse anyone of anything; all I had to do was suggest that something was not right. I would show the list to one of the president's own men and ask him if he did not find it a little odd that what looked like a record of financial transactions involving witnesses in this trial should have come from a computer that only someone inside the Executive Office of the president could have used. Let him explain it; all I had to do was ask the question. The more I thought about it, the more convincing it became. When I finally fell asleep, sometime after three, I had thought about it so often, seen it so often in my mind — question and answer, then question and answer again — that I had completely forgotten that the people who were behind all this might have thought about it as well.

I woke with a start and for a moment did

not know where I was or if I was really awake. It was pitch-black; I could not see a thing. A shattering, strident sound ripped through the night, piercing straight into my brain. It was a gunshot! No, it was a fire alarm! I jumped out of bed and started for my clothes. But it stopped, and then, as I began to see the gray outline of the room, it came again. Muttering at my stupid, irrational fear, I reached down and picked up the phone. The clock on the bedside table read seven forty-five. I had overslept.

"Did I wake you?" asked Gisela after I murmured hello. There was a crisp energy to her voice.

"I tried to call you last night, but you weren't home. I left a message to call whenever you got in," I mumbled incoherently.

I sat on the edge of the bed, running my hand through my disheveled hair, as I tried to remember where I was supposed to be. My arm began to hurt, and for a moment I could not figure out why. I could hear her soft breath as she cradled the telephone under her chin so she could use both hands.

"Why didn't you call me?" I asked.

"I thought it was too late. I knew you were all right; I knew that you had been released from the hospital; but I thought you should sleep. Are you really all right?"

"I'm fine," I said, wincing at the sharp pain that shot through my arm. "Are you coming back this morning, to cover the trial?"

I was on my feet, prowling the room, moving my arm a little each way as I tried to think.

"Don't come back today. Stay there. I'll get a flight down late this afternoon, as soon as I get out of court. Can you meet me at the airport?"

"Yes, of course; but why . . . ?"

"I have to see your friend. You have to arrange it. Promise whatever you have to. I won't reveal his name; I won't do anything he doesn't want. But I have to talk to him. Tell him that after what happened yesterday, he doesn't have any choice. None of us does."

I stopped, caught my breath and then said more easily, "We can have dinner together tonight. Then, tomorrow, in the morning, you can come back to New York with me."

It took longer to dress with my bandaged arm, but I made it outside just as the car pulled up. There was a kind of solace in the easy cheerfulness of the driver's eyes and the rhythmic songlike banter of his voice. He talked all the way down Central Park West, through the street-choking traffic, all the way to Foley Square. He dropped me at the front of the courthouse, instead of the back. After what had happened, all the protesters were gone, the only placard left held by a frail determined old woman, asking that God bless the United States. It seemed, under the circumstances, a brave and decent thing to do.

"I need a ride to the airport later today, but I don't know when."

With two fingers bunched together, he tapped the cell phone he carried in his shirtfront pocket. "Anytime you like."

"And I'll need a ride back from the airport first thing in the morning."

He could calculate a profit faster than any banker I knew.

"You'll be wanting then to go from the airport to the apartment, then from there to here. I understand this right? Good. Always a pleasure to do such good business with you."

I was early, but Haviland had already arrived. He had acquired the habit of getting there before anyone else, so in the safety of the counsel table reporters could not badger him with the same questions he had been asked a hundred times before. Haviland and I had just begun to talk, when Caminetti tapped me on the shoulder and asked if he could have a word.

"I got calls this weekend from the White House and . . . ," he said.

"Who in the White House?"

We were standing between the two counsel tables, our backs to the crowd. With his shoulders hunched forward, he was staring down at the floor. He did not like being interrupted. He turned his head just far enough to give me an irritated glance.

"The White House . . ."

"Someone tried to kill Browning; the Secret Service agent who was there to protect him was shot in his place. What do I care what the White House wants?"

Caminetti shook his head and turned up his palms. "I'm sorry about what happened. I'm glad you're all right. But we've still got this trial, and the White House keeps calling. They don't know what's going on, and neither do I. What are you doing? You dropped a subpoena on . . . ?"

"What about it? Are they going to move to quash it? Is the White House going to let everyone think they've got something to hide?"

"You don't understand. They don't know anything about . . ."

Before he could say anything more, the bailiff's booming voice announced that court was in session. Caminetti and I both moved back to our places. Charles F. Scarborough greeted the jury with a long, thoughtful glance.

"As all of you know," he began, "there was an attempt yesterday morning on the life of Thomas Browning. Mr. Browning is scheduled to be a witness in this case. It is even more imperative now that you not let your personal feelings influence in any degree whatsoever your judgment about the credibility of this or any other witness in the case. That is your duty. You must do no less."

Without another word, he turned to Caminetti and invited him to call his next witness. We were back in court. No matter what might happen outside, the rules never changed.

"The People call Ezra Whitaker," announced Caminetti as he busied himself with a file.

It took a moment before it registered, then I was on my feet. I did not know anything about this witness: He was not on the prosecution's list.

"May counsel approach?" I made it sound as if there was nothing particularly wrong, that it was just some minor matter that needed to be addressed.

The three of us huddled together on the far side of the bench, out of the jury's view. "He's not on the list," I complained.

"That's right, Your Honor," admitted Caminetti without apology. "He's new. We just learned about him."

"This is Monday morning. You learned about him this weekend?" I asked with a skeptical smile.

Caminetti's eyes were on Scarborough. "We didn't have court Friday. That's when I first learned about the witness and the evidence he had."

"You learned this on Friday, but Mr. Antonelli didn't know anything about it until now — here — in court?" Scarborough got right to the point. "What evidence does he have?"

"A signed statement from a woman who witnessed the victim's death."

"From a witness?" I asked, incredulous. "Without any notice you suddenly produce a witness, not to what happened, but to what some other witness supposedly said?"

"Wrote," corrected Caminetti, dropping his eyes from Scarborough to the floor. "Wrote. It is a signed statement."

Scarborough fixed Caminetti with a profoundly inquisitive gaze. Beyond the immediate question, it sent a warning that he had better be careful, that he was on dangerous ground.

"I assume there is some reason why you propose to put Mr. Whitaker on the stand rather than the person who authored the statement you wish to offer into evidence?"

Raising his eyes before Scarborough finished his question, Caminetti listened with the same rigid impatience that he did to everything that made him wait.

"The written statement — that witness is dead. Whitaker was her lawyer. She had left . . ."

Scarborough cut him off. "In chambers."

Caminetti followed Scarborough, and I followed him. Scarborough threw open the door to his chambers, Caminetti caught it and with a short jab with the heel of his hand sent it flying back a second time. With a sideways step, I slipped in behind him and let the door slam shut.

"You would be well-advised, Mr. Caminetti, not to try my patience too much more than you already have."

Scarborough stood in the middle of that richly appointed room, his feet planted on a thick silk carpet, surrounded by thousands of gleaming leather books and a dozen luxurious, priceless paintings. His hands on his hips, he glowered at the New York district attorney as if Caminetti were a servant in danger of being dismissed. With the instincts of the street, Caminetti, ready for any challenge, spread his feet and glared right back.

"I have a witness. What's the problem?"

"Problems, Mr. Caminetti. There are several. First, this witness is not on your witness list. The defense was not given notice. Second, you want to offer into evidence the statement of a witness who is not available to testify, which means the witness cannot be subject to cross-examination by the defense. A defendant has the right to confront the witnesses against him. Third, if the statement is offered as a 'dying declaration' exception to the hearsay rule, there first has to be a showing that the declarant was aware that she was dying or knew she was in imminent danger of death when she made it. Fourth, and most important of all, I have the feeling, Mr. Caminetti, that you are playing fast and loose not just with the rules of evidence, but with the rules of the court. I am not going to allow it."

Caminetti bit hard on his lip. He blinked three, four times in rapid succession. His whole body seemed to tense.

"This witness has evidence crucial to the prosecution. This witness . . ."

"Let me see the document," demanded Scarborough, stretching out his hand.

"It's in the courtroom."

"Get it." Caminetti started to turn. "No, tell me what it says."

Caminetti glared with resentment at being ordered about. Quickly, he brought himself back under control.

"The statement says that Evelyn Morgan saw Jamison Scott Haviland push Anna Malreaux out the window at the Plaza Hotel December twenty-fourth, nineteen sixty-five. It says that she did not see it clearly enough to know if he had planned to kill her or had done it in a moment of anger. It says that Thomas Browning asked her to say it was an accident because everyone had been drinking and people would think it was his fault. She said she wanted to clear her conscience before she died."

"And it's signed and dated?"

"That's right."

"When is it dated?"

"Three years ago."

"When did she die?"

Caminetti shrugged. "A few weeks ago, a month maybe. Her lawyer started going through her papers for probate. That's when he found it."

"Then it isn't a dying declaration," mused Scarborough, stroking his chin; "but I suppose it could be argued that it is a statement against interest."

He put his hands behind his back. The expression in his eyes became more pensive. Caminetti began, not exactly to relax, but to become less hostile. He followed Scarborough's change of attitude with a searching, catlike glance.

"It has to be against the declarant's penal interest," I objected in a halfhearted attempt to move Scarborough in a different direction.

He raised his eyes and smiled. "She could have been charged with lying to the police, obstruction, even conspiracy." Scarborough slapped his forehead. "Of course! The statement is a confession of a coconspirator. Because if the statement is true, she conspired with both Browning and the defendant to cover up the crime."

He began to pace, his head bent, his eyes

busy and intense. A few moments passed. He stopped abruptly and peered intently at Caminetti.

"And the lawyer — this Whitaker — got hold of you, told you what he had found?"

"That's right," said Caminetti in a cautious voice.

"When? When did he first get hold of you? When did he first tell you — when did you first learn — about this statement?"

There was something forced and artificial about the way Caminetti stared back, as if he had to make a conscious effort not to let his eyes dart off somewhere else. Was he lying, or was he trying to hold something back?

"Friday." After a slight hesitation, he added: "He apparently called once or twice before. But Friday was the first I heard."

"Other people in your office knew about this before you did?"

With a quick toss of his head, and an even quicker tight-lipped smile, Caminetti dismissed it as a matter of no importance. "We've gotten hundreds of calls. It takes a while to sort them out."

Scarborough would not be put off. "You first knew about it Friday — morning or afternoon?"

"Morning," replied Caminetti, his voice again cautious and controlled.

Scarborough's gray trimmed eyebrows rose in a majestic arc. "And you did not advise Mr. Antonelli until now, when you could have given him the weekend to prepare?"

"I had a lot of things to do that day."

Scarborough's head bolted forward, as if he had been struck a blow and was instinctively striking back.

"Listen to me, Caminetti! I've been on the bench a long time, and that, without question, is the worst excuse I've ever heard. You 'had a lot of things to do that day'! You say anything like that to me again and I promise you contempt of court will be the least of the things you have to worry about!"

Caminetti took a step forward. Scarborough lifted his chin and with his eyes dared him to take another. Caminetti did not move.

"I apologize, Your Honor," he said, stepping back. "That was a stupid thing to say, but I was busy, and I simply forgot. If Mr. Antonelli needs time, of course he should have it."

We went back into court and solely for purposes of getting it on the record, I objected to the testimony of the witness on the ground that there had been a lack of notice and that, in any event, the statement of Evelyn Morgan was hearsay and inadmissible. The objection was duly noted and immediately overruled. I sat back and listened to Caminetti lay the groundwork for Ezra Whitaker and the bombshell he was about to explode.

"This will be the prosecution's last witness," said Caminetti on his way toward the witness stand.

He made it sound so normal, so routine — I did not catch the significance of it until he had already asked Ezra Whitaker to state his name. There were two names on that list of names and numbers I had been given, two witnesses Caminetti was going to call, but now he was only going to call one. A sense of panic crawled up my spine; my throat went dry. If he did not call them both, if he called only that drug-addicted witness to what Haviland had supposedly said to him in treatment, I had nothing to argue, nothing with which to raise a question about the strange and unlikely coincidence that two different witnesses, both of them crucial to the government's case, were on a White House list of people who had for some reason apparently been paid. My neck felt damp; my legs grew weak. My heart was racing, my breathing short. They must have found out that I had the list, they must have realized that using both of those paid-for witnesses put them too much at risk. Or maybe it had been nothing but chance. Maybe they did not know anything about what I had. Maybe they had just decided that with Whitaker they had all they needed. I darted a frantic glance at Haviland, but he could not give an answer to a question I could not ask.

"And you were Mrs. Morgan's personal attorney, and that's how you happen to have her personal papers?"

"Yes, that's correct. I had been her counselor and legal advisor for many years."

It was the slow-flowing thick-smooth voice of the southerner of a certain type, the ones trained by habit and history, as well as shrewdness and cunning and excessive self-love, never to utter a word that did not ooze sincerity with every vowel. Whitaker's silver-gray hair curled smartly at the back of his neck.

Ezra Whitaker. Why did that name sound familiar? What was there about it that reminded me of another name . . . ? Then I knew, or thought I knew. I leaned over and riffled through the papers thrown together in my briefcase until I found what I was looking for. Setting it on the table in front of me, I ran my finger down the edge of the first page, but his name was not there. Nor was it on the second page or the third or any of the rest; and then I was on the last page, certain it must be there, a name that started with *W,* the last name on that list of Byzantine transactions. But Ezra Whitaker was not on the White House list. I began to have a sickening, empty feeling in my stomach: the growing certainty that there was nothing I could do, that Jimmy Haviland was going to lose.

Caminetti was finished with the preliminaries. Whitaker put on his glasses, held a sheet of embossed stationery in his hands, and began to read. A woman with no earthly reason to lie had sworn on her immortal soul that she had once called a death an accident when she knew it was not; lied because she was young and frightened and because it was what Thomas Browning, whom she knew and trusted, had asked her to do. The air went out of the room; everything went flat. There was no more hope, no more expectation; just the sense that it was over now, that a man they heard enough about to like had killed a girl he was supposed to have loved; that another man, one they admired and respected, a man who had just yesterday nearly been killed, a man that most of them wanted to win the next election, had lied about a murder and done it for the worst reason of all: because he was a coward, afraid of what others might think.

"Do you wish to cross-examine the witness, Mr. Antonelli?" asked Scarborough. The face he showed the jury was unchanged by what he had heard; unchanged except for what I thought, or perhaps only imagined, was a new and deeper sadness in his eyes.

The document, that signed statement confessing her participation in a conspiracy of lies, could not be true. This woman — Evelyn Morgan — could not have seen what she said she had; but I had no way to prove either that she had lied or that the document itself was false. Whether Ezra Whitaker was himself a liar or the innocent victim of an ingenious scheme, I had no way to know.

"Your Honor, I have no questions, at least not yet. Mr. Caminetti has indicated that this will be the prosecution's final witness. I would ask that Mr. Whitaker be kept under subpoena and that we recess until the morning, at which time I will either cross-examine the witness or begin the case for the defense."

Scarborough looked at Caminetti. "Under the circumstances, that seems a reasonable proposal. I'm sure you won't object." With a cursory nod, Caminetti agreed.

As soon as the judge left the courtroom, the crowd began to rush outside, anxious to report on what appeared to be a crippling blow both to Thomas Browning and the defense. I turned to Haviland, whispering under the noise. "Do you remember anything about Evelyn Morgan, anything at all?"

There was a lost look in Haviland's eyes. He did not answer; he just shook his head.

"It doesn't matter," I told him, trying to revive his spirits. "You didn't do anything. That's the truth of it."

It was the truth, and we both knew that it was not nearly enough.

"Tomorrow I'll have something that will change everything. You'll see."

My empty promise had no effect. The look in his eyes, that anguished, ghostlike glance, had deepened, become more troubled, more at war with itself.

"Do you think I could have killed her,

done what they said, and then forgotten, burned it out of my head, imagined that it never happened? Do you think I'm mad, that I've lost my mind?" he asked with a wretched, heartbreaking stare.

23

As soon as we were in the car, Gisela started to talk about the attempt on Thomas Browning's life and what had happened at the trial.

"Everyone thinks Browning will have to withdraw." Both hands on the wheel, she gave me a sympathetic glance. "The White House doesn't want to look smug, especially after the shooting. They say they can't comment on a trial; but they have that look in their eyes. They know it's over. There is talk that they'll send up Reynolds's name as soon as the chief justice is dead."

I did not care what the White House thought; I did not care what anyone thought.

"Were you able to arrange it? Will he talk to me?"

She darted a glance in the rearview mirror. "I don't know. When I called him, he said I had a wrong number. A few minutes later, he called me. He would not talk on the telephone. We met at a coffee shop. He thinks he's being followed; he thinks his telephone is tapped."

"The White House?" I asked. "He thinks they know what he did?"

"No, they're watching everyone."

"Everyone who works in the White House?" I asked.

"He doesn't work in the White House."

"I thought this was your White House source, the one who told you about the investigation, the indictment . . ."

"I did not say he was someone inside the White House." She gave me a quick, apologetic glance. "I couldn't tell you; I can't tell you. I promised I would not say anything about him."

If he was not in the White House, how had he obtained access to the White House computer system — the one that Browning said was restricted to the executive office of the President?

"Where does he work?"

"I don't know."

"You don't know, or you can't tell me?"

"All I know is that it's secret, and that it's important, and that he seems to know everything that is going on."

"You said you didn't know if he would talk to me. That means he didn't say no," I remarked, clinging to the last hope I had.

"I told him I was picking you up at the airport. He said he would call tonight."

We drove into Georgetown, but instead of turning to go to her house, Gisela pulled up in front of a restaurant. Two blocks away, on the other side of the street, was the place where in that dim private up-stairs dining room I had had lunch with Joanna. I wondered what must have gone through her mind these last few days. First the attempt to assassinate her husband, then the revelation that the case against Jimmy Haviland now included the deathbed confession of a woman Thomas Browning had asked to lie. Nothing could have prepared her for this.

"Could he have?"

"What?" I asked, looking up from the dinner I had scarcely touched.

"Could he have done that — asked that woman to lie?"

"Browning? No," I said, wondering whether I still believed it. "No," I repeated, the doubt, minuscule at first, now a little more advanced. "I'd be surprised."

The doubt to her seemed real. Reflected back, I became irritated, angry, as if the only doubt was hers.

"Browning is too intelligent to have done

that," I insisted. "And he was in love with Annie. He was not Thomas Browning then; he wasn't the man everyone knows now: the famous politician, the man a lot of people think should be president. He was not the former senator, or the former head of Stern Motors; he wasn't the former anything. He didn't want anything to do with the company; he certainly would not have covered up a crime because of what might happen to its reputation."

Perhaps I had only been trying to convince myself that Browning could not have done what they said, but the more I thought about it — the more I remembered about the way things had been — the more certain I was that I was right.

"Browning was in love with Annie Malreaux. That's what they all forget. He was in love with her! He would have given up everything he had, gone off somewhere the other side of the world, if she'd been willing to go off with him. Ask someone to lie about her murder — to save Jimmy Haviland, who had just killed the girl, the only girl, he loved? It doesn't make sense."

But Gisela had not known Browning then; she only knew him now. What I remembered, she could not quite imagine.

"But wouldn't he have worried that people would think it was his fault? Wouldn't he have been concerned with what it would do to his chances later on?"

"His chances?"

"He knew he was going to be running one of the largest companies in the world. He must have thought about the things that would allow him to do. He must have thought about his reputation."

"His reputation? Whatever he was thinking about the day Annie Malreaux died, I'm sure it wasn't that."

Gisela was not quite convinced. She was about to ask me something else, when the waiter interrupted to tell her that she had a call. When she came back to the table, I could tell from the look in her eyes who had called and what he had said.

"He'll meet you tonight. Eleven o'clock at the Lincoln Memorial."

We lingered over coffee until half past ten. When we got back in the car, I looked up and down the street, watching to see if, when we left, anyone was following behind. Half a block away, a beige colored Chevrolet pulled out at the same time, but when we turned at the corner, it kept going straight. At the Lincoln Memorial, instead of stopping, we crossed the bridge, drove another mile, then doubled back. Gisela dropped me in a secluded spot about a hundred yards away and then found a place to park the car and wait.

As I climbed the white marble steps, I caught a glimpse of someone in a tan overcoat with the collar pulled up, standing on the other side of the statue, pacing back and forth. He watched me with a kind of indifference, as if he did not care if I kept coming or not. Then, suddenly, he turned and disappeared. I began to move more quickly, each step quicker than the last, until I reached the base of the statue. I stopped and looked around. I heard a woman's voice from somewhere in the distance below.

"Have you seen enough? It's getting late. We should go."

Then I saw him, the man in the coat, catching up with the woman whose voice I had just heard. He was a tourist, a visitor, someone who wanted to see the Lincoln Memorial the way it looked lit up at night.

I hovered near the statue, hoping that the next person who came along would be the man I was there to meet. I checked my watch. It was eleven o'clock exactly. Five minutes went by, then ten. A car pulled up below, a door opened, and someone stumbled out. There was a peal of laughter as a hand reached from inside and pulled him back. The car raced away, and I was again alone. I went down to where Gisela was waiting in the car.

"Give it a few more minutes," she suggested.

I trudged back up the steps, gazing with curiosity at Lincoln's wise and melancholy face. Browning had understood that after Lincoln the word, at least the spoken word, would suffer a decline. How had he known that? How had he grasped so early what so many still did not understand? That in our frenzied effort to do a dozen things at once, we had forgotten that it takes time to do one thing well. I looked at the statue and thought about Browning, and about the speech he had given that day at the edge of the park while thousands pressed forward, eager to catch every word. Browning understood the power of the word. At eleven-thirty, when there was still no sign of Gisela's anonymous friend, I walked down the steps and told her we might as well go.

We got back to Georgetown and parked the car. I waited while Gisela, fumbling in the dark, unlocked the door. The telephone began to ring, and Gisela dashed toward the kitchen while I stood in the narrow hallway trying to find the lights.

"I think it's him," she said, her hand over the receiver. "There's someone on the line. I can hear him breathing, but he won't speak."

I took the telephone from her hand and held it next to my ear. There was nothing, not a sound.

"Who's there?" I demanded.

"One hour." That was all; just those two words, then the line went dead. "One hour?" I exclaimed, staring at Gisela, baffled.

Something caught her eye. A half page, torn from a small spiral notebook, the kind reporters use, had been left on the kitchen table.

"This is from him," she said, handing it to me.

" 'National Cathedral. Alone. Park the car across the street and wait,' " I read out loud.

"He was here," she explained. "While we were at the Lincoln Memorial, he was here. He must have come down the alley in back."

She went to the back door. The chain that locked it from the inside hung loose. The metal plate that held it had been pried off.

"He must have wanted to make sure no one was following us," I remarked, wondering what made him so cautious and afraid.

I borrowed Gisela's car. A few minutes before one in the morning I parked across the street from the cathedral where official Washington gathered for a final farewell whenever someone died for whom the whole nation would mourn. In a few days, or perhaps a week, it would be the chief justice's turn.

There were other cars parked on the street, and there was traffic on the road. A few lights flickered from windows in the neighborhood. The headlights of a car flashed in the rearview mirror. I raised my hand to shield my eyes. The car sped past and I took a deep breath, wondering how long I was going to have to wait. Then, suddenly, something cold and hard was pressed against the base of my skull. He had opened the door, slipped inside the back seat, and I had not heard a thing.

"Don't turn around."

It struck me funny: With a gun pressed against my head, I was too scared to move.

"Drive."

"Where?" I asked, a stupid stammer in my voice.

"Anywhere. Just keep your eyes straight ahead on the road."

I pulled away from the curb and within a few blocks was completely lost. Gisela had given me directions to the cathedral; beyond that I did not know where I was or how to get from one place to the next.

"Why didn't you use the list? What are you waiting for? Don't you know what's at stake?"

Once I began to drive, he sat back against the seat, not directly behind me but in the middle, behind the split between the two front bucket seats. Despite his warning, I glanced in the mirror. The gun was now held in his lap, pointed almost casually to the side. I caught in the shadows a brief glimpse of his face. He was in his forties, I thought, with heavy lines in his forehead and troubled, anxious eyes. He did not seem like someone eager to be out at one in the morning, involved in a clandestine meeting with someone he did not know and about whose competence he clearly had doubts.

"You're a friend of Gisela's, and Gisela is a friend of mine. Why did you think you needed a gun?"

"Do you know who I am?" he asked in a voice that surprised me. It had the texture of a well-read man. "You don't even know my name," he went on. "Gisela would not tell you anything about me I did not want her to tell. I don't know why I trust her, but I do. You're fortunate, Mr. Antonelli. I wish I had . . ."

He stopped in midsentence. He did not need to say another word. It was all there, in the space between and after the words, that sense of something you know you can never have. I had heard it before, in Haviland's voice and in Browning's voice as well, when they talked about Annie Malreaux.

"She has not told me anything. Until tonight I thought you worked inside the White House. I thought . . ."

"The White House?" he interjected with a short, rueful laugh. "Now listen to me. I haven't got much time. I'm only going to tell you this once. This is dangerous, more dangerous than you know. Everyone is being watched. The case against your client was fabricated; it's all lies and half-truths, it's . . ."

"I know that; I know that's what they've done. But I need proof."

"They bought Fitzgerald," he went on, appearing to pay no attention to what I had said. "He wasn't in treatment with

606

Haviland. He's never seen him in his life. Do you understand what I'm telling you? Fitzgerald wasn't there. But you won't be able to prove it. They changed the records, added his name and a medical file. You think the government can make people disappear? They can create witnesses who don't exist; they can make them be places they have never been."

"Witnesses who don't exist . . . ? Evelyn Morgan? They made her up? But Whitaker wasn't on the list."

"Whitaker isn't involved. Evelyn Morgan is what he said she was. She knew Browning. She was probably at the Plaza the day Anna Malreaux died. The rest of it — the statement — that's what I meant."

I started to ask a question, but he placed his hand on my right shoulder and told me to make the next right turn.

"Pull up at the next corner and let me out." He reached over and on the passenger-side seat dropped a zippered black plastic bag, the size a slim laptop computer would fit inside. "It's all there, everything you'll need. No," he cautioned me when I reached toward it. "Not now."

"But there might be something I need to ask, I . . ."

"I've taken too big a chance as it is. Now

607

pull over and let me out."

I kept driving. There were too many things I had to know.

"I said pull over."

"The name — used by whoever kept track of the payments, the routing of the money — Lincoln Edwards. Who is it?"

"It's all there," he repeated.

"Why are you doing this?"

"I took an oath to protect and defend the United States. Nobody gets to go around trying to convict somebody of a murder he didn't commit just because it's the only way they've got to destroy the only person they might not be able to defeat. One of the problems with doing something like that," he added with a kind of grim satisfaction, "is that someone finds out about it, and then all you've done is give them the chance to get you first. It's like chasing someone in a circle, thinking you're sneaking up on him, only it turns out he's sneaking up on you."

He pointed to a vacant curb half a block ahead. "Pull over there."

"You're not in the White House. How did you get all this?"

He placed the gun inside his jacket. I stopped the car and with the engine still running turned off the lights.

"You understand that we've never met? This ride never happened. Whom do I work for? You've heard of the CIA — the National Security Agency? You haven't heard of us."

"What about the assassination attempt? Was the White House involved?"

"You were there. What do you think? What did he look like to you? Some lunatic with a cause? Or a cold-eyed assassin who could come right at you, get close enough to feel your breath and then, after he pulled the trigger, walk away?

"Don't trust anyone: These people are everywhere. Your best friend could be working for them. Look what they're doing to your client. Do you think it stops with him?"

He left and I sat there a minute with the lights out, so that no one would see him go. When I was sure he was safely away, I pulled out from the curb and headed down the street, my mind full of what he had said.

It took me a while to find my way back to Georgetown and to Gisela's house. She greeted me barefoot at the door, dressed in a blue silk nightgown. Her eyes, dark and mysterious, as intimate as the night, made me forget everything except how lovely she was. All I wanted was to crawl into bed with her and never leave.

She noticed the zippered bag I held under my arm. "You have it, then — what you need?" She took my hand and led me down the narrow hallway, through the dining room, to the kitchen in back. "You'll need to work — yes? I'll make some coffee, then I'll go to bed so you won't be disturbed."

"What can you tell me about him — your friend, the man I just talked to, the one who gave me this?"

Gisela bent her head a little to the side. "I promised I wouldn't."

"He said he did not trust anyone, but that he trusted you. He's still in love with you, you know."

She accepted it as a fact of existence, that men fell in love with women, and women fell in love with men, not always with each other and not always at a time when it could work.

"If there is one person who would always do the right thing, even if it would cost him everything to do it . . ." She gave me a long, searching look. "Did he tell you how dangerous this is — what you're doing? Is it worth it?"

She made the coffee, poured me a cup

and kissed me briefly on the side of my face. "We're on the plane together at seven. Maybe you can sleep for an hour or so."

I pulled her down onto my lap and she nestled her face against my neck while I held her close.

"This is going to be over soon," I said. "Why don't we go away somewhere for a while, before we decide what we're going to do next?"

"Yes."

"Yes?" I asked, laughing quietly, not only at her charming, funny voice, but also at how much I had wanted her to say that, to tell me that there was something to look forward to, that the end of the trial did not have to be the end of us. When I was young, when I thought I might be falling in love with Joanna, I did not think much about when things would end. Now, it was almost the first thing on my mind, the fear that happy endings were tales told by idiots to strangers and to fools.

"Yes, we'll go somewhere, anywhere you like," she whispered before she slipped her arm from around my neck and went upstairs to bed.

I tried to imagine what it would be like to have her alone and not worry about what was going to happen next. It was the dream I might have had with Joanna, if I had not been so full of my own ambition, and so foolish as to think that things always, or even very often, turned out for the best.

I was losing time. In six hours I was going to be back in court. I emptied the contents of the zippered pouch onto the table and went to work.

On our way to the airport and again on the plane, I barely spoke a word. I was still concentrating on what I had learned, reviewing it, organizing it, reorganizing it in my mind. On a reporter's notebook borrowed from Gisela, I jotted down the questions that had to be asked and the answers I hoped to elicit. I listed them in the order they should be asked, looked at them, then tore up the list and wrote another; looked at that, and then did it again. It still was not right; I started all over. In the car from La Guardia, I crumpled up the last list I wrote and tossed it on the floor. We were coming into Manhattan, crossing the bridge; there was no time to try again. But it did not matter now; I had reviewed it so many times, thought about it in so many ways, that when it counted, when I had to face the witness, the questions would organize themselves. It was like being back in law school, pulling an all-nighter, getting ready for an exam. When we had a class together, Browning and I would go over the material so often that, at the end of it, when the dawn was breaking and we were both giddy without sleep, instead of tossing questions at each other and getting answers back, we would do it the other way around: give an answer and get the question. I would have studied for days to get to that point; Browning could do it even when he had not started until the night before.

The courtroom was empty; I was the first to arrive. The maroon leather chairs in the jury box had a sedate, elegant look, as if they were going to be used for the board meeting of a rich and powerful corporation instead of by a dozen average strangers called from their normal anonymous existence to decide whether someone should live or die. A deputy came in from the side entrance, the same one through which the bailiff, the clerk, the court reporter and the judge would eventually come. Wearing dark blue pants and a black leather belt, a shiny white shirt stiff with starch and a blue tie, he had three blue stripes on his sleeve. I had seen him every day in court, a big, burly man who went about his business quietly and quickly, but he had been a part of the background, not someone to whom I had paid any serious attention. I was tempted to ask him what the stripes meant, whether they referred to his rank, but the door opened again and the court reporter came in and began to set up her machine, and a few moments after her, the clerk. The pale yellow sun slanted through the narrow windows high above the jury box, daybreak in what was, now that I thought about it, the only world I knew.

The double set of double doors in back swung open with growing regularity as the stream of reporters and spectators began to swell. Sitting beside me, Haviland drummed his fingers against the hard surface of the table that, from the look of it, had not been cleaned or polished in years.

"Are we going to have a good day?" he asked in an even-tempered voice.

I had come to admire Jimmy Haviland, more every day, more than I had ever thought I would. He was the one accused of murder, the one whose reputation, even if he was acquitted, would never be the same; but throughout the trial his emotions had been more closely guarded, kept more under his own control, than I had been able to keep my own. I gave him a confident look, which this time was real.

"A very good day."

The bailiff let out a sudden cry. Everyone sprang to his feet, but nothing happened. The eyes fixed on the door shifted with a kind of wrathful fury to the bailiff, expecting some show of contrition. A slight movement of his eyes warned us that we had better stay where we stood. A smile of vindication quivered briefly at the side of his mouth as, not two seconds later, the door flew open and Charles F. Scarborough bustled across the front of the courtroom.

"Bring in the jury," he bellowed, rubbing his hands as he greeted the courtroom crowd with a cheerful grin.

"Mr. Antonelli," he fairly shouted, swiveling around to face me after the jury had filled the box and he had welcomed them back. "How would you like to proceed? Do you wish to begin with a cross-examination of the prosecution's last witness, or do you wish to begin the case for the defense by calling the first witness of your own?"

"I have a few questions for the prosecution's last witness, Your Honor."

"Very well. Would the bailiff ask Mr.

Whitaker to return to the witness stand?"

Ezra Whitaker was admonished that he was still under oath. As I approached the witness, Scarborough leaned forward to watch.

"Yesterday you testified that the statement of Evelyn Morgan implicating the defendant, Jamison Haviland, in the death of Anna Malreaux, was among her private papers. You found it when, as I believe you put it, you started going through her papers for probate. Is that correct, Mr. Whitaker?"

Whitaker sat with one leg crossed over the other and his head held high. "Yes," he said in a deep slow drawl. "That is correct."

"And that document was signed in her hand?"

"I handled Mrs. Morgan's legal affairs for a great many years. I was quite familiar with her signature."

"And she apparently signed this document three years ago."

"Again, that's correct." Whitaker tugged at his left lapel and then, with the back of two fingers, brushed lint from off his tie. He looked up. "Yes, that's correct," he repeated, puzzled why I had not immediately moved on.

"When exactly did Evelyn Morgan die?"

"Six weeks ago."

"Six weeks?"

"Yes."

"And when did you first see it? What was the date on which you first saw this document, this signed statement of Evelyn Morgan?"

Whitaker stroked his chin. "Let me see. Two weeks ago tomorrow."

"That is the first you knew about this? This woman you had known for so many years had never mentioned anything about it to you before?"

"No. I was quite stunned when I read it. Mrs. Morgan was a very gentle woman, a refined woman, from one of the best families around. The idea that she would have had any knowledge of a crime, that she could have been involved in keeping that crime a secret, is, I must say, completely foreign to everything I knew about her."

"I understand," I remarked with a certain detached sympathy. "Were there any instructions concerning what you were to do with it?" Before he could answer, I asked, as if the question had just occurred to me, "Was it even directed to you? I mean, was it inside a sealed envelope, with your name on it, with some language to the effect that it was to be opened only in the event of her death?"

Whitaker shook his head. "No, my name was not on it. I first . . ."

"Had it been left with you for safe-keeping, or was this document simply found among her other personal papers?"

"It was never given to me."

"It was not under your control? It was not locked up in your office safe, or at least kept under lock and key?"

"No, as I say, she did not give it to me."

"But you were her lawyer. You had drafted her will?"

"Yes."

"You had that in your office, didn't you?"

"Yes, of course. She had a copy, of course, but . . ."

"But though she understood that you had her will, and that you would be handling her estate, she never thought to entrust you with this very important document that she apparently wanted no one to see while she was still alive. Doesn't that strike you as a little odd?"

"I can't say why she did what she did. All I can tell you is that, again, it was among her private papers."

"In an envelope?"

"Yes."

"Among her private papers which she kept . . . where?"

"In her desk at home."

"Locked in a drawer?"

"I don't believe the drawer was locked — no."

"She died six weeks ago, and you discovered the document two weeks ago. About how long had you had her private papers before you discovered the document?"

"I suppose I must have had them for a week or so," he said with a vague smile on his lips.

"So for two or three weeks after her death, those papers, including that signed statement, were still there, in that unlocked desk drawer in her home?"

"Yes, of course. Her sister brought them to me. She had gone through Mrs. Morgan's things."

"The envelope it was in — you say it was sealed?"

"Yes."

"So until you opened it, no one — not her sister, not anyone — could have known what was inside. Would that be correct?"

Whitaker inclined his head a hairbreadth to the side. "Yes, I believe that would be correct."

"One last question," I said as I started

walking back to the counsel table. "Because you were so familiar with Mrs. Morgan's signature, I assume you did not think it necessary to have that signature authenticated by anyone else — a handwriting expert, for example?"

"No," he answered, wondering why I would ask. "There wasn't any reason to."

"No, of course not," I said as I looked from the witness to the bench. "No more questions, Your Honor."

I waited until Ezra Whitaker had left the witness stand and had reached the doors at the back of the courtroom.

"Your Honor, the defense calls, as its first witness, Arthur Connally."

24

Arthur Connally came into court with the impatient swagger of a man used to having everyone look to him for direction; he took the oath as if the implied suggestion that he had to swear to tell the truth was a personal affront.

"You are the chief of staff to the president of the United States, correct?"

Caminetti bounced up from his chair. "Leading."

"Yes, it is," I remarked, cool and indifferent.

Throwing up his hands, Caminetti staggered forward as if the burden of correction was too great. "It's his witness."

"Mr. Connally has been called by the defense, but he isn't our witness," I replied, ignoring Caminetti as I focused on the judge. "He's on the other side. Permission to treat as hostile, Your Honor."

I moved from the front corner of the counsel table, through the shaft of light that cut across the floor, until I was standing directly in front of the witness stand. I was close enough to the jury box to touch the railing with my hand. Tucked under my arm was a single thin file folder.

"Before you were the president's chief of staff, you managed his campaign, correct?"

Connally's head was bent to the side, a look of angry suspicion in his eyes. His mouth, barely open, scarcely moved when he grunted his reply.

"That was the campaign in which Thomas Browning was the other leading candidate for the Republican nomination, correct?"

I started to taunt him with my eyes, to let him know that I was in charge, that I could keep him there, answering questions, for as long as I liked.

"Would you be kind enough to take a look at this?"

I stepped close to him and removed from the file a single sheet of paper. He took it with a certain staged reluctance, trying to show his contempt. He held the sheet of paper with his thumb and the tip of his index finger, as if anything that came from my hand must be unclean. But the gesture was too obvious and he realized he had gone too far. He studied it a moment and then looked up.

"Have you ever seen this document before?"

"I read about it."

Turning my back on him, I faced the jury. "That was not my question."

"I don't understand your question."

The eyes of the jury had gone to Connally; I waited until they came back to me. Smiling to myself as if I had heard this same predictable testimony a hundred times before from witnesses who had something to hide, I lowered my eyes.

"Read it," I said.

"What?"

"Read it!" I shouted as I wheeled around and stared hard at him. "You have it in your hands. Read it out loud!"

Connally looked at Caminetti, expecting him to do something. Caminetti looked at Scarborough, expecting the same thing. Scarborough looked at me, expecting an explanation.

"I want the jury to know what it is he's looking at; and I want there to be no mistake that the witness has actually read and understands what is written on that page. This is the copy Mr. Caminetti gave me of the document the prosecution entered into evidence, the signed statement of Evelyn Morgan, the supposedly eyewitness account of what happened to Anna Malreaux."

"Supposedly?" cried Caminetti, bolting to his feet.

"Exactly! Supposedly!"

"Very well," interposed Scarborough, motioning with the back of his hand for Caminetti to sit down. "Proceed."

Connally read the short, damning statement of Evelyn Morgan, and then, as if it signaled a triumph, the proof of something he had said, or if he had not said, believed all along, gazed at me with a vindictive smile. "As I say, I read about it."

"In the newspapers?"

"Yes, in the newspapers." He bent forward, his elbows on the arms of the witness chair, gripping his hands together. I might still be asking questions, but he was in control now. "I think everyone read about it." Shifting his weight, he brought his left hand up to his chin, stroking it with confidence and satisfaction.

"It's pretty much the same allegation you made yourself, isn't it? In the last campaign — against Thomas Browning."

Connally's hand flew out to the side, a dismissive gesture that rejected both what I had said and what it implied.

"That a woman had died — been murdered — in a hotel room in New York, and that Thomas Browning had been involved. Surely, you remember this — South Carolina, the primary you had to win, because if you lost it nothing could stop him from getting the nomination."

There was no answer. Connally just looked at me as if none of this was of any concern to him.

"Are you going to sit there, under oath, and tell us that you don't know anything about that? That you never heard of anything like that being said about Thomas Browning during that campaign, that campaign you led?"

Caminetti was on his feet. "Relevance, Your Honor? I don't know where counsel thinks he's going with this, but . . ."

"I'll show relevance, Your Honor," I promised. My eyes were riveted on Connally as I gripped the railing of the jury box. "Answer the question," I insisted with all the force I could. "You knew about this rumor, didn't you?"

Connally shrugged. "There are rumors in every campaign."

I kept gripping the railing, my hand almost numb. "You were in charge of the overall campaign. You had people whose job it was to research the background, the history, of the opposition — correct?"

I began to walk around, a few steps one way, then a few steps back, concentrating on everything that was said.

"Anyone who did that — anyone competent, anyone who knew what they were doing — would have gone all the way back to the beginning, to the earliest days of Thomas Browning's life, to his family history, the story of how his grandfather had built Stern Motors, the way Thomas Browning had been raised. That's what any campaign would have done, isn't that correct, Mr. Connally?"

He agreed that there was nothing exceptional in doing any of that. Every campaign, at least every campaign for the presidency, wanted to know everything there was to know about the other candidates in the race.

"And that would include a candidate's personal life — whom he dated, whether he was ever engaged, whether he was ever involved in an illicit affair — correct?"

Connally was no fool. He understood perfectly the evil necessities forced upon you by an imperfect world.

"Yes, I'm afraid the process has become much too intrusive. No one is allowed even a small mistake. Things get blown way out of proportion."

"I'll take that as a yes. Now, you had people checking up on Thomas Browning's personal life, the girls he dated when he was in school . . . Annie Malreaux. And that meant someone must have learned how she died, must have learned she fell out a window during a party, a party given by Thomas Browning." I raised my head and searched his eyes. "You knew that, didn't you? I don't mean someone in the campaign, I mean you. You knew that Annie Malreaux fell out a window Christmas Eve nineteen sixty-five; you knew that Thomas Browning was there when it happened. Answer the question, Mr. Connally. Do you want me to ask it again?"

"No, you don't have to ask it again. Yes, I knew that. So what?"

" 'So what'? Well, let's see. The facts were that she fell out the window and that Browning was there. The rumor, the one that somehow got started in South Carolina when everything — the campaign, the nomination, William Walker's one and only chance for the presidency — was on the line, was not that she fell, but that she was pushed; not that it was an accident, but that it was murder, and that

Thomas Browning was involved. And that rumor started with you, didn't it, Mr. Connally?"

Anger, cold and implacable, stalked through Arthur Connally's deep-set hostile eyes. "That's a lie. I did no such thing."

Suddenly, it hit him: a way to prove that he was not lying and, better yet, prove it out of my mouth.

"Don't you remember what you just had me read? There was a witness. It wasn't some rumor someone made up. It was the truth, and someone had started to talk. That's what happens, you know; that's how things come out. Someone tells someone and then he tells someone else."

I had begun to move away from him, slowly, so I would not miss anything he said. When he was done, I faced him across the courtroom. The witness stand seemed to fall back into a darkened corner, caught between the jury box on one side and the judge's bench on the other. I gave him a look that called him a liar.

"Yes, I see. That must have been what happened. Not some vicious rumor you started or helped to start for purposes of your own, but the truth, making its way into the light after all these years because, of course, as that old saying goes,

628

'the truth will out.' "

I dropped the file I had been holding and picked up another, thicker one, in its place.

"Now tell us this, Mr. Connally: As chief of staff one of your responsibilities is to decide who gets to see the president?"

It was a different line of questioning. Connally watched me as I came toward him, trying to guess where I might be going with it.

"There is some of that," he replied in a guarded voice.

I was halfway there, moving toward the witness stand in a rapid stride, the file dangling in my left hand.

"You are also responsible for the flow of information into the Oval Office: not only what the president sees, but the form it takes — whether, for example, a proposal from someone in the administration goes directly to the president or whether other members of the administration have the chance to comment on it first?"

Connally rolled on his hip, giving me his shoulder as he faced toward the jury. "There's a system in place, a process in which . . . ," he began to explain.

"Yes, as a matter of fact nearly everything goes through a sophisticated computer system — isn't that right, Mr. Connally? A system that's under the control of someone with the title staff secretary — correct?"

His eyes cut away from the jury. "Yes, but . . ."

"And the staff secretary reports directly to you, because everyone who works in the White House is responsible to you — correct?"

I was right in front of him. We were just feet apart, staring at one another, hostile and intense.

"Would you be kind enough to please identify this?" I asked as I took a step back and reached inside the file.

"It's a blank sheet of paper," he replied after he looked at what I had given him. A thin smile of contempt curled along his lower lip.

"Would you please look at it again — the line across the top. Do you see it there — 'EOP'? Doesn't that indicate 'Executive Office of the President'?" I lowered my eyes and then, in a slow half circle, raised them to the jury box. "And the rest of it — those different letters and marks — doesn't that indicate that this has been generated from inside the White House system, and not only that but — I think it's called an

'IP' number — the individual computer terminal from which it was sent?"

Connally looked at me with a kind of weary indifference. He had better, more important things to do than listen to the meaningless jargon that could only possibly matter to some useless computer hack.

"Yes, I suppose it does, but I don't . . ."

"And you're aware, are you not, that while this information doesn't normally appear at the top of a message, it is easy enough to have it printed out?"

"Yes, I suppose, but . . ."

"Who is Lincoln Edwards?"

"Who?" he asked, indifference giving way to exasperation. "Lincoln Edwards? I don't think I know that name."

I showed him another sheet of paper, holding it in my hand, folded over so that he could see only the part I wanted him to see, the e-mail address at the very top.

"This is from the White House system. It has the same address as what I gave you before. Notice the name of the sender."

Connally looked at the document and then looked at me. "Lincoln Edwards."

"Yes, Lincoln Edwards. But you say you don't know anyone by that name. That's strange, isn't it? You run the White

House — you're in charge — yet there is someone working there whose name you've never heard? Of course, quite a few people work in the White House, don't they? But, then, how many of them would be sending messages directly to the president himself?"

Connally grabbed at the paper. "Go ahead," I said, letting it go. "See for yourself. POTUS. That's the famous acronym, isn't it? President of the United States."

He held it with both hands, reading what had been sent from Lincoln Edwards to the President.

"Here, you might as well have the rest." I removed from the file the five remaining pages from the list of names and numbers that included two of the witnesses the prosecution had originally intended to call.

"What's this?" demanded Connally as if I owed him an answer instead of the other way around.

"It's a list of names and numbers; it's a list of monies paid and the extraordinary lengths to which someone went to keep secret what he had done. It's a list that among other things includes a record of payments made to two witnesses in this trial, one of whom has already testified, the other of whom has not yet been called."

With a sidelong glance at Caminetti, who was sitting at the edge of his seat, clenching his teeth, I added: "Perhaps the prosecution is saving that one for rebuttal." My eyes darted back to Connally. "Tell me, is it your testimony that in addition to Lincoln Edwards, the name — there, right on the list, a little farther down — Gordon Fitzgerald . . . you've also never heard of him?"

"He was a witness in the trial, wasn't he?"

It was stunning how well he could lie: the blank look of total incomprehension with which he managed to mask both his knowledge and his guilt. Was it the short-lived memory of the politician, eager to forget the evil he had committed because of the good he was convinced he could still achieve? Jamison Haviland might face the executioner, but all his death would mean to Arthur Connally was that William Walker was one step closer to a second term.

Connally's question echoed false and discordant in the hushed stillness. I walked to the counsel table and lifted up a paper-bound directory.

"This is the White House telephone book. No one named Lincoln Edwards is listed inside it. The question becomes, Mr. Connally, how did someone who doesn't work in the White House have access to a White House computer? And how was he able to communicate directly with POTUS, the president, himself?"

Connally did not immediately answer, and I did not give him time to think.

"All messages — and there must be millions of them each year — that go through this system are stored, kept, made part of the historical record, by law — correct?"

"Yes," he admitted. He was leaning forward, gripping the arms of the chair, all his senses alert.

"It's impossible to remove anything — the hard drive, everything, stays in place — correct?"

"Yes, that's true."

"And you've already testified that each computer has an identification — an IP number. Each computer is assigned to someone and that person has his own password, the word that gets him into the system — isn't that correct?"

"Yes, but I . . ."

I tossed the White House directory on the table and picked up another file. Holding it open in front of me, I walked at a slow, steady pace across the courtroom floor, passing through the shaft of sunlight, into the shadowed corner formed by the witness stand and the jury box.

"This is a list of computer assignments inside the White House. I have drawn a circle around your name. Do you see it?" I asked as I handed him the sheet.

"Yes," he replied in a cautious, tentative voice.

"The computer assigned to you is identified by a number, correct?"

"That's right."

"Good," I remarked, nodding politely as I took back the sheet of paper. I started to ask him another question, but then, as if I had just remembered something, I walked quickly to the counsel table and picked up the file I had had before.

"I almost forgot," I said as I hurried back. "This, the one I showed you before, the list of names and numbers, the one with Gordon Fitzgerald's name, the one sent by that Lincoln Edwards who doesn't work in the White House and whom you don't know — Take another look. See the number there at the top, that tiny codelike line — the identification number? Now look at this again," I said in a voice that was suddenly hard, cold and unforgiving. "Look at the identification number of the computer assigned to you." I shoved the document in front of his face. "It's the same, isn't it? It's the same because, you're right, Lincoln Edwards doesn't work in the White House — you do. You're Lincoln Edwards. You took that name so that if someone happened to stumble on a printed copy of it, they wouldn't know — not without some knowledge of the White House system and the way each computer was assigned — they wouldn't know it was you, the White House chief of staff, the president's former campaign manager, the president's closest friend, who was behind all of this, this conspiracy to buy perjured testimony, to forge documents, to do anything you had to do to bring about first the indictment, then the conviction of an innocent man because it was the only way you had to destroy Thomas Browning before Thomas Browning could defeat William Walker in a fair election!"

"That's a lie!" cried Connally, shooting straight up from the chair. "You can't accuse me of . . . !"

"Accuse you? You accused yourself! What do you think you've done here, claiming you never heard of Lincoln Edwards when, as these documents plainly show, Lincoln Edwards is you! But there's more to it than that, Mr. Connally. We're not quite through. There's one thing I haven't yet asked you about."

There was one more document left. I pulled it from the file and while everyone watched folded it carefully in half. I held the bottom half in front of Connally's eyes.

"What does it say, Mr. Connally? Read it out loud, so the jury can hear."

When Connally saw what it said, he refused. "What does this have to do with me?"

"Here," I said as I gave him the document. "Read the whole thing; read it from the very beginning; read out loud to the jury this message that Lincoln Edwards — that you — sent to the president of the United States."

Unfolding it, he started to read. "To POTUS, from Lincoln Edwards. We used this in South Carolina. It worked then, it will work even better now . . ."

The hand that held it dropped into his lap. He looked at me with a puzzled expression, as if he could not understand how anyone had found out.

I had worked on it so hard, pulling it all together in my mind, that now when I finished what he had started it was like a finger drawing each letter on a steam-covered mirror.

I read more from the e-mail. " 'It worked then, it will work even better now. We have a witness to say that the girl was pushed out the window and that Browning covered it up. This woman was at the hotel when it happened. Her statement will come out as a written confession found among her papers after her death.' "

I looked at Connally. "Isn't that what it says? Did I leave anything out? Isn't that exactly what you said to the president? And isn't that exactly what you did?"

Trembling with rage, he glared at me and did not say a word.

"There is one other thing, though, isn't there? The date you sent this to the president. It's three weeks before Mrs. Morgan's lawyer discovered her 'posthumous confession' in a sealed envelope that had been found in a desk drawer in her home."

I waved my hand in a gesture of disgust. "That's all. No more questions. No more lies!"

Caminetti was already on his feet, protesting.

"Do you have any questions you wish to ask this witness, Mr. Caminetti?" asked Scarborough with a stern glance. "If not, counsel in chambers. Now, if you please!" he cried as he stalked off the bench.

He was furious, pacing up and down that opulent room as if he wanted to beat his fists against the wall. The moment Caminetti and I came through the door, he began to jab his finger in the air.

"Tell me you didn't know anything about this! Tell me this is all a great shock and surprise! Tell me you haven't used your office to aid and abet a scheme of perjured testimony and forged evidence. Tell me that you didn't know anything about this. Tell me — or I swear to you that if it's the last thing I ever do, I'll have your job, your license, and your freedom. Oh, yes, make no mistake, Mr. Caminetti — I'll make certain you're prosecuted for everything the law can invent. I'll make sure you go to prison for so long that by the time you get out no one will remember why you went."

Caminetti's face was ash white, but whether it was from anger or fear I could not tell.

"I don't know anything about any of this. I've never seen any of what Antonelli just produced in court. I don't know where it came from, and I don't know how he got it."

With his legs spread wide apart, Scarborough held his hands behind his back. A grim, determined look on his face, he searched Caminetti's eyes.

"Is there any reason to doubt the authenticity of the documents? The witness authenticated them himself, did he not, when he acknowledged the identification numbers and described the system that produced them?"

Under pressure, Caminetti was forced to agree.

"Then there is no question what we have to do, is there? All right, then, back to court. But don't think for a moment that the matter ends here. There will be an investigation into the conduct of your office. There should be no question about that. Are we clear?"

"We took the case and the evidence we got. We had no reason to think anyone lied. How could we have known about something that apparently was only known inside the White House itself?"

"Antonelli found out," replied Scarborough, unmoved. "You're not supposed to take the evidence as it comes; you're supposed to see if it's true." A look of bitter disappointment blazed in his eyes. "Doesn't anyone care about anything anymore except whatever it takes to win?"

He ordered us back to court. As I followed Caminetti down the narrow corridor I began to feel a sense of relief. It was almost over. There was nothing more I had to do, no more witnesses to question, no more arguments about the law. Caminetti was just about to open the door when he turned around and looked me straight in the eye.

"I didn't know anything about this."

That was all, a simple statement of fact, given without apology or any suggestion that one was required. That was all he owed me, and that was all he gave. He did not wait for my reaction; he was not interested in anything I might have to say. He opened the door and walked quickly across the front of the courtroom to his chair.

The silence inside the courtroom was uneasy, the tension electric, as everyone waited to see what would happen next. Minutes passed, and it seemed like hours. Nothing could happen without Scarborough, and the wait went on. It was so deathly quiet I was afraid to whisper anything to Haviland for fear that no matter how softly I spoke it would be overheard. All I could do was look at him once and nod, a gesture that had no more meaning to him than that things were under control. I glanced over my shoulder, hoping to catch a glimpse of Gisela's face. I knew she was there, probably in the back, but I could not find her; and so I sat back and fiddled with my tie and wondered how much longer it would be.

The door flew open and Scarborough, all business, marched to the bench. His lips pressed tightly together, he glanced at the jurors in a way that seemed to acknowledge not just the part they played, but the paramount importance of what they did. He did not look at Caminetti and he did not look at me.

"There are some cases — not many, but a few — in which something happens that removes any doubt about what the outcome should be. When that happens it becomes the obligation of the court to make certain that justice is done and that the proceedings come to a stop."

Scarborough paused and for a moment gazed out at the courtroom packed with reporters holding their collective breath as they waited for what now seemed inevitable but had yet to be said.

"It is the opinion of the court that after the testimony of Mr. Arthur Connally the evidence against the defendant, Jamison

Scott Haviland, is not sufficient to sustain a verdict of guilty. Therefore, acting on its own motion, the court directs that a verdict of not guilty be entered on the record. The defendant is free to go. The jury is thanked for its service in this case." Scarborough rose from the bench. "Court will be adjourned."

The courtroom was bedlam. The jury quickly filed out of the jury box. Carrying her machine, the court reporter followed right behind. Caminetti shook my hand, and then, without hesitation, shook hands with Haviland, wished him good luck, and then vanished into the crowd, giving short, efficient answers each time a question came booming over all the noise.

Gisela was standing on her tiptoes at the back of the courtroom, following Caminetti with her eyes. She held a cell phone to her ear, covering her other ear to keep out the noise. She began to talk rapidly, intent on each word, no longer interested in Caminetti or anyone else. Hoping to catch her eye, I waited for a moment, but she stared straight ahead, too caught up in what she was saying to look around. When she put away the phone, I called out to her, telling her to wait, but she did not hear me and I lost her in the crowd.

I grabbed my briefcase from beside the table and, with Haviland close behind me, managed to find our way out the back.

"What are you going to do now?" I asked as we stood on the street outside.

"Annie's mother is here. You were going to call her as a witness," he reminded me. "I think I'll take her to dinner. I haven't seen her in years. Why don't you come along?"

"No," I said, "but give her my best." Jimmy turned to go. "She never had any doubt," I called after him. "She never believed for a minute that you had anything to do with Annie's death."

He turned and smiled and for just a moment in that dazzling shiny New York sun he looked exactly like the Jimmy Haviland I used to know, years ago, when we were both still young.

25

A snowstorm had turned Central Park white. The sun had broken through in the early afternoon, but the air was still crystal cold. Wearing an ankle-length fur coat, a long cashmere scarf wrapped around her head, and dark glasses to protect her eyes against the glare, Joanna passed unrecognized as she crossed Fifth Avenue and came toward the bench where I sat waiting at the edge of the park.

"You must be freezing." She touched the lapel of my sports jacket with her gloved hand. "Not even a sweater!"

"I'm all right. It feels good; besides, the sun is out, so how cold can it get?"

We began to walk, neither one of us speaking a word. After a block or so, she looked up at me and smiled.

"Let's go through the park. We have time."

She took my arm, and we followed a path that did not take us too far from the street.

"I won't ask if you were surprised to hear from me. You must have known I'd call."

"I didn't know that at all. To tell you the truth, I didn't think I would see you again after that day we had lunch in Georgetown."

Her hand tightened around my arm. She walked slowly, more slowly with each step she took, hanging on to me as if we were two old friends who had all the time in the world and could do anything we liked.

"I made a reservation for lunch — Is that all right?" She swung around so she could see my face. A strange, lonely smile crossed over her mouth. I could not see her eyes — the dark glasses she wore were impenetrable — but the mood was unmistakable.

"It's all right," I said quietly. "Everything is going to be fine."

"Fine? No, I don't think so; never fine, never that."

The smile took on the aspect of a brave front, a refusal to yield another inch to what she felt inside.

"You're going to keep the apartment, aren't you?" she asked as she let go of my arm and we again began to walk.

"Jimmy Haviland couldn't afford to pay

me anything. I didn't take the case to make money."

"You never did anything for money; that's why you're so good at what you do."

That was the way she remembered me; but then, she had not known me in years.

"I made a lot of money doing what I do."

"But even if Jimmy Haviland had been able to pay you something, you would not have taken money from him." She shook her head emphatically and began to walk a little faster. "But you weren't just defending him, were you? You were defending the famous Thomas Browning." Joanna stopped and searched my eyes. "That is what the case was about. If there was any doubt about that before, there certainly isn't now. You were defending Thomas Browning, and besides that, you saved his life. There isn't any amount of money that can ever pay what you deserve. He wants you to have the apartment. It was his idea. He owes you that much, and more."

I laughed at how insistent she seemed. "Do you know how much that apartment must be worth?"

"I don't know what anything is worth. But it isn't enough, not for what you've done."

She looked at me a moment longer, a strange quizzical expression on her mouth; then, for no apparent reason, she tossed her head and laughed. She skipped ahead a few steps, knelt down and scooped up a handful of snow, packed it tight and with the awkward stiff-armed motion of a girl who had never been athletic, let it fly, pink and silver under the glimmering sky.

"You need a place to live in New York!" she cried in a vibrant, full-throated voice. She scooped another handful of snow and threw it as far as she could.

"Why?"

"Because you've reached that age." She took off the dark glasses and looked at me, something sad and nostalgic in her eyes. "Don't you remember? That summer, here in New York, when we'd go for walks here in the park, and you would see someone the age you are now with a young woman the age I was then. Remember what you used to say? You used to tease me with it. You'd say that you were going to come back to New York when you were that old, because it was the only place you could be with a girl that young and not be arrested!" The memory of it enlivened her, made her forget everything that had happened since. "And so now here you are, just as you said," she went on, her eyes sparkling with a mischief of their own, "with an apartment on the park, and — what shall we say? — a woman considerably younger than yourself."

"Gisela?" I blurted out, embarrassed without quite knowing why.

Joanna seemed delighted. "Gisela Hoffman, yes. Don't look like that! Did you think it was some kind of secret, that no one knew? Half the men in Washington envy you, a man your age with a beautiful young woman like her."

Joanna took my arm and gave it a gentle tug. "You never thought about it, did you? — the difference in your age. I think that's charming," she said, walking now with a more carefree step. "And so like you. You were always like that, so caught up in what you were doing that you didn't always notice what was going on around you. But do you think that's any different than those other men, the ones you used to tease me about, the ones we used to see here, in the park? Do you think they thought very much about the differences in age? Or do you think they just did what they wanted to because they could?"

We were getting near the end of the park. There were more people on the pathway. A few of them looked at Joanna and then looked again. She put on the dark glasses and held my arm tight.

"Is it serious — you and the girl?" Before I could answer, she added in a solemn-sounding voice, "I hope it is. It would be nice to think of you happy and content. It would help make some sense out of all this."

I started to explain that I did not know what it was, how serious it could be, or if it could be serious at all. We had planned to go away somewhere after the trial, somewhere we could spend time alone, but the trial had unleashed a firestorm which, as Joanna knew better than I, had only just begun.

"It's been almost three weeks. She's been here two weekends, and I've been down there once. She had to report on the trial; then, after Arthur Connally had to resign . . . Well, you know everything that's happened after that: one major story right after the other. And now these rumors about whether the man who shot Agent Powell had links to forces overseas. So, is it serious? We'll see."

"But you're going to stay here, in New York?"

"You mean now that I have a decent place to live?"

"It's a little like the place my parents had. Remember?"

I put my arm around her shoulder and hugged her. "I think about your father a lot."

"He was almost as sad you left as . . ." She shook her head. "No, I promised myself I wouldn't do that. Not today."

We reached the sidewalk outside the park, across the street from the Plaza Hotel. Grinning at the way my breath blew cloudlike into the blue frigid air, I took her hand as we dashed through the traffic to the other side.

"Connally resigned in disgrace; Walker is trailing badly in the polls. Do you think he'll pull out or try to fight it to the end? He doesn't have a chance of winning, though — does he?" I asked, chattering away as the doorman held open the door and we went inside. "Browning is going to be president. No one can stop him now."

"Thanks to you," said Joanna in an odd, distant voice. "It's what he's always wanted. I think he'll be a great president. No, I'm sure he will. And he owes it all to you. How strange that is, that it should have worked out like this."

At the entrance to the grill where she had made reservations, she pulled me off to the side. "Do you mind if we don't have lunch? I'm not hungry, but I could use a drink."

At a table in the far corner, Joanna sat with her back to the room. She slid her arms out of her coat and let it drop over the chair. She untied the scarf and with a furtive glance over her shoulder removed the dark glasses from her eyes.

"We had lunch here a couple of times that summer. Remember that?"

There was more than nostalgia in her eyes, more than quiet desperation; there was something close to fear. Puzzled, and a little worried, I was about to ask her what was wrong, when the waiter brought our drinks and Joanna's mood abruptly changed. She began to talk about that summer in New York, and she could not stop.

"Remember I had that job at J. Walter Thompson, the big advertising agency?"

Joanna's eyes had a sheen to them, a kind of glaze, as if the light inside them was shining on something old, something lost.

"Do you remember the man I worked for? Mr. Everett? We were so formal in those days, I must have known his first name, but I've quite forgotten what it was."

She took another drink, put it down and, watching her reflection, smiled into the glass.

"I imagined he must have wanted to be a writer. He graduated from Yale in English Literature. But he got married instead and took a job in advertising."

She finished off the drink, but she did not want another. "I have to go."

"You have to go?" I asked as she started to push back her chair. "But I thought there was something you wanted to talk about. When you called . . ."

She pulled her chair up to the table. "That must have been what you thought it would be like for you. Is that what it was? That if you took the job with that Wall Street firm, you'd never be able to do what you had always dreamed of doing?"

I started to say something, though what it was I don't really know. The dreams I had had then were not the dreams I had now.

"Yes, you're right. There is something I wanted to talk to you about. There is something you need to see."

We left the grill, but instead of leaving the hotel, she led me to the elevator. When she pushed the button for the eighth floor I felt a dim, inexplicable panic, a strange sense of foreboding, the whispered secret that you had always known, this thing that until now you didn't know you knew at all.

"Joanna? Are you sure?"

Her eyes did not move. They stared straight ahead until the elevator came to a halt and we stepped into the corridor where in the haunted confines of my mind I could still see the faces and hear the voices that had been there once before. At the end of the corridor, Joanna reached inside her purse and found the hotel key. She unlocked the door to the corner suite that faced out onto Central Park and went inside.

Rushing across the room, Joanna threw open the window. "Look! Isn't it wonderful?" She glanced over her shoulder for just an instant to make sure I agreed. "You can see everything from here."

She pointed into the distance, toward the side of the park bordered by Central Park West.

"Where I lived then, where you live now. And there, on the other side — See? We're neighbors, you and I."

She turned away from the window and drifted back toward the door. She stood there for a moment, moving her eyes around the room.

"You remember that day? When you were here? You left sometime in the middle of the afternoon, didn't you?"

Her eyes moved back to mine. The saddest smile I think I have ever seen settled on her frail, trembling mouth.

"That was the reason I came," she continued, "because I thought you would be here. I wanted to come earlier, but it was Christmas Eve and I went shopping with my mother and I remember I bought a dress because I wanted to wear something new for you. I had not seen you since the end of summer, when you went back to school, and you were not coming back and I had not stopped thinking about you. And then, I heard you were coming down for Thomas's party, and I had to see you because I thought that there was still a chance we could start all over and that maybe this time you would not want to leave, that maybe this time you would want to come back."

I started toward her. "Don't," I said, shaking my head, but it was too late. It had been too late for years.

"No, I have to," she said through bitter tears. "I had come to find you, but you were gone, the way you had gone before. I couldn't find you, and what I found instead was Thomas and that girl, Annie Malreaux. Thomas was a child, a baby; all that astonishing intelligence — he understood everything, except himself. I came in, looking for you, and Thomas was standing there — right over there," she said, pointing to a spot next to the window. "He had this look on his face, gleeful, triumphant — like a child! They were going to get married. That's what he told me when I walked in and asked about you, that they were going to get married. They were going to run off and do it, get married and then go to Europe somewhere and never look back. I came to find you and I found them. I told him he couldn't do it: that there were things he had to do; that he had responsibilities. I told him he couldn't throw it all away. She told me that Thomas could do whatever he wanted to, that they both could, and that I had no right to interfere. That's when it happened, right there."

Joanna gazed at the window, the only emotion a kind of wonder, as if after all this time she was not any longer quite certain that it had really happened and that it was not instead a bad dream, and that if she tried hard enough, she could wake up and never have to think about it again.

"I shoved her. I was so angry that after everything he had done he would just give it up. I shoved her hard. I remember the look on her face. It struck her as funny, what I had done. She started to laugh, but then she stumbled, and then she fell, and in that instant, the instant it happened, everything changed. All that time I had been protecting him, from his grandfather, from all the people — people like her — who wanted to use him for what they could get; and then, in that instant, he started protecting me.

"It was an accident. I didn't mean for her to die. I didn't; I swear it's true. I wanted to tell the truth, to tell the police what happened, but Thomas would not allow it. He knew it was an accident, he knew I didn't mean it, but he knew what would happen if anyone found out. He told me it was not just a question of a scandal, but that I could go to jail. He was in love with her, he was going to marry her, and now, because of me, she was gone, but he protected me because nothing could bring her back and because I had always protected him."

A grim expression moved deathlike across her eyes. "How much we grew to hate each other because the only tie between us was this sense of obligation that could never quite be met. Yes, we had two children — both of them conceived while we each imagined we were making love with someone else."

I had no more sympathy left. "What about the trial? What about Jimmy Haviland? What about me?" I asked. "There was not any White House conspiracy, was there? Thomas — Thomas Browning — was behind all this? He used Haviland? He used me?"

It had become a habit, and the habit had become instinctive. She had to protect him. It was all she knew.

"They used it the last time. That is how they won. They would have done it again, and it would have been worse — it would have destroyed Thomas — because someone would have discovered the truth. There was not any choice. Don't you see that? The choice was made here, Christmas Eve, nineteen sixty-five, when I pushed Annie Malreaux and she stumbled and fell. It was an accident, and it ruined our lives."

"But what about Haviland — what about what he had to go through? And what about what my great good friend Thomas Browning did to me? Using me to prove a

658

White House conspiracy that did not exist."

"You have to decide what you want to do about that. It's the reason I brought you here and told you what I've never told anyone. If you want to tell the world what I've told you, I won't blame you for it. But is it always better to know the truth?"

I turned away and stared out the window, across the park, shining with snow the way it had that day, years before, when Annie stumbled and died. From the first time I saw it, an island of quiet sanity in the shouted madness of the city's rush to keep moving forward, faster every day, driven by the vanity of its claim to be the best and by the fear that if it even once slowed down it might become second-rate, I had been drawn to it, made to feel that it was the place I eventually wanted to be. Everything that had ever happened to me in New York — everything important — had happened here. And now this.

Thomas Browning was a genius and he had played me like a fool, and like most things ingenious it had been simplicity itself. There were people all through government who knew he would be a better president than what they had; there were people in the White House who owed their loyalty to him. I had been right, after all. The evidence against Jimmy Haviland had been manufactured by the government, but it was a part of the government that Thomas Browning controlled. The only thing I did not know is whether the decision to tell me what he had done had also been his, or whether Joanna had done it on her own. I turned around to ask, but Joanna spoke first.

"Do you know the worst memory of all? The memory of all the things I missed, the things that never happened, the things that might have been and never were."

When we said good-bye outside the Plaza, we both knew that there was nothing more to say and that we would never see each other again. It had been her idea to tell me everything because she thought she owed me that, and because she had to tell someone and I was the only one she could trust. Browning would never know unless I decided to take what she had given me and use it for some purpose of my own. Should I do that? Should I tell the world what I knew and destroy forever Thomas Browning's chance for the presidency? I wanted to let that question somehow answer itself; but it kept coming back, taunting me with cowardice and indecision.

On Friday evening, Gisela came up for the weekend and in the sweet savagery of the night I forgot Thomas Browning and what he had done; I forgot about the trial and about Jimmy Haviland; I forgot about everything except the sheer delight I took in being with her. We slept till noon, and then, like Saturday's children set free in Manhattan, we crossed the park under a brilliant azure sky and climbed the crowded steps to the Metropolitan.

We wandered through the Greek and Roman exhibits, and I listened to Gisela with her European education tell me things I did not know.

"What was it like at the funeral?" I asked, curious what she thought about the service held for the chief justice at the National Cathedral. "Any tension?"

"Between Browning and the president? They didn't sit near each other. The president came alone. Browning was there with his wife."

"Joanna?"

"I forgot, you knew her, didn't you?"

"I saw her this week. We had a drink together, at the Plaza."

Gisela led me down the marble hallway,

past the statuary and into another exhibit.

"Did she tell you anything interesting?"

"You could say that."

Before she could ask, I told her there was something I wanted her to see. The crowds were thick, pulling in all directions at once. I stayed in front of her, guiding her through.

"Can we look at this first?" she asked, squeezing my hand. "There must be five Picassos here."

As we stood in front of the first, her eyes brightened. "I don't think he's going to run. I think he's going to get out." She looked up at me, an eager smile on her mouth. "That's the rumor now. They say that Walker hasn't decided to run a second time, that he's 'praying on it.' Maybe God will tell him the same thing the public-opinion polls say: 'Browning has a huge lead.'"

Gisela looked back at the canvas, but a moment later smiled at me again. "I have news you could not have heard. Jamison Scott Haviland . . ."

"Jimmy? What's happened?" I asked, remembering what Browning had done.

"What's happened is that the only people who don't think he should run for Congress are the ones who think he should run for the Senate. He's become a hero, the decorated war veteran who became an innocent victim of a White House conspiracy. The money is there, whatever he wants to do. Your friend Thomas Browning seems to have done a few things on his behalf."

"Did he?"

"You look a little strange," said Gisela. "Is everything all right?"

"I want you to see this," I said as I took her hand and led her into the next room. It was still there, on the wall in the far corner, *The Boy in the Striped Sweater*, the painting by Modigliani that had once caught my attention and held me there, staring at it, remembering the Thomas Browning I had once known.

"Does it remind you of anyone?" I asked after she had examined it from several different angles.

"No, but I like it quite a lot. Why, does it remind you of someone?"

"You don't think it looks like Thomas Browning?"

"No. I don't see that at all. Do you?"

I looked at it again.

"I suppose it reminded me a little of what he looked like then, when we were in school together. It was a long time ago," I added as I put my arm around her shoulder and led her away.

Outside the museum, I bought us pretzels with mustard, and then we wandered aimlessly into the park.

"Aren't you going to tell me?" asked Gisela, laughing as she wiped mustard off her chin.

"Tell you what?" I was dazzled by how she looked. I did not want her ever to change.

"What Mrs. Browning — your friend Joanna — said."

"What she told me, I'm not sure you'd believe. It's a great story, though; a story that I suppose could change the world if anyone knew. But I won't keep you in suspense. I'll tell you everything she told me."

"When?" asked Gisela, her burgundy black eyes pulling me deep inside.

"I lived here, in New York, a long time ago — one summer, when I was in law school. You know what I used to think about then? How one day, when I was old enough to have a little gray hair, I wanted to have an expensive apartment right on Central Park and be madly in love with a gorgeous young woman barely half my age, someone who looked exactly like you."

She was up on her tiptoes, her hand on

my shoulder, teasing me with her dark, haunting eyes.

"When are you going to tell me, tell me what she said, the story that could change everything?"

"Soon," I said with a distant smile. "A few weeks after Thomas Browning finishes his second term. It's all written out, in a sealed envelope I've never opened and probably never will."

"That's probably wise," she remarked as she let the subject drop.

Almost imperceptibly, Gisela's mood began to change. She stopped talking except when I said something first. Even then, she made only brief, largely noncommittal replies. Something was on her mind, but when I asked her what it was, she said it was only work. There was so much going on, so much she had to do. Washington was chaos and, as the only reporter for her paper, she had to try to cover it all. At dinner she told me that though she did not want to leave, she could not stay: She had to get back to Washington that night. Next weekend might be better; perhaps we could have more time then. When I suggested I come down to Washington for a few days, she said it would only make her feel guilty because she would not be able to spend as much time with me as she would like.

After I put her in a cab for the airport, I wondered if everything she told me had been the truth. She had said it a little too quickly, and with a little too much reserve. It was like watching someone hold her breath while she tries to get all the way through a lie. I told myself that I was imagining things because I was disappointed, that I had no reason to be jealous of her work; but no matter how many reasons I came up with, none of them could quite banish the feeling that things were not right. Perhaps she had met someone else, someone more her own age.

The next morning, having barely slept, I went for a long walk in the park, past the bench where I once had sat with Joanna's father; past the place where, just a few days before, I had watched her throw snowballs as if she did not have a care in the world. I must have wandered around for an hour or more before I found myself back on the sidewalk across the street from where Thomas Browning lived when he was in New York. Sitting on the bench where I had waited for Joanna, I traced the route she had followed as I remembered how she had looked, bundled up against the cold.

Then I saw her, the last person I expected to see, leaving the building, an overnight bag slung across her shoulder.

"Gisela!" I shouted across the traffic and the noise.

She looked up, a puzzled, guarded expression in her dark, impenetrable eyes. She saw me and her eyes went cold, as if her name had been called by a stranger she had never met and did not want to know. A car was waiting; the driver held the door. She slipped inside and never once looked back.

I turned and walked into the park, feeling lost and lonely and more than ever a fool. Thomas Browning had left nothing to chance. He had exploited every weakness I had. But then, I should not have expected anything less: He had always known how to use the people he needed.

When I reached the other side of the park, I looked down Central Park West. From somewhere far away yet whisper close, I listened to Joanna's voice, that voice I had heard that night she introduced me to her parents, telling them that we had just met and that she was going to marry me the day after tomorrow. I should have stayed in New York, stayed and married her. Annie Malreaux would still be alive, married to Thomas Browning. And Browning and I would have gotten together every so often — perhaps at the bar at the Plaza — and talked about all the good times we had had in law school and afterward. We would have complained, the way middle-aged men do, about where the country was headed; and then, because we would have grown happy and content, kidded each other about our lack of ambition. It would have been a good life, so much better than the lives we led instead.

About the Author

D. W. Buffa was a defense attorney for ten years. The author of five acclaimed novels featuring attorney Joseph Antonelli — *The Judgment* (nominated for an Edgar Award for Best Novel of the Year), *Star Witness*, *The Legacy*, *The Prosecution*, and *The Defense* — he lives in California.